HACKED

A CHAMPION SECURITY NOVEL

LUCY LENNOX

MAY ARCHER

HACKED

Well-known computer security infiltration specialist Jasper Huxley has never met a system he can't hack. Whether his assignment is accessing a highly-classified Pentagon server or modifying his high school report card, he's always got a botnet, an exploit, or a little bit of social engineering he can call up to get the job done. But there are certain things he can't finesse, no matter how hard he tries.

• Beating the infuriatingly adorable, adorably infuriating Kevin Rogers in the Enchanted Javelin Toss to qualify for the Horn of Glory Conqueror's Tournament. (*Robbery.*)
• Sharing a house and—worse—a network with Kev. (*Gah.*)
• Being forced to allow a non-trained, non-serious, and non-resistible civilian to take part in a critical intel operation. (*•side-eyes Kev*)
• Keeping Champion Security's system safe from increasingly sophisticated black hat threats. (*Once again… Kev.*)
• Maintaining his distance from the man haunting his thoughts… especially when he learns that Kev's a virgin. (*At least for now.*)

In short, when Kevin Rogers is in the picture, the safe and peaceful life Hux has managed to construct for himself gets suddenly and irrevocably… hacked. (*And it's all Kev's fault.*)

1

KEV

SmittyKitty clearly needed my fuzzy dice... and I was in the mood to give them to him.

Watching new guys play Horn of Glory wasn't generally a hobby of mine. If I wanted to watch a bunch of cocky know-it-alls fuck around—and I did *not*—I could find a plentiful supply in my real life since my cousin-slash-best-friend Carter had fallen in love with a life-sized GI Joe doll named Riggs, who came complete with a huge entourage of overgrown "security expert" badasses including his boss, Champ, and—in a shockingly unpleasant turn of events—my Horn of Glory archnemesis, Jasper "HogMasterHux" Huxley.

As of two weeks ago, Champ, Hux, and the whole crew of Champion Security had practically moved into our house while they pinpointed a vulnerability in their security, where they'd proceeded to steal my cheesecake brownies and gobble up the bandwidth in my dedicated internet connection.

Not that I was bitter about that or whatever.

But Smitty was the exception to my newbie rule and

had been since the first moment I'd noticed him trespassing on my HOG homestead looking for abandoned tools and seeds a few weeks back.

Not to blow my own, erm, *Horn*, but I was kind of a big deal in the game. Even the rankest newbie knew the only players allowed on my land were me and Carter, and encroachers would meet the business end of my rhubarb wand. I'd messaged Smitty to give him a chance to retreat before I turned him into compost, because I was a nice person like that.

HogDocKev: *You seem to have gotten off course, Swamp Minion.*

I'd waited for him to apologize or pretend he'd wandered past my wards accidentally, but he hadn't done either.

SmittyKitty: *Oooh, scary. *yawn**

I'd leaned toward my computer screen, my finger hovering over the obliterate button, but I'd had to admit, this was… new. It had been a hot minute since someone in the game—besides HogMasterJerkface, obvs—had dared to disrespect me. So I'd typed back.

HogDocKev: *You want to battle? *eyeroll* I don't battle newborn babies. Accrue some actual game play time and we'll talk.*

SmittyKitty: *Puh-lease. Like it would be a fair fight even then. You can't be killed. Not when you have BOTH the Apple Butter Booster AND the Hedgerow of Health booster. The odds are stacked against me.*

HogDocKev: *Yeah, cause I stacked them myself through hard work and commitment. I completed every quest needed in order to obtain both boosters. I have earned every pip I've ever spent in this game.*

SmittyKitty: *Sure you have. You're like a knight in shining armor, Sir Pipsalot. And did it ever occur to you that those quests were only open to ranked players? Just like almost all the quests* *required to compete in Ascendant's Class in the Conqueror's Tournament require a certain ranking. New guys have to work twice as hard, and it's still not a level playing field.*

HogDocKev: *I'm not apologizing for playing HOG longer than practically anyone. Move along.*

SmittyKitty: *Just saying, Pip, I could beat you in any fight… if the fight was fair.*

After that, he'd turned around and stalked off my land… and I'd let him go, for a bunch of different reasons.

For one thing, destroying a newbie would be a hollow victory. And for another thing… Smitty intrigued me. I liked his frankness and confidence. I liked the way he challenged me. And I liked that he made me rethink stuff I took for granted, like which players were eligible for quests and tournaments… and what I could do to make the game more fair.

Since then, I'd kept an eye on the guy, and what I'd seen had intrigued me even more. I learned he used he/him pronouns, lived in the upper peninsula of Michigan, and worked as a cashier at a pet supply store. The only thing I was unsure about was his age, so I ran his chat strings through an AI assessment tool, which estimated his age to be around late twenties, early thirties.

I also knew that he was a really talented player.

And that he continued to call me Pip, even though—or maybe *because*—it bugged me.

Tonight, I'd watched him swindle a marauding red panda out of his rubies—which required serious strategic thinking skills—but Smitty hadn't gotten ten paces in his air speeder before he was beset by a pack of lightning orcs who'd watched the whole showdown and wanted the rubies for themselves. Without fuzzy dice in his air speeder to up his transportation points, Smitty was a goner.

HogDocKev: *Hey, Smitty. Your air speeder needs these. Enjoy!*

After sending the dice as an in-game gift, I sat back and stretched, moving my eyes off my monitors for the first time in hours. I rubbed my eyes and adjusted my glasses.

It was late… or early, maybe. Somewhere in the 5:00 or 6:00 a.m. range, according to my internal clock. I'd been watching Smitty for maybe half an hour, but I'd been playing Horn of Glory since midnight. With the new Valentine's theme release, it had been easy to lose track of time. There were a million reasons I loved a theme update in the game, but this one had been extra special because Carter and Riggs had gotten married yesterday on Valentine's Day.

Riggs was a good guy—even if he had terrible taste in friends—and I was genuinely thrilled he was joining our family. He made Carter happy, which meant I was happy too. Mostly.

But I couldn't deny that Carter's wedding made me a little melancholy too, which was why I'd left while the party was still in full swing and jumped online. I wasn't a fan of too much socializing, even when I was in the best of moods, and my HOG life was way easier to deal with than my real life.

Now, I'd completed a scavenging quest through the Infernal Wood, my orc horde was surrounded by heart-shaped fairy lights, my villagers had enjoyed a champagne toast, and the pink and red fireworks had continued on for hours over the icepack townships.

I was satisfied that my HOG world was running smoothly, and it was officially time for me to get back to my real-world work—namely, investigating the security breach that had caused Riggs's team to invade the calm quiet of my house. The sooner I figured it out, the sooner they'd all leave me to my peace and quiet… and my cheesecake brownies.

But the moment I clicked the key to switch programs, the edges of my monitor flashed, and a cultured British voice that I may or may not have created to mimic Henry Cavill's said, "Good morning, sire. I regret to inform you that your internet speed is critically low."

My internet?

Motherfucker.

I growled, then typed the keys that would turn on the security feed I'd installed on the first floor the day that the Champion Security invaders had arrived.

Sure enough, the bandwidth thief was sitting at my kitchen table, bold as you please, where he'd crafted himself a mini-lair complete with three monitors.

HogMasterHux.

The man who'd not only attacked me in a cranberry swamp upon first "meeting" me in Horn of Glory last summer, stealing every pip in my pack and all my health nuggets because "That's how the game is played, HogDoc. Watch and learn."… but who'd then had the absolute *gall* to not be an utter ignoramus with a face like a potato and hair like a troll doll when we'd met in real life.

Why should Jasper Huxley get to be a muscular, brilliant, sexy, crinkly-eyed Zac Efron look-alike with a smile so bright it could power a small city? It was utterly unforgivable.

Also, the man was way too well-groomed and well-rested for this hour on a Sunday, damn it.

"For fuck's sake, Huxley," I said into my comms and had the pleasure of watching Hux jump three feet as my voice broke the silence. "Why are you at my house at this hour?"

"Because according to Riggs, we work here now." Hux

scowled and addressed his words to the clock on the wall, then scowled harder and addressed the area by the refrigerator, unsure where my camera was. "And it's not a house — it's a fucking *estate* with ten billionty rooms. And unlike *some* people, I'm dedicated to my job, so I'm doing it. Go away."

I growled again, off mic. Go away? When he was in *my* home?

I really hated it when people assumed I was a freeloader who lived in my family's basement because I was too lazy to get a job and make money. I mean, I *did* live in the basement, but that was because I'd built my lair here. And I had plenty of my own money, both earned and inherited.

"Bold talk for a man who'd been working his Horn until I startled him," I spoke into the mic in a bored voice. "And don't try to pretend that you were on that Horn for work purposes, HogMasterHux, because I can see from here that the device sitting on that table is a blue star-sapphire third-gen Horn, and I know for a fact that the Horn device you're supposed to be analyzing for Champ is a sparkly peach first-generation one." Just to grind his gears, I added, "And I know this because I supplied the decoy Horn that saved the day on your mission, *remember*? I'm..." I paused for dramatic effect. "...kind of a hero."

Smug? *Moi*? Maybe just slightly.

I could practically hear Hux's molars squeaking. "I remember it a little differently," he told the light fixture on the ceiling. "Now, go watch cartoons and let the grown-ups do their work."

God, he was infuriating. I pushed my glasses up on my nose. "Stop stealing my fucking internet and maybe I will."

"You can't possibly need all of it," he bit out —*erroneously* —addressing himself to the vase of Valentine's Day roses in the center of the table. "What the hell was Champ thinking, making us work alongside a bunch of fucking civilians? If I have to spend one more day here, I'm quitting."

"Quitting? Oh noes! Oh, *gasp*! Wherever will Champ find someone with your amazing skill set, Huxley? Oh, wait, no, I know. Amos Nutter has that overly aggressive alpaca who spits constantly. Betcha five bucks nobody would realize he wasn't you for a full forty-eight hours."

Hux made a high-pitched teakettle noise of rage. "This is why no one wants you around, Kevin Rogers. Because you will do anything to get attention. But I'm *not* gonna give it to you anymore." He clapped a pair of headphones over his ears and began banging his head in time to some music I couldn't hear.

Oh. My. God.

Attention? Me? The guy who'd avoided attention his whole life like vampires avoid the sun? How could one human contain as much *wrong* as Jasper Huxley? I burned with fury at the injustice.

I briefly brainstormed ways to create a targeted signal disruptor that would work only on Hux's headphones so I could force him to listen to Neil Diamond's "Girl, You'll Be a Woman Soon" until the resulting earworm dissolved his brain into applesauce.

When that vision didn't satisfy my lust for vengeance, I contemplated outfitting the kitchen with some kind of laser I could use to vaporize people—one particular person, really—at will.

Then I sighed. I was pretty sure this was how regular geniuses turned evil.

And the truth was, I didn't want Hux *harmed*, I just wanted his charming, poison-ivy-eyed, mean-spirited self out of my home as quickly and safely as possible… which meant getting to the bottom of Champion Security's infiltration problem.

I'd already begun checking over the scans I'd set up the night before, and even set a couple of new ones to run, when a new message notification from Horn of Glory popped up on my screen.

I expected to see some kind of acknowledgment from Smitty—was a thank-you too much to hope for?—but I quickly forgot about him because the message was from someone way more exciting.

Anomaly451: *Hey, honey! How's my Valentine? I missed you today!*

My heartbeat kicked up a notch at the endearment.

I'd waited a long time to be somebody's *honey*. Twenty-five long years, in fact.

Take that, Huxley. Plenty of people want me around, fuck you very much.

Anomaly451, whose real name was *Adam*, was a HOG player I'd "met" in an online tournament a little over a month ago. Unlike Smitty, who had a chip on his shoulder the size of my homestead, or HogMasterHux, who was the sort of person who'd commandeer a man's orc forces without so much as a by-your-leave, Adam was sweet.

When I'd harvested a record number of snowflakes and knocked him out of contention for the tournament prize, Anomaly hadn't been upset. Instead, he'd plucked a bouquet of snowflowers to congratulate me. Then he'd chat-requested me, and… well, the rest was history.

We'd been online boyfriends for weeks. We'd started having regular Tuesday night chats. I'd told him all about the computer lair I'd constructed. He'd asked my advice on system security for the projects he worked on. And, in a development that had filled me with 90 percent excitement and only 10 percent crippling anxiety, he kept begging to meet in real life so he could "see my setup"—which was code for helping me cash in my virginity card at long last—and I was pretty sure I was going to agree. Soon.

Like, *really* soon.

Could be any day now.

But I couldn't exactly invite the guy over to my house while it was invaded by a nest of hot-as-fuck security operatives, could I? "Pay no attention to the waves of high-octane testosterone luring you toward the ripply-muscled badasses, Adam! Come down to my dark lair and spoon me!"

Yeah, no. There were limits to how much humiliation a man could endure.

HogDocKev: *Hi! It was good. Haven't gone to bed yet. How was work?*

When Adam had told me he had to work on Valentine's Day, my brain had immediately tried sabotaging me by suggesting he had someone at home to celebrate with, but I'd resisted. I was not the doubting, jealous type. Besides, Adam told me all the time that I was the first thing he thought of each morning. That he'd never met anyone like me. That he didn't want us to rush into anything too fast or to become exclusive too quickly, but that he considered me his boyfriend. His *Valentine.*

Having him message me first thing this morning just confirmed it.

Anomaly451: *Meh. Work was a shit show because my boss is incompetent. And you remember that huge research project I mentioned to you? Looks like it's gonna be more time consuming than I thought, and the deadline is getting tighter. You know how it goes.*

Anomaly451: *Actually, I guess you don't exactly, do you? Lol. Trust me, it's annoying. Not nearly as fun as staying home and playing games all afternoon!*

I shut my mouth with a clack.

So, okay, maybe there were a couple of things about our new relationship that I wished I'd handled differently. One was the time I'd explained to Adam that I came from a long line of prestigious doctors, when he asked why my username was HogDoc. Another was telling him that I was a self-employed consultant, when he'd asked what I did for a living.

I hadn't explained things well enough, clearly, because he'd jumped to some conclusions about my work ethic that reminded me a lot of Hu—erm, *certain people's*—bullshit conclusions, and no matter how many times I tried to correct him, he didn't seem to get it.

Consequently, I never brought up his work anymore so he wouldn't make comments about mine.

HogDocKev: *You know I do other things besides play all day. I'm an inventor. I mentor college kids interested in STEM careers. I make a chicken tikka so good you'd cry.*

Anomaly451: *Sure, sweetness. I know. I didn't mean it like that! Just that I wish I had more free time. Time I could spend playing HOG with you.*

Awww. I melted. Was that the cutest thing ever? Pretty sure it was.

I was being an idiot. A prideful, overly sensitive idiot. And it was Hux's fault. Just because *he* didn't take me seriously, that didn't mean Adam didn't.

HogDocKev: *Sorry. I'm a little touchy this morning, I guess.*

Anomaly451: *No need to apologize, darling. What's got you feeling prickly?*

See, this was what I liked so much about Adam. He asked me questions about my life and seemed interested in the answers. I debated where to begin.

HogDocKev: *Well… my cousin got married yesterday. You remember me telling you about him?*

Anomaly451: *Of course. KevsCuz. The guy you share your homestead with.*

I felt a bittersweet pang.

HogDocKev: *Yeah, him. But we don't share a homestead anymore. He and his hubby will be sharing their own homestead now.*

I'd even gotten them a rare pair of mated swans for their roof as an in-game wedding gift.

Anomaly451: *Ahhh. And now you're carrying on all alone?*

I blew out a deep breath, and stupid tears prickled behind my eyes. Adam understood me on such a fundamental level, it felt like magic.

HogDocKev: *Exactly! That's it exactly. Thank God you understand. I'm happy for him, truly. But…*

But Carter was my best friend. More like a brother than a cousin. He'd been looking out for me since I was a socially awkward middle schooler and my parents dropped me off at our grandfather's house for a visit… then decided it'd be better for all of us if I just lived there permanently.

It was hard not to feel a little lonely, knowing someone else was Carter's priority now.

Anomaly451: *Say no more, angel. Defending a homestead the size of yours all by yourself this close to the tulip harvest? What a pain in the ass!*

Anomaly451: *I don't blame you for being angry at your cousin!*

I blinked. Okay, so maybe Adam didn't magically understand me. But he made an effort, which was more than Hu—erm, *certain people*—did. Right?

Another new message notification popped up onscreen.

SmittyKitty: *What'd you send me this for???*

I rolled my eyes. Speaking of annoying people determined to misunderstand me…

I heaved a sigh as I switched chat windows.

HogDocKev: *It's fuzzy dice. So your air speeder will go faster. Buzz buzz vroom vroom? Maybe you can avoid the lightning orcs next time.*

SmittyKitty: *Don't remember asking for your charity, Pip. Also, FYI, air speeders aren't motorcycles. They don't make noise. And if my motorcycle started buzzing, I'd check out the bearings before I had a catastrophic engine failure, just sayin'.*

Oh, for God's sake.

HogDocKev: **eyeroll* First off, I was racing air speeders before your Horn was even manufactured, whippersnapper. Second, it's kindness, not charity. Don't people do nice things for one another in the UP?*

HogDocKev: *Third, stop calling me Pip.*

Three dots swirled next to Smitty's name for a long moment. Then finally, he responded.

SmittyKitty: *The UP?*

HogDocKev: *Dude. The Upper Peninsula of Michigan? Where you live?*

The second I sent the message, I smacked my forehead.

Wow, Kev, tell me you're a creeper who's been stalking the newb's bio without saying you're a creeper who's been stalking his fucking bio.

SmittyKitty: *They do. For friends. But you and I are not friends… Pip.*

HogDocKev: *We could be, if you wanted. I could help you out. No strings.*

SmittyKitty: *Not interested. I'm not playing the game to amass an empire.*

HogDocKev: *Lolz. That's what most players say when they haven't yet amassed an empire. You ever meet a player named HogMasterHux?*

SmittyKitty: *??? Should I have??*

HogDocKev: *Guess not. You two have a lot in common, that's all.*

SmittyKitty: *Incredible natural talent?*

HogDocKev: *A love of looted goods and a chip on your shoulder. Hux is a great Horn player, but he's not a *team* player. You can't trust him.*

I sighed. Why was I wasting time trying to explain fucking *Huxley* to *Smitty*, the only person in the world who disliked me as much as Hux did?

HogDocKev: *Just watch out for Hux, that's all. And try not to be like him.*

HogDocKev: *Anyway, the dice are yours. Go in peace.*

I closed the chat window and went back to my chat with Adam, but the green light by his name had gone dark. He'd left me some unread messages, though.

Anomaly451: *One day, when you're ready, I can move into your homestead, and then you won't be alone anymore. I'm a kickass scout, and between my gift for strategy and your spellcasting abilities, we'll be unbeatable!*

Anomaly451: *#HOGPowerCouple!*

Anomaly451: *Which reminds me, what are you up to next weekend? I'm working remotely at the end of the week. I could be in Tennessee by Friday. We could celebrate V-Day in a whole new way. Lolol. *eggplant emoji**

Anomaly451: *I want to know what you look like. And I respect our promise not to google each other or send pictures, but a man has needs. *eggplant emoji* *eggplant emoji**

Anomaly451: *Plus we can quest together while I'm there! If you and I team up, I can qualify for the Ascendant's Class in the Conqueror's Tournament at HOGCon in Vegas in a couple weeks. You're going, right? Because the new HOG Power Couple needs to form an alliance!! We're gonna dominate.*

Anomaly451: *Hello? Earth to Kev?*

Anomaly451: *Guess you fell asleep without saying goodbye.*

Anomaly451: *When we meet in person, I'll have to make sure* *to keep you awake. *eggplant emoji* *eggplant emoji* *eggplant emoji* Let me know about this weekend!*

My stomach flipped. Next weekend was very soon.

Possibly too soon for all that eggplant.

But the tournament at HOGCon… Hmm.

I'd considered playing in the tournament more than once. Despite having some of the highest posted scores in the game, and maybe the highest number of game-play hours (Hux and I were usually neck and neck at the top of the leaderboard), I'd never competed in an in-person prizewinning tournament before. Social anxiety was a bitch sometimes.

But if Adam and I were boyfriends, a HOG power couple, and we could meet in Vegas, away from prying eyes and rogue badasses…

I toyed with the corner of my glasses nervously.

Anomaly451: *I have quite a bit of work to do today, so I've got to go, but starting the day talking with you is the best thing I could have hoped for, sugar. XOXO*

Damn it. I'd wasted my time chatting with Smitty and being annoyed at Hux when I should've been focused on the guy who actually cared about me. Story of my damn life.

I read the message again and again. *Sugar.* I didn't know anyone who used that endearment unironically in real life, but I decided I liked it.

I typed out a message he could read next time he logged on.

HogDocKev: *Sorry I missed saying goodbye. Good luck with your work! Let's talk about Vegas!*

I stared at the screen some more, thankful I was alone so no one could see the giant grin on my face. And then another message popped up on my screen.

SmittyKitty: *Thank you for the dice, I guess.*

SmittyKitty: *FYI, someone (not me) crossed your border and is looting your magical jelly and jam cellars. I think it might be the Hux guy you mentioned. Now you and I are even. Have fun storming the castle, Pip.*

What the…

I clicked over to the correct monitor and found the orc horde that was supposed to be guarding that section of my property wasn't just ringed by heart-shaped fairy lights anymore, they'd been *tied up with them.*

Meanwhile, HogMasterHux was systematically—nay, *gleefully*—destroying my carefully organized jelly cellar, upending a ten-gallon drum of boysenberry preserves to the delight of my champagne-drunk villagers.

What. The. Fuck.

He thought *I* was the attention-seeking child around here? *Me?*

Ohhhh, the lasers in the kitchen were *so* happening. But first, I was going to march up there and—

"Pardon me, sire," Henry Cavill interrupted politely as my monitors flashed. "But your scan is now complete, and an ongoing vulnerability has been detected."

I clicked over to the tool I'd been running, and my heart sank when I saw the system vulnerability the computer had found.

Fuck.

This was going to make Huxley *miserable*, which should have made me happy. Instead, it was the absolute last thing I wanted to see.

Hux and I were going to be stuck with each other for even longer.

2

____

HUX

"Don't listen to him. He's about as close to a cybersecurity expert as that ham sandwich you're picking at," I said, trying for the millionth time to dissuade my boss, my coworkers, and the assorted other people in the Rogers family's kitchen from giving any credence to the warnings Kev was spouting.

Kev ignored me. He folded his arms and leaned back against the kitchen counter—white marble, naturally, because the Rogers family had only the best—looking annoyingly cute and approachable with his lean frame, artfully messy hair, and dark-framed glasses that had probably cost more than my truck.

Meanwhile, I was still recovering from back-to-back sleepless nights and yesterday's impromptu afternoon housewarming party for Champ and his boyfriend, who were officially shacking up in the historic Victorian Champ had recently renovated. It was a Monday morning, but I looked and felt about as fresh as week-old flowers, which had put me in a not-great mood.

Then Kev had started spouting about something that his scans—his unnecessary, unauthorized, unsubstantiated scans—had found the day before, and my mood had slid from not-great right into fucking-awful.

"I believe Hux is under the false impression that there'll be flashing red lights and warning sirens to indicate a systems breach," Kev told Champ, "when in reality, there is a new kind of intrusion Champion Security is specifically vulnerable to, called—"

I leaned toward him, bracing a hand on the big wooden table I'd commandeered as my desk since Kev refused to share the space in his stupid super-secret lair. "Need I remind you that I was trained by the United States military?" I cried. "Stop acting like I got my experience from a STEM summer camp. *Some* of us worked damned hard for our cybersecurity education, and *some* of us continue self-educating and pursuing advanced certificates as the latest tech is released. Some of us even teach cybersecurity classes at the local community college!"

Kev wrinkled his nose pityingly at me before addressing Champ once more. "You know what they say. Those who can, do. Those who can't, teach."

Champ opened his mouth, hopefully to defend me, but I beat him to it. "I do *and* I teach! You don't do either. You sit all day in your basement gaming chair and challenge cloud mavens to enchanted javelin tosses."

Kev turned his head to me in slow motion and pushed his glasses up. "Your jealousy is both obvious and unattractive, Huxley. As you know, it took thirty in-game hours of training to get to a high enough level of enchantment where I could best the track and field mavens. Unlike certain people who call themselves 'masters' of Horn of Glory, some of us are *dedicated*."

I gritted my teeth. He was right—if I'd learned nothing else about Kevin Rogers, I'd learned that he was committed and diligent, especially when it came to one of the many things he was passionate about.

Take, for example, his quest to make me lose my mind.

I'd come a long way from my formative years growing up in a tiny house in an unincorporated part of Pennsylvania, where my Marine dad had managed to find a mechanic job after separating from the military. I'd traveled a lot of places, met a lot of people, seen and done a lot of things, both good and bad... but *nothing* in the entire world had ever riled me as much as Kevin Rogers did, every moment of every day, with every word that came out of his weirdly pouty mouth.

That was dedication, alright.

"Also..." Kev pursed his lips thoughtfully. "Remind me again how well you did with the javelin toss? Will HogMasterHux be making it to the Conqueror's Tournament?"

"I... I had connection issues," I said between clenched teeth. "I was in Malawi that week, *as you know*. The lag time made accuracy impossible."

Kev made a tsking noise. "Only a poor craftsman blames his tools, Huxley. SmittyKitty scored higher than you, and he's a newb."

I squeezed my eyes shut and inhaled a slow, deep breath.

Every once in a while, I wondered if I was too hard on Kev. If maybe I should apologize for having stolen his pack during our very first encounter in the cranberry swamp, back when Horn of Glory was in its infancy and we were two of only a few dozen players worldwide, before our paths had ever crossed in real life. It had been a shit thing to do, after all, and Kev was a decent guy... sometimes.

I hadn't handled a lot of things in the game (or in life)

the right way last summer. There had been extenuating circumstances, yes, but that was not an excuse. So, I'd decided, earlier this year, to slowly phase out the old "Hog-MasterHux" account and come back to the game under a new identity, as a guy who'd play more fairly and value connections over tournament wins.

I'd decided that having my new persona, SmittyKitty, make amends to Kev would be part of that do-over. I'd vowed not to assume the worst every time Kev opened his mouth—or his chat window. I'd reminded myself we didn't need to be rivals because the game was plenty big enough for both of us.

But then the fucker had done one insufferable thing after another—like assuming my new alter ego was trying to loot his homestead when I *absolutely had not been*, or warning my new alter ego that HogMasterHux wasn't a team player when I *absolutely was*, or saying something as smug and ridiculous as "only a poor craftsman blames his tools, Huxley"—and *wham*. I was back to looting his jam cellar just for shits and giggles and wanting to grab him with both hands and shut his big mouth with my…

I blinked in horror.

Fist.

My fist. Obviously.

My fingers clenched on the tabletop.

Yes, okay, my first thought had been to say *mouth*, but that was an error because I fucking refused to find this privileged know-it-all attractive.

"Alright, children, that's enough." Champ rolled his eyes tiredly.

I sighed. "Regardless, Kev, you're not a professional security expert, so you need to back the fuck off. When I say Champion Security's systems are clear of current vulnerabilities and intruders, I know what I'm talking about."

I glanced back over at Champ, urging him with my eyeballs to trust the man he'd hired for this job.

Thankfully, he got the message. He stood up from the kitchen table and leaned over to press a kiss against the top of his wedding-planner boyfriend's head and then one on his cheek. "Then I guess we're heading back to the office. Good luck at your meeting, baby. I love a destination wedding as much as anyone, but hopefully, you can convince them that actively searching for the Bermuda Triangle is more of a honeymoon thing."

Quinn rolled his eyes. "Your lips to God's ears."

Kev shook his head as I passed him. "You're making the wrong choice, Huxley. My scans found a vulnerability, and you won't even entertain the idea that—"

I stopped and spun to look at him. He shut his mouth with a clack and swallowed nervously.

To the casual observer, Kev Rogers was a nerd-boy wet dream—a Clark Kent, attempting to conceal his Superman looks, intelligence, and shrewdness from the rest of the world with nothing more than a pair of black glasses and an aw-shucks-please-underestimate-me attitude—and somehow, unbelievably, it worked.

But I was not a casual observer, and I did not underestimate him.

No one as gorgeous, as wealthy, as smart, as sexy, and as funny as Kev Rogers could be as fucking sweet and insecure as he pretended to be.

He was looking for attention. He wanted my job. He was trying to drive me insane.

And that was why I tried—as hard as a red-blooded human with a massive, debilitating hard-on for gorgeous, nerdy guys possibly could—not to give it to him.

"I ran my own scans, Kev," I said breezily. "They detected *nothing*."

He huffed out a breath, and I saw that he was tapping his index finger to the side of his thumb—one of his odd nervous tics. "You and I might have our differences, but you *know* I wouldn't lie about something like this."

"Sure. I know that," I said sincerely. Then I leaned into his space a tiny bit, getting a whiff of his vanilla-and-coffee scent. "But *you* know I'm damn good at my job."

"Yes! But that's why we have redundancies! That's why two pairs of eyes are better than one! You can be good— you can be *great*—and still miss something—"

"But I didn't," I said firmly, ending the conversation— and, hopefully, my entire acquaintance with Kev—once and for all.

Since I was highly motivated, it didn't take me long to pack up as much of our tech gear as possible, along with my beloved pet rabbit, Rodrigo, and load everything in Champ's truck. We made a minicaravan as we drove away from the mansion. Elvo and Riggs rode in Riggs's big truck, Jordan and Champ followed in Champ's, and I brought up the rear in my Jeep with Foo Fighters blasting from the speakers.

Part of me wanted to shoot the bird out the window at Kev, as a symbol of my annoyance for his interference in my job, but then again, he *had* helped us by providing that decoy Horn for our last job.

And I supposed, if I thought about it, that we *had* put him out a tiny bit by taking over several rooms in his home as our satellite offices while I worked on patching our systems...

And...

I sighed.

Okay, fine. Kev meant well. There, I said it.

He had a big heart. That wasn't up for debate. He did. He just… he was also a nosy know-it-all who was always *right there*, invading my life, trying to steal my job and my sanity. Putting a little distance between us for the first time in two weeks was going to be a huge relief.

When we returned to the Champion Security office, even the sight of our octogenarian receptionist didn't dim my euphoria.

"Mornin', Herman," I called as I sailed past him with my beloved PC tower under one arm and my rabbit carrier in the other. I strode through the large central desk area we called the mosh pit and headed for my office—the big room in the back dominated by a giant wall-mounted screen and the conference table where I conducted briefings—which we called the war room.

After a few more trips back and forth with more gear, I was finally installed back in my happy place.

I let out a deep breath. *Home. At last.*

I figured most people wouldn't have felt as deeply about their workspace as I did—after all, I didn't *actually* live at the Champion Security office; Elvo and I shared an apartment in an old craftsman down the street. But I'd had a hand in designing every aspect of my war room when Champ had started Champion Security, from the monitors and conference table to the design of my desk. There was more Jasper Huxley in this space than there ever would be in the apartment I was renting.

I patted my desk before flicking on the giant wall screen and starting up my computer. After logging in, I made my way to the break room for a fresh cup of coffee. If I felt a little light on my feet while stirring in the sugar, there was no one to see me twirl other than myself.

I took a sip on my way back to the war room, and when

I looked up, I stopped so suddenly, hot coffee sloshed over my hand.

"*Motherfucker*," I shouted, staring through the glass windows at the giant monitors on the wall.

Everyone in the mosh pit turned to see what the problem was.

Scrolling across the screens in an old-timey dot-matrix font was a message that could only be from one meddling, too-much-time-on-his-hands, not-so-juvenile delinquent.

Jasper Huxley can no more protect his "systems" than throw an enchanted javelin through the Ring of Evenlore.

After the message scrolled through the first time, a video popped up showing me in real time, slack-jawed and coffee-stained.

"He... he..." I coughed out. Had the air suddenly lost all oxygen, or was I choking on my righteous indignation? "He got into my system. How the fuck...?"

Champ sighed and turned to me in resignation. "We packing back up?"

Kev was going to be the death of me.

"No. Absolutely not! Go back to that man's evil lair? Are you joking? Besides, there's no danger. The only person infiltrating our systems is him!"

I could tell what Champ was going to say before he said it, because it's what *I* would have said in other, non-Kev-related circumstances. "If Kev can get in..."

I gritted my teeth. I pulled out my green Horn and shot off a private message to HogDocKev.

HogMasterHux: *You will pay for this, Gourd Goblin. If you thought things were bad before, you're about to learn differently.*

And then I quickly moved my entire troll army toward his magical kelp forest and burned it to the ground.

When I was done, I nodded to myself in satisfaction and slipped the Horn back into my pocket.

I glanced up to find Champ watching me. His expression was incredulous. "This is when you choose to play your video game? Really? Interesting choice, Huxley."

I opened my mouth to speak, but he cut me off with a growl. "Pack. Up. We're headed back to the Rogers' house."

"But surely we can find another place—"

"The only thing wrong with the Rogers' place is your ridiculous feud with Kev! So suck it up, buttercup, and learn to get along. I'm not wasting days trying to find another safe place to set up when HOG Corporate—which is not just the manufacturer of your little Horn game, let me fucking remind you, but *Champion Security's biggest client*—is expecting an update this week, and we currently have *no update to give them*," he said fiercely. Then he straightened and smoothed his shirt. "Besides which, Kev found the vulnerability when our scans didn't. I don't care if you like him or don't like him. I don't care if he sent a mystical fire tornado whirling through your bamboo bayou. He's fucking *useful*. So let him help you."

Let Kev Rogers help me? When the man was clearly trying to show me up so he could ingratiate himself with my boss?

Death. First.

"Please. Kev couldn't wield a fire tornado if his homestead depended on it," I scoffed, waving a hand. "And I'd never plant bamboo. That shit'll take over your whole—" I finally caught the dangerous expression on Champ's face and belatedly shut up. "Erm. Yes, boss. On it, boss."

Champ walked away, muttering something about being trapped in a pun-tastic nightmare.

I patted my PC tower gently. "We can do this, baby," I whispered. "We're going back to the bad place, but it'll be okay. Daddy's here."

When we got back to Kev's house, I got Rodrigo settled back in his cage, but I couldn't seem to settle myself.

I felt restless and hostile. My skin was too tight, and I had trouble focusing on the job, which sucked because my number one priority was figuring out how Kev had infiltrated my system so I could shut that shit down.

I set up my computers on the giant kitchen table—again—and got to work. Maybe if I kept my eyes on my own tech, I wouldn't see Kev and do something that would land me in jail.

As the guys set up around me, I concentrated on taking deep breaths and trying to relax.

Kev might have been born into a cushy situation—handsome, plus rich, plus a loving, supportive family equaled the trifecta of cushy, as far as I was concerned—but there were things I could do that he couldn't, precisely because I hadn't grown up with silver spoons in each hand.

Like, Kev would never have the drive that made me the first person in my blue-collar family to graduate from college or that led me to be an All-State rugby champion, despite being six inches shorter than most players in the league (not to mention having zero natural talent for sports).

He wouldn't understand the kind of loyalty and work ethic that had been ingrained in me by my former-Marine dad or the brotherhood that had formed between me, Champ, and our other teammates when we served together.

Kev didn't get that sometimes you fucking *had* to succeed because failure wasn't an option…

Or that letting down my team would crush my soul.

After several hours of trying to find the vulnerability and failing, I was at my wit's end. Champ eyed me over the giant mug of coffee he'd brought over from the fancy machine on the kitchen counter. "Take a break, Hux. We need to talk strategy."

"I can't," I argued. "I've got scans running, and I… I fucked up by not finding this myself. I need to make it right."

"You fucked up," Champ agreed with no heat. "But that happens. Nobody's perfect. That's why we work as a team. Our success or failure isn't all on you, okay?"

But it was. The tech part of it was.

And the fact that his words reminded me of what Kev had said earlier… well, that made me clench my jaw tight.

Champ lowered his voice, and his eyes met mine in concern. "Is there a reason why you won't ask Kev for help? Beyond the gamer rivalry, I mean. Anything I need to know?"

I felt like Champ was managing me, and I hated that. I hated being someone who *needed* to be managed.

So I was sure as hell not gonna admit something as childish as "Kev Rogers has everything I've ever wanted, and I'm not gonna let him take my fucking job too." Not when I knew how silly that sounded.

"Nah. We just work differently, that's all." I shrugged. "But I can work with him if I have to. No problem."

We both knew I was lying.

"Right. We're moving to the den for a planning session. Nonnegotiable," Champ added before I could argue again. "We need your input before the meeting with HOG Corporate."

I gave one last, longing glance at my machine, then logged out and followed him through a small hallway into the wood-paneled room we'd taken over for our strategy sessions. There was a giant sectional sofa in front of the stone fireplace, with two comfortable chairs making up the rest of the seating area. A low wood coffee table filled in the empty space between the seating and the hearth. Thankfully, the furniture had been deliberately selected to withstand the abuse of ten men treating it like their own personal playground.

Champ pulled one of the chairs around in front of the fireplace to face the rest of us scattered across the sofa and spoke solemnly, "First things first: you did a fucking incredible job on Saturday. I wanna thank you all."

We all exchanged glances, and I saw Jordan and Elvo nod. Champ was never stingy with praise when we'd earned it, the same way he never hesitated to call us on our mistakes.

"We didn't have a lot of time to plan this one," he went on. "We were flying by the seat of our pants, but we made it happen. I think it's safe to say that when I assigned Riggs a mission last November, none of us expected this—"

Riggs snorted. "Now, that's an understatement. Let's see… Since last November, Champ's forced me into a shitty personal protection assignment in Venezuela with a rich doctor—" Riggs counted off on his fingers.

Champ rolled his eyes. "Yeah, my bad. I see how poorly that worked out for you and your new husband."

"We got kidnapped by the head of a notorious drug cartel," Riggs continued counting, "only to learn he wasn't *actually* the head of a notorious drug cartel. We found that HOG Corporate's missing lead programmer was being held at the cartel's compound also. We rescued Buck, then found out that he'd stolen a Horn device full of cartel data." He shook his head. "I definitely hadn't *expected* any of that."

"Don't forget falling in lurve in the jungle with the doctor you were sent to protect." Elvo batted his eyelashes and made a bunch of teasing kissy noises. "That was the most unexpected of all."

One corner of Riggs's mouth tipped up, and he didn't

seem embarrassed in the slightest. "It was," he agreed, glancing at the shiny new piece of hardware on his left ring finger. "But what Carter and I have… that's the part that makes all the rest okay."

I restrained an eye roll and a gagging noise only with incredible strength of will.

Look, it wasn't that I didn't believe in love, or think it was cool, or whatever. But the idea that love could make a person change their whole interpretation of events, elevating an utter clusterfuck into something that was "okay" simply because love came out of it? Lolz. *No.*

Love might be a sweet power-up in the game of life, but it would never be my reason for playing.

"I'm personally still trying to process that the Horn Buck stole contained information on the cartel's associates," I cut in before the conversation devolved into a full-on love-fest. "No, wait, lemme back up a step. I'm still trying to process that a drug cartel was conducting business through Horn of Glory in the first damn place."

Jordan snorted. "You sound so outraged, Huxley. How *daaare* they use your precious game to launder money?"

The others laughed. I didn't.

"Frankly, *yes*." I folded my arms over my chest. "I mean, is nothing sacred to these fuckers?"

"Clearly not," Champ growled. "Since two days ago my ex-boyfriend attempted to use the love of my life as a *human shield* so he could steal back a device he believed was the cartel's Horn."

Everyone stopped joking and went quiet immediately, squirming guiltily.

Clearly, Champ was still enraged that his ex, a DEA agent named Vince Parler, hadn't been trying to get his hands on the cartel's Horn because he wanted a big promotion and a corner office in DC as we'd originally thought, but because he was working for the Cartel de la Luna. And I knew that what really pissed Champ off was that his sweet, sassy Quinn had ended up in serious danger during the course of our operation.

Even knowing that the wedding we'd staged had worked—that Vince had fallen for the bait and had stolen a decoy Horn full of practically impossible-to-decrypt data that would keep his cartel bosses busy and off our backs—hadn't calmed Champ one iota.

And I couldn't blame Champ for any of that.

"The question is," he went on, leaning forward slightly, "what are we going to do with the information on the cartel's Horn now that we know Vince was involved? The only reason we didn't let the government handle the investigation from the moment we realized what Buck had stolen was because our client was involved—"

"And HOG Corporate's stock would tank the second the media ran a story about a connection between a drug cartel and the biggest gaming sensation in a decade," Elvo concluded. "HOG's competitors would have a field day with it, and we'd almost definitely lose our client."

"Correct." Champ massaged the spot between his eyes, like hearing it all laid out was overwhelming. "None of that's changed, but it's a secondary concern now. We have evidence in our possession that could help take down Cartel de la Luna, and we know that a DEA agent has been compromised." He dropped his hand and gazed around at each of us. "We initially planned to pass the data on the Horn to the DEA while keeping Horn of Glory out of the story. I don't know how we could possibly do that now, which makes things... complicated."

"A clusterfuck, you mean," Jordan sighed, tilting their head back to the ceiling.

We all exchanged uneasy glances… and then my phone buzzed with a text.

KevTheAnnoyingOrcHoarder: *Your rabbit is in my lair again.*

Seriously? It figured that when the asshole actually contacted me, it would not be to apologize for embarrassing me in front of my boss earlier, or to make amends for spying on me in my kitchen-lair yesterday, or even to give me actual pertinent information about my *supposed* system vulnerability, which my scans still hadn't fucking identified, it was to tell me he'd kidnapped Rodrigo.

Like a fucking stalker.

I closed my eyes and took a deep breath before tapping out a response.

Me: *I was very careful to latch his door after the last time, and Rodrigo lacks opposable thumbs. If my rabbit is in your lair, it's because you opened the damned cage door to let him out, convinced him to follow you down there with treats, and then opened your biometric locks.*

Me: *If you harm him, I will go full Liam Neeson on you.*

KevTheAnnoyingOrcHoarder: *Oh, fuck off. You have ZERO room to talk after what you did to my kelp forest!! I have been relocating angry refugee mermen all afternoon.*

KevTheAnnoyingOrcHoarder: *Besides, I would NEVER hurt Rodrigo. In fact, I rescued him. I heard him crying in there. Pretty sure it sounded like, "Help, I'm owned and ignored by the worst HOG player in gaming history." Sorry, Hux. My hands were tied. I'm not a monster.*

Me: *I don't ignore him and you know it! That's why I brought him out here. That's why I agreed to let you give him a bedroom, so I could continue his regular nap routine even while I'm working.*

Rodrigo's bedroom here was bigger than my own room back at my apartment, but whatever. Rodrigo enjoyed the peace, and Kev had space to spare.

KevTheAnnoyingOrcHoarder: *Oh, right! I forgot about The Bunny Song! Fortunately, I have a video I can call up whenever I need reminding.*

KevTheAnnoyingOrcHoarder: *In fact, maybe THE WHOLE INTERNET needs reminding.*

I gritted my teeth and tried not to remember the time two nights ago when I'd accidentally left Rodrigo's bedroom door open and Kev had witnessed me carrying him around like a baby, singing to him about what a good bun he was and how much I loved him, before putting him down for a nap.

My face had been scarlet red for an entire day after that.

If he had a video and posted it… oh, God, I was going to kill him.

Elvo leaned over to set his coffee down on the table, calling my attention back to my *actual* priority. I put my phone in my pocket and ignored the next buzz.

"The situation doesn't have to be a clusterfuck," he said. "We could go higher up at the DEA and find someone we trust to give the information to. Someone who's not connected to Vince."

Jordan frowned. "But how can we know who we can trust? We can't assume that Vince was working alone."

"We have no reason to believe he's pulled in anyone else at the DEA, though," Champ pointed out.

"I guess," Jordan agreed. "It's just… as soon as we give the government the data, the way they handle it is gonna be out of our control. If the DEA fucks up the investigation — purposely or not — or they decide the evidence isn't enough to pursue a case, we'll have implicated our biggest client in a massive public relations scandal for no reason at all. How much of a slam dunk is this evidence?"

Champ looked over at me. "What we know so far is that the data on the cartel's Horn is a list of high-ranking cartel member names and their corresponding Horn of Glory usernames, right?"

I nodded. "If the Cartel de la Luna is using the Horn of Glory game as a front for their large drug transactions, this list is the key to understanding who's doing what."

Jordan ran their hands through their hair. "Yeah, but this has never made sense to me. How can you use a game as a front for tracking large shipments of drugs?"

Their eyes flicked to me, so I did my best to explain. "Two things you need to know about Horn of Glory. One, it allows you to spend actual money to purchase *pips*, which are HOG's in-game currency—"

"Like you'd buy coins in a different type of game app, or extra lives or skins. That's not unique," Riggs said.

"Not at all," I agreed. "What makes HOG unique is the *second* thing you need to know. While Horn of Glory keeps a record of certain information, like pip purchases, IP addresses, and total game-play hours, the majority of your user info is stored on your individual device."

Several pairs of eyes watched me with similarly blank expressions, so I tried again.

"Okay, here's an example. Let's say that I go and spend ten thousand American dollars to purchase ten thousand pips with my credit card. You with me?"

Everyone nodded.

"Once I make that purchase, HOG Corporate will keep a record of it. *HogMasterHux, who is playing on his green Horn with serial number 12345, purchased ten thousand pips for ten thousand dollars.* They'll also track where I am every time I'm playing—the internet address where I logged in—so they'll know I'm in the Thicket now, and last summer, I was up in Pennsylvania for my dad's thing, and so on. And they log my total game-play hours. Still with me?"

"So far," Champ agreed.

"They do not track what I *do* with my pips once they're on my Horn, just like the bank doesn't track what I do with my cash when I withdraw it from the bank. So I could bury my pips in a coffee can on my homestead like an old prospector. I could buy a couple of Ferny Redwoods and then chop them into kindling." I shuddered at the very idea. "I could spend it all on rutabagas that die in a Root Vegetable Blight, leaving me with nothing but sad memories. *Orrrrr—*" I looked around the assembled guys. "—if I'm the sort of person who wants to do illegal, criminal things, I could take my pips and buy sixteen hundred bushels of sparrowflox powder from a player named *Nabo-Enojado7*—who, according to the list, is none other than Mauricio Leon, a known cartel member—"

"The fuck is sparrow powder?" Jordan demanded.

"Sparrowflox." I tried not to sound like I was explaining simple things to a toddler, even though that's kind of how I felt. "It's a magical substance that allows a creature to heal faster, and it's incredibly common, which makes it not particularly valuable... *in the game.*" I paused. "But according to our intel, to the cartel it represents cocaine."

"*Ohhhhh,*" Elvo said, eyes wide. Then he frowned. "Wait, no, still don't get it."

I tried hard not to smile, and fucked-up as it was—because I was still *seriously* pissed at him—I had to stop my eyes from traveling around the room, trying to seek out Kev's. Working together on the wedding op for the last couple of weeks, I'd gotten used to having someone else in the room who spoke my language, and I... I missed it.

I was also dying to check my phone, which continued to buzz with unread messages in my pocket, but I resisted the urge.

"Okay," I said patiently, continuing my example, "so now I can take my sixteen hundred bushels of sparrowflox, and I can sell half of it to a user in Haiti who'll give me ten thousand pips for it—"

"Wait, that's as much as you paid for your *whole* inventory," Jordan argued.

"Exactly. Hell of a profit margin, right? And I can sell my pips *back* to the game and get my cash back. Meanwhile, the Haitian user can sell theirs to a user in Dallas, and so on and so forth."

"Who the hell is spending these crazy amounts of money in the game?" Elvo demanded. "How could HOG Corporate not see exactly what's happening here?"

"You need to understand just how much some people spend to play this game every single day. It's not just bad guys who are purchasing thousands of dollars' worth of pips. I haven't put a dime of my money into the game, but I'm the exception to the rule. I'd be willing to bet that nearly every ranked player in the game has paid to give themselves the upper hand," I said disgustedly, thinking of Kev Rogers and his immunity boosters.

I mean, I didn't know for sure that Kev was buying them, but the chances of him earning them the hard way was practically nil.

"And there's the sheer volume of the game to consider," I went on. "If this was a game with a couple dozen users, they could *never* hide that kind of money. But there are millions of HOG players and tens of millions of transactions each month." I hesitated, then admitted, "That's also probably why HOG doesn't have much interest in eliminating this problem."

"Explain," Champ demanded.

"Well. If I put ten thousand dollars in HOG's bank account today to buy pips and then cash in my pips and withdraw my money next week, HOG has been collecting short-term interest on my money. That's not gonna earn you a ton on ten thousand dollars, but on a million? Ten million? *More?*"

Elvo whistled. "Yeah, I see."

"It's a very handy way to launder money because it's basically untraceable..." I leaned forward slightly. "*Unless* you have a list that links usernames to real-life names. Because once you know *that*, you could subpoena those people's Horns, and their device will show exactly what they did with their pips and their sparrowflox and where they were when they did it. So, thinking practically, if we're able to look at HOG's financial data for these cartel members, and we see that the Dallas username has just purchased a lot of pips..."

"We'd know they were probably about to make a large purchase, and we'd be able to watch for an incoming drug shipment to their location. If we got their Horn, then we could create a trail showing the flow of money back from Dallas, to Haiti, to Venezuela..." Champ said excitedly.

"And connect them to the cartel," I agreed. "Yeah."

"Wait. Hold up." Elvo narrowed his eyes. "You mean the *DEA* could issue subpoenas and create a trail. Not '*we.*' Why would *we* have any interest in doing their job for them?"

Champ hesitated. "We wouldn't... unless we could figure out a way to get the DEA the info they need to take down the cartel without implicating HOG Corporate like we'd originally hoped to do." He shrugged. "It always comes back to the same thing."

Elvo shook his head. "I don't see how you keep HOG out of this. How do you explain the money-transfer thing to the DEA without talking about *pips* and *sparrowflox powder?*"

Champ sighed. "You're right. We're gonna have to talk to Jacob Horn and tell him we're going to the DEA about Vince and the stolen Horn."

He didn't need to say out loud what we all knew—that in the hierarchy of priorities, getting a cartel off the streets was way more important than any client's reputation, let alone our own.

I saw the tension in his face. Once we'd passed off the decoy Horn to Vince and Quinn was safe, Champ had thought for one shining moment this case was finally over. Now it looked to be as far from over as possible.

Riggs had been mostly quiet, so when he spoke, the rest of us snapped our heads over to him. It was clear his mind had been following a different path. "What if Vince is undercover? I know his name is on the list of cartel associates from the Horn, but what if he's a plant in the cartel to help bring them down? Doesn't that make the most sense?"

To spare Champ from having to say it, I answered for him. "There are a number of indications he's not. There are limits to what a government agent can do even when under-cover. There's no record of a warrant for the wiretap on our office. There's no justification for the intimidation and bribery he used with Quinn. And, frankly, if the DEA wanted Tommy Drakes's Horn, they would have gotten a warrant for it. Finally, Vince Parler is a known DEA agent. If he was undercover, they would have tried to erase him from their public records or something. Either that or he'd have to have done something incredibly bad to convince the cartel to trust him."

Champ's nostrils flared. "We all know that's the case regardless."

Riggs reached over and patted Champ's shoulder. "We don't know his reasons. They could have something on him."

Champ shook his head. "I appreciate what you're trying to do, Riggsy, but that wouldn't excuse him taking the low road instead of going to his agency for help. People are dying from the illegal drug trade, and if there's anyone who knows how bad the effects are, it's a trained DEA agent."

"Do we know why Vince is on leave from the DEA? And, if not, can we find out?" Riggs asked.

"The most I could find out from my sources is that he requested personal time." I shrugged. "I'll put out some feelers to see what excuse he's using, at least."

Riggs nodded.

When my phone buzzed a fourth time, I pulled it out to see Kev's messages.

KevTheAnnoyingOrcHoarder: *Did I mention I relocated my mermen into your Nymph Preserve? I sense a population boom coming. You're welcome.*

KevTheAnnoyingOrcHoarder: *Also, Rodrigo says he likes me best.*

KevTheAnnoyingOrcHoarder: *Yes, I speak bunny. I'm multi-talented.*

KevTheAnnoyingOrcHoarder: *Rodrigo says he wishes to wear a bowtie and tiny sweater vest, and to pose for a classy photo shoot. *shrug* I don't make the rules, Huxley.*

I repressed a flare of amusement and powered my phone off. Kevin Rogers was the most annoying human on earth... and I didn't want to think about why I felt lighter after reading his texts.

"Okay, so we're agreed?" Champ glanced at each of us in turn. "We're meeting with Jacob Horn tomorrow, and we're going to tell him what we know—and that we're turning the information over to the government so they can do an official investigation?"

We all nodded, some of us more reluctantly than others.

I felt a wave of affection for the teammates I considered my family. They were a bunch of assholes sometimes, but when the chips were down, we were all committed to doing the right thing…

Even Kev.

I couldn't help but pull my phone out one more time and shoot Kev a message back.

Me: *No bowties. Sweater vests are fine, but nothing around his neck.*

He didn't hesitate.

KevTheAnnoyingOrcHoarder: *Deal. I hadn't thought of that.*

And only because he said that, only because he admitted I might know something he didn't, did my ego finally allow me to send the text I should have sent an hour ago.

Me: *I need you to tell me how you infiltrated my systems this morning.*

KevTheAnnoyingOrcHoarder: *Dude. I tried to tell you earlier.*

I rolled my eyes. Of course he had to say his I-Told-You-So's. Honestly, I'd have done the same.

Grudgingly, I typed back:

Me: *You did. And I should have listened. But I need to know our vulnerabilities in order to keep Champion Security safe.*

KevTheAnnoyingOrcHoarder: *I know. So bring me a big cheesecake brownie on your way down here and I'll show you.*

I closed my eyes and leaned my head back on the sofa. The other guys were standing and stretching, grabbing half-empty coffee mugs from the table, and wandering out of the room.

"Hey." Riggs kicked my foot with the toe of his boot. "You okay?"

I straightened in my seat. "Yeah. Good." Aside from struggling to admit that a full-time couch potato—an elitist *child*—could possibly know more about cybersecurity than I did, I was peachy.

"Look…" Riggs hesitated. "I know you and Kev are like oil and water. And I told myself I wasn't gonna interfere—"

I lifted an eyebrow. "Then don't."

"—but the guy is family now."

"Pfft. Your family."

"*Our* family," he countered. "Part of the Champion Security family. And I know he can be shy and awkward—"

"I think you mean diabolical and evil."

"—but he's a good person. I care about him. He's like a little brother to me now. So, I don't give a shit if you trash-talk each other or get into a steel cage death match in the game—"

I snorted.

"—but in real life, maybe you could try to get along."

Riggs took one look at my pursed lips and narrowed eyes and held up his hands in surrender. "And now I'm going back to not interfering."

I rolled my eyes. Too little, too late. "Did your new husband put you up to this?"

"What? No, Huxley. Believe it or not, I'm still capable of having my own thoughts and opinions."

My disbelief must've shown on my face because it was Riggs's turn to roll his eyes. "I can't wait for you to actually fall in love someday. I'm going to laugh my ass off."

I pushed myself to my feet. "Well, no danger of that happening anytime soon, big guy. Tell Carter your ass is plenty safe."

Riggs blushed—literally blushed—which was so unlike him that I had to smother a smile as I turned and left. But as I stalked down to Kev's lair, I found myself gritting my teeth as I replayed the conversation.

Me? Try to get along with Kevin? Yeah, no. Kev needed to stop invading my work, invading my *thoughts*, and then

we'd get along just fine. The man spent all day in his basement lair, challenging other full-time gamers to quests while
the rest of us worked our asses off to support ourselves and
try to improve the world around us in some way.

And I was *not* bringing that bunny-napper a brownie.

*I will not call him a spoiled dilettante to his face. I will not call
him a spoiled dilettante to his face…*

That promise to myself lasted all of twelve minutes in
his presence.

And then I couldn't hold back.

3

———

KEV

"Huxley, Huxley," I said in my best Marlon Brando impression, swiveling my chair around to face the door after I'd buzzed the lock that allowed Hux to step into the semi-darkness of my lair. "We have known each other for many years, and this is the first time you come to me for counsel, for help." I stroked the rabbit on my lap thoughtfully. "But you don't ask me with respect. You don't offer friendship. You come to me on this, the day of my daughter's wedding—"

Hux's booted feet *thunked* against the polished black floor as he walked toward me, and the light from the fractals spiraling and morphing across the giant screens that ringed the walls reflected off his messy hair and set jaw.

I tamped down a giddy flare of excitement when he came to a stop less than a foot away and leaned a hip against my enormous glass desk.

He rolled his eyes so hard I was surprised he didn't give himself an aneurysm, but the edges of his lips twitched like he was holding back a smile at *The Godfather* reference. "Can it, Don Kev-leone. The *only* reason I'm here is because

Champ asked me to work with you. And gimme my bunny back."

I shouldn't have taken as much delight in teasing Hux as I did, but it was fun to poke at the giant chip on his shoulder. It was even more fun knowing that someone understood my weird sense of humor, and even though Hux rarely gave me the satisfaction of laughing, I never doubted that he got my jokes.

"Thought I told you to take that thing off his neck," Hux said as he reached for the rabbit on my lap. When he leaned close to grab hold of Rodrigo, I caught a whiff of Hux's familiar scent. There was something about it that made me a little wobbly, which was ridiculous since I was pretty sure it was simply a low-budget sandalwood deodorant stick from the grocery store.

I turned my chair back toward my monitors quickly.

When Hux reached for Rodrigo's R2-D2 bow tie, he realized it wasn't on a collar. "Is this… *glued to his fur?*"

I kept my eyes on my monitor bank. "Not glue. Calm yourself. I already told you, *I* am not a person who takes out his aggressions on innocent mermen… or bunnies. It's just lube."

"You used *lube*? On my *rabbit*?"

I tossed him a glance over my shoulder. "Could you stop making it sound weird? How do you think parents get bows to stick on their babies' heads? They use lube. Google it."

Hux made a scoffing noise. Then he murmured reas-suring platitudes to Rodrigo as he delicately picked the bow off his fur and rubbed at the tiny spot of goop there. "You don't need a bow to be cute, do you, sweet boy? No you don't. No you *don't.*"

I did not want to find his bunny-talk endearing… but I did.

Just like when I'd pulled up my security feed from the

kitchen earlier and caught part of a conversation between Hux and Champ, I hadn't wanted to find their interaction entirely relatable… but I had.

I fucked up by not finding this myself, Hux had said, sounding legit heartbroken over his error.

In that moment, Hux hadn't been the arrogant jerk who'd dismissed my skills and blown me off spectacularly that morning. He'd looked almost… nervous, like he was worried Champ might kick him off the team for not meeting expectations or something.

Or maybe I was hella projecting because that's how I would have felt.

Either way, sympathy had tarnished the shine of being proven right, and now I couldn't even gloat, which was annoying. How dare Huxley be vulnerable and multifaceted when disliking him was the only thing that made me feel better about his attitude toward me?

In an effort to ignore the man making sweet kissy-faces at his rabbit, I checked my Horn for new messages.

Anomaly451: *Hey, sweetie! Security question for you.*

I relaxed into my chair and grinned at the screen. At least someone recognized my intelligence and sought me out without being forced to.

HogDocKev: *Yeah! Shoot.*

Anomaly451: *If you wanted to secure digital information so no one can hack it, how would you do it?*

HogDocKev: *Uh. Wow. That's… broad.*

Anomaly451: *Lol. I guess it is. I'm writing an article on it and I'm consulting with a few subject matter experts, so I thought, why not ask my own boyfriend?*

HogDocKev: *You're so sweet! Okay, let me think…*

Anomaly451: *We can chat over comms if you'd rather! Or, I could ask you this weekend! (Hint, hint.) I'm about ready to get out of DC and see some Tennessee beauty. Namely YOU.*

Yeah, the Tennessee thing so wasn't happening—as evidenced by the interfering jerkface standing beside me—but the idea that Adam had sought me out made me feel good. Before I could respond, though, Hux dropped Rodrigo back in my lap, sans bow tie.

"There. That's better," he grumbled. He looked at the design on my *Star Wars* polo shirt and snorted out an appreciative laugh. "Nice shirt."

"Oh, uh." I glanced down at my chest like I hadn't already seen the quirky design a million times, mostly to hide my blush. Of course Hux was the one other person on the planet who got it. "Thanks."

He leaned his ass against my desk and folded his arms over his chest. "Now, talk to me about this vulnerability. I still can't believe I missed something large enough for you to gain access to the system and run a script."

Hux was medium height—maybe three inches shorter than my five-eleven frame—but unlike me, he was *built*. Every part of him, from his thighs, to his abs, to the tattoos on his forearm revealed by his rolled-up shirtsleeves, was packed with solid muscle. I didn't want to notice it, especially not at that moment, but the way he was leaning put it all on display.

I swallowed hard and fumbled my Horn back into my pocket. "You didn't. I mean, you *did*. But, uh… only sort of." Great job, Kevin. Really articulate. "Getting in to run the script was easy. You know the best way to gain access to a system isn't to hack your way in with brute force—" I began.

"No shit. It's social engineering." Hux sounded bored. "Call someone and pretend you work for their IT department, then ask for their password. Or write an email pretending to be from their credit card company and see if they'll follow your bad link. Blah, blah, blah. Wait…" He paused for a second to narrow his eyes at me. "You can't possibly think I was dumb enough to fall for any of those things."

"No! Not exactly. Um." I took a deep breath and carefully didn't look at Hux because just the sight of him kept tripping me up. It was truly unfair that someone so jerky should be so hot. I tapped my index finger against my thumb once, twice, three times, five times, eight times, thirteen times to calm myself. "You know social engineering's not all about telling lies, right? So, an opportunistic person might wait until their target left their desk to, say, collect their bunny's travel cage in the other room—" I chanced a glance at him.

"Wait... *wait.*" Hux blinked, and then his entire face went red. I'd seen him angry—often—but not like this. "You... you used the bunny against me? You accessed my system and programmed it to run that script when we got back to the office?" he whispered. "You made me look like an ass in front of my boss, Kevin. *Fuck you.*"

I blinked at him in confusion. "Wait, what? You... you already knew that I'd accessed the system to run the script. I mean, that's why you're back here at the house—"

"But I thought you'd accessed it through an actual vulnerability, asshole!" Hux straightened and ran a hand through his messy hair. "I didn't realize it was because you'd *created* a vulnerability just to exploit it."

"No. I... I didn't! I mean, technically I did, but only because—"

Because there was an actual vulnerability in the system, and he wouldn't listen to me. Because I wasn't sure how else to get his attention. Because I'd been desperate and, yes, pissed off, and I'd wanted to get through his ironclad ego any way possible just so he'd take my warning seriously. Take *me* seriously.

"Because you wanted attention again," Hux finished. "You wanted to save the day again."

"No!" I insisted angrily, pushing away from my desk. "Not at all. That's not it *at all*."

In fact, after overhearing Hux's conversation with Champ, I'd decided to admit my wrongdoing and draw Hux a map to the vulnerability so *he* could find it, fix it, and be the hero himself, because I was a giver like that. I'd been working my way up to my confession with my messages about Rodrigo earlier, but then Hux had demanded the information before I could offer it.

Now, with Hux's eyes flashing fire and his jaw clenched as he stared me down, I was starting to regret being so soft-hearted. Because the truth was that Hux *had* fucked up by not finding the threat, then compounded that fuckup by not listening to me, and doubled down on the fuckup by leaving his computer unattended. The fact that he was blaming me when I'd tried again and again to be helpful was...

Well, it was *hurtful*. And that made me angry.

"I mean... technically, you're the one who left your computer unguarded, so really, *you* made *yourself* look like an ass, wouldn't you say?" I clapped back. "I admit that I—"

"My computer was unguarded in a trusted space!" Hux's hands tightened into fists—a kind of clench-release, clench-release that made my throat go dry. "Jesus, fuck, Kev. I was here in your house with all known agents."

I tilted my head and wrinkled my nose at him curiously. "Are you... are you serious?" I demanded. "Knowing someone isn't the same as trusting them, Hux. Look at what Champ's ex did. Doesn't matter if someone is a 'known agent.' Unless you'd trust them with your *life*, you don't trust them with your system." That was Cyber Security 101, right there.

Hux's face got redder—like, concerningly red—probably because deep down, he knew I was right. "Clearly, it was a mistake thinking I could trust *you*." His words hit me like poison, bitter and caustic. "Why the hell would you sabotage me in front of my team? Do you have any idea how hard I work to make Champion Security safe from intruders? This isn't a game, Kev. There's a lot at stake here. We're dealing with cartel intel. A cartel that murders people."

Like I didn't know that? Like my own cousin hadn't been kidnapped by the cartel people and I hadn't stepped in and helped to get him back safely?

I focused on keeping my breathing steady so I wouldn't yell at him for being so condescending. In my calmest voice, I said, "Then it seems extra important to keep your systems secure by logging off your machine when you step away from it, hmmm?" Honestly, that was IT Security 101.

He rubbed his face with his hands the same way he had when we'd worked together to decrypt the data on the cartel's stolen Horn—like he was disgusted and weary in equal measure. "Christ, you exhaust me. Is that all? You're saying the single vulnerability in Champion Security's system is the one time I left my own machine at the hands of a rabbit-napper?"

I opened my mouth to admit there was more to it, that there was an actual vulnerability, but then Hux shifted his weight toward me, and a wave of his signature scent hit me, making me dizzy again.

"No, I..." I shook my head to clear it, and my gaze caught on the stark black ink of his tattoos, which shifted as the muscles beneath them shifted. Even when he was angry at me, the man was impossibly distracting.

I tried again. "I just meant that I..." But then Hux ran his hand over his face again, and I became hyperaware of his callused hands and long fingers as they scraped along his chin, and I had to look away and close my eyes to get my breathing back under control.

Good freaking gravy. What the hell was wrong with me?

But even as I thought the words, I knew. Obviously, I knew. Sexual frustration could make a man desperate, and considering I was about to enter my twenty-fifth year of sexual drought, it was no surprise that I was starting to feel like I was back in high school, popping wood every time the breeze blew.

I'd had a kinda-sorta sexual encounter with Anomaly —*Adam*—a few weeks back, and it had been great, but… well. If I was being honest, it hadn't quite lived up to my fantasies. When I'd imagined my first time, I'd envisioned sensual touches and husky pleas, not an MUD—a Multi-User Dungeon—where we typed our commands to one another.

You've taken off your shirt and now you're naked.

You love it when I play with your sensitive nipples.

Your dick is enormous and hard, and when I touch you, you moan.

It had been fun, sorta, and Anoma—*Adam*. Jesus, why was that so hard to remember?—seemed to really enjoy it, which made me feel good, but… Well, if the universe had intended for a man to type and jerk himself at the same time, he would have been born with three hands, you know?

I'd thought about setting up a hookup through an app. Adam had said many times that he didn't expect me to make a commitment or be exclusive yet, even though he was committed to me in his heart. But… I'd gone this long waiting to have sex, and now I wanted it to mean something. To be more than an anonymous fuck.

My brain flashed an image of Hux naked and sweaty on top of me, grunting into my ear—most likely something bossy and rude. I imagined my bare legs wrapped around him as I arched up against him.

Whoa. Where had that image come from?

And why did it get me more excited than all the MUD commands put together?

Hux's nostrils flared. "That's it, huh? Nothing to say for yourself?" He shook his head. "This is why we don't work with fucking *civilians*. You have no idea what trust and teamwork mean."

The fantasy bubble I'd been floating in popped, and I sucked in a sharp breath as I came back to reality.

This was *Huxley*, for goodness' sake. The menace who'd destroyed my fucking kelp forest. The man who made me painfully aware of just how socially awkward and useless he believed me to be.

And no matter how vulnerable he'd sounded with Champ, that didn't make us friends. It never would.

Stupid me for forgetting.

I grabbed Rodrigo and shoved him in Hux's arms. "Take him. Take your damned rabbit, okay? And get out of my lair."

I wanted Hux gone, immediately. If I tried to explain the actual security vulnerability my scans had found, he'd spend more time in here confusing my sex-deprived brain, making me think about all sorts of shit that could never actually happen.

Instead, I'd use the administrator account I'd given myself when I'd accessed Hux's system to run the script, and I'd patch the damn vulnerability myself. Hux never had to know I'd been in there again.

Hux settled the rabbit with gentle hands, but the look

he shot me was hard. "Kicking me out? You have an important HOG date or something?"

I stuck out my chin. "Maybe I do. My boyfriend was asking my advice on a technical issue, actually."

He looked deeply suspicious and maybe a little angry. "Your boyfriend? Wait, you mean *Anomaly451*? The HOG player you mentioned the other day? You're official now? Have you met in person?"

"N-no. Technically, we haven't met yet. But he's my *boyfriend*," I said stoutly. "Online. And he's none of your business."

"Bullshit."

I squawked in outrage. "It is not—"

"First off," Hux went on, leaning toward me, "there's no such thing as an online boyfriend. Until you're in the same room with the guy, you can't know if you have chemistry. Do you like the way he smells? The way he smiles? The way he looks at you? The way he carries himself?"

"I— It doesn't matter. That's shallow stuff—"

"Does looking at him make your dick swell, even in a crowded room?" He spoke the words casually while cuddling Rodrigo to his chest, which should have made it impossible to take him seriously, but the intensity of his eyes nearly made me swallow my tongue. "Does he make you laugh? Does he know how to get under your skin? Does he make you want to be around him all day long? Does he make you think, 'Now, *that* is a man who could take me apart piece by piece and put me back together'?"

"I— He—" My mouth was too dry to complete a sentence.

"No," he concluded. "He couldn't possibly. Because you don't really know him. And second… It is for sure my business if someone's fucking with family, Kevin."

I blinked at him. "F-family? Me?"

Suddenly, a miracle happened. Jasper Huxley blushed and looked away. "You know what I mean. Champion Security and any of the people connected to it."

My heart hadn't slowed down since the Hux-naked-on-top-of-me scene had paraded its way through my skull, but now, my breathing ticked up to join it.

"Right. Well, Adam's not fucking with me. He's... he's kind. He makes me feel capable and cared for. Unlike certain people."

"Mmhmm. Anomaly sounds like a real prince." Hux huffed out a laugh. "I hope for his sake he doesn't leave his system unguarded when you're around."

Ughhhh. Infuriating!

"I could have done something so much worse, and you know it!" I said hotly. "If I'd *actually* been untrustworthy, if I'd *really* wanted to fuck things up for you, I could have! I was being helpful."

"Yeah, sure. Thanks for the help, Kev." He leaned toward me again, and this time, I held my breath so I wouldn't get lost in the Jasper Huxley Sensory Vortex. "Stay away from me, and stay away from my shit. Got it?"

He strode out of the room, and the minute the door swung shut behind him, I pushed my chair back from the desk and leaned back in my chair.

"Henry, engage locks," I commanded.

"Yes, sire."

As soon as the locks snicked tight, I groaned out loud in the soundproof room.

Hux was going to drive me insane.

But before I could do anything dramatic—like, say, loot Hux's crop of rainbow parsnips and salt his field—my alarm went off, reminding me that I had a lunch date.

I groaned again but jumped to my feet quickly because my date hated to be kept waiting.

I was so distracted by the encounter with Hux that I completely forgot to answer Adam. Instead, I ran a hand through my hair, made sure my glasses were on straight, grabbed my car keys, and got on the road to Nashville.

"I started to wonder if you forgot how to get here, it's been so long since you were home," Grandfather said after we sat down in the private dining room at his golf club, which was exclusively set aside for members.

"I just saw you on Saturday at Carter's wedding," I reminded him.

"It's not the same," he lamented. "When you decided you wanted to live with Carter in Licking Thicket, I figured you meant for a few weeks. But I suppose I should have known it was permanent when you took Oprah along. You always loved that stuffed duck more than was reasonable for a grown— Oh, gin and tonic for me, please, Maggie," he told the uniformed server who had, of course, appeared at our table at the moment of peak embarrassment for me, because that was how I rolled.

I felt my face go hot and tugged at the collar of my shirt. "Erm. Just water for me. Thank you."

The pretty blonde smiled. "You must be Dr. Rogers. Your grandfather talks about you all the time."

"Really?" I blinked. "I… yeah, I am." My cheeks went even hotter if that were possible.

"It's so cool how cardiology runs in your family. I'm a premed sophomore at Vandy, myself." She pressed a hand to her chest.

I opened my mouth, then shut it again. I'd mostly made peace with the fact that, despite having my doctorate, I was the only nonmedical person in my family of renowned medical pioneers and philanthropists, but every once in a while, the old sting rose to the surface. "That's, uh… You're thinking of my cousin Carter. I'm the *other* Dr. Rogers. The black sheep."

"This is *Kevin*. The one who's a talented computer… erm…" Grandfather waved a hand in my direction as though expecting me to supply the word. "Inventor person."

I nodded seriously. "Yes. I personally invented computers."

"Oh. Wow." Maggie, who, tragically, had been born without the ability to recognize sarcasm, got a little pucker between her eyebrows. She looked from my face down to my polo golf shirt—which had a tiny embroidered Yoda with a five iron over my heart along with the words "May the Course be With You" spelled out in rainbow letters— then to my grandfather and back to me. "That sounds… difficult?"

"Not really," I said modestly. "The time travel was the trickiest part. Once I had that down, the rest was easy."

Maggie stared at me in utter confusion.

Grandfather coughed lightly. "We'll both have the turkey club sandwiches and side salads," he said with a firm smile. "Thank you, Maggie."

She forced a smile and nodded at him, but she kept frowning at me, even as she walked away, like she low-key questioned the genetics that had led me to be a Rogers.

Girl, same.

Grandfather lifted an eyebrow at me, and I sighed and squirmed like a little kid who'd been caught misbehaving. "I was only joking."

"I know, Kev." He sounded fond but a little out of his depth, as usual. That my grandfather loved me to the ends of the earth, I had no doubt whatsoever. But he didn't know quite what to do with me, either, and never had.

"I don't like salad. And I dislike being treated like a child," I muttered… exactly like a child.

"I know that too," he said cheerfully. "But making you eat your vegetables is a habit I'll never break, even when you're a hundred." He winked. "So, how are things in the Thicket? How are the newlyweds?"

"Oh, fine." I waved a dismissive hand. "Carter went right back to work, and so did Riggs. Literally, nothing changed." I pondered this for a second. "Except Riggs's name, I guess. He's a Rogers now."

Grandfather made a supremely proud and satisfied noise, as though he'd personally engineered this outcome… which I supposed, in a way, he had. "Proof that not all Rogerses have to be doctors," he said pointedly.

I smiled, just a little. "Yeah, I know." At least, I knew it in theory. "So, um… Mom emailed me," I said a moment later, after Maggie had delivered our drinks.

Grandfather's mouth pursed in a way that had nothing to do with the lime in his drink. "Did she?"

"First time since…" I sucked down some water and thought about it. "Hmm. I think since my birthday last year? She's been praying for me every day, though."

"Of course, of course! Too busy praying to pick up a phone, presumably." He rolled his eyes. "What else did she say?" The way he asked the question made me suspect he knew the answer.

"Oh, the usual. That Shepherd Church is doing some amazing things in Burundi, providing needed medical care, and she knew I'd be interested in helping them out. She said I could go over and volunteer if I wanted… or just make a donation if I'd feel more comfortable doing that."

He made a rude noise. "Yes, your father contacted me about a donation also." His voice was strained the way it always got when he talked about my parents. I knew he didn't agree with most of their parenting choices, and I tried not to feel bad that I'd driven a wedge between Grandfather and his only living son.

"What did you say?" I wondered.

"The same thing I hope you said." He lifted an eyebrow. "To take a long walk off a short pier. The Rogers Family Foundation doesn't give financial support to charities that aren't actively pro LGBTQ+, and neither do I." He narrowed his gaze. "That *is* what you told her, right?"

I couldn't restrain my smile. Some people pitied me for the way my parents had left me to be raised by my grandfather, but I figured I was pretty lucky, all in all. If the first family members I'd had to come out to had been my parents... well, I might not have come out. Ever. Instead, I'd had Carter and our grandfather, and they'd been fierce champions for me, always.

"That's what I told her," I confirmed. "I might have considered volunteering, but we both know I'm no use to a medical charity when I have no first aid skills."

Grandfather didn't waste breath arguing about whether my parents felt that way. He reached across the table and took my hand, which also made me feel like a little kid, but in a *good* way. "More fool them if that's what they think, Kevin. You've saved hundreds of lives in your own way. You're intelligent and kind and *good*."

"Sure. Not to mention devastatingly handsome," I joked since I didn't want to argue about it.

I wondered if I could get my grandfather to call Hux and tell *him* what a good person I was. I figured Hux was at that moment telling Champ I was a menace, simply because I'd tried to help him out.

I quickly changed the subject after that by pulling up some glamour shots of Rodrigo in his tiny vest, to my grandfather's delight... but as we ate our sandwiches, it was harder to stop thinking about it.

One of the downsides—okay, maybe the only downside—to being born into a wealthy, philanthropic family was that I'd very quickly become aware of all the sadness and unfairness in the world, and that made it genuinely hard to feel like I'd done enough good to make up for the advantages I'd had in life.

Yes, I gave tons of money away. Yes, I'd developed some patents that I'd given away too. But my grandfather was a huge philanthropist. My parents had devoted their lives to their work. Heck, Carter's parents had *died* on a medical aid trip when he was just a kid, and Carter himself had worked with Doctors Across Continents for years.

I wanted to do more. To truly help people in a tangible way, like they all did.

Which was maybe why it pissed me off so much when Hux continually reminded me how useless he thought I was. It hit a little too close to home.

Grandfather and I chatted about a few projects he'd been working on, as well as some research I'd been doing, and our lunch passed quickly and happily.

As I drove back to the Thicket, I felt better than I had in a long time. I'd needed some time away from the house, away from the overpowering group of ex-military personnel who'd taken over my peace like a team of caffeinated rhinos trapped in a tea shop.

But after the interaction with Maggie, I also felt a little bit guilty for making Hux look incompetent in his job.

Yes, my intentions had been good... mostly. And yes, Hux was a jerk who'd chosen the worst possible interpretation of my motives and who should have *listened to me*. But also... there were many less-embarrassing ways I could have accomplished my aim. So why had I picked the one that would provoke him the most?

When I finally got back to the house, Champ's team was still hard at work around the kitchen table. I avoided them and slunk down to my lair the back way so I wouldn't have to make annoying small talk with anyone.

Guilt made me get to work immediately on fixing the security vulnerability… but when I actually settled to work, what I found was enough to send a wobble of dread into my stomach.

Someone had already taken advantage of the vulnerability and tried to take control of one of the servers on the network.

Fuck.

After another hour of hacking my way down several rabbit holes, I discovered the intruder was working from a local IP address. Of all the HOG joints in all the world, how was the hacker here in the Thicket? Unless…

On a hunch, I took another tack and hacked into HOG's location-tracking system, asking my system to run a scan on Vince Parler's current location.

"Understood, sire. We'll notify you once it's complete," Henry Cavill assured me.

Then I began the slow, meticulous process of accessing employment records at the DEA so I could figure out what excuse Vince had given them for his leave of absence.

I needed to remember my plan from yesterday: help Champ and Hux's team close this case once and for all so I could get these meatheads out of my house once and for all. So I could go back to my regular, peaceful, Hux-less life. So I could have the freedom to invite Adam for a visit, and we could burn my virginity card to ashes.

I closed my eyes and gritted my teeth. *If you wanted them gone, why did you infiltrate Hux's system to get them back here?*

"Because he needs to know he isn't Mr. Perfect Cyber-security Expert," I muttered under my breath.

Which was also true. But my flipping stomach suggested the real reason had way more to do with the goofy gamer who fairly reeked of competence when people were looking… and who baby-talked his bunny when they weren't.

Jasper Huxley was a dreamy combination of expert gamer, tech-savvy professional, and fun to be around. He made his friends laugh, and if I was ever fortunate enough to find myself in his inner circle, I'd consider myself lucky as all heck.

I opened my eyes and focused on my work. Maybe impressing Hux with my own tech abilities and protecting his team was the first step in gaining his respect.

4

———————

HUX

Jacob Horn was not a calm man.

"Dammit, Champ, I was counting on you to get us out of this PR disaster," he said, pacing behind the chair at the head of the conference table in Horn of Glory's executive offices. Weak February sunlight glinted off his fancy watch and the bald spot at the crown of his head. "I took a chance on you, even though there were plenty of other, better-established companies who wanted my business, because I trusted you to get the job done. And now you're saying you've *failed*?"

Ugh. I bristled. I couldn't help it. There was nothing I hated more than indiscriminate use of the f-word, especially when it wasn't warranted. Champ hadn't *failed*; our team had made a choice—the correct one—and I wanted to punch Jacob Horn in the mouth for suggesting otherwise.

Clearly, I wasn't feeling very calm either.

To be fair, my mood wasn't all about Jacob Horn. I was still seriously angry about Kev's antics from the day before. Who violated the integrity of a man's system for the sole purpose of embarrassing him? Who mooned over a pissant

HOG-champion wannabe like fucking *Anomaly451* as though he was God's gift to e-boyfriends?

"He makes me feel capable and cared-for," Kev had claimed. Puh-lease. Like Kev Rogers, with his pretty face and off-the-charts intelligence, had ever had a reason to feel bad about himself?

I'd been so worked up I'd tossed and turned all night, and when I'd finally fallen asleep, I'd had a crazy dream — one where I'd sat buck naked in Kev's expensive leather chair in the middle of his tricked-out lair, pushed Kev to his knees, threaded my hands into his thick hair, and made him choke and gasp his way through a very *thorough* apology blow job while wearing nothing but those damn black glasses. One where I'd shown Kev that Anomaly wasn't the only person who could make Kev feel capable and cared for.

I'd woken with the smell of vanilla and coffee in my nose and a raging erection — *me, having wet dreams about Kev Rogers? Christ. What was the world coming to?* — which had riled me further.

"I'm waiting, Mr. Champion," Jacob Horn prompted. "For some explanation."

I felt a migraine brewing behind my eyes, so I fingered my earring and took a deep breath. I directed my gaze out the window to the pasture full of grazing cattle on the far side of the employee parking lot and focused on counting cows to chill myself out.

The Horn of Glory Corporation headquarters was a modern chrome-and-glass building that would have been right at home in New York or Miami or even Nashville. Here on the outskirts of Licking Thicket, surrounded by fields full of cows and alfalfa, it looked a little like an alien spaceship that had crashed to earth.

I'd always figured they'd chosen to locate here partly

because Horn of Glory had been created by a Thicket local and partly because we had the best of both worlds, with the affordability of rural Tennessee and the proximity to Nashville's technical talent pool. Even knowing that, though, it had still struck me as strange.

It was as if Amazon or Boeing had suddenly decided to move their corporate offices to the tiny northwest Pennsylvania town where I'd grown up so their executives could gaze out the window at the Elks Club, where my former-Marine dad had spent his evenings, and the Lutheran Church, where my mom still spent her days, and the tiny field where my runty ass had begun and ended my high school football career all in the same game.

Why would anyone in their right mind do that?

Watching Jacob Horn rant and pace, I figured I understood. Anyone who had to deal with the man for more than a few minutes needed some cheerful, pastoral scenery to look at, or they might lose their shit entirely.

Champ, who had far more practice being professional than I did, kept his usual calm and controlled demeanor. "We greatly value HOG Corporate as a client, and I feel like we've gone above and beyond in order to fulfill our duty. However, I'm not in a position to break federal law by withholding data critical to a DEA investigation." He took a breath. "We would love nothing more than to find a way to keep the company name out of it, but unfortunately, we seem to have run out of options."

Jacob pinned Champ with a stare. "There is no limit to the budget for this."

Champ's chin dipped. "I understand. But it's not an issue of money. It's an issue of legality, not to mention moral obligation. I cannot condone the obfuscation of information that would potentially enable the DEA to take down a drug cartel. We need to turn this list of names over to the government."

Jacob sighed and ran his fingers through his hair. Whatever product he used was damned good at its job because his salt-and-pepper combover landed perfectly in place again. "Then I really need to insist that you give me some time to prepare. I need to put together a response team, consult my attorneys, and determine how to prevent a disastrous devaluation effect."

Champ nodded thoughtfully, like we hadn't already anticipated this. "Understood. But I'm afraid we can't give you long."

The two executives he'd brought into the meeting shared expressions of concern. I understood their worries, but I also knew Champ was right. We could no longer justify holding on to this information without any compelling reason other than "our client's company will look bad, so we'll look bad too."

I shifted in my chair when the executives began discussing strategies to manage key stakeholders. Corporate-speak wasn't something I was comfortable with. I was a Marine who was the son of a Marine, which meant I was way more familiar with discussions of deployments than depleted market share.

Champ glanced over at me and must've seen that I was both bored and on edge—a dangerous combination. He barely restrained an eye roll. "While we discuss timelines, why don't you take this opportunity to gather the user data you mentioned from the technical team, Huxley?"

I shot out of my seat like a rocket and was halfway down the hall before taking a breath of relief, but that relief was short-lived. My Horn yodeled with an incoming message just as I reached the elevator.

Shit. I thought I'd set the thing to Silence Mode days ago.

I gave an embarrassed smile to an older gentleman, who gave me a disapproving look, and quickly pulled my Horn out of my pocket to check my notifications. If fucking Kev had *re*-retaliated for my kelp-forest-burning retaliation, I was going to *re*-re-retaliate so hard that legends would be told about the force of my…

Oh.

When I saw the message on the screen, I realized my error. When I'd left that morning, I'd accidentally grabbed my new blue Horn—SmittyKitty's Horn—instead of my usual green one. And while the message was from Kev, it wasn't retaliatory at all.

HogDocKev: *Yo, Smitty, I have kind of an odd question. Do you ride motorcycles?*

HogDocKev: *You mentioned something the other day when we were messaging about air speeders. The reason I ask is because if you do, I can send you some Harley-Davidson safety gear IRL.*

HogDocKev: *I just got a box of airbag jackets in a bunch of different sizes. Happy to send one if you'd like.*

I stared at the message, remembering the box emblazoned with the Harley-Davidson logo that Riggs had carried down to Kev's basement lair yesterday. I'd assumed it had been motorcycle parts since I'd recently learned Kev owned *three* motorcycles, but clearly, I'd been wrong.

I sighed and felt a little of the tightness ease from my shoulders.

Just when I thought I had the guy figured out and could write him off entirely—sexy punishment blow job fantasy notwithstanding—Kev went and showed that he didn't quite fit the "spoiled rich attention-seeker" pigeonhole I kept trying to cram him in.

He was sweet and generous sometimes. Maybe even most of the time. Maybe to everyone but me.

I typed a response.

SmittyKitty: *Why'd you order more than one?*

HogDocKev: *I didn't order them. They just keep sending them.*

SmittyKitty: *Because they like you???*

HogDocKev: *Ha. No. I wrote a piece of code that they use in the sensor software for the airbag deployment so I guess I'm technically on the development team. *shrug**

I stared at the Horn screen and reread his message several times before trying to type a response.

SmittyKitty: *You…*

I deleted that and reread his message again.

SmittyKitty: *You helped write the code for airbag deployment sensors in safety jackets?*

HogDocKev: *Yeah.*

HogDocKev: *I mean, no.*

HogDocKev: *I mean, I didn't develop it specifically FOR that purpose…but yes, I own the patent for it.*

My curiosity was so intense I ended up on the basement level of the HOG building before realizing I'd missed my floor. I pressed the button for the second floor and typed again.

SmittyKitty: *What purpose did you develop it for, Pip?*

While waiting for a response, my brain started snapping puzzle pieces together. Someone—maybe Riggs—had mentioned once that Kev was independently wealthy, but I hadn't believed them. He'd been raised by his obscenely wealthy grandfather, who was a fixture in Nashville high society. I'd just assumed Kev had a giant allowance from his granddaddy that enabled him to buy his NASA-level tech and live a life of couch-potato idleness.

HogDocKev: *This is kind of embarrassing.*

HogDocKev: *Okay, so I was in the rocketry club in high school…*

HogDocKev: *(That's not the embarrassing part, FYI.)*

I stepped out of the elevator just in time and found my mouth curving up in a smile. Kev was geeky, like me, but he owned it and never apologized for it. I could respect that.

HogDocKev: *This guy in my class, Wayne Montrose, was your classic bully. Used to give me wedgies and call me Heavy Kevvy, the Supergeek.*

HogDocKev: *(That's not the embarrassing part either. Not my fault Wayne was an asshole.)*

I snorted and parked my ass against the wall by the elevator as the dots by his name swirled.

HogDocKev: *Anyway. Wayne lived a few streets over from the school. So one day I tricked out one of our rockets with an accelerometer, a gyroscope, and GPS sensors, and then added a balloon filled with paper penis confetti to the rocket.*

HogDocKev: *When the rocket reached certain parameters (i.e., the ones that meant it was over his house), it triggered a pin snap that burst the balloon and showered his house with dick… right when his mom was hosting the governor's wife for a garden party.*

I barked out a laugh, which caused a woman walking past me down the quiet hallway to startle and jump back. After murmuring an apology, I stared back at the screen, hoping for more of Kev's ridiculous story.

HogDocKev: *But while I knew the confetti was biodegradable, since it was paper, I hadn't even CONSIDERED that it might contain dyes that weren't great for the environment until someone in Green Club chewed me out later.*

HogDocKev: *That's the embarrassing part. Still makes me cringe.*

I shook my head. I hadn't believed it possible for someone to be so brilliant, so devious, and so strangely innocent at the same time… but I was starting to believe it now.

HogDocKev: *After the in-school suspension, I was given some whispered advice by the rocketry advisor to patent the technology. It was supremely satisfying to show up a few years later and give them enough money to sponsor the rocketry club and the Green Club for decades to come. Score one for the Dick Rocket.*

I wanted to hear more—to hear other stories of young Kev and his antics—but I wasn't sure what to say or how to ask. And the uncomfortable thought twinged in my mind that maybe Kev wouldn't have shared that story at all if he'd known he was telling it to *me*.

SmittyKitty: *Love that. Massive respect for the Dick Rocket Man, Pippy.*

HogDocKev: *Aw. Thanks. *smiley face**

HogDocKev: *And my name's still not Pip.*

I hesitated, then sent the text I would have sent if I hadn't known HogDocKev was wealthy Kev Rogers in real life. It was a test, I told myself firmly. A way to confirm that, behind all the quirky, sweet stories, he was still the entitled, attention-seeking asshole I'd known for months.

SmittyKitty: *You know, you could sell that Harley gear for cash. Make a killing. Or do a giveaway of some kind. You'd get loads of admirers.*

HogDocKev: *Nah. I hate attention and I don't need the money right now. I need the good karma, and I like knowing I helped someone out.*

HogDocKev: *Anyway, let me know if you want it. No strings, I promise.*

Ugh. I shook my head as my chest squeezed pleasantly.

When I spotted the developer I needed to talk to, I quickly slipped the Horn back in my pocket and followed her to her cubicle with a little lightness in my step that for sure hadn't been there before hearing Kev's ridiculous dick-rocket story.

How fucked-up was it that Kev pissed me off like no one else… and cheered me up like no one else too?

No strings, Kev had said. He'd said that to Smitty before too. But somehow, with every damn word he typed, I grew more conscious of the tether growing between me and the guy I didn't want to like.

I spent the next hour gathering the data I needed to be able to track the IP address of each Horn user on our cartel list. Our team had voted to simply turn over our information to the DEA, and we would, but we'd also anticipated that Jacob Horn would ask for a short-term stay of execution while he and his PR team prepared for the fallout. During this waiting period, it was going to be my job to keep track of the cartel members on the list, monitoring their locations and any large cash transactions being processed through HOG's system from these accounts.

Once the developer gave me access to the system, I lost no time calling up all of the reports on my phone. As predicted, the twelve users were spread out over the US, as well as Central and South America. The most surprising location, however, was the one associated with Vince Parler's username.

According to HOG user data, Vince had been accessing the game from right here in Licking Thicket as recently as an hour ago.

My stomach twisted unpleasantly. All of our intel suggested that Vince had headed for a private airstrip and fled town after obtaining the decoy Horn… which made sense because Vince had to know that if Champ caught him, he'd tear him limb from limb for threatening Quinn.

If he was back—or if he'd never left town in the first place—we needed to find out why.

I waited impatiently for Champ to finish small-talking the bigwigs, and as soon as we got in his truck, I told him we needed to assemble the team ASAP.

Champ's eyes had met mine, and whatever he read there made him sigh gustily as he sent out a group text.

Champ: *Team meeting. Twenty minutes, at the safe house.*

I frowned down at my phone as he drove us across town. *The safe house?* Was that what we were calling Kev's mansion these days? Pretty ironic since every time I entered the place, I felt off-balance and out of control.

When we got back, Champ called Quinn to check in, and I stopped to make sure Rodrigo was okay—I pretended I didn't notice the fresh dill leaves mixed in with his usual hay or that he was freshly groomed—then made my way into the den. I plugged my laptop into the enormous wall-mounted TV and prepared to take my usual seat on the leather sofa, but I stopped short.

Kev was curled up in my spot, fast asleep like freakin' Goldilocks, those black glasses askew and his plump pink lips parted like a nerdy little cherub. His Horn was clutched in his hands like he'd dozed off while playing—or maybe right after texting Smitty about dick rockets—and my fingers twitched with the need to smooth back the clump of messy hair that had fallen across this forehead.

I'd never felt an urge like that before *in my life*, and I didn't like it.

Out in the hall, Elvo signaled his arrival by yelling, "Heya, boss! How'd the meeting go?" at the top of his freaking lungs, and Kev's eyelids fluttered open.

"Hux!" he whispered happily, and then he blinked in sleepy confusion, and his expression turned more wary. "Uh. Hey. D'you get my message?"

It was my turn to blink confusedly. Wait, *fuck*. Was he

talking about his message to Smitty? Did he know Smitty and I were the same person?

While I stood and stared, waiting for him to lose his mind, Riggs and the others came into the room and took action.

"Kev, dude, we're gonna have a meeting in here," he said in a low voice, placing a hand on Kev's shoulder from behind.

Kev, who must've still been half-asleep, startled. Confusion filled his eyes for a split second before he realized he was at home and among friends.

"Oh. Yeah, no, of course." He rubbed his eyes with his fingers. "Sorry. I was waiting for Hux — I mean, for all of you. I texted Hux a few minutes ago, asking if we could meet because I have some information for him — I mean, for all of you."

Ohh, he'd been asking if I'd gotten his *text* message. Nothing to do with Smitty at all. My guilty heart resumed beating.

I dug my silenced phone out of my pocket and saw the notification at the same time Kev said, "You guys need to know… Agent Vincent Parler's business in the Thicket isn't finished just yet."

My gaze flew up to his face, and I blinked. "You knew? How'd you figure it out?"

"Hold up. Huxley, since when did *you* know that?" Champ demanded, narrowing his eyes at me as he took his seat.

"Since a few minutes ago," I said. "That's why I asked you to call this meeting. While we were at HOG Corporate, I tracked Vince's Horn. His IP address shows that he's here. In fact, he might have never left."

Kev cleared his throat and shot me a look that was almost apologetic. "Actually, *he* did leave. I dug a little deeper, and CCTV in St. Louis shows Vince entering his hotel there about…" He checked the time on his phone. "Forty-five minutes ago."

I took a seat on the far end of the sofa and twisted toward Kev while the rest of the guys took seats around us.

"Not possible," I scoffed. "That Horn was active here in the Thicket all morning."

And what the heck had Kev been doing, anyway, scanning CCTV cameras for a suspect in *my* investigation?

Kev's forehead crinkled in concern, as if he was worried something was wrong with me. "You do know both things are actually possible, right?"

Fuck, he was annoying. "Well, yes, of course I do. Theoretically. But if that's true…"

I broke off, not wanting to accept the ramifications of what this meant.

Kev finished my sentence. "It means Vince has a partner," he agreed softly. "Yeah. Or a team. Someone else who was… using his Horn."

The distaste in Kev's voice was palpable, and when his eyes met mine, we shared a rare moment of total wordless understanding. I wouldn't trust my Horn to anyone unless it was a life-or-death emergency, and I knew Kev felt the same.

"M'kay, sorry to disturb your beautiful moment of nerd unity—" Champ began.

I startled guiltily and saw Kev's face flush beet red before both of us glanced away.

"—but is it possible to mask the location with like… IP addresses or VPN or something?" Champ went on. "I don't know much about that stuff, but surely—"

"No," Kev and I blurted at the same time. We exchanged another quick glance, and Kev pressed his lips together firmly. He waved a hand as if giving me permission to continue leading the meeting *I* asked Champ to call.

I rolled my eyes. "Horns don't… Look, it's complicated to explain, but the short version is that *no*, there's no way to do that on a Horn."

"Besides which," Kev interjected because apparently he couldn't keep still, "I, um… I hacked into the security system at the Silage Motel, where Vince was staying, and the person going in and out of Vince's room wasn't Vince."

I narrowed my eyes at him. "You did what?"

Kev lifted his chin defiantly. "I hacked the security footage after I realized Vince's Horn was still here but he wasn't. I figured it was important to know for sure where Vince was, and I wanted to help. And since you didn't bother replying to my text, I figured I'd just… go ahead and do it." He swallowed hard and added waspishly, "Especially since that way I'd know it was done correctly."

I opened my mouth to shred him into quark-sized pieces for overstepping *yet again*, for ham-handedly pushing his way into *my* fucking case, for being an untrained civilian asshole… when I noticed his pointer finger tapping spasmodically against the side of his thumb, and I shut my mouth with a clack.

When I looked closely, I could see all the other little signs of anxiety Kev was trying to hide. It was there in the tiny pucker between his eyebrows, in the slight quiver of his lips. He was waiting for me to ream him out, and he was dreading it, but he'd gotten the footage anyway.

I wanted to help, he'd said.

I like knowing I helped someone, HogDogKev had told Smitty earlier.

Fuck. I could let him have a moment of glory, just this once.

I took a deep breath and blew it out. "I would have handled it just fine, but… thank you. For making this more efficient." I shrugged. "So what did you find?"

"Well…" The combination of excitement and wariness in Kev's expression was so comical, and I had to restrain myself from grinning. "I went back through their security footage and found an instance of Vince entering the room with the man at the same time. I'll forward you still photos of the instances, but there isn't really enough of the second man to get a good look at him. Just enough to confirm that they definitely know each other."

I powered past my annoyance that this intel was coming from Kev instead of me and glanced around the room at my team. "So, signs suggest there's definitely a partner involved."

"Maybe," Elvo said thoughtfully. "But the guy at the motel could be a hookup or even a friend."

"A friend Vince entrusted his cartel-connected Horn to?" I asked dubiously. "That's a mighty close friend."

"I trust my cousin Carter more than anyone on the planet," Kev said. "We shared a homestead before… you know." He shot Riggs—the cousin-marrying homewrecker—a resigned look. "But I wouldn't just leave him with my Horn, especially if it was connected to an op. Would you?"

Champ closed his eyes briefly. "Shit. So the other guy *is* a partner."

"Yeah, almost certainly. And, um." Kev licked his lips and stole a glance at me. "That's not all." His face took on that half-apologetic look he'd worn before, and it raised my hackles. What the hell else had he done?

"Out with it," I demanded.

"You, ah… You might be wondering why I hacked into HOG Corporate's system to find Vince's location in the first place?" His finger tapped the side of his thumb again. "Well, I was… I was looking into your system vulnerability today, and I discovered Champion Security's systems are still being targeted," he said in a rush. "Someone here in the Thicket attempted to hack into one of the servers."

"Looking into—? But you said the only system vulnerability was—? And how did you access the system *today* when I—?" I was only confused for a split second before the answers hit me, one after the other. "Motherfucker! You lied about being the only vulnerability in my system? Jesus, Kev. And when you accessed my computer to run the script yesterday, you made yourself a fucking admin on my account so you could get back in later, didn't you? You *asshole*."

The sense of betrayal was overwhelming. Any sliver of goodwill I'd begun to feel for Kev Rogers was gone faster than an air speeder with a coveted Apple Butter Booster.

I sent Riggs a boiling-hot glare. *How the fuck am I supposed to get along with this guy when he keeps pulling shit like this?*

"Wait, Hux. Let me explain," Kev said quickly, holding out a hand toward me.

I jerked away before he could touch me. "I'm such a fucking idiot. You had to have admin privileges to load the program." I ran a hand over my face. Why hadn't I seen that before?

Simple. Because even after yesterday, I'd still trusted him deep down.

"I cannot believe you had the balls to make yourself an admin of my system when you *know* how shitty that is, Kevin. You *know*, more than anyone in this room."

Kev winced and had the decency to look guilty, but I didn't care. It hadn't been enough for him to humiliate me in front of my team yesterday, but he'd actually withheld information so I could look even more incompetent today.

I jumped to my feet, and Champ jumped up to restrain me, like he worried I might attack the gnome-fucking *betrayer* on the other end of the sofa… and maybe he was right.

"My intention wasn't… I mean, I wasn't going to… I mean… I *tried* to tell you about the vulnerability yesterday, and you wouldn't listen to me," Kev insisted, his words tumbling over themselves in his rush to get them out. "So, yes, I accessed the system and ran that script to make a point. But when I tried to confess, you jumped to conclusions again. You were already so angry, and I… I knew if I told you everything, you'd be nuclear-fallout-level angry, which you are—"

"*No shit!*" I yelled. "Because I keep trusting you, and you keep fucking me over!"

"But I didn't fuck you over! I wouldn't! I thought if I could just take care of it myself, that would help make it up to you. I was trying to…"

I leaned toward him and said in a low, menacing voice, "Tell me you were trying to help, Kev. Tell me. I dare you."

Kev swallowed convulsively.

"If you wanted to help *me*, you would have told me what was going on from the beginning. You would have let me handle it," I said in that same tone.

Riggs leaned forward, like he, too, was ready to physically separate us. "Can someone please explain what's going on to those of us who don't know what the hell you're talking about?"

Kev opened his mouth but quickly snapped it shut when he saw my face. I turned to Riggs and gave him a super-simplified version.

"There's a vulnerability in the system, and the bad guys tried to exploit it."

"You mean they've figured out that we have the info from the original Horn and they want to access it?" Champ demanded, pushing me into my seat before sitting back down.

"No." I sat on the edge of the cushion, careful to maximize the space between me and fucking Kev the Civilian. I was *itching* to get back to my computer so I could see what the fuck Kev had done to my system… and ensure he never had the opportunity to do it again. "They have no reason to believe that we have the data, let alone that we've decrypted it. They're probably trying to monitor our communications. To see whether we've given up the investigation, to figure out how much we know and who we suspect."

"But if they got into our systems," Elvo said, "maybe they found the Horn data too."

"They didn't get into our system," I said confidently. "There are multiple layers of protection to prevent that. It's like they're peeking through a hole in our fence—which is not the same as crossing the yard, bypassing the alarms, and picking the locks to get inside our house. You feel me?"

Elvo nodded slowly.

"And furthermore…" Part of me wanted to glance at Kev in smug satisfaction—or maybe to see his eyes flash with appreciation and respect—but I forced myself to stay focused on Riggs. "Even if they did get through our security, they wouldn't find what they're looking for. I keep all of the HOG data offline. It cannot be hacked. Our OPSEC hasn't been compromised."

Then I did turn to Kev, only so I could explain in my sweetest voice, "OPSEC means Operational Security, Kevin. It's a term we used in the military," as though Kev were a particularly dim child who couldn't make that logical leap.

His jaw tightened. "Thank you, Huxley, but I'm familiar with the term, thanks to Wikipedia and, you know, *television*."

"Mmm. I bet you get most of your experience from the internet and television," I said condescendingly.

Kev's eyes flared, and he turned a violent puce color, which was odd—that had been a half-assed insult at best since we both knew Kev had multiple degrees in computer science and sure as fuck hadn't gotten them by watching TV—but whatever.

I ignored him and turned to Champ. "Still, this is serious. Unless Vince became a hacker since you two dated, this confirms he's working with someone. That raises the threat."

Champ looked up at the ceiling. "That fucking asshole," he muttered before focusing back on me. "Who could Vince be working with who has those kinds of skills?"

Kev opened his mouth to speak again, then inhaled sharply and stopped himself.

"Oh, by all means, answer," I said, sweeping a hand from him toward the rest of the team. "Since I didn't get a chance to actually *see* the fucking breach in my own damn system, I'm sure you know best."

Kev cleared his throat. His finger and thumb *tap-tap-tap-tap-tapped* frantically, like a hummingbird's wings, but I hardened my heart and refused to feel sympathetic.

"The vulnerability they tried to take advantage of..." Kev glanced briefly at me. "Hux is oversimplifying. It's not as straightforward as a hole in a fence. The security he built is actually quite complicated and technical. So for Vince's associate to not only find it but to know how to slip in under the radar means we're not dealing with a casual keyboard warrior or some teenager who works part-time at the geek shop at the mall. He's well trained."

"Government, then?" Champ asked. "DEA?"

Kev shrugged and glanced my way, looking for permission to speak.

I folded my arms over my chest and gave him the barest of nods. Kev could praise my security all he liked, but I was still *livid*, and I had no plans to change that.

Kev sat up straighter. "Could be. If so, they're likely in a very technical position there," Kev said. "We're talking a security analyst, cybersecurity forensic analyst, or a pen tester. I can't imagine someone would have these skills and not be using them to earn a better living."

Champ huffed out a humorless laugh. "Presumably, the better living is coming from the cartel, kiddo."

Kev grimaced but nodded.

I exhaled. "Kev's right," I said, though no one seemed to be doubting him. "Cybersecurity's always changing. It wouldn't make sense that someone doing another job—let's say special agent, scientist, or administrative role—would have the time to keep current on the latest hacking intel in a way that allows them to actually use it. It's one thing to understand the concept; it's another to be able to pull it off without leaving a trace."

Riggs's face was crinkled with confusion. "But he did leave a trace, right? That's how Kev realized he was here in the Thicket."

"Kev had already found the vulnerability, so he had an idea of what he was looking for. Besides, even if the hacker is good, Kev's better," I answered without thinking.

The silence in the room clued me in to the compliment I'd inadvertently given my archnemesis.

I focused on my hands as if the jagged edge of one of my fingernails held the key to eternal life. Heat filled my skin everywhere and left me slightly damp. I swallowed and prayed for someone to say something.

Finally, someone had mercy on me.

Unfortunately, it was Kev.

"Anyway!" he blurted. "The good news is I fixed the breach." He pinned his bottom lip with his top teeth before flicking his eyes away and lowering his voice. "I mean. It wasn't a bad breach. Only… um… a little janky thing. I patched it. You guys should be good now. Maybe. Hopefully."

I didn't want to ask—I really, absolutely didn't want to give Kev the satisfaction of asking—but my mouth opened anyway, and words tumbled out.

"What janky thing?" I growled.

"Oh, ah… The public-facing SSH access on the Cisco router." He waved a hand.

I felt my face go even hotter, and my fingers tingled slightly. Good fucking God. That wasn't a "little janky thing." It was a big fucking mistake that Kev had caught and fixed.

Less of a hole in the fence and more like a wide-open gate inviting people inside.

"*Fuck*," I muttered.

"Sounds like we owe you one." Champ stood and clapped Kev on the shoulder. "Thank you." He turned eyeballs in my direction, like he expected me to say the same.

Kev's eyes flicked to me, obviously nervous about my reaction.

I wanted to rage at him some more.

I wanted to ask everyone in the room how grateful or trusting they'd feel if some guy noticed their front gate wide open and, instead of *alerting them*, had come inside and made himself at home.

I wanted to thank Kev for keeping our system safe when I hadn't.

And another part of me—the biggest part—wanted to punch myself in the face for fucking up in the first place.

So instead of saying any of that, I simply stood up, muttered, "Looks like I have work to do," and walked my ungrateful ass out of the room.

5

KEV

I tried not to feel dejected after Hux left the room. Really, what had I been expecting from him? Effusive praise? Why was I surprised by his surly attitude when the man was 100 percent made up of surly attitude? Yes, he'd complimented me briefly — and I could admit to a moment of happy smugness at his words — but he'd also treated me like the unemployed freeloader he still thought I was.

"Hey, thanks for the assist, man," Elvo said, shaking my hand before he left the room.

"Hmm? Oh, sure. No problem," I murmured, Hux's angry glare still playing on an endless loop in my brain.

I'd known he was going to be annoyed that I'd touched his precious system. I would have been if the shoe had been on the other foot. But why couldn't he see that I'd done it for the right reasons? That my intentions had been good?

"Great job, Kev," Riggs said, pulling me in for a one-armed bro-hug. "You showed real initiative."

"Huh? Oh, cool," I mumbled, but it was hard to summon a smile when my mind couldn't stop replaying

Hux's smirky smirk as he said, *"I bet you get most of your experience from the internet and television."*

How had Hux guessed that I'd never had sex with anyone but Anomaly and that the closest I'd come to seeing someone's orgasm face was in porn? Did I emanate virgin vibes?

Could Hux tell that I'd been dreaming about his smile before they'd woken me up a half hour ago?

I swore by the many moons of Vulcan I had never been so mortified.

"Don't mind Hux. He's taking this case hard," Champ explained, clapping my upper arm with one giant hand. "It happens like that sometimes. He feels personally responsible for the security of our systems, you know? And guilty when he thinks he's let us down. When he's in the right frame of mind again, he'll thank you too."

I mumbled something agreement-ish and nodded along, but as I stared at the spot on the sofa where Hux had been sitting, I knew Champ was either lying or delusional.

Jasper Huxley was determined to find the worst possible interpretation for everything I did, always.

And I was tired of it.

I looked around the empty room and set my jaw. All my life, I'd felt less than. My grandfather and Carter loved me, but they didn't understand me. The computer science geeks like the ones I'd met in college understood me but didn't love me. And the rest of the world—whether it was bullies like Wayne Montrose or my own dang parents—didn't do either.

For the longest time, I'd figured that was my fault—that I must have some flaw in my code that made it impossible for me to have the easy friendships that other people took for granted. I'd spent years cutting myself off from the real world, living almost entirely online—working on algorithms and data structures, developing technology, and playing massive multiplayer online games like Horn of Glory—because when I interacted through a computer interface, I knew the rules and how to achieve things. I rarely made mistakes. Other users sought me out to collaborate with me, learn from me, and spend time with me.

And it had been satisfying. Safe. Easy.

Then my cousin had gotten kidnapped a few months back, and everything had changed.

When Carter went missing, I'd been frantic to help him, but I hadn't had the first clue how. In Horn of Glory, I had a cache of weapons and an army of orcs on air speeders to command. In real life, I had few practical skills and not a single contact I truly trusted not to take advantage of me to gain access to my name and wealth.

I realized I'd tried so hard to hide from the world I had no resources to help my family when they needed it. If Champ's crew hadn't been on the case... *ugh*. It made my stomach flip to imagine what might have happened to Carter or to my grandfather when he heard the news.

Since then, I'd resolved not to feel powerless anymore. I'd talked to a therapist who'd given me strategies to manage my social anxiety. I'd forced myself out of my lair. I'd visited Grandfather often. I'd reached out to new people, both online and in real life, and made an effort to forge connections, which was how I'd become friends with SmittyKitty. I'd tried to use my resources to help others. I'd chatted with Anomaly and let things develop instead of walling myself off. I'd tried to assist Champ's team as much as possible.

And I'd felt... better. Not powerful, exactly, but definitely more in control.

So it was incredibly lowering that Jasper Huxley, with his secret smiles and piercing eyes, his sandalwood scent and his bunny-talk, could make me feel vulnerable again with just a few angry words.

I hated how much his opinion mattered to me. I hated that even though the rest of the team was giving me kudos for a job well done, none of it made me happy because the guy I respected most was angry at me.

In frustration, I slapped my palm against the doorframe on my way out of the room—which accomplished nothing except giving me a sore hand—and stalked down to my lair.

The more I thought about it, the more I realized that I had as much right to be angry as Hux did.

Heck, I had *more*.

I ignored the sick twisting in my stomach calling me a liar and placed my fingerprint on the pad that unlocked my lair. The door opened with a quiet *whoosh*.

"Henry Cavill?" I demanded.

"Sire?" the AI replied smoothly.

"Pull up the record for the IP address I was looking at earlier. Also, please show me the camera feed from the second floor of the Silage Motel from the last twelve hours. Playback at two times speed."

I was going to find out who Vince's associate was. I was not going to let Hux's bad attitude stop me from helping Champ's team.

"Yes, sire. Processing now," Henry agreed. "Sire, you have one unread email from Professor Homsy at Vanderbilt with the subject 'Request for Project Assistance.' You have one unread text from Carter Rogers that reads, 'Come join me and Riggs for dinner tonight if you're home.' And you have one unread Horn of Glory message from Anomaly451 that reads—"

"Reply to Carter, please," I interrupted the AI. "Tell him, 'Not tonight, cuz. Home, but working. Thanks anyway.'"

"Yes, sire. Message sent."

"Thanks." The other messages could wait because I had work to do. "Oh, and Henry? Could you open..." I hesitated.

I'd been about to ask him to open the feed from my camera in the kitchen, but I thought better of it. I didn't want to watch Hux stomping around angrily. That would be pathetic.

"...I mean, could you, um, order me a pizza, please, from the usual place? I'm going to be here a while."

"Yes, sire," Henry replied gently, making it clear that even the AI thought I was pretty pathetic already.

It took eighteen hours to track the mystery man down, but when I finally did, the results were worth the effort. I raced upstairs and skidded to a halt in the kitchen. When my socks didn't get the message, I nearly wiped out before grabbing at the kitchen island.

"Found him!" I gasped, waving my tablet in the air and straightening my glasses.

Five pairs of bleary eyes looked up at me. The giant kitchen table was cluttered with half-filled coffee cups and half-empty takeout boxes—an indicator that our house-keeper and cook, Mrs. Carmody, must have long abandoned her post—and through the window, I saw the sky was just beginning to lighten.

"Found who?" Elvo asked.

"Dude, why haven't you answered Carter's texts?" Riggs demanded.

"Is that the same shirt you were wearing yesterday?" Jordan wanted to know. "Have you not slept yet?"

"Erm." I looked down at my T-shirt. "Yes? And no. But

it doesn't matter because…" I paused for dramatic effect. "I found Vince's guy. The hacker from the motel. The motel hacker." My brain pulsed from a heady mixture of excitement, fear, and four liters of Dr. Pepper.

No one else seemed as excited as I was, though, and once I replayed my words, I realized they weren't nearly as impressive as I'd thought.

"Shocker," Hux said dryly, barely glancing up from his computer screen. "Did you find that he was… at the motel?"

I noted that Hux was dressed in the same tight-fitting black T-shirt and ass-molding cargo pants he'd worn the day before, but no one made snarky comments at him. *Hmph*.

I ignored him and focused on Champ. "The guy's name is Linus A. Dixon of Rosecommon Drive, Falls Church, Virginia. And he is, as we suspected, a security analyst for the DEA."

"Wait, you actually ID'd the guy?" Champ pushed back from the table and made his way over to the coffee maker, though his eyes remained fixed on me. "How'd you do that?"

Hux grumbled angrily, "And who the fuck authorized you to?"

Once again, I ignored Huxley. "Well, first, I spent hours and hours trying to enhance the security images from the motel that I forwarded to you, but that got me nowhere—"

"No shit," Jordan confirmed, rubbing their eyes. "I've been trying the same. No dice."

"And I ran plate numbers on every car in the lot—" Elvo yawned.

"Same," I agreed eagerly. "But all the cars were tied to other rooms."

Elvo nodded. "Right. Our guy must enjoy walking."

"I tapped into the motel's security cameras." Hux closed his eyes and stretched his neck from side to side. "But other than getting a middle-of-the-night pizza delivery, our guy hasn't moved. So how the hell did *you* get an ID on him?"

"Right. About that. See, I remembered a conversation I had with…" I darted a look at Huxley and licked my lips before giving Champ a nervous smile. "…with *someone* the other day. We agreed that the best way to gain access to a system isn't brute-force hacking but social engineering…"

From the corner of my eye, I saw Hux's head snap up and felt his eyes boring into my skull like lasers.

"So I brought the guy a pizza," I concluded. "I walked up to his door and knocked."

Hux shoved himself up from the table much faster than a tired person should have been able to move. He lunged toward me, grabbing my upper arms roughly and pinning me with an intense glare. "You did *what*? Have you lost your fucking *mind*, Kevin Rogers?"

My heart hammered in my chest, and my eyes went wide. "I… I…"

Champ laid a hand on Hux's chest. "Let go," he said, his low voice deep and commanding. "That's inappropriate and unprofessional. Huxley, you're scaring him."

Champ's last words seemed to penetrate Hux's frantic anger because Hux let go of me instantly and lifted his hands in the air in a "don't shoot" posture. His face fell. "I… I'm sorry. I didn't mean to scare you."

I shook my head, unable to speak for a moment. How could I explain that *fear* was not remotely what I'd felt when Hux had grabbed me and his eyes had locked on mine? That my heart was racing for an entirely different reason?

"You didn't," I managed to choke out. "I'm not scared of you."

Hux clenched his hands into fists and nodded once. "I still shouldn't have touched you like that."

You shouldn't have let me go, I wanted to say, but I managed to close my mouth before the words could escape.

This is not the time or the place, Kevin. Not the guy either, I reminded myself.

"Okay," I said instead.

Champ nudged Hux out of the way, but I could still feel Hux's eyes roving all over me as if to assess whether or not I'd come away from the hotel unscathed. Maybe I should have been insulted—I mean, honestly. I was capable of simple tasks!—but I couldn't work myself up to it. It felt too nice to imagine that he cared about me.

"You shouldn't have done that," Champ said calmly. "You're not a trained operative. We don't know who we're dealing with, but we know Vince is dangerous. You could have been recognized. You could have been hurt—"

I held up my hand to stop him. "I wore a baseball hat, a Pizza Plaza sweatshirt with the hood pulled up, and the thick plastic glasses I had in high school, which, trust me when I tell you," I added wryly, "render me invisible to all men. He was busy doing something on his Horn and barely glanced in my direction before he slammed the door. I apologized and said I had the wrong room, then I left. End of story. But I was wearing a hidden camera, so I was able to run his face through facial recognition when I got home and discover his identity."

I tapped on the tablet to send the data file to Hux's work email. "That's everything I got. I'm sure you can take it from there."

Hux didn't look mollified by this, but he returned to his computer and began typing. My eyes stayed on him, hungrier than ever. As annoying as he was, he was also, somehow, a comfort. Of all the fit and capable people in the room, I felt most understood by him. I still felt the strong grip of his hands around my arms, even though he was no longer holding me. His eyes had been filled with a mixture of surprise and fear.

He'd worried about me. About my safety.

Champ pointed me to an empty chair at the table. "Let me get you some coffee. You look dead on your feet."

I shook my head. "I'm used to it. It's okay."

"Nothing about this is okay," Hux muttered without taking his eyes off his monitor. "Should have been me. Should have been someone on the team."

Once again, I wanted to meet his anger with anger and retort that I was perfectly capable of knocking on a door without dying, but I noticed a muscle ticking in Hux's jaw, and I remembered Champ's explanation from earlier. *He feels guilty when he thinks he's let us down.*

He really *had* been worried for me.

"You were working it from another angle," I said softly. "It's not like you've slept either."

Hux looked up at me. "How do you know?"

Heat filled my face and made me look away. "Just guessing."

I wasn't going to admit that I remembered what he'd been wearing the day before because that would be weird… wouldn't it?

And I was definitely not going to say that I always had a sixth sense about where he was or what he was doing, or tell him that his presence had tugged at me like gravity from the first moment we met, or admit that sometimes it took all my self-control not to track his devices or spy on him digitally just to make sure that he was okay. He'd think I was a stalker and have an even worse opinion of me than he already did.

Besides, it wasn't like that. Not really. I had my own…

person. Adam was my boyfriend. And online boyfriends were *so* a thing, no matter what Hux thought.

Hux focused his attention on his computer while Champ and the rest of his crew sitting resumed a discussion they'd clearly already been having about how to best protect their client.

Carter appeared eventually, kissing Riggs on the cheek and getting himself coffee.

"Nice to know you're still alive," Carter said pointedly, sliding a bowl of apple slices in front of me.

I winced. "Yeah, I'm sorry I didn't get your texts. I haven't checked my phone or my Horn since…" I paused to consider. "Shit, yesterday afternoon?"

Carter's eyebrows went up. "That's… unusual."

I nodded. It was unprecedented, really. And now that I'd realized it, I began to feel a little twitchy about the fact that I'd left all my devices down in my lair. But I also didn't want to miss a moment of what was happening up here, so I forced myself to calm down.

I nibbled on my apple slices while Carter said his good-byes and left for work, then got up to find something more substantial in the pantry.

I returned to the table with a plate of cheese and crackers just in time.

Hux muttered, "Fuck me," before pushing his keyboard away and glancing up at his boss with a mixture of triumph and trepidation on his face. "Champ, this Dixon guy served in the army with Hiram Oliver, who's the current head of the Inspection Division of the DEA."

Champ's lips tightened as he inhaled. "Meaning, we don't know who we can trust there."

Jordan's eyes darted around the table. "What if we approach the wrong person about their rogue agent?"

Riggs nodded and tapped his finger on the table before

saying what everyone was thinking. "We need to proceed with caution. Find a contact we can trust. Surely we know someone who—"

Elvo sighed heavily. "No. What we need to do is find the Horns ourselves."

Champ's and Riggs's eyes widened, but Elvo held up a hand before anyone else could speak. "I know. *I know.* I was the one who wanted to turn this over to the DEA from the start. We don't have their resources or their authority. This should be their mess to clean up. I still believe all of that. And I don't give a rat's ass about Jacob Horn and keeping HOG's name clean. Not anymore." He shrugged. "I'm sorry, boss, but it's the truth. I know they're our client, but they're in this up to their eyeballs, profiting off the cartel's financial transactions. They had to know the game had this potential, and they haven't bothered to stop it yet. So I was not about to go to jail just to protect a bunch of cartel-enabling one-percenters, you feel me? This face is too pretty for prison." He tapped his own cheek, and Jordan snorted.

Hearing it laid out like that was sobering, and from the looks Hux, Riggs, and Champ were exchanging, they felt the same.

"But I'm also fucking tired of constantly reacting to shit. Of waiting for *them* to make a move so we can counter it. Of not knowing who we can trust and feeling like we're one step behind at all times." Elvo set his jaw. "Nah, man, I want this shit to end so that we can move on with our lives, and the best way to do that is for us to conduct this investigation ourselves. We need to gather all the evidence, wrap it in a bow, and present it to the DEA, the DHS, the DOJ… hell, the CDC if they wanna sit in… in a way they can't ignore or hush up. We can still protect our client, probably —the details of this case don't have to be public, and the alphabet agencies would lose all kinds of credibility if we told the media that not one but *two* DEA agents were conspiring with Cartel de la Luna—but better still, we can make sure that these assholes can't come after us. Never do an enemy a small injury, right?" He leaned forward in his seat. "So we take them down."

Champ's eyes closed for a beat. "That's… inspiring, Elvo. And I'm not saying I disagree with you. But you're talking about us—our small team—finding twelve Horns. *Twelve.* Each one held by a known cartel associate. And we don't have warrants. We can't legally obtain those Horns in a way that'll be admissible in court—"

"We don't need to," Elvo argued. "The Horns aren't the buried treasure; the drugs and the financial transactions are. The Horns are the treasure map that will tell law enforcement where to look for them."

Champ seemed unconvinced, but Riggs nodded, and a slow smile spread across his face. "I like it."

Champ shot him a disapproving look. "Settle down, cowboy. These fuckers are spread all over the world. How do you propose—?"

"Not all over the world," Jordan argued. "They're all contained in this hemisphere, in the US, Canada, and South America. And two of the South American ones will be in the US for the Ascendant's Tournament at HOGCon, which is coming up soon." Riggs lifted an inquiring eyebrow, and Jordan shrugged. "What? Literally everyone knows that."

"Not everyone," Champ grumbled. "Some of us actively avoid knowing." He sighed. "I hate this fucking game. Fine, then. Elvo, grab your whiteboard, and let's make a plan."

I continued eating my cheese and crackers, totally engrossed as the team brainstormed around me. They made a list of all the names they were tracking and where the associated Horn was currently. Hux told Elvo which names to put a star next to, as those represented HOG players who were expected to be in Las Vegas for the tournament. I found myself nodding along as they came up with their plan.

"You need someone to play in that tournament," I advised around a mouthful of cracker. "That'll be your best chance at getting close enough to those two Horns."

Hux nodded. "I can do it."

"But you can't," I reminded him gently. "You were disqualified after the javelin toss, remember? You need three high-level quest achievements in order to qualify. Not to mention, you need a hundred game-play hours in the thirty days leading up to the tournament, and you're hardly ever on anymore." I swallowed. "I mean, that I've noticed. Not that I *would* notice. In fact, I definitely wouldn't. Unless someone notified me that HogMasterHux was looting my jam cellar or torching my kelp."

Champ groaned slightly and shook his head. "Please tell me that's all a euphemism for something," he begged Riggs, who patted his shoulder comfortingly.

"I can qualify if I play as Sm…" Hux's face reddened. He snapped his jaw closed before trying again. "Uh. If I play as soon as I'm done here and as often as possible over the next week."

"That would require you to complete quests back-to-back, while also playing enough to restore your health points and restock your power-ups, while also doing all the groundwork for the op, unless you have some super-secret method of qualifying that I don't know about," I scoffed.

Hux set his jaw and glanced away.

Right. I rolled my eyes. For the love of Commander William T. Riker. I didn't care if Hux was being protective or guilty—the man was so pigheaded it made me want to scream. He couldn't do it all. He shouldn't have to do it alone. Not when I could help.

I mean, yes, I'd never actually appeared at an in-person tournament before, and, yes, the idea was more-than-slightly terrifying. But I'd already been toying with the idea just as an excuse to meet Anomaly, and now I had even more incentive.

Hux's gaze caught on my hand, which rested on the table, while my fingers *tap-tap-tapped* out a Fibonacci sequence of their own volition. I quickly trapped my hand between my thigh and my chair and assumed a confident expression. "I can do it," I told Champ breezily. "I have plenty of game-play hours, and I only need to complete one more quest. Easy peasy."

"You never go to in-person tournaments." Hux made the statement sound like an accusation.

I shrugged. "There's a first time for everything."

In fact, if I played my cards right, I might have more than one first time while I was in Vegas.

But Hux, my own personal wet blanket, was shaking his head. "No. Absolutely not. You… you're not a member of this team, and like Champ said, you're not a trained operative. Besides, we can get at the Horns another way. You don't… I mean, *we* don't… need to be in the tournament itself. We can approach the cartel guys while they're walking through the hotel and pick their pockets. We can get into their rooms, uh… somehow… and steal them. We can…" His voice trailed off, probably due to a distinct lack of decent ideas.

I lifted an eyebrow. "Uh-huh. How about if I qualify for the tournament just in case?"

The look Hux shot me was almost feral. What the heck was his problem?

"*I* will qualify for it," he growled. "You can… you can provide support from here in the Thicket."

"Why doesn't Kev qualify, and then Hux can borrow his…" Jordan began reasonably, but they broke off immediately when Hux and I sent them matching incredulous stares. "Oh. Whoa. Right, no. Just kidding. *Ha!*" they said, wide-eyed. "Forgot that's a violation of the first HOG-zealot commandment."

"Unlike *some* people, I would never use a teammate's gear without permission." Hux shot me a look that proved I was absolutely not forgiven for accessing his system earlier. "And I wouldn't touch Kev's Horn with a ten-foot pole."

"Is *that* a euphemism?" Champ whisper-demanded, leaning toward Riggs again.

Riggs shook his head.

"Right." Champ cleared his throat and straightened in his seat. "I believe I'm the one giving the orders around here, Huxley, and Kev has shown that he can be a valuable asset on this operation several times. It's ridiculous that he was downstairs following the same leads that we were working on, wasting time and duplicating effort, when you could be working together. So, thank you, Kev. I'd appreciate it if you could do that. I can't imagine being in a gaming tournament room at a Vegas hotel would be all that dangerous. You'll be our backup plan."

I nodded solemnly and forced myself to be a magnanimous winner. One who didn't stick his tongue out at Huxley, no matter how great the temptation.

I was on the team… sort of. I could be professional.

But when they moved on to discussing the other cartel members and how they'd attempt to gain access to each of their devices, I started feeling twitchy again with the need to lose myself online. I decided to head back downstairs and register for the qualifying tournament. That way, I could scope out the competition and strategize.

On my way downstairs, I took Rodrigo from his room and tucked him under my arm. As soon as I was comfortably ensconced in my gaming chair under my fuzzy blanket with Rodrigo in my lap, I pulled out my Horn and immediately winced at the volley of old messages waiting for me.

The onslaught had begun more than fourteen hours ago, around three o'clock yesterday afternoon.

Anomaly451: *Hey, sexy! You forgot to answer my question yesterday for the article.*

Anomaly451: *It's okay, though, bc you can answer it tonight. Let's get on comms!*

Anomaly451: *Our Tuesday chats are the best night of the week! *heart emoji**

Anomaly451: *At least until I come to Tennessee this weekend? (Please say yes!)*

Anomaly451: *Let me know what time you want to log on, baby doll. Can't wait to talk to you and pick that golden brain. *wink emoji**

The next texts came a few hours later.

Anomaly451: *Kev?*

Anomaly451: *Angel face, the system says you haven't been on in hours. I'm waiting!*

Damn it all. How could I have possibly forgotten that Adam and I had a standing chat date on Tuesday nights? I'd never had to set a reminder before since I was almost always online, and last night, I'd been so busy that it hadn't crossed my mind.

God, he must've been so worried. Guilt coiled in my stomach as I continued reading.

Anomaly451: *Kev, that asshole SmittyKitty is lurking around your kumquat orchard. Should I run him off?*

Anomaly451: *Never mind. On it. A boyfriend's job is to protect his territory!*

Shit. I guess I'd neglected to tell him Smitty and I were friendly.

But also… a brief flash of annoyance burned off some of my guilt. I knew Adam meant well, but what was it with people thinking I couldn't handle things? It was one thing when it came to Hux worrying about me in real life—my breath caught as I remembered his hands on me before I pushed that unhelpful thought away—but there was almost no one in the world as qualified as me when it came to Horn of Glory.

And since when was my territory his?

I continued reading the old messages.

SmittyKitty: *Okay, this Anomaly451 asshole just messaged me. He considers me an "enemy combatant" who's "lurking on your perimeter" and he's threatening to attack me if I don't "state my purpose" in being here.*

SmittyKitty: *WTAF is this?*

SmittyKitty: *I swear to fuck, I am DONE dealing with enti-tled assholes today.*

SmittyKitty: *Oh, this keeps getting better. Asshomaly says if I'm hoping to lure you into an alliance when I'm at HOGCon, I'm too late because you're HIS. What in the dumbfuck outlandish possessive bullshit is he spouting? You're not going to HOGCon, are you? You never go to in-person competitions.*

SmittyKitty: *Whatever. This motherfucker is yapping like a chihuahua in heat. Excuse me while I explain to him in detail that he does not own HOG and he does not own YOU, Pip. *cracks knuckles**

I rolled my lips, fighting a smile. It felt a little disloyal to Anomaly that I was so excited at the idea of Smitty putting him in his place, of us being on the same side for once. I couldn't even care about that stupid nickname.

SmittyKitty: *Done. And FYI, you have shit taste in online boyfriends.*

SmittyKitty: *I'm here to be FRIENDLY. I came by to bring you marmalade since I know you're low on jam right now due to the, ah… unfortunate circumstances the other day.*

I snorted. Unfortunate circumstances meaning Huxley willfully destroying my jam cellar. It was really sweet of Smitty to try to make up for Huxley's asshole behavior.

SmittyKitty: *Besides, why does Anomaly think you need protection? Your weapons cache is legendary.*

Yes! *Thank you.* Great question.

SmittyKitty: *Like, yeah, I get it, you have a hard-on for the HogDoc. Take a number and get in line.*

SmittyKitty: *Fuck. Delete that. I didn't mean… It's almost midnight. Long day. I don't know what I'm saying.*

SmittyKitty: *Double fuck. Why doesn't this game have a message delete function? Delete it from your brain, okay?*

SmittyKitty: *Anyway. I left your marmalade under your cheddar tree. So. Good night, Pip. Have fun storming the castle.*

I laughed out loud at his awkwardness and found myself grinning goofily at my screen, thinking all sorts of warm and gushy friendship thoughts.

Everyone knew marmalade was the most potent of the Preserve Power-ups after the Apple Butter Booster. It was an objectively great gift to give any player, but to me, it was even more meaningful. I couldn't remember the last time someone had given me something for no reason. Sometimes, players asked to barter, and more than one tried to loot, but I was pretty sure no one had voluntarily shared resources with me since last summer, a couple of weeks after I'd started playing the game, when I'd gotten my first Top 10 Ranking. Folks figured I didn't need their help—and that was true. But I hadn't realized just how isolating that had felt until… well, until now.

A moment later, I forced myself to keep scrolling through the remaining message notifications, and my warm feelings quickly evaporated. An hour after Smitty's last message, Anomaly had messaged again.

Anomaly451: *It's after one in the morning, sweetie pie!! You are SO late!*

Anomaly451: *I guess you're upset at me? Did you take something I said the wrong way again?*

Anomaly451: *I hate how you overreact and never give me the benefit of the doubt.*

Anomaly451: *I've tried every way I can think of to show you that I care. I keep offering to come and visit you, but you keep putting me off.*

Anomaly451: *Are we boyfriends, or not? Am I coming to visit you Friday, or not? Are we allies in the HOGCon tournament in Vegas, or not?*

Anomaly451: *Whatever. Some of us have jobs to get to in the morning. Bye.*

I blew out a breath, kinda glad that I'd been deep into facial recognition scans when these messages had come through last night. Turned out you learned a lot about a person from the way they treated you when they were angry.

Hux, for example… his anger was bright and clean. Sure, his overprotectiveness and dismissiveness drove me up a tree, but at least he was never manipulative.

Meanwhile, the guy I was supposed to be dating hadn't managed a single "Everything okay, Kev?" when I hadn't shown up last night. Instead, he'd jumped straight to calling me overly sensitive and made himself a victim.

Was this just how relationships worked, where if one person made a mistake, the other person got a free pass to be a jerk about it? Because if so, I wasn't a fan. I felt unsure and more anxious than I had all day, even when I'd been interacting with a dangerous cartel member.

Consequently, I wasn't overly friendly as I opened a chat window and messaged back.

HogDocKev: *Work emergency here last night. It's resolved now. Sorry I didn't have a chance to let you know.*

HogDocKev: *FYI, Smitty is a friend. Don't harass him.*

HogDocKev: *I'm definitely not up for a visit this weekend, and I'm not sure about the rest of it.*

I closed the chat with a decisive click and shook off my negative feelings. I strolled through my kumquat orchard to the cheddar tree and found a barrel of marmalade waiting for me, just as Smitty had promised.

I whistled as I rolled it to my recently rebuilt jam cellar, savoring the sweetness of having made a Horn of Glory friend—one who'd given me back a little of the pure, unadulterated happiness that had made me fall in love with the game in the first place.

I wanted to do something really nice for Smitty in return. Something bigger than fuzzy dice for his air speeder. Something more meaningful than the Harley equipment he didn't seem to want. Something like…

Oh.

As soon as the idea occurred to me, I opened a chat window before I could talk myself out of it. I hugged Rodrigo to my chest in excitement, pushed up my glasses, and began typing.

HogDocKev: *Hey, Smitty. I just decided that I'm going to HOGCon in person for the Conqueror's Tournament.*

HogDocKev: *I know you said you can't qualify for the tournament in Ascendant's Class because of your ranking, and that sucks. FWIW, I sent HOG a strongly-worded email about changing their rules.*

HogDocKev: *But in the meantime, you'll be automatically* *qualified if you agree to form an alliance with an already-qualified player… like, for example, ME.*

HogDocKev: *So, what do you say?*

HogDocKev: *There's a 100k pip prize we can split.*

HogDocKev: *And I think it would be a lot of fun.*

HogDocKev: *And I really admire the way you play. I think I could learn a lot from you.*

HogDocKev: *But no worries either way, man. Thanks for the marmalade.*

The moment I hit Send on the final message, I stared at my chat window and snorted. *Thanks for the marmalade?* Jesus Christ. I was officially the biggest dork in Tennessee. Hopefully Smitty didn't expect too much suaveness from his friends.

But I also felt good and strong. Like my impulsive choice had been the right one.

"Sire?" Henry Cavill said smoothly, rescuing me from my thoughts. "You asked to be informed when HogMasterHux next signed in to the game. He's undertaken the Rooster Domination Quest, level three."

My heart skipped a beat, then began pounding in frantic double time.

Huxley. Shit. He was clearly serious about qualifying for the Conqueror's Tournament, and he was for damn sure gonna have something to say when he found out I'd just entered into an unexpected alliance.

In fact, I thought, feeling the ghost of his fingers on my upper arms and the heat of his gaze, he was going to lose his ever-loving mind.

And I was looking forward to it.

6

HUX

HogDocKev: *There's a 100k pip prize we can split.*

HogDocKev: *And I think it would be a lot of fun.*

HogDocKev: *And I really admire the way you play. I think I could learn a lot from you.*

HogDocKev: *But no worries either way, man. Thanks for the marmalade.*

I read through the messages on my SmittyKitty Horn for the forty-fifth time since they'd come through an hour ago, trying to make them make sense.

Kevin Rogers wanted to form an alliance in the Conqueror's Tournament with a barely ranked newbie?

Yeah, no. I still didn't get it. What the fuck was he thinking?

Why hadn't he asked his stupid asshole e-boyfriend? Hell, why hadn't he asked *me*, especially now that we were working together?

"Whoa! Dude, you're dying!" Elvo leaned into my space and pointed at my monitor, which was hooked up to my *other* Horn—my HogMasterHux Horn. On the screen, my avatar was attempting to catch and subdue as many enchanted roosters as possible to complete my quest… or at least he *had* been until Kev's texts had come through and distracted me. Now, HogMasterHux was crouching in the middle of a chicken pen with his hands over his head, getting pecked by overly aggressive poultry and rapidly losing health points.

"Shit." I powered off Smitty's Horn, tucked it back into my pocket to deal with another day, and zeroed in on the game—the *mission*—that should have been my sole focus. I pulled a handful of charmed corn from my pocket and got to work. In short order, the screen flashed, and golden eggs fell like rain to celebrate my win.

"Ah, now I get it!" Elvo said admiringly. "You were just playing dead to lull the roosters into a false sense of security, weren't you? You had those cocks eating out of your hand." He shoved my shoulder before he walked away, "I shouldn't have doubted you. You're the master, after all."

"Yeah." I smiled wanly. "I try."

A message popped up on my screen.

HogDocKev: *What the heck was that duck and cover move? LMAO.*

HogDocKev: *Rodrigo and I have so many questions.*

I closed my eyes and shook my head, unable to stop the smile pulling at my lips.

Of course *Kev* knew it hadn't been an intentional move and hadn't hesitated to call me on it. It was annoying… and also weirdly comforting.

HogMasterHux: *Lies, Kevin! Rodrigo never judges me.*

HogDocKev: *Rodrigo thinks it's ridiculous that you're going all out to qualify for the tournament when I'm already almost qualified.*

HogDocKev: *Why can't you trust me, Hux?*

My smile fell away, and I quickly disconnected from the

game so I could begin running some more in-depth searches on known cartel associates.

Kev was wrong. My insistence on qualifying for the tournament myself had nothing to do with trust and everything to do with protecting him. Protecting him from having to participate in an in-person tournament when even talking about it this afternoon had made him look a little peaky… and protecting him from learning the truth about the "newbie" player he'd just asked to form an alliance.

I fucking *hated* deception. Ever since Marc Pine had pretended to be my friend back in high school, only to lie to our coach about who removed all the showerheads from the locker room during Prank Week and get me kicked off the team, I'd vowed to be aboveboard in all my friendships, and I had. And while I wouldn't say Kev and I were friends precisely—what did you call someone you wanted to kiss the shit out of but also strangle? What was the word for a person you understood so well, in some ways, that it was like you were the same person, but who also confused the crap out of you in other ways, with the twisty turns of his brilliant, terrifying, mystifying brain?—that didn't matter.

My tiny little lie of omission was quickly becoming a plain old lie, and I knew I needed to either confess everything or stop interacting with him as Smitty, but I hadn't been able to bring myself to do either.

There was something different about the way that Smitty and Kev related, without all the bullshit complications that Kev and I had when we were interacting as ourselves. Smitty got to see a more vulnerable, approachable side of Kev while I brought out all his prickles and vice versa. That was why, after lashing out about Kev's system breach the day before, I'd logged on to Horn of Glory as Smitty to deliver Kev a barrel of apology marmalade.

I thought of what my days would be like without Kev

bantering with Smitty and telling tales of his earnest do-gooding, and my stomach clenched. Almost against my will, the man had become a fixture in my life... and I didn't want to give that up.

"Okay, what gives?" Jordan asked, forcing me to look up. "You've been abusing your keyboard for an hour, and you usually treat your equipment like it's precious and delicate."

"It hasn't been an hour," I argued. But when I checked the enormous clock on the wall, I saw that it had actually been a little longer than that. *Huh.* I'd been too caught up in thoughts of Kev to notice.

It was becoming kind of a habit.

Jordan set an energy drink in front of me, and I nodded a thanks to them as I popped it open. "I dunno. I guess I'm still kicking myself for missing that vulnerability yesterday," I said, which wasn't a lie. "You know how much I hate being shown up by an amateur."

Jordan made a noise through their nose and took a seat at the table near me. "He's hardly an amateur. Didn't you hear Carter tell Champ about Kev's contracts at one of the big sensor tech companies? They hired him to create some kind of algorithm that works with environmental sensors. Apparently he was going to do another doctorate, this one in microsystems technologies or some shit, but companies kept asking him to consult on their projects, so he hasn't yet. I don't see why he'd bother doing more college if companies are already willing to pay him top dollar."

"But..." I stared at them. "Kev sits in the basement and games all day." Even as I said it, though, I thought of the dick-rocket and knew there was more to the story—more to *Kev*—than met the eye.

Jordan laughed. "No, bro. Riggs says he games *while* he's coding—or whatever you call that computer language shit. He multitasks, which makes zero sense to me, considering he made killer money on some tech patents. I don't see why he doesn't just game all day. I would."

"*Riiiiight.*" I couldn't help but snicker. Jordan was the most energetic person on the team. They'd made a point of learning every job at Champion Security, mostly to stave off boredom, and loved fieldwork more than any agent at the company. "Sure you would."

Champ strode into the kitchen and circled a pointer finger in the air. "Strategy meeting in the den. Ask Kev to join us."

He grabbed Elvo's whiteboard, where we'd scribbled the name of each Horn user from the cartel's list along with the current location of their device, and disappeared in the direction of the meeting room.

After grabbing my laptop, I followed Jordan to the den. Riggs was already seated on the far sofa, texting on his phone.

I pulled out my phone to text Kev.

Me: *Champ wants you to join the strategy meeting now in the den.*

KevTheAnnoyingOrcHoarder: *Stepped out for a massage. I'll be home in ten.*

I stared at my phone as I dropped onto the sofa. He was getting a massage? Why? And where? Whose hands had been all over his skin?

Was it a relaxation massage? A sports massage to treat an injury? Was he okay?

My brain threw up a helpful image of Kev's lean body, barely covered by a towel, on a massage table in a small room, his oiled skin gleaming in the dim light and his face blissed-out by therapeutic touch and meditation music. In my mind, it was *my* hands reaching for him, *my* hands making him moan and sigh… and just like that, I knew I was in trouble.

It had been a long time since I'd been in bed with a man —not since last summer, when I'd been home in Pennsylvania mourning my dad, looking for a night of distraction. It had been even longer than that since I'd consciously let myself fantasize about the feel of a man's skin beneath my fingers, his breath in my ear. And when it came to Kev, I'd cut off any and all lustful thoughts behind a sturdy fire door in my brain, then ruthlessly wet-blanketed any stray sparks that tried to escape.

But now that I'd cracked open that door, I couldn't stop my thoughts of Kev from rushing through it like errant flames greedily searching for oxygen…

And my whole brain exploded like a flash fire, searing all my rational thoughts to ash.

I imagined inching the modesty towel lower, my slick fingers gliding down his spine, until his entire body was bare to me, and there was no need for modesty at all.

I ran a hand down my thigh over my jeans. My body was dense and muscled, very different than Kev's. What would it be like to feel his slimmer form?

I rubbed a hand over my stubbled face and stared at my phone, remembering how Kev's cheeks flushed when I teased him. Would they turn the same shade of pink when he was aroused? Would his breathing hitch if I dragged my finger over the curve of his ass? Would his legs spread for me automatically? Would I need to coax him?

"Elvo, my dude, you brought enough snacks for twelve people," Jordan taunted, their voice barely filtering into my reverie. "Can you say *oral fixation*?"

My throat went dry.

I'd dreamed once about Kev getting on his knees for me in his lair, and it had been so hot I'd woken up rock hard.

Now, my mind went in a whole other direction, where Kev turned over on the table, his eyes shining up at me in trust and wonder from behind those stupidly, sinfully sexy glasses.

I wanted to slide my hands over his pecs and abs. To take the warm, salty weight of him on my tongue. Was he cut or uncut? Trimmed or not? It suddenly seemed incredibly wrong that I didn't know this and crucial that I find out.

"Aww. Poor Riggsy. Toss the boy a snack or something," a female voice joked to raucous laughter. "Look at that sexy pout, you guys."

Fuck, I needed to stop—I needed to stop *immediately*—but the pull of the vision was too strong. Instead, I imagined Kev's lips, Kev's sexy pout.

Sometimes, when he was concentrating hard or trying to hold back some emotion, he'd pull his lower lip into his mouth, sinking his teeth into it. It was almost as much of a tell as his finger tapping.

He'd do the sexy lip bite when I got my mouth on him, I'd bet every pip I had on it. I'd fucking make sure of it. His eyes would go unfocused. He'd moan too—long and loud, his voice hoarse and helpless. And he'd forget all about his stupid e-boyfriend, as well as every other guy he'd ever been with. All the power and skill in that fiercely brilliant brain of his would be focused on me and me alone. On what I could do for him, what I could do *to* him.

And when he came, he'd say my name like—

"Hux?" Kev waved a hand in front of me, then leaned down to peer into my face. "Hey," he said softly. "I got here as fast as I could." His glasses slid down his nose, thanks to his awkward position, and he pushed them back up impatiently. "Y'okay?"

My gaze found his and caught. *Held.* And all the breath left my body.

Good God, he was beautiful—like, all the way beautiful. His eyes, his body, his mind, his soul. And I... I wanted him.

Badly.

And maybe that shouldn't have been an earth-shattering revelation, but holy fuck, it felt like one. Like the world had turned upside down or become a chiaroscuro image of itself so that all the things that had, up until five minutes ago, driven me crazy *about* Kev now drove me crazy *for* him.

I sucked in a deep, desperate breath, and when I did, I could practically taste the lavender oil that some stranger had rubbed into Kev's skin, overlaying his usual scent. For the first time in my life, I had the possessive urge to haul a man over my shoulder, cart him into the bathroom, and scrub him down until he smelled like my Kev again— bracing coffee and wholesome vanilla.

Whatever caveman look he saw on my face made Kev's eyes flare wide, and then he frowned in confusion. My breath came hard and fast. I opened my mouth to say some- thing, probably something extremely unwise—

"Huxley? Are you seeing visions over there or some shit?" Champ demanded. "Because you're looking like that kid in that movie that one time, with the big eyes and the 'I see dead people' thing. You know the one I mean?"

I blinked, looked away, and slid back on the sofa all at once. "Uh, no. I'm good," I croaked. I cleared my throat. "Just reflecting on the fact that you can't make a movie reference that's not two decades out of date, old man."

Kev took a spot on the other end of the sofa. I felt his eyes on my face, but I couldn't make myself look at him again.

Holy. Shit.

This—*this!*—was why I'd refused to acknowledge, even to myself, how smart and kind and gorgeous and talented Kevin Rogers was. This was the subconscious reason I'd been desperately trying to shore up my defenses with lies about how spoiled and lazy and annoying he was. Because, just like when the spring rains came back in Pennsylvania and weakened the soil, once I'd *really* admitted to myself just how gorgeous and handsome and *good* Kev was, once I let myself acknowledge how badly I wanted him, it had triggered a catastrophic landslide that slid my feelings from cautious tolerance, straight past amicable friendship, and down into the pit of utterly infatuated lust.

I was so very screwed.

"We're the same age, Huxley," Champ said hotly. "Anyway. If you're done, we're gonna go over the specifics of this operation—"

"Operation Horn Hunt." Elvo smacked his hands together.

Jordan shook their head. "I told you, we are *not* calling it that."

"I like it," Kev said. He shot me a look, like he expected me to deliver my usual line—the one about his opinion not counting because he wasn't part of the team—but I couldn't make myself.

I was tongue-tied and sweaty. Overwhelmed when I really needed to focus on the op.

The differences between Kev and me were very, very real. He was still an incredibly wealthy socialite with a trust fund, and I was a former Marine who couldn't afford his apartment without a roommate.

He came from a long line of doctors and philanthropists who supported LGBTQ organizations, while my dad had never gone a day without grease under his fingernails and had blamed the bad influence of books and computers for the fact that his son hadn't turned out to be a straight, all-American jock.

He had a ton of friends and family who loved and supported him, and I had... well, the people in this room, and that was it.

A guy like that would never want a guy like me... but that didn't make me want him any less.

"Okay, so to recap for those who weren't in the last meeting—" Champ nodded to Yolanda and Sasha, who'd seated themselves on the floor by Riggs without me even noticing their presence, for fuck's sake. "We're planning the best way to get the twelve missing cartel-linked Horns."

"And we're gonna turn it over to the alphabet agencies and hope that mutually assured destruction is enough of an incentive for them. If they want us to keep quiet about their rogue agents, they need to keep quiet about HOG's involvement," Sasha finished, nodding his head. "Yeah, I read the report."

"And we're further hoping," Yolanda continued, "that if we get the data from the Horns, they can use it to track the movement of drugs and money, to find other players involved in their distribution chain or patterns in the movement of drugs or money. Maybe they'll find specific, actionable information about a big shipment or transaction they could bust in person."

"Exactly," Champ agreed. "Okay, so we're all on the same page."

Riggs raised his palms to the ceiling and pumped. "Mission Hornapalooza begins."

Jordan shook their head again and this time added a groan. "Riggsy, no. That's worse than Operation Horn Hunt."

Kev raised his hand like he was in third grade, which was both ridiculous... and ridiculously adorable. When

Champ nodded, Kev fixed his glasses before saying, "Uh. Just to say, you guys, getting Horns off dangerous men isn't going to be a walk in the park. Even with all your expertise, it's gonna be hard."

Elvo opened his mouth to say something, but Champ jabbed a finger at him from across the room. "Say one word about Operation Hard Horns, Elvo. Just *one*," Champ warned, "and watch what happens."

Elvo shut his mouth with a clack and muttered something that sounded like, "No fun."

Champ made a satisfied noise, but his face went tight as he turned back to Kev. "We know. That's why we're gonna start with the easy ones and work our way up." His gaze flicked around to each of us. "Assuming there are some easy ones. What've we got?"

Elvo pointed to his whiteboard, where he'd listed the name of each suspected cartel operative. "Hux dug up more info on each of these guys, and I ordered them based on my best guess about ease of access. This doesn't necessarily correspond to the order we should go after them in—we'll need to figure that out separately, based on their proximity to each other, our team resources, et cetera—but it's a good jumping-off point. M'kay." He tapped the top line. "Horn Number One is a low-level aviation tech in Haiti. He should be easy to distract in a busy cargo hangar. Horn Two spends a lot of time in a dance club in Miami. He should be an easy mark also."

He continued down the list, pointing out what we knew about each target and our best chance of gaining access to their Horns. When he got to Horns Six and Seven, he sighed. "These next two are the ones who are expected in Vegas for the Conqueror's Tournament. If our research is right, their data will be critical. They're much bigger players in this distribution chain than the aviation tech in Haiti or the dock worker in Houston."

Kev nodded. "I can handle them. Who else?"

I opened my mouth to argue with him once again—to give all the very valid reasons why that idea sucked—but Riggs kicked my shin, and Champ shot me a *shut the fuck up* look from the other side of the room.

The edge of my phone dug into my clenched fist.

Fuck. Champ was clearly committed to having Kev involved in this.

Well, that was that, then. I couldn't tell Kev that I was Smitty. Not now, anyway. If Kev got angry at me—and he would—he might decide not to participate in the mission, and Champ would kick my ass or possibly fire me for fucking things up.

It was a relief to have that decided.

I felt a slight pang of regret when I realized that this also meant SmittyKitty would have to do a vanishing act—turn down Kev's offer of an alliance, withdraw from the Conqueror's Tournament, probably slide away from HOG altogether—because there was no way Kev and Smitty could both be in the tournament without him finding out.

But there was a kind of relief in that too, and I felt it immediately. I'd already decided I didn't want to deceive Kev anymore, but that felt especially important now that I'd admitted to myself that Kev wasn't my adversary. He was my... I swallowed hard. He was my something else entirely. Maybe I didn't need to be Smitty anymore.

I wrenched my attention back to the matter at hand as Elvo continued. "SummonerStallion is Horn Number Eight. He lives in a compound in New Mexico. Damned impossible to breach, but he also brokers thoroughbreds. I figure we can arrange to buy one of his horses and meet with him that way."

Champ scribbled something on the notebook in his lap. "Sounds good. Jacob Horn said there's no budget limit, so he can be the proud new owner of a horse when this is all said and done. Who's next?"

"Horn Nine—AnarchyBarbie75. *She* owns a chain of beauty salons in Mobile, Alabama."

That didn't seem like one of the hard ones. "Why isn't that on our easy list?" I asked.

Elvo lifted an eyebrow at me. "She also runs illegal guns from the back room of several of the salon locations. So you can get a manicure *and* a machine gun. Kind of a one-stop shop, if you will."

"More like BadassBarbie, am I right?" Jordan snickered.

Champ sighed. "Fucking hell. Why? Why me?"

Elvo rolled his eyes and went on. "Meanwhile, Horn Ten is a user named HOGFireChampion, who is…"

Kev snorted. "Deluded? Because, seriously, I've never heard of this so-called 'champion.' You?"

He looked at me, and I shook my head. "Nope," I said, popping the *P*. "And if neither Kev nor I have heard of them, they're not a champion."

"Exactly." Kev grinned—one of his bright, powerful grins that made the recipient glow like the sun was shining directly on them. I'd never actually been on the receiving end of one before, and it scrambled my brain just slightly. "But it's cute that they think that," he concluded smugly.

Shit. Smug Kev was even more attractive than quirky, nerdy Kev.

Definitely, definitely screwed.

I swallowed hard and looked away. "You were saying, Elvo?"

Elvo hmphed. "I was *saying* that HogFire-not-a-Champion is a human resources executive at a large textile plant in Dalton, Georgia." He shrugged. "Doesn't scream 'I run with drug dealers,' I know, but like Cartel Barbie, this guy is known for being a gun nut. He owns two hundred acres of land and runs organized hunts on the regular. He also owns his own small plane and has private landing strips, both at his home and at the land."

"We need a woman," I said. "That kind of guy would be easily taken in by an attractive, flirty younger woman."

Champ nodded. "Honeypot, agreed. Yolanda?"

"Yep. On it," Yolanda said, getting out her phone.

Kev winced. "Um. I think you'd do a great job in any other circumstance, Yolanda, but… that kind of guy probably isn't going to go for a mature Black woman."

Yolanda's eyes creased with her laughter. "That's the fucking truth. But you haven't met my wife." She wiggled her eyebrows.

Champ grinned. "Katie is a stunning white woman who served with us in Afghanistan. She's a personal trainer now here in the Thicket. She'd love nothing more than to pull one over on a good old Georgia boy."

Kev's cheeks turned pink from embarrassment. "Oh."

Elvo tapped the next name on his whiteboard. "This one's tough. Horn Eleven is GreenBerryTemptress… who lives at the JollyBrook Residential School for Boys, just outside Cape Camden, Missouri."

"A kid?" Jordan demanded. "Seriously? The cartel is recruiting teenagers now?"

"More likely, an adult that lives there," Champ said grimly. "A teacher or administrator. But if everyone there is hooked up to the school Wi-Fi, even if we gain access to the school, how will we know whose Horn it is?"

"Wi-Fi jammer," Kev and I said simultaneously.

We exchanged half-smiles, and I waved a hand, inviting him to continue the explanation.

He blushed—fucking *blushed*—then said, "If we wait for the GreenBerry person to log on, then we can use a short-range Wi-Fi signal jammer and just walk up and down the halls, waiting for them to be kicked off."

"What if they're using a cell signal?" Champ demanded.

I shook my head sadly. The poor guy really didn't understand the fundamentals of Horn of Glory. "Horns don't have that capability. They access the internet through Wi-Fi only, whether that's through a regular internet connection or a mobile hotspot."

"Well." Kev coughed lightly. "Commercial Horns don't, that's true."

I turned to stare at him. "You rigged up a Horn that…"

"Has a satellite uplink? Yeah. I mean, how did you think Carter and Riggs communicated with us from that plane in Venezuela?"

"I…" I shook my head. "I *didn't* think, I guess."

"Well," he said with a proud smile, "maybe it's time you did."

Holy fuck. How had I not realized how much of a turn-on this man's tech-nerd genius was? I looked away immediately and shifted so I could draw a throw pillow over my lap.

I was light-years beyond screwed. I was ready to throw Kevin Rogers on the carpet and kiss him senseless if he said one more brainy, sassy thing… and then what would happen?

Nothing good, for all the reasons I'd already considered.

"What about Horn Twelve?" I asked Elvo a little desperately.

"Hmm? Oh, Horn Twelve is Vince." He grimaced sympathetically at Champ. "You're still keeping track of his Horn, right?" I nodded in confirmation. "So, I'm guessing we'll take his data here in the Thicket, at the motel. That one's Number Twelve because it's gonna be tricky for... personal reasons."

Champ sat up straighter. "No it won't. There ceased to be a personal connection between me and Agent Parler when Quinn's life was put in danger," he said coldly.

Some would argue that made it more personal, but I wasn't going to suggest it.

"Fair enough." Elvo nodded. "One more thing to consider: we need to execute these plans quickly. Before the Conqueror's Tournament. If we get caught while downloading the data from any of these Horns, the other names on this list might change their patterns or increase their security."

With that in mind, we moved right into making travel plans and splitting into mission groups to try and knock out as much of the low-hanging fruit as we could. Jordan called in several of our teammates who'd been working from home as well as a few who'd been on other missions. Champ had even asked Kev if he'd run the tech part of the operations so that I could take a spot on one of the retrieval teams. By the time Mrs. Carmody announced it was dinnertime, we'd arranged the first few Horn missions and had plans to leave the following morning.

When the meeting ended, I forced myself to walk out of the den toward the large dining room, even though every instinct pulled me toward Kev's side. Behind me, I overheard Champ ask Kev if he could speak to him privately after dinner. Champ's business voice was easy to recognize, and I knew he was going to go over the specifics of hiring him to be part of the team for the next couple of weeks.

What I didn't know was how I felt about that.

I hated how my skin prickled with awareness when Kev finally entered the dining room a little while later and took the empty seat next to mine.

I hated how my body swayed toward him as if there was a mystical vacuum effect caused by Kev's presence that somehow sucked away the air between us.

But yet I found myself leaning into him like a plant in darkness seeking the warm, bright, life-giving force of the sun.

I wanted to rage at the idea that we needed additional tech help, at the possibility that I might be replaced on the team.

But I also wanted to rejoice at the knowledge that someone as competent and knowledgeable as Kev would have our backs.

My brain wanted to warn Champ in no uncertain terms that Kev and I were a powder keg, and putting us together would cause an explosion.

But my stomach swooped in anticipation every time I looked at Kev, because I was pretty sure the explosion was inevitable… and deep down, I couldn't wait for it to happen.

7

KEV

My lair was already set up like a command center, but it hadn't truly been used like one since the time Carter and Riggs were trapped in a cartel compound in Venezuela.

Today, I was back in my happy place, with comms to all three of the team leaders in the field, and my bank of wall monitors tapped into dozens of surveillance images. I juggled multiple requests for information, communicated critical countdowns, monitored the location of every Champion Security asset in the field, and even hacked into two different security systems.

When the first mission was over and the Horn data had been extracted safely, I'd let out a huge sigh of satisfaction and cracked my aching neck, flush with a kind of cocky confidence. I had this. I was *made* for this.

Just then, the leader of the second team had announced that his team was in position to approach the next Horn, and did he have go-ahead?

I'd scrambled to get up to speed on that mission, pulling up maps and locations in Alabama, tapping into security feeds and even placing a perfectly timed distraction call to our target to discuss her car's extended warranty. But literally the moment I hung up, the third Horn retrieval team touched down in a new city, ready to acquire the third Horn, and suddenly I was managing two missions at once.

After that, the first team got into position for their second retrieval of the day, and things spun wildly out of control. I forgot what time zones people were in—heck, I forgot what time zone *I* was in—and the last time I'd eaten. Rodrigo, the most patient pet in the universe, had gotten tired of my lack of attention and wandered off to curl up in a corner of my lair, and I'd had to pee really badly for... God, who knew? Hours? Possibly days.

I wished Hux were there with me, and not only because I wanted to apologize for ever doubting that he was a fucking tech god and beg him to tell me how he handled all these comms and requests for surveillance information without his brain imploding like a dying star, but because his presence was bracing and comforting, even when he was teasing me. Even when he was giving me shit. Even when he was frustrating me so badly that I could feel my temperature rising like a cartoon thermometer, growing redder and redder until the top popped off.

I also wanted him there so he could explain the seriously mixed signals he'd been giving me right before he left, starting with the laser eyeballs during the meeting that had made every muscle in my body quiver, proceeding through the dinner where he'd practically sat on my lap, and ending with the weirdly formal, weirdly sweet, and just plain weird *handshake* that he'd given me right before he'd left with one of the teams.

"Line of sight is clear, Team Two. I'm shutting down the power to the fence now," I said before quickly switching channels so I could listen to Team One as they moved around a townhouse.

In the middle of all of it, a Horn message from Adam flashed up on one of my monitors, and I groaned.

Anomaly451: *Kev, we need to talk.*

Anomaly451: *I want to apologize for some of the things I said the other day. I miss you, angel. I'm tormenting myself thinking about how hurt you must've been.*

Anomaly451: *I want you so much. I think it's time we take our relationship to the next level. Become exclusive. You're the only guy I think about, sweetie.*

Anomaly451: *I know I blew my chances of seeing you this weekend, but what about next week? I can take some vacation days. I can stop there on the way to Vegas, and we can head for HOGCon together.*

Anomaly451: *#HOGPowerCouple, right?*

I groaned again, so loudly that my voice echoed around the room.

I did not want to have that discussion. Not while I was doing this job… and maybe not at all. The things Adam was offering now might have been exactly what I wanted to hear a week ago, but now…

Now a muscled, tattooed, bunny-talking badass was busy retrieving the third Horn and needed my undivided attention.

I turned off my Horn of Glory notifications and focused on the work. A hot bead of sweat inched its way down my spine. This job wasn't for the weary. If only I had an octopus's arms or cloning technology.

The rest of the day went by at light speed. Thankfully, the missions Hux's team had been on were straightforward and close enough that his team landed Champion Security's plane at a private airfield outside Licking Thicket in the early evening hours and drove home.

I watched them on camera as they exited a giant Suburban, and Hux led them up the front steps to the house, talking and laughing. They all looked grimy, exhausted, and satisfied. One of the Champion Security guys I hadn't met yet said something to Hux and shoved him lightly. Hux grinned his irreverent, cocky grin and said something back, and a small part of the tension I'd been carrying eased.

They were home. They were *safe*. One out of three teams, anyway.

I quickly rolled my chair across the workspace and tapped a button to activate the speaker hidden in the hedge by the front door.

"*Jaaaasper Huxxxxley,*" I intoned.

Hux jumped a foot—seriously, I needed to make that happen every single day—then folded his arms over his chest, and his eyes narrowed. "Kevin."

Just hearing his voice did things to my insides.

"Need you in the lair." I hesitated. "Please?"

If Hux was surprised that I was actually inviting him into my Fortress of Solitude, he didn't show it. He stared at the nearest security camera for a long moment while the other guys slapped him on the shoulder good-naturedly and preceded him into the house. Then he nodded at me once and stalked down to my lair faster than I'd thought possible.

As soon as I buzzed him in and the pocket doors shut behind him, I felt the sting of tears in my eyes. There were a lot of things I wanted to say, a lot of questions I wanted to ask, but there was no time.

"I… I need help," I admitted before he could say a word. "I know I said I could handle it, and I can. But I… It's been a long day, and I'm afraid I'm going to miss something."

His normally stern face softened, and his eyes flicked up to the monitors for the first time. "Yeah. I'm here." He slid into the seat next to mine, still wearing his tactical pants and formfitting shirt, and put on a headset. "What've we got?"

The following few hours were much easier. Not only were we down to only two of the missions scheduled for the day, but there were two of us. We each took charge of one of the missions, and when I needed help with something, Hux was there. It wasn't the first time I'd seen him in action, but it didn't matter. Every time I saw him in his element, I got a little vibration in my solar plexus.

He was amazing.

When the mission I was managing finished successfully, I switched gears to help Hux while still letting him take point. I watched him out of the corner of my eye, admiring his control and confidence, which I knew came from years of training and experience.

It was possible that he was right about his training giving him an advantage in certain situations… not that I planned to tell him that.

Because I was studying him so closely, I noticed immediately when his body stiffened, and I focused back on the monitors just as things began to go wrong.

"Elvo, left. *Left*, dammit," Hux hissed into his headset. "Three guards in north corridor pursuing from your four o'clock. Steady on. Guy with a cleaning trolley ahead on your right. Careful. Good… *fuck*."

His fingers flew over his keyboard, looking for a safe extraction route. This particular mission involved breaking into a high-security penthouse apartment in Chicago. We'd known it would be a challenge, which was why only the most experienced members of the team were involved.

Elvo's voice sounded shockingly calm for someone being pursued by multiple armed guards. "So I said to the chick, 'Lady, I'm just here to work you out. If you want *that* kind of exercise, you're going to have to call someone else.' And you should have seen the look on her face. Priceless." He ended his strange half story with a soft chuckle into his phone.

"What's he doing?" I whispered to Hux.

"His cover," Hux said absently while still typing away between various surveillance screens to find the best way out of the building. "He's there as a personal trainer to the lady in one of the other penthouse units, remember?"

It explained the running suit and gym bag over his shoulder, but I didn't remember this cover at all. Maybe I'd already lost it in the sea of mission data I'd had to cram the night before.

I squawked when I spotted the guard around the next turn. "Hux! Stop him!" I said, pointing at the monitor.

"Guard ahead on corridor to left. Suggest approach and inquiry to nearest exit," Hux said calmly into his headset.

My heart thundered. "You want him to deliberately go up to this guy?" I whispered in shock, as if afraid the guard would hear me from hundreds of miles away.

"Elvo is the best at playing stupid. Just watch," he said, not cracking a smile.

I felt a faint dizziness wash over me as images of a violent shoot-out flashed through my head, but I kept my eyes glued to the surveillance monitor. Hux tapped the command to have the audio play over the speakers.

"Excuse me, uh, sir? Do you work here by any chance?" Elvo's voice sounded like the gym rat I'd seen at my local grocery store a few times. "I could sure use some help finding my way outta here."

The guard stopped short and stared at him. "What are you doing here?" he challenged. "Who are you visiting?"

Elvo's dimpled smile appeared, and he hooked a thumb over his shoulder, pointing several floors up. "Mrs. Healy in PH-3 with the floofy white dog. She calls it

Fiona, but I call it a city noise ordinance violation, amirite?"

Score one for mission intel. I'd been the one to come up with those details while helping them prep for the op, so I couldn't help but bask in the glory a little.

The guard's body relaxed. "Can't say I disagree. What's your business here? If you're visiting the penthouse floor, why are you on floor eleven?"

Elvo blinked. "Well, that's the problem, see. I decided to take the stairs—you'd be surprised how little time I get for my own workouts when I'm training my clients—but I lost count of what floor I was on. I saw the number one and exited the stairwell, but now I see it's eleven, not one, and dang if I can't remember where the stairwell is. This place is like a maze trapped inside an escape room, bro." He flashed a goofy grin.

"Too much," I whispered under my breath. Hux nodded. The tension returned to his shoulders.

The guard's eyes narrowed. "You didn't tell me your business."

"Personal training. Mrs. H. gets worked out every Monday, Wednesday, and Friday at seven. Usually she works with Tony, but Tony had a rough night last night after we all went out for our buddy Samir's birthday. Big three-oh, so we gave him hell, you know? Stayed out way too late, though." Elvo shook his head and laughed. "Just wait till Samir learns what it's like when your body can't handle late nights anymore. Thirty. Fucking baby."

I grabbed Hux's arm and squeezed. "The trainer's name is Tommy! Oh God. The guard is going to kill him!"

Hux hissed the correction through the mic, but Elvo didn't react. The man was damned good at his job.

Finally, the guard's face loosened into a small grin. "No

shit. Wait till he hits forty. That's when your warranty runs out."

The guard kept talking as he led Elvo toward the elevator bank and down to the lobby. Hux and I watched with wide eyes, waiting for the moment the guard would turn on him.

"Do you think he knows that lady's personal trainer enough to remember his name?" I asked my worry out loud.

"No way to know," Hux murmured. "But he's not going to *kill* him, Kev. You watch too many movies. Apartment building security guards aren't usually trigger-happy madmen. The most he'll do is ask him to leave and escort him out. Which is what we want."

I started to pull my hand away from his arm when I realized I was shaking with nerves. Maybe I wasn't cut out for this kind of high-stakes work.

"Hey," Hux said with a frown, turning his eyes away from the monitors to glance at me. "Are you okay?"

"Yeah, of course," I said, faking a smile of reassurance. From the way Hux's eyes widened, I must not have done a good job of it.

Elvo's laughter came over the speakers. "Home free, my dudes. Thanks for the help. That deserves an iced coffee and a giant piece of cake. Driver, take me to Dough!"

Considering his driver was Jordan, I wasn't surprised to hear a faint "Fuck off" over the speaker before the comms disconnected.

I let out a breath and forced a tiny smile. "Good. It's all over. Well, until tomorrow."

Hux swiveled his chair around and took my hands in his. His skin was warm and dry, and his grip was strong. "Your hands are shaking."

I closed my eyes and inhaled the sandalwood deodorant

smell I'd come to associate with him, the scent that sent my heart skittering around like a shiny metal pinball shot into play in an old-fashioned machine. When I was around Hux, sometimes it really did feel like there were chimes and lights, nervous anticipation of some kind of high-stakes payoff. If only the ball stayed on course, if only I could use the paddles to keep it in play a little longer.

Hux's hands moved to my face.

"Kevin?" he asked softly, his thumbs stroking my cheeks. I could hear the worry in his voice, and I attempted to pry my eyes open. I knew that every second I spent hiding behind my eyelids was more proof I wasn't up for this challenge, wasn't cut out to be on the team, and I didn't want him to think I was weak, but—

"You know, the first time I managed comms on an op like this, I threw up?" he said conversationally. He laughed lightly. "Oh, I was fine while it was going on—running a translation program so my guys in the field could talk to their informant in Dari, monitoring surveillance feeds, the whole nine. And then the team finished their extraction, got back to the plane, went wheels-up... and I spent the next fifteen minutes praying to the porcelain gods. Just *blurghhhh*. Sometimes adrenaline hits late like that, you know? Totally normal."

I peeked at him through my lashes. "Yeah?"

"Oh yeah."

"But you didn't get overwhelmed while the mission was still happening, did you?"

"Well, no." Hux's thumbs stroked soothingly over my face again. "But I wasn't managing two ops at once all day long on my very first day. You got thrown in the deep end. And I know I keep saying this, but—"

"But I don't have the training," I sighed, closing my eyes again. "I know."

I felt Hux nod. "It's a big deal, Kev. But still…" He hesitated. "You did amazing. Really. And what you did at the end, putting the success of the op above your pride and pulling me in here when you got overwhelmed? That's…" He coughed lightly. "Well. Some of us still have trouble taking help when it's offered, let alone asking for it, as some smart-ass recently pointed out to me. Two sets of eyes are better than one, he told me. That's why we have redundancies. So… maybe he needs to take his own advice, huh?"

I sucked in a breath, opened my eyes, and forced myself to look at him. The double divot of worry between his eyes. The late-day shadow on his cheeks. The still-bright eyes that always seemed to be hiding some kind of mischief. And… the tiny black dot of the tragus piercing in his left ear.

Before I realized what I was doing, I'd reached out with my finger to trace the little earring. I'd always been curious about it. "Is this for migraines?"

Hux's whole body went still. Watchful. And when I lifted my eyes to his, I realized just how close we were.

He frowned, like he was trying to read my mind and figure out what I was thinking. If he found an answer, maybe he'd be so kind as to let me know, too, because right now, I felt like I was stepping out onto a rickety bridge over a deep valley with nothing to hold on to.

"Uh…yeah," he said in a rough voice. It was more like a guttural grunt of agreement, the kind that deepened the vibration in my solar plexus and brought back the bead of sweat running down my back.

"Does it help?" I asked.

Hux's eyes dropped to my lips. I could feel the warmth of his breath against my cheek.

"A little." His breathing seemed to hitch just before the tip of his tongue came out to wet his bottom lip.

I moved my fingertip slowly down from the tragus piercing to his earlobe. He was even closer now. Too close for my gaze to focus on him properly… or at all. "No other piercings?" I whispered.

Hux tilted his head slightly until his nose grazed against my cheekbone. "Not up here."

His lips curved up, and I stopped breathing entirely. What… what exactly had he meant by that? "Huh?"

My brain shorted out, imagining other places he could be hiding piercings. I wanted to see them. I wanted to enjoy the investigation itself.

My fingers twitched against the skin of his neck, a slight, grasping little movement. Maybe that movement was somehow responsible for triggering what happened next. Hux's head turned, causing his lips and nose to skim against my cheek. I turned reflexively after that and brushed my lips across his. Would I have done it on purpose? Heck, no. I would have overthought it and held back. But my brain wasn't functioning enough for intention.

And once I felt his lips on mine… it didn't matter why I'd done it. It didn't matter who'd done it first or how it had happened. It only mattered that it was the most exhilarating feeling I'd ever had.

Hux pulled back slightly and froze, giving me that watchful, mind-reading look again. His eyes roved over my face, assessing me with the same care and utter absorption he'd had while monitoring the op earlier, and I could practically see the gears turning in his brain. *Is this okay? Is this what Kev wants?*

I wasn't sure what expression my face was making, and speech was entirely beyond me, but I hoped he *could* read my mind and could pick up the message I was trying to convey.

Yes, it's okay. So very okay. More, please. More, now. Show me how it could be.

Hux's whole body seemed to come alive at once. He surged forward and clasped my face between his hands again. Strong fingers tilted my head exactly where he wanted it, and his warm, firm mouth took charge of mine.

Our knees knocked together, Hux wrapped one strong arm behind me and yanked, and I found myself half-sprawled across his lap, still kissing him. I linked my arms behind his broad shoulders and held on tight, because if I fell on the floor and caused this kiss to end prematurely, I would never forgive myself.

I needed him. Needed him like a honey troll needed firefly moss to complete its den. Like a mage needed green-berries to complete his Eternity Quest. Like a... *fuck*. Like a very human man who'd just discovered, for the first time in his not-quite kiss-less life, why so many musicians sang songs about this.

I felt light-headed and floaty but also more profoundly aware of every square inch of my body than I'd ever been before. The cornsilk texture of the hair at Hux's nape, the sweetness of his mouth, the hardness of his thighs supporting me.

My brain was a janky montage of snaps and fizzling sparks. I wanted to moan in appreciation, but since I was more likely to break out in hysterical giggles, I forced myself not to make a noise.

I was kissing Jasper Huxley. Correction: Jasper Huxley was kissing *me*. And I didn't care how we'd gotten here or what was going to come next. I just never, ever wanted this kiss to end.

8

HUX

This kiss needed to stop.

It was ridiculous. Inappropriate. Outrageous.

A post-op adrenaline rush gone terribly wrong.

Possibly the stupidest thing I'd ever done.

But, I thought as his fingers stroked over my neck and my gut tightened, it was also turning out to be the most enjoyable.

It was impossible to believe that I'd deluded myself into thinking I didn't want this man. I wanted him *desperately*— wanted to kiss his soft lips until he begged for air, wanted to hold his slender, willing body against mine until we were fused together. Even the thought of stopping made my arms tighten around his back to pull him against me more firmly.

I used my other hand to gently remove his sexy glasses before setting them on the desk. The tip of his nose was pink from my whiskers, and his lips were red and shiny from my kisses.

"*Fuck*," I whispered hoarsely as another wave of desire swamped me. I cupped the back of his head and pulled him in to fuse our mouths together once more.

All I could think of was tearing his clothes off and running my hands all over his naked body. I couldn't decide what I wanted more: to suck his dick or fuck him. Either would be good, and whichever I didn't do first, I could do next.

Right when I'd decided to start by sucking him off, I heard a loud buzz. Both of us were so startled, we tumbled off my chair into a tangled heap of limbs on the floor.

Kev spat out a curse and scrambled to get up. "The door. The *door*!"

"Kevin? Huxley?" came a muffled call.

Realizing one of my teammates was likely on the other side of the door was like waking up from a fever dream to a bucket of very cold water.

What the fuck was I doing kissing Kevin Rogers?

I stood up and straightened my clothes—adjusting my pants, in particular—before running fingers through my hair in hopes of taming whatever Kev's fingers had done to it.

"Your glasses," I whispered, pointing to them on the desk.

"This never happened," Kev said, pointedly not looking at me. He shoved his glasses on crookedly, swiped at his mouth with one shaking hand, and turned to face his monitors.

I blinked at his back. "What?" I asked stupidly.

I was the one who was supposed to regret it, not him. It had been his idea, after all.

Hadn't it?

"You and me. Never happened," he repeated, reaching over to a button on his desk so that his door opened with a *whoosh*.

"But—" Before I could argue with him—because no matter how much had changed between us in the past day, if Kev said a thing *didn't* happen, I was going to say it *did*—Champ came through the door into Kev's lair, and I belatedly dropped into the second chair.

"Uh." I cleared my throat. "Hey, boss. I was going to open the door for you. Forgot Kev had everything automated. Good day, huh? Almost half the Horns accounted for! Feeling pumped about planning to get the next few. How about you?"

Champ narrowed his eyes suspiciously, his gaze pinging from me to Kev and back again. In my head, I heard Kev saying, *"Too much,"* just like he had when Elvo had tried to oversell his story, so I clamped my lips firmly together and gave Champ a bland look.

"Yeah," Champ agreed finally. "It *was* a good day, and I'd like to plan the next missions… which is why I texted you several times to come upstairs for a team meeting." He raised one blond eyebrow. "Might wanna check that your phone is operational."

"Oh. Uh. Yes, sir," I mumbled, reaching for my phone on Kev's desk. I was mortified.

Champ grunted in response, still looking back and forth between Kev and me. "Everything good here?"

"Everything's great here," I informed him. "Really… great."

"Yeah. All good," Kev said softly without turning around.

"Hmm." Champ folded his arms over his chest. "Kev, if Huxley drives you crazy, you'd let me know, right?"

"Hey," I squawked in protest.

"Yeah, no. I… nothing happened," Kev assured him. "We'll be up in a minute."

The moment Champ left and the doors slid shut behind him, I shot Kev a glare. "Something happened. It very much happened. And it's going to happen again, Kevin Rogers. Get used to the idea."

I stormed out before replaying what I'd said in my head. What the fuck had I been thinking? It was going to happen again? Was that supposed to be a threat? Had I just threatened Kev with… a *kiss*?

I smacked my forehead. "Stupid fucking fucker," I murmured. "You should have agreed with him." Because Kev was right. Our lives would be noticeably easier if we pretended nothing had happened.

Easier, maybe. But not better.

I groaned and headed upstairs. It was time to focus on work. We had more Horns to target.

I managed to successfully avoid Kev for nearly twenty-four hours while the Champion Security teams traveled to Haiti and New Mexico.

This was great in the sense that I'd managed to take several breaths without searching for his scent, go entire minutes without listening for his voice in my ear over comms, and string multiple thoughts together that didn't revolve around kissing, holding, or shaking the man.

It was also a serious fucking error because while I was doing my best to ignore him, Kev and Champ had somehow gotten it into their heads that Kev should join us in the field for our next retrieval so he could "gain experience" on an easy op before he took a starring role in Vegas. I wasn't sure who had decided this was a good idea, but they were dead wrong.

Which was how he'd ended up on the op in Miami with us.

Champ's voice came through my ear. "Confirm eyes on the target, Team One."

As the other members of the team checked in one by one, I peered through the hazy smoke at the throng of dancers swaying hypnotically on the floor of Azul, Miami's hottest nightclub, searching out our target, Freddy Rosendo. Our plan tonight had involved surrounding Freddy on the dance floor, which was how I'd found myself shirtless under a black leather jacket and half-deafened by electronic dance music. But it was very difficult to focus on our target when one of my team members had decided to trade his nerdy graphic tees for a cropped mesh top, his baggy khakis for low-slung jeans, and his geeky black-framed glasses for contact lenses and purple glitter eye makeup.

Kev's body was fine with a capital *F*. Apparently he'd been hiding some serious abs and arm definition under his baggy clothes, but now that it was on display, I couldn't take my eyes off him... and neither could half the people in the club.

My dick had been hard for two hours, and my back teeth hurt from clenching them.

"Huxley," Champ's voice broke into my thoughts again. "Confirm."

Kevin Rogers was a distraction to this mission. As long as he was here, how the hell could our team —namely *me* — stay focused on the target?

Belatedly, I pushed the button on the side of my watch that engaged my mic. "Yeah," I managed. "Got it."

"Good," Champ said. "Everyone close in a little."

As a group, we danced closer to each other, subtly tightening the circle around our target. Kev's hip brushed mine, and I sucked in a breath. Someone knocked into him, pushing him against me again. This time, Kev lost his footing and stumbled. I reached around him with both arms and pulled him in tight to my bare chest to keep him from falling.

"Oh," he said as his sweat-slick skin touched mine. His hot breath made shivers dance down my neck. The club lights flashed across his face, lighting up the sparkles near his eyes in rainbow colors.

My arms tightened as I stared at him. He was just a tiny bit taller than me—almost unnoticeable in our day to day since I was much more muscular and we rarely stood this close—but I liked it. I liked the way he had to tilt his head just slightly to look at me, leaving no doubt that he was focused on me just like I was on him, and—

From the corner of my eye, I saw Elvo close in from behind Freddy while Yolanda, who had poured herself into a dress comprised mostly of black plastic lacing and safety pins, distracted him. Once Freddy was engrossed in dancing with Yolanda, Elvo would swipe the Horn, hand it off to me to download the data as quickly as possible, and slide it back into the guy's pocket.

Fuck. We were here to do an important job. I was on the clock.

The surprising press of Kev's dick against my hip made focusing on the job impossible until Champ's voice hissed into my ear again. "Okay, *now*."

Kev's eyes met mine, and we let go of each other at the same time. Elvo shoved the Horn into my hand while Jordan swayed over to Kev, putting their hands on Kev's hips. Kev lifted his hands in the air, shifting in time to the music, blocking me from Freddy's view completely.

I tore my eyes away from Jordan's hands on Kev's skin and forced myself to concentrate. I leaned over slightly, pretending to dance up on Kev's hip, letting my leather jacket fall open to further obscure my movements. I connected the Horn to a high-speed transfer cable and offloaded a backup of the entire system within a minute. My watch buzzed to let me know the transfer was complete, and I disconnected the Horn.

"Done. Ready for handoff," I murmured, tapping the mic button.

However, just as I handed the Horn off to Elvo, Yolanda's tense voice sounded in my ear.

"Losing him, boss. Target is heading off the dance floor."

Champ's voice, calm as ever, replied. "I see him. He's heading to the back corridor by the bathrooms. Elvo, take the Horn and head for the bathroom. Jordan, cover the front entrance to the club. Yolanda, follow Elvo and distract Freddy in the corridor—I don't know how. Ask for his number, maybe?—to give Elvo a chance to slide the Horn into his pocket. Hux and Kev, wait for my signal, then proceed to the corridor also, to provide backup for Yolanda and/or provide a distraction so everyone can get away clean. Maybe another rousing shouting match about the time Hux grabbed Kev's, uh… berry." He made a strangled noise. "Christ, I hate that game."

As Jordan moved out of the way, Kev's eyes met mine, and like magnets, the two of us moved toward each other, swaying in time to the pounding beat.

"Should I remind them that *I* was the one who stole *your* greenberry?" Kev asked, his voice a soft whisper in my ear.

"So you admit it was mine, then?" I ground out, not thinking about greenberries or HOG or any other damn thing but the man in front of me, the man swaying in my arms. "You prevented me from ascending to mage status for the whole summer on purpose?"

"You… you deserved it for killing my bronze goose," Kev countered. He swallowed hard. His eyes were dilated, and he sounded almost drunk as he continued. "Poor Jaunty. Besides, I couldn't let you ascend before me. It's no fun playing without you."

"*Now*, Huxley," Champ commanded.

I closed my eyes for half a second, muttered a curse under my breath, then grabbed Kev's hand and moved quickly toward the corridor, pulling him behind me. Further down the hall, Yolanda reclined against the wall in a studiously sexy pose. Elvo and our target were nowhere to be seen—probably in the men's room. I pressed Kev against the wall and moved in close to him.

"We're providing distraction," I reminded him before brushing my lips against his cheek.

"R-right." His hands rose and fell in a nervous flutter. "And this is distracting?"

"Oh yeah." The attraction that had grown between us once I stopped choking it off was by far the most distracting thing I'd ever encountered in my entire life. "Way better than fighting about your duck."

"G-goose. Jaunty was a… a…" Kev broke off with a hard swallow, his breaths coming fast and shallow against the sweat at my temple.

I slid my lips down from his cheek toward his mouth, taking my time in case he wasn't up for it, in case he wanted to pull away and try something else. But he didn't.

Instead, he leaned against the wall, spreading his legs slightly so I could insinuate one thigh between his. His hands fisted the edges of my leather jacket to pull me closer, and they fell like a cocoon around us both, hiding the bare skin of his sides and hips from anyone else walking by.

The club reeked of sweat and manufactured fog, of a hundred spilled drinks and twice as many clashing colognes, but when he got close, all I could smell was coffee and vanilla and…

"Are you wearing cherry ChapStick?" I demanded.

"Uh…" Kev blinked and licked his lips like he needed to check. "Yes?"

A rogue wave of lust swamped me. Nothing that innocent and endearing should be so damn sexy, but then, this was Kev Rogers. A study in contradictions. The exception to every rule. I couldn't help but smile.

"Stop laughing," he breathed against my chin. "It isn't funny."

"No," I said, brushing his lips with mine. "Definitely not funny." And then I took his mouth with a hard, hungry kiss, the kind of kiss that had been hovering in the air between us while the music thumped and the dance floor writhed. The kind of kiss that tasted like the promise of hours-long sex—the sweaty, sticky kind full of tongues and mouths, sucking and nipping, exploring and touching abso-fucking-lutely everything on this man's body.

I felt his groan shudder through him. My hands moved down to his hips and clutched him tightly. I pressed my hard dick against his and ground into it, moving my hands around to grab his ass and pull him even tighter against me.

It was dirty and wrong. Inappropriate for coworkers—not to mention enemies… frenemies… archnemeses—but spot-on perfect for this dim corridor in a late-night dance club in Miami. We were making a scene… but that was the point.

Somehow, Kev's legs ended up around my waist, his back pressed against the wall again and my mouth sucking marks down his neck. His hair stood on end from my seeking hands, and the mewling sound he made had me on the verge of embarrassing myself in public.

At some point, I heard someone talking in my ear, but I didn't care. All I cared about was using every single minute of this "distraction" to taste and feel and hump every bit of Kevin Rogers I could.

"Mm-hn," Kev moaned. "But, nnggghhh… hnghhh. Wait… whut… wait… wait!" He pulled back and stared at me dazedly. "We gotta go."

"Huh?" I leaned in and kissed his swollen lips again. And again. "What? Go where?"

"I think… I think Champ said we're supposed to go." He looked around us and suddenly jerked out of my hold, stumbling to the side until I grabbed his arms. He looked at me with wide eyes. "They're gone!"

I looked around the empty corridor. *Fuck.*

The comms unit crackled in my ear before Jordan spoke, their voice full of amusement. "Where the hell are Hux and Kev? Did they miss the part where providing distraction to cover our getaway only works if they remember to leave?"

Champ's voice took over, sounding distinctly unamused. "I don't have eyes on them. They're in a camera blind spot. Hux, find Kev and get your ass out front to the vehicle. Now. Otherwise, we'll send someone back in for you."

I bit out a response. "Copy. On our way."

After taking a firm grip of Kev's hand, I once again pulled him through the crowded club, this time much less eagerly. We ignored the blatant come-ons and people who accidentally stepped in our path, and when we finally hit the outside, I took a deep breath of muggy Miami air and tried to clear my head.

Halfway down the block, the back door opened on our rented SUV. Kev dropped my hand and strode down the sidewalk, leaving me to catch up.

"Sorry, guys," he said as he scrambled inside and took a seat in the third row. "We were…" His voice trailed off, and he blinked at me as I climbed into the second row. His face was bright red, and his eyes were still wide.

I wanted to pull him onto my lap and wrap my arms around him. Instead, I faced forward, closed the vehicle door, and stared out the darkened window into the night.

"Making a scene?" Jordan asked with fake naiveté and real glee.

"Contributing to the distraction?" Yolanda supplied, shooting me a wink.

"Sucking face?" Elvo suggested in a low voice before I elbowed him hard in the side.

"Caught up in the crowd," I said firmly.

The car made its way through the half-empty city streets. My teammates discussed the success of the op in a low buzz, but I tuned it out.

Flashbulb memories of making out with Kevin snapped through my vision until all I could see was his kiss-drunk expression. I could still taste cherry ChapStick on my lips and feel the swell of his ass against my palms. Despite my teammates laughing and joking around me, I'd swear I could make out the sound of Kev's breathing, of his racing heart.

All I could think about was getting him in my arms again. Putting my mouth and hands on him. Taking everything I wanted from him and not letting him go until he lay debauched and spent in my sheets.

My leather jacket was stifling, so I tore it off. Jordan chucked me the T-shirt I'd left in the car before the op, and I dragged it over my head, then sank back against the seat. I closed my eyes and focused on slowing my breathing.

Inhale, one, two, three… *coffee and vanilla.*

Exhale, one, two, three… *the feeling of Kev's smooth skin beneath my…*

No. This was not okay. It wasn't professional. Hell, this was Kevin Rogers.

Kev the Civilian.

Kev the Annoying Orc Hoarder.

Kev, my freakin' archnemesis since the first day I'd acquired my Horn.

Kev, who was brilliant—and had the degrees and patents and Harley-Davidson team gear to prove it.

Kev, who had a housekeeper and a trust fund and a lair that was bigger than my parents' house.

Kev, who was kind to rabbits and newbie players… and even to me when I didn't deserve it.

Acknowledging that I wanted him was one thing. Pursuing it would lead to infinite levels of disaster.

I had to take a giant step back. To approach this logically. To—

"Hux?"

Kev's whispered question was almost too low to hear, unless you were a total sap who'd somehow become completely attuned to the man. I turned my head and found him huddled in the corner of the seat against the door. His arms were wrapped around his knees.

"What is it?" I asked, hoping I didn't sound as annoyed as I felt.

"Do you think I could borrow your jacket? I mean, if you're not using it? The air-conditioning is… a lot."

Was there air-conditioning? I was clearly too hot to feel it.

Before I realized what I was doing, I'd turned around and lurched up onto my knees in the seat. Instead of chucking my jacket at him, I motioned him forward so I could reach the leather jacket around Kev's shoulders. I fussed over him for several minutes, murmuring for him to put his arms down the sleeves so I could zip it up to keep some warmth inside.

Once he was covered up, he smiled softly. He mumbled a thanks and closed his eyes, leaning his head against the window.

I turned back around and put my seat belt back on. The vehicle had gotten very quiet all of a sudden, but I didn't dare meet any of my teammates' gazes. I already knew at least one of them would be giving me "what the fuck?" eyes, and the last thing I needed was for them to see the answering confusion in my own.

I had no idea what the fuck I was doing, that was the scary truth.

So, instead, I closed my eyes and tried not to listen for any scrap of sound from behind me. I tried not to imagine his sweet body wrapped in my jacket, infusing it with his signature scent.

I failed.

When we pulled up at the private airstrip where our plane was waiting, I realized Kev had fallen asleep. Yolanda woke him up gently and helped him climb out of the SUV and head to the tarmac.

I clenched my hands into fists to keep from taking over, but I also made sure to grab the seat next to Kev's on the plane the minute Yolanda turned away.

When the small plane reached cruising altitude, Kev fell back asleep. If someone helped nudge his head down onto my shoulder to make him more comfortable… well, it was nobody's business but mine.

And if, later that evening, that same someone got on his Horn and obtained a peace offering—for a truly exorbitant price. Goddamn inflation—and left it on the doorstep of a certain HogDoc's homestead… well, that was nobody's business but mine either.

9

KEV

After landing back in Tennessee in the small hours of the morning, I fell into bed, crusty eye glitter and all.

Big mistake.

I woke up Saturday morning feeling like I'd been on a drag queen bender. My hair was sticky, my face was scratchy, and purple glitter had made its way inside my underwear. Vague memories of stroking myself to images of Hux in the club before I'd finally zonked out last night flitted through my brain, but I banished them before they could take shape.

I had no idea what was going on with Hux. I didn't know why he blew hot and cold, why sometimes he made me feel like I was the best, smartest version of myself and other times like I'd never be able to earn his respect. I didn't understand why he'd kissed me like he wanted me, tucked me up in his jacket... then seemed able to turn it all off and barely mutter good night when we'd landed back in Tennessee like it had all been part of the op.

And maybe worse than all that, I didn't understand

what I wanted from him. Approval, yeah. Friendship, sure. More of those drugging kisses that made me feel like I was flying? *Fuck...* I really did.

So, what did that mean for my relationship with Adam? God, I was a terrible person. I hadn't thought of him *once* the night before.

An online boyfriend is not a boyfriend, Hux's voice whispered in my brain. *Do you like the way he smells? The way he smiles? The way he looks at you? Does he make you think, 'Now that is a man who could take me apart piece by piece and put me back together'?*

I ignored my throbbing cock, dragged myself out of bed with a groan, and headed straight for the shower.

"Henry, set the shower steam to high and play the *South Pacific* soundtrack. Start with the one about washing that man right outta her hair."

"Unfortunately, that selection is unavailable, sire," the AI voice replied. "I've also crossed Gloria Gaynor off the accessible music list. Might I suggest Cyndi Lauper's 'Girls Just Want To Have Fun'?"

The unmitigated gall! It turned out there was a reason why the concept of a sassy, all-knowing AI had never caught on.

"Play Ingrid Michaelson 'Hell No,'" I said through gritted teeth.

The AI deliberately disobeyed me, which, to be fair, he didn't do often. Only when he really thought I needed protecting.

"Playing 'Gonna Make You Sweat (Everybody Dance Now)' by C & C Music Factory."

I stripped and slumped into the shower stall, submersing myself under the wide rainfall showerhead and letting the hot water pound down on my shoulders. The upbeat dance music didn't have Henry Cavill's desired effect the way it normally did. I was perfectly capable of sulking despite the magnetic beat.

"Play 'This Is Why We Can't Have Nice Things' by Taylor Swift," I called over the sound of the pounding water.

"Playing 'Roar' by Katy Perry," he replied calmly.

I sighed. The computer knew me well. Within minutes, I was bellowing along with the song, feeling empowered and determining I wasn't going to obsess over Jasper Huxley anymore. I had a job to do, and I was quickly becoming an integral part of the team. Plus, I had a full docket of my own projects today, which had nothing to do with Champion Security.

Eye of the tiger. Katy had it right when she belted out that song. I needed focus.

This attraction… *thing* with Hux was nothing more than a distraction, just like he'd said in the club last night. We'd had a brief moment of adrenaline-fueled lust the other day, followed by a moment play-acting on an op, and… and, okay, one really sweet, unguarded moment with a leather jacket. In between, though, Hux had done his best to ignore me. So I was going to force myself to do the same.

As I dried off, completed my skincare regimen, and finger-combed some product into my hair, I told Henry to read my latest Horn of Glory messages.

"Yes, sire. First message, from Anomaly451. Received, 6:26 p.m. Yesterday. 'Hello, sweetness. I hope you're not still upset. I wish we could be together right now. I can't wait to see you in Vegas.' Would you like to reply?"

I sighed, feeling a tangled web of guilt and annoyance tighten around me. If the man was my boyfriend, it was wrong that I hadn't even thought of him while losing myself in Hux's kiss the night before. Then again, Adam hadn't been acting like much of a boyfriend this week, when I hadn't immediately agreed to an alliance or to meet up for sex.

But maybe he was having a bad week. Maybe the article he was writing was more stressful than he'd let on. Maybe he'd gotten caught in DC traffic. Maybe the real problem was that I wasn't great with people or relationships.

Which is why the first person you've developed a major, monster, take-me-right-now crush on is a guy who spends his days finding inventive ways to insult you and trolling you in Horn of Glory.

I blew out a breath. "Yes, please reply. Say, 'I'll definitely see you in Vegas. We can talk after the tournament. When do you arrive?'"

There. That was nice. Appropriately friendly without implying the kind of commitment that would make me feel even guiltier if I accidentally jacked off to thoughts of Jasper Huxley again.

"Message sent," Henry announced.

"Great. Is, um… is there any message from SmittyKitty?"

"No, sire. SmittyKitty has not logged in since Wednesday when he read your last message. Would you like to send him a new message?"

Henry Cavill sounded vaguely disapproving of this idea. I didn't blame him.

"No, thanks," I said glumly.

It wasn't like I'd expected the man to drop to his knees in gratitude at the offer of an alliance or whatever… but I hadn't expected him to drop off the face of the planet either. We'd gotten to be friends, or so I'd thought.

I needed another round of Katy Perry, stat.

"Thank you, Henry," I concluded. "You can —"

"Next message, from HogMasterHux. Received, 3:47

a.m. Today. 'There. Now you can stop complaining. This time, think up a better name for it.' Would you like to reply?"

Hux had messaged me?

What did he mean, a better name?

I grabbed my Horn and logged in for the first time since hopping a plane to Miami the day before, and the moment my avatar appeared in front of my homestead, I understood what Henry was talking about.

There was a golden duck on my front porch — the larger, rarer, and far more expensive cousin to my bronze goose, Jaunty, that Hux had done away with the previous summer. A golden duck increased your health and happiness points exponentially, and there were only a few in existence, so Hux must've called in a bunch of favors to make this happen.

But… why? What the hell did it mean? Was it a friendship sort of duck? Or a courtship sort of duck? Or a "Hey, sorry I gave you a giant boner last night — oh, and the night before — but I don't actually find you all that attractive, so have this duck in lieu of hot sex, you giant loser," sort of duck?

Interpersonal relationships had a language I hadn't heard spoken often enough to become fluent, and as far as I knew, there was no translation app available. I could maybe ask Carter if he was around later. He was smart about this stuff.

"Would you like to reply?" Henry prompted.

"No," I said firmly. "Not at this time. Any more messages?"

"No, sire."

"Okay, then." I pulled on some clean jeans, my glasses, and a wash-worn Champion Security hoodie I'd stolen from Riggs and headed for the door. I had a busy schedule this morning, and I needed coffee before I attempted to accomplish anything—

"Sire, one of your scans has caught some keywords in an online HOG forum involving SummonerStallion."

I turned around and folded my arms over my chest. "Way to bury the lede, Henry Cavill. Jesus." I shook my head. Clearly, my AI needed some reprogramming. "Send the details to my phone, please."

"Yes, sire. Done."

As I strode down the hall, I read the information Henry had sent, then headed upstairs to share it with the team.

When I got to the kitchen, several people were gathered around the table, looking as fresh as if they hadn't been on a late-night op in Miami the night before. I made my way to the coffee machine with a grumble.

Riggs approached with his own empty mug. "Morning, Kev. You're just the guy we needed to see. Hux needs help on our next op."

Hux didn't look up from his keyboard. "I don't *need* help."

Oh. Great. We were back to this? How delightful.

I mentally checked "courtship" and "friendship" off my list of duck-gift-motivations, and I forced myself to look at the coffee maker and not at Huxley's bed-rumpled hair and gorgeous, closed-off face.

"Ignore Hux," Riggs said with a grin. "He's cranky because his rabbit's depressed."

"Fuck off." Hux rubbed his eyes tiredly. "That's not what I said."

I paused with the coffeepot in my hand. "Rodrigo? Is he okay? Is he sick? Because sickness in rabbits can turn serious really quickly and—"

"I know. He's fine now," Hux said gruffly. He darted a glance in my direction, and his voice softened. "I took him to the emergency vet to be sure, and she said he was just bored because he was in his cage at my apartment most of the day yesterday and the day before."

"Oh." I filled Riggs's mug. "But you could have left him here, you know. Mrs. Carmody thinks he's adorable—"

Hux's fingers gripped his computer mouse so hard that the plastic audibly squeaked. "This isn't his house. He shouldn't get too used to it."

I frowned harder. "But—"

"Discuss the rabbit later," Riggs said. "Right now, we need to worry about the next Horn." He leaned against the counter and took a sip of coffee. "We need someone who can engage our target in the game for the better part of this afternoon and evening so we can identify which family member is actually using the Horn. Somehow, Hux thinks he can do it while he's also running surveillance for the op at the same time—" He rolled his eyes in Hux's direction.

"I absolutely can," Hux grumbled.

"—but we think it would be better if he had backup," Riggs concluded.

Champ took a bite out of a slice of toast and made a noise of agreement. "I've approved another day of consulting fees if you're up for it, Kev. Certainly don't feel obligated if you have other commitments."

I mentally reviewed my day. "Yeah, no, I can do it. I have a Zoom presentation for some grad students at MIT later this morning, but I'm good after that."

Riggs knocked his shoulder into mine and raised an eyebrow. "How much is *that* consulting fee?"

"More than Champ's gonna pay him," Carter teased, breezing in from the direction of their bedroom. He snagged Riggs's mug and took a long sip while Riggs watched him with a look that managed to be simultaneously besotted, amused, and hotly possessive, probably because of the way Carter's new wedding ring glinted under the overhead lights every time his hand moved. "You still able to meet me to sign the papers today?" Carter asked.

Riggs's face softened as he looked at my cousin. He reached out and smoothed down Carter's blue-and-silver striped tie before pressing a kiss to his lips, and I very definitely did not sway against the counter, remembering the feel of Huxley's lips on mine or envisioning his face wearing that same affectionate, proprietary expression.

"Wouldn't miss it for the world, Doc," Riggs said. "And I can't wait to see the look on Marisol's face when we tell her about the scholarship later."

"What scholarship?" I asked. "Who's Marisol?"

Carter turned to me, his handsome face alive with happiness in a way that I'd rarely seen it before Riggs came into his life. "You remember the young woman in Venezuela last year? Well, she really wants to become a cardiologist since there's a huge need for them in her area, and my husband had the brilliant idea that we could sponsor her and her grandmother to move here for her education."

"And *my* husband had the brilliant idea that the Rogers Family Foundation could pay for it," Riggs said, wrapping his arms around Carter from behind.

"Oh." I forced a smile. "Wow. That's so..." Impressive. Heroic. The perfect embodiment of the Rogers family's commitment to selfless philanthropy that was helping people live longer, better lives every day.

Meanwhile, I was busy... what? Zooming with grad students for an exorbitant fee? Waiting for Smitty to message me back? Working on one tiny component of some artificial intelligence that might or might not prove useful in diagnosing cancer a decade from now, if the sun didn't implode before then?

Ugh. I forced myself to delete the self-pitying thoughts from my brain. I was on edge and off my game today.

"That's incredible, Carter," I said sincerely. "You two make a great team."

I poured myself two cups of coffee, securing one inside an insulated tumbler with a lid and filling my favorite Grogu mug with another.

Hux shifted his gaze from the computer and eyed the two cups in my hands. "Expecting company?"

"Huh? Oh! No, this is me attempting to convince myself that I was in bed early last night. That whole op was nothing but a bizarre dream," I said blandly.

I waited for him to make a snarky comment, but he didn't. His eyes narrowed, but he didn't laugh or smile, and I shifted my feet awkwardly. Hux always got my jokes.

"Okay, well." I cleared my throat. "Thanks, for… you know." I felt the weight of everyone's stares, and I couldn't bring myself to say *the duck*. "Letting me know about Rodrigo."

I turned my focus to Champ and not the man sitting in front of his computers, exuding magnetic sexuality while low-key glaring at me. "I'm going to prep for my presentation. I'll be back up here by one. Will that work with the op?"

Champ closed his laptop and stretched. "Yep. We'll go over the plan and have you start after that. Appreciate it."

I nodded and moved to leave but then stopped. "Wait, I almost forgot. That guy in New Mexico? The horse breeder? He said something in a HOG forum last night about traveling to Santa Anita. That's a horse racetrack in California. According to the website, there's a big race coming up, but it's next weekend, the same time as HOGCon in Vegas." I shrugged. "He was upset that he would be missing a livestream of the event."

Champ rolled his eyes. "Of course both things are at the same time."

Riggs shrugged. He kissed the top of Carter's head and moved to take his seat at the table. "It's no big deal, boss. We'll split into two teams. You know this is our best chance to get the breeder's Horn. It's impossible when he's at home in his compound."

As they began strategizing, I grabbed a banana, a microwavable oatmeal cup, and my two coffees, then returned back to my lair. The rest of the morning went by quickly. The grad students were more fun and engaged than I'd expected, so I took extra time to answer questions at the end of the presentation.

By the time I went back upstairs, I was feeling considerably better about the world and my contributions to it. And then Huxley opened his big mouth again.

"Nice of you to join us, HogDoc. Why am I not surprised that you made a commitment and then immediately disrespected it?" he said sourly as soon as I entered the den and took my seat on the far end of the sofa.

I narrowed my eyes. Was this really the same guy who'd held me the night before? Who'd whispered hot words in my ear, who'd gotten hard as he pressed up against me? Who'd sent me a golden duck? It was like he'd had a personality transplant and become the same asshole he'd been at our first meeting.

"What commitment did I make, exactly?" I shot back.

"To help us with this op. You want to play like you're a teammate, but then you don't take the job seriously."

I tilted my head and made a big production of looking at my watch. "I'm literally here. For the job. And it's one-oh-four." I glared at him. "Subtract a minute for your wind-bagging and another minute for when I stopped on the stairs to answer a text from Champ—which I did because I *respect my commitments* —and I still made it upstairs less than two minutes after the agreed-upon time. Are you telling me that you've never arrived at an internal meeting two minutes past the start time?"

Elvo watched us like a tennis match while sipping from an energy drink.

"Oooh, I know the answer to this one!" Jordan stretched their hand in the air.

Hux glared at his teammates. "Just… just sit down," he said, though I was already seated. "Your excuses are only wasting more time."

Elvo snorted his drink across the table and started to choke with laughter. When he finally pulled himself together, I could have sworn I heard him mutter, "Just fuck already," under his breath.

His words made my face ignite, and I suddenly couldn't bring myself to look in Hux's direction.

Images from the night before flashed for the millionth time through my head. The feel of Hux's strong grip on my ass, the smell of sandalwood on his leather jacket, the taste of lime on his tongue as it took complete ownership of my mouth.

The press of his thick erection against my thigh.

When Champ kicked off our strategy meeting, where he described how and why he'd need me to keep the target totally engaged for the next several hours, I managed to stay focused and nod at the appropriate points, but I was way too aware of the man beside me. Tension rolled off him in waves, and when the meeting finally adjourned, Hux immediately jumped to his feet.

"Grab your Horn, and let's get started," he commanded.

I pushed up my glasses and stared at him. "Huh?"

He wiggled his gaming device so it became a blue blur mere inches from my face. "Your Horn? The thing you're going to need for this op? Hello? You were paying attention, right?"

Elvo stood also, barely restraining a shit-eating grin. "Whoa. Someone oughta charge money for this show. The sexual tension is…" He fanned at his face. "Phew. Hottest thing I've seen since… eh, two weeks ago when Champ and Quinn were dancing around each other, wouldn't you say, Jordan?"

Champ rolled his eyes and shoved Elvo toward the door.

"Mmm," Yolanda agreed, shutting her tablet and giving me a wink. "Alpha male pheromones. *Grrr.*"

It was my turn to glare at everyone, ending with Huxley. "I left my Horn downstairs, where it's wired into my monitors. I'm going to play there."

"Fine." Hux rolled his eyes. "Let's go."

"I don't recall asking you to come."

"Yeah, well, maybe that was all a *bizarre dream* too." He made a rolling motion with his hand. "Can we just cut to the part where we do our jobs, please?"

Be professional, I reminded myself.

I stood, not realizing just how close that would bring us until our chests nearly brushed, but I refused to take a step back. "Bring the bunny," I countered.

Okay, so not the *most* professional thing I'd ever said.

Hux pursed his lips but finally nodded once, his eyes hot on mine.

I very definitely did not repress a shiver. I nodded back, then put my chin in the air and stepped around him, leading him downstairs.

~

Having Hux in my lair always made me feel a stew of emotions. Excitement, nerves… the urge to ask him to stay and play with me awhile.

But I pushed the stew away and remembered the trust that Champ and his team had given me. And I would rather die before letting them down.

Eye of the tiger.

"How exactly will me distracting them in the game help us get this guy's Horn?" I asked, handing Hux a long HDMI cable so he could connect his laptop to one of my large wall monitors. I conveniently plucked the bunny out of his hands so Hux could deal with the cable.

It was no secret Rodrigo preferred my lap over Hux's, and I was determined to give him extra attention. No bunny should feel lonely when I was around.

"Not a guy—a woman. We're working off the assumption that the Horn belongs to Camila Dacosta. She's married to Anthony Dacosta, who is a highly rated heart surgeon in Houston. We initially wondered if the Horn was his because of some ties he might have had to Gustavo Santiago, the head of the cartel."

"Doesn't that seem more likely?" I asked.

"Why? Because she's a nice, rich lady?" Hux said hotly. Then his shoulders slumped, and he sighed. "There's been enough active game play during Anthony's surgery times to give us doubt," he said more calmly. "They do have two teenagers who could be using the Horn, and though the game play has been during school hours, that's obviously inconclusive. But to me, the biggest giveaway is the username, OnCallWidow."

Hux reached for the bunny. I pretended not to notice. "That's pretty circumstantial if you ask me. Lots of people's names don't align with their real lives. For example, some people believe they're *masters* of the game—"

"Yeah, yeah." Hux cracked his neck from side to side like he was trying to dislodge tension. "We've had this conversation before. Get new material—"

"—and I hate to be the one to explain this to you, buddy…" I reached out and placed my hand on his tattooed forearm, setting my face into my most solemn, earnest expression. "But sometimes people lie on the internet."

Hux's lips twitched, and he moved his arm away, but when he sat down, I saw him rubbing his fingers over the spot where I'd touched him, even though I knew for a fact that I couldn't possibly have hurt him.

Hux rolled his chair closer to the desk and sat up straight. "Focus, HogDoc. I finally tapped into the Dacostas' exterior cameras. One of the teens is performing in a matinee theater production this afternoon with her drama club and will definitely not be able to play during those hours."

"Won't the mom go to the play too?"

He shook his head. "There are like eight performances, and she's already been twice. Meanwhile, the other teen is home sick."

"And what about the surgeon?"

"Speaking at a medical convention in Salt Lake City. He flew out early this morning, and the Horn's data shows it still at home."

I winced. "Yeah, that's less circumstantial. So, if it's the wife's Horn that's being used as a front for cartel trans-actions…"

"Then sweet Mrs. Dacosta, former debutante and current secretary of the neighborhood garden club, is a very bad girl," Hux finished with a grin.

"Woah."

"Mmhm. So get to distractin', HogDoc."

I hopped on my Horn and maneuvered through the

game, grabbing a few easy pips and using them to upgrade my enhanced birdseed to enchanted birdseed. I sprinkled it on the path ahead of me and then entered the username of our target. My character immediately appeared next to her in the game, so I quickly checked her stats—high game-play hours, but very few tournament wins, which made sense if she spent a lot of time in the game for nefarious purposes—then typed out a greeting.

HogDocKev: *Love those rain pearls on your hat! They're always sold out when I have enough pips to get some.*

OnCallWidow: *Thanks. You should see my collection. *winky face**

HogDocKev: *OMG, you collect them? How cool! I collect unicorn tail wigs. I even have the limited edition commemorative one they only made for the royal jubilee.*

Hux muttered, "Braggart," under his breath after reading the messages on the large monitor.

OnCallWidow: *Wait, I've heard of you! You're the guy who has the Hedgerow of Health booster AND the Apple Butter Booster, right? That makes you almost immortal! You're probably the best player in all of HOG.*

"Debatable," Hux commented. "Some might say patently false."

I flashed him a quick grin. This was the Hux I was used to, snark and all.

HogDocKev: *I've just played longer than most people. The game is harder for newbies than it is for longer-standing players like you and me, you know?*

Hux made a sort of strangled noise.

"What?" I lifted my chin. "My friend Smitty explained it to me, and he was right. More people need to be aware if we want things to change."

OnCallWidow: *Yeah, sure. Whatever you say. So, is it true* *you grow hexing thorn fruit? The poisoned kind that can even kill an orc who's been charmed with sparrowflox? Could you show me how?*

I sighed. "Some people aren't ready for change, I guess."

"Cartel operatives, not a demographic known for their commitment to fair play."

"True."

HogDocKev: *I can. I usually only share my secret with people who help me on quests. But we can do one right now if you w —*

Hux reached out a hand to stop me before I could finish the message. "Too much." He flicked a glance at my face. "Back off a little. Trust me."

I deleted my last line and added a new one.

HogDocKev: *I can. I usually only share my secret with people who help me on quests. Let me know if you'd be interested sometime.*

As I moved my character away from OnCallWidow, I saw Hux nod in approval. Then, like he couldn't help himself, he added, "Not that hexing thorn fruit are so impressive or whatever. I mean, I've done just fine without them."

I turned toward him. "Would you like to know how to grow them?"

"*Pfft*. No." He paused. "Maybe."

"Because I only share that secret with people who can manage to be civil to me two entire days in a row," I said sweetly.

"Me?" Slashes of red appeared on his cheekbones. "I'm civil. I'm not the one pretending last night was a bad dream."

"I… What?" I blinked at him for a second before the penny dropped, then once it did, I smacked his arm. "You idiot. I meant that I was so tired from all the dancing I needed caffeine so I could convince myself I'd had a proper night's sleep. And I didn't say a *bad* dream. I said bizarre." I lifted one eyebrow. "Which is accurate."

"Oh," Hux grunted, his cheeks redder than ever. The second recorded occurrence of Jasper Huxley blushing. "I might have misunderstood. I'm running on about two hours of sleep between the op and the vet visit."

"And the sourcing of a certain golden duck?"

He shrugged and turned his face away. "No, that… no."

"Thank you," I said earnestly. I hesitated, on the verge of saying something way too sweet about how he didn't have to do every damn thing by himself, or maybe to ask what *he* thought about last night, when my notifications pinged again.

OnCallWidow: *OMG, really? Yes! Anytime. How about today?*

Hux's excited smile spread across his face like a sunrise. "You got her."

"*We* got her."

HogDocKev: *Sure. We could do one today if you want. I'm trying to qualify for the HOGCon tournament and I need to complete one more level eight acquisition quest.*

OnCallWidow: *Level eight?*

HogDocKev: *Yeah. I figured that wouldn't be too hard for a player with your playing hours… but never mind! It's fine if that's a little too dicey for you!! We can quest together another time!! Later!!!*

The dots beside her name swirled for a long moment while Hux and I held our breath.

OnCallWidow: *Wait, no! That's fine. I've done a level eight quest before. Once. Did you have one in mind?*

Hux snickered. "You're good. Now she's got something to prove. And all those exclamation points make you look so friendly."

HogDocKev: *I want to acquire the Duchess of Moon Flowers.*

Hux stiffened, and his gaze burned the side of my face. "Wait. That's a four-person quest, Kev. It's gonna take…"

"A whole afternoon," I confirmed. "Yeah, obvs. How'd you think this would work? An easy quest won't give us the time we need."

Hux gestured toward the monitor. "She's not advanced enough to help you for shit on something that big. She has everything to gain, and you have everything to lose."

I ignored him.

"Kev, I don't care how many boosters or golden ducks you have, you're not actually immortal. If she fucks you over in this quest, your health points will dip. Your ranking will tank. Forget not qualifying for the Conqueror's Tournament—you could become vulnerable—"

"I know. Which is why I need to make sure the rest of my team is solid." I tapped out another message.

HogDocKev: *I already have a healer and scout lined up to help, but I could really use someone with strong enchanting spells.*

Hux cursed under his breath. "You have to raid the grackle nesting grounds for eggs. Grackle eggshell powder is the only thing that will knock the duchess out long enough for you to kidnap her."

"I know."

"You've tried this before. And failed."

"I *know*," I said again, trying to maintain my patience.

"Who are you tapping as your healer?"

I lifted Rodrigo to rub my face against his fur. "You don't know him. Guy named SmittyKitty."

Hux's whole body went still. "He..." He cleared his throat. "He's a newb."

I shrugged. "But I trust him."

"Fuck," Hux said under his breath.

OnCallWidow: *I'm in! When are we doing this?*

The tension in the lair was palpable as Hux's fingers flew over his keyboard to check his surveillance feeds. "Her car hasn't left the house, but I don't have eyes inside. We'll need to have a pizza delivered or something right when the action gets good. Maybe if we see who comes to the door, we can get conclusive proof it's her."

HogDocKev: *Sounds great. Let me get my team.*

OnCallWidow: *Ready when you are.*

I immediately switched chat windows and sent a message to Smitty, though the light beside his name wasn't on.

HogDocKev: *Smitty, please please please tell me you're free to run a quest with me today. I need a healer.*

Hux stood, stretched, and yawned loudly. "Welp! I'm gonna go grab a coffee, I think. Want anything?"

Coffee? *Now?* I frowned. "No. There's a minifridge with soda in the corner—"

"Mmm, yeah, but I really want that flavored syrup Mrs. Carmody buys. And while I'm up there, I might grab a snack. So. Be back in a few. Maybe ten minutes, tops."

I pushed up my glasses and stared at him in confusion. His mood swing this morning had been strange, but this was borderline bizarre. I'd never seen him act this way before an op.

"Hux, for real, are you… okay?"

"Me? Never better. *Never. Better.* Be right back."

As the doors slid shut behind him, I shook my head, then tried as best I could to dismiss him from my thoughts. I had bigger fish to fry.

I opened my Anomaly chat.

HogDocKev: *Adam, remember how you said you wanted to quest with me if you came to visit?*

I felt my face heat as I wondered why that wording sounded dirty. Hopefully he didn't read it that way since I'd only meant meeting up with him at the tournament. But it was too late to change the wording since the message was sent.

Smitty was right—there really should be a delete option.

Anomaly451: *Hi, sweetie. Of course! I can't wait to hold you in my arms in person. I can be there tonight!*

HogDocKev: *Actually, I'm working on one of my qualifying quests today and hoped you might be able to act as the scout. Do you have time? Pretty please?*

Anomaly451: *Anything for you, doll. What's the quest?*

A message from Smitty popped up on my monitor, and I switched chats without replying.

SmittyKitty: *Sorry, Pip. I'm not online today. Working. *sad face* But kick some ass, okay?*

My stomach lifted at the nickname—I'd become kind of attached to it—then dropped when I read the rest of the message. I'd really been counting on Smitty's help.

HogDocKev: *I understand. Work comes first.*

SmittyKitty: *I can recommend a couple of players who might be able to help. GorkyCat12 and LongSallyK are both good healers.*

HogDocKev: *Thanks, but I've got someone else I can ask. He's a kickass healer and an all-around excellent player.*

Not that I'd say so to his face.

HogDocKev: *Hit me up tomorrow if you're on. Let's chat about Vegas!*

But Smitty had already logged off, and the message remained unread.

A notification from the other chat pinged.

Anomaly451: *Babe?*

I shook off the convo with Smitty and focused on explaining the plan to Adam. Once I finished up, Hux came back and handed me a small bowl of cut-up strawberries and carrot pieces. "For Rodrigo," he said, not making eye contact with me.

"I need you to be our healer," I said without preamble, plucking out a piece of strawberry to offer to the bunny.

"Me?"

I shrugged. "Don't sound so surprised. Smitty's good too, but he's not nearly as experienced as you are. I'd have asked you first, but you were gonna be focused on surveillance. I figure between the two of us, though, we can handle the surveillance and the game. We're just watching her house, and I can set up a motion-detector alert on the cameras."

"You want me to be your healer?" Hux asked. He cleared his throat and looked a little flustered, probably feeling like I did—that it was weird and kinda cool to be on the same side in the game for once. "Who's going to scout for us?"

"My friend Adam."

"Anomaly," Hux repeated in a flat voice. "Your fake internet boyfriend."

I shot him a look. "Don't. You barely know me. You sure as heck don't know Adam."

"I know enough," he said darkly.

I held up a hand. "We're not talking about this right now. We need a decent player, and he's available."

He fumed for a moment, then held up his hands in surrender. I tried not to look at the sexy ink on his arms, but it was impossible. "Fine. Let me run upstairs for my Horn. Be right back."

Had he left his Horn upstairs when he got his snack? So odd.

While he was gone, I coordinated a comms channel for our team and set up an extra headset for Hux. Once I heard OnCallWidow's voice, I knew we had what we needed. She was definitely an adult woman and didn't sound anything like a teenager.

"Hey," I said in a cheerful voice. "You can call me Kev. Nice to meet you."

"You can call me Cam. Thanks for this. I'm stuck at home with a sick kid today."

When Hux got back, I handed him another HDMI cable so he could run his game on another one of my big monitors. We settled in with game play on two monitors and the surveillance feed on a third. I muted my microphone and told him about Camila giving us identity-confirming information.

"Good work," Hux said. His words made me feel way prouder than I had any right to feel. I hadn't actually done anything to get that information out of her; she'd volunteered it. Still, I loved impressing him.

"Hey. Are we doing this or what?" Adam said in a bored voice. It wasn't the first time I'd heard his voice over comms, but something about hearing him live made me feel nervous and a little on edge.

I unmuted my mic, feeling my face heat. "Hey! Glad you could make it. Thanks for helping us."

Hux rolled his eyes but thankfully kept his mouth shut.

I quickly made the introductions—though it soon became clear that Adam and Hux had history. We laid out a strategy and discussed it for a while before happily embarking on the quest.

It became a shitshow immediately.

"HogMasterHux, are you even seeing how low my health points are right now?" Adam demanded. "Some healer you are! Jesus Christ, this troll is going to take me."

"He's a level three garden troll," Hux said, his eyes never moving from the screen. "Heal *yourself*. I'm battling a Summer Spider over here, for fuck's sake. Do you know how strong a Summer Spider has to be if she's still alive by February?"

"Oh my gosh, where are you guys?" OnCallWidow tittered. "I lost you cuties somehow in the swamp, and now

I can't find you. Can someone send out a homing butterfly?"

"I don't have a free hand right now," I gritted out between clenched teeth, trying to truss up a mother grackle so I could steal her eggshells. I'd managed to sneak almost all the way to the nest while she was sleeping, but then Adam had sent a stray bolt of mage-light arcing across the nest, and the mother had immediately moved to protect her hatchlings from the nearest threat—namely *me*.

"HogMaster! Heal me, you trollfucker, or you're going to have to do the rest of the op without a scout!" Adam warned.

"Good," Hux muttered. "Since Kev and I have been ten leagues ahead of you since the outset, I'm pretty sure we're scouting for oursel— Oh, shit! Kev! There's a second grackle behind you!"

My avatar turned before I'd even had time to process his warning, and I launched my bespelled claymore at the second grackle like a lance, catching him on the shoulder. While the mother grackle squawked and cooed worriedly at her mate, I grabbed as many of the empty eggshells as I could carry and hopped out of the nest, taking a slight dip in health points as I rolled headfirst down the side of an embankment.

I let out a shaky breath. "Thanks," I said quietly. I couldn't turn to look at Hux, but I felt his tension ease a notch.

"Always," he said. Then he sent me an influx of restorative health points that fell on my avatar like diamond rain.

"What the fuck?" Adam screamed. "Dude, I needed those health diamonds. I'm dying!"

"You keep saying that, but you never follow through," Hux said sadly. "The HogDoc is our leader for this quest, Anomaly. He needs health more than any of us."

"Some leader," Adam barked. "He just threw away his sword."

"Ooooh," OnCallWidow said. "Yikes."

I ground my back teeth together as an uncomfortable silence spread over our comms.

"I… I didn't mean it like that," Adam said quietly. "I'm just… Honeybunch, this would be so much easier if we were in the same room together. I think I'm delayed a few seconds—"

"Bullshit." Hux sounded bored. "This has nothing to do with lag. This has to do with your inability to play the game. Someone once told me only a poor craftsman blames his tools."

I snorted before I could stop myself, and the sound carried. I tried to cover it with a cough.

"Oh! Oh, hey, Anomaly! I see you! Yoo hoo!" OnCall-Widow yelled. "Finally, we're back together, boys. What'd I miss?"

Hux and I shared an eye roll.

From that point on, it only got worse.

Adam insisted on baiting Hux, calling him names and demanding health points in a whiny voice.

Hux relentlessly dragged Adam for not spotting threats and for missing literally every target he aimed at.

Cam seemed determined to flirt with both of them and giggled every time she got lost… which was often.

Worst of all, Hux and I seemed to be the only ones capable of focusing on the mission itself.

"Adam, there are three cypher slyths behind the bell tower!" I warned.

"Stop yelling! Kev, if our relationship is going to survive, you need to work on your communi— Wait, shit! Where am I? Where did you go?" Adam demanded.

"Ooopsy!" Cam singsonged. "My spell went wide, and I

hit you instead. But it's okay—I sent you a shit ton of sparrowflox powder, so you didn't die; you just respawned back at the platypus pasture! Sorry, my bad!"

"Nonsense, Cam," Hux said blandly. "Best thing you could've done for our team."

"Hey! I heard that, asshole," Adam snapped back. "How are you gonna sneak up on the duchess without a scout?"

"Better question is how we would sneak up on her *with* you," Hux retorted. "You are the worst—"

I shot him a look. "It's fine, Adam. You can catch up. Take the shortcut. And Cam, that's... an awful lot of sparrowflox powder you donated." I gave Hux a significant look. "Adam should thank you."

"Fuck that. It's gonna take me an hour to find you again! You can't go on without me! If you complete the quest and I'm not there, I won't level up to Ascendant Class!"

"Oh, crap!" Cam wailed. "You guys, I have to pick up my other kid from a school thing in an hour, and I can't drive while I play! Can we restart the quest?"

"No fucking way! Just leave your Horn, and you can catch up when you get back," Adam said. "Problem solved."

"I can't! If I leave the Horn here, my other kid'll find it and fuck everything up. He's a pain in the ass, especially while he's sick."

Hux sat up and slammed his feet on the ground, turning to me with big eyes and making a dramatic wrist-rolling gesture, like he wanted me to draw this out.

"Uh, well," I said, trying to figure out his plan. "If you can enchant your avatar to attach to mine, then we can cross the Blue Butter Bridge while you're gone. But you still need to leave your Horn connected to Wi-Fi somehow."

Hux grabbed my arm and spoke into his headset,

sounding way calmer than he looked. "Why not leave your Horn on your front porch or something so it stays on Wi-Fi but your sick kid doesn't find it?"

"Oh, perfect!" she cooed. "Fuck, Kev, I'll need a power-up if you want me to do that enchantment on the bridge trolls. I'm running low."

"On it," I said, accessing my stores to find what she needed.

"Be right back," Hux mouthed. I nodded and kept playing, slowing the pace down to buy Hux some time while he ran down the hall.

When he returned, we muted our comms.

Hux was clearly in go mode. "Champ's got Yolanda and Sasha in place to get the data off the Horn while Cam's gone."

I felt my eye bug out. "What?" I hissed. "Are you crazy? There's a kid in that house!"

"That's why I asked Cam to leave the Horn outside."

Things were spiraling out of control. "It's freaking Texas. What if someone shoots a gun?"

Hux's face softened into amusement. "No one's going to shoot someone for picking up a gaming device. They'll dress up like utility workers or something and pretend to be at the wrong house. This is exactly what we hoped would happen. We're prepared for this. It'll be fine."

"Okay. Yeah." I blew out a breath. "Okay."

Hux's brows furrowed, and he grasped my fingers with his. "You're doing that tapping thing again." He brought his other hand up to clasp around our joined hands as if to warm mine. "What's going on in that head of yours?"

I stared at his strong fingers and remembered them trailing across my cheek the night before—clenching on my ass the night before. I felt a bolt of lust go through me.

So much for my resolution to ignore the man. I was

fantasizing about him while on comms with my sort-of boyfriend.

I swallowed. "Nothing worth talking about. I'm fine." I yanked my hand out of his grip and faced the monitors again.

"Are you nervous?" Hux's voice held genuine concern.

I ignored him and unmuted my microphone. "Cam, let me know if you need a Pumpkin Butter Booster before the bridge crossing, okay?"

Hux studied me for another minute before focusing back on the game.

My nerves went from a level ten to a level million over the course of the following hour. What if something went wrong? What if Cam figured out what we were doing? What if we lost the quest *and* I didn't qualify for the tournament in Vegas? What if…?

"Babe," Hux murmured, reaching over to massage my shoulder. I jumped a foot high. His touch was like an electrical current, and I wasn't quite sure if it was a good shock or bad. "Deep breath."

"What? No. I'm okay. It's fine."

"You're not fine," he said softly, moving his microphone away from his face and clicking to mute both of our headsets. He set my Horn on the table before taking my hands in his again. "Talk to me. How can I help?"

"Fuck, I don't know," I admitted. "I'm good at this. I know I am. And I really want to help the team. To contribute. But then when I think about someone on the team getting injured, I lose my cool. I'm afraid I'll ruin everything!"

As I sputtered, Hux's eyes got bigger. When I finally petered out, he moved his hands up to cup my cheeks. "Of course that's what it's about for you. You need to help."

I blinked. "Well… yeah. I'm not a world-renowned

cardiologist, so I'm limited in what I can do, but if I *can* help, why wouldn't I? Anyone would do the same."

One side of Hux's mouth went up. "No. They definitely wouldn't." He leaned in closer until his face was the only thing I could see. "You are doing amazing, Kev. Truly. Even without training, even without experience. Just keep being your usual friendly self. You have a gift of putting others at ease. People like you. They want to spend time with you."

My chest hitched as I tried to draw a breath. "You once told me no one wanted me around."

Hux huffed out a laugh. "Since when do you listen to me? You're a great leader and an incredible player. We all learn from watching you and playing with you." His mouth twisted up in a smile. "Even HogMasters like myself."

I snorted, which seemed to be what he was looking for if his answering grin was anything to go by.

"Keep playing, Kev. That's all you need to do. Keep playing."

The feel of his dry, warm hands on my face and the scent of sandalwood coming off his clothes grounded me. I wanted to crawl into his lap and lay my head down on his shoulder. There was something about him that both riled me up and calmed me down.

How was that possible?

I looked into his eyes. They held warmth, understanding, and... *kindness*, restoring me as surely as any health diamonds.

"Okay," I breathed. "Yeah. I can do that."

He used his fingertip to gently push my glasses up before softly swiping his thumb across my cheek. "I know you can. I got your back."

I nodded. "I know."

He tilted his head and stared at me with a strange intensity. "Do you?"

I nodded again, more slowly this time. "Yeah. Yeah, I do."

Our eyes stayed locked for another few beats while my heart thundered wildly and my palms poured sweat.

Only this time, it wasn't because of nerves about the op. It was because I was suddenly in an even more dangerous situation than that.

I wanted to lose my virginity at long last, not with my online boyfriend, but with the man who hated me most in the world…

10

HUX

The following hour was nerve-racking, even for me. Yolanda and Sasha barely made it to the location on time, and Camila almost decided to take her Horn with her to the school "just in case."

Thankfully, Kev was a master at using the game to get people to do what he wanted. He sweet-talked her into leaving it on the front porch by making a kind of joke. "Unless you live in a neighborhood like mine where someone else might take off with it."

He lived in a mansion on a gated estate with a professional ex-military security expert armed to the teeth on a normal day. No one in his neighborhood would have dared take a Horn from the front porch.

Except for me.

Kev had left his Horn out by the hot tub several days earlier, and I'd brought it inside to keep it safe, not realizing that Kev had only run into the pool house bathroom for a quick minute. He'd thrown a hissy fit when he'd returned to the hot tub and found it missing.

When Yolanda and Sasha pulled into the neighborhood

and realized it was a gated community, I thought Champ was going to lose his mind. He hovered behind Kev and paced back and forth like a caged lion, which only served to make Kev more of a nervous wreck than he already was.

"Hux," Champ said in his commanding voice. "Hack into their systems and put Yolanda and Sasha on the approved-entry list."

Kev's eyes widened behind his glasses, but I spoke before he could respond. "It doesn't work like that," I said softly, even though my gaming comms were muted. "There's no time. Give them a chance. They're good at this shit."

They passed the turn to the gatehouse, pulled down the road to another turnoff, and parked before coming back into the neighborhood as a pair of runners.

Kev's face went pale. "Camila's house is a mile and a half away from the gatehouse!"

I reached over to squeeze his arm. "They're fast. They run PT sprints for breakfast."

It was excruciating to watch, but they made it in under ten minutes. We'd discovered the school run would take a total of fifteen minutes if Cam didn't have to wait around for her kid. That left them less than five minutes to steal the data and get the hell off the Dacostas' front porch.

Stupid fucking Anomaly's voice came over comms. "Huxley, are you *trying* to lose us this quest?"

I blinked at the game monitor and noticed my character was being held over the side of the bridge by a very large Squall Orc.

"Shit," I blurted, quickly throwing a wind hand counter spell at him and deploying a mystic bubble chute. "Sorry," I muttered when I finally landed safely back on the bridge next to Kev.

Kev met my eyes with a soft smile. Nerves were still

clear in his expression, but I could see his relief that I'd saved myself. "You did good."

We continued across the next section of the bridge without too many additional challenges, but I could tell the stress of the op was seriously affecting Kev's equilibrium. He was low-key trembling, and his voice was shaky. I wasn't sure others would be able to tell, but I could.

I wanted to pull him into my lap and wrap my arms around him. I wanted to end the op and close everyone out of his lair while I distracted his big brain from the stress of the day.

Who was I kidding? I simply *wanted him*.

Any way I could get him.

Champ's low voice behind me, talking to Yolanda on the op comms, wasn't helping lower the tension in the room. The surveillance camera pointed at the Dacostas' front porch showed Yolanda's scramble to get the device connected to the cable and USB drive while Sasha pretended to stretch out an injured ankle.

I muted my game comms and switched to the op comms to walk them through it as calmly as I could. Out of the corner of my eye, I noticed Kev's pointer finger tapping the side of his thumb again, so I reached over and squeezed his hand without thinking.

"Take a breath," I said softly. He hesitated a beat before nodding, and I felt another thread of connection grow between us, one that tied us together every bit as firmly as Cam's avatar had enchanted herself to Kev's in the game.

And one that was probably just as imaginary, I reminded myself.

This was still Kev. Rich, gorgeous, brilliant Kev. And in reality, Kev needed a guy like me about as much as he needed—

"Trouble!" Anomaly squawked, nearly blowing out my

eardrum. "Kev, I'm being attacked by Hospitality Squirrels! I need you to kill them and save me!"

I pulled my hand away from Kev's, hoping like hell Champ hadn't noticed, and engaged my mic. "Anomaly, for fuck's sake. Hospitality Squirrels won't hurt you; they just want to take you to their den—"

"I know, dumbass! But I've never seen so many! They're overpowering me! I'm going to have to fight them." On the monitor, I saw Anomaly reach into his pack.

Kev shut his eyes for a half second and straightened in his chair, trying to overcome his anxiety so he could help his team. "No! If you get aggressive, they'll turn on you! Stay calm and—" He broke off with a gasp as a Nix Shell exploded, sending creeping amaranthine shock waves across the field, temporarily paralyzing everything in their path.

"Oh, you absolute jackass! You fucking selfish piece of — That shell is going to paralyze *us* too!" I yelled, too furious to think.

Kev didn't hesitate. He switched to his cache, extracted a woven blanket, coated it with protective Niobe Tears, and threw it over our avatars one second before the purple haze spread across the screen.

At the same moment, in a quiet neighborhood in Texas, Yolanda finished transferring the data and bolted off the Dacostas' porch. She and Sasha hit the sidewalk half a second before Cam's luxury SUV pulled onto the street. They turned the corner and were halfway back to their vehicle by the time Cam pulled into her driveway.

Kev made a whimpering noise and closed his eyes in relief. My jaw ached with wanting to reassure him, to thank him, to tell him how fucking impressive he was... and to yell at him for insisting on being part of this stressful, high-stakes mission in the first place. I was proud as fuck… and also hated that we'd involved him.

"Done," Champ said, blowing out a breath. "Good work, you two. Come find me later." He patted Kev's shoulder and sauntered out of Kev's lair as if it had been a regular day at work… because of course, for us, it had been.

I felt a rare wave of resentment toward my boss. Did he not see that Kev hadn't been trained to deal with this shit?

Cam's voice came over the headset. "I'm back. What'd I miss? Why is everything all purple?"

Kev and I climbed out from our blanket once the danger had passed. Anomaly tried stammering insincere apologies, but Kev cut him off.

"It's… it's fine. These things happen. Let's just finish this quest, okay? Everyone ready?"

The only thing I was ready for was pulling Kev from the room, throwing him up against the wall in the hallway, and recreating our scene from the club last night, kissing him over and over and over until he was trembling with want instead of fear and had forgotten all about this stupid mission.

"Yeah," I muttered, yanking my headset more firmly in place. "Ready."

We finished the bridge crossing and moved to the final and most challenging stage of the quest. It took three more hours to finish, three hours of near misses and tense communication with our asshole scout and our drug-dealing enchantress. Three hours of sitting next to the kindest man I knew, who was trying his hardest to keep it together. Three hours of inhaling his familiar scent and trying not to notice the way he crinkled his nose to lift up his slipping glasses without using his hands.

Three hours of trying to convince my dick it didn't

belong in his irresistible body. Three hours of imagining what it would feel like to hold him down and take him right here in his lair.

And three hours of arguments from the angel on my shoulder—who sounded an awful lot like Champ—who reminded me why getting involved with Kevin Rogers would be an incredibly stupid and shortsighted choice.

"Got her!" Kev cried when he successfully slipped the sleeping duchess out the tower window and into Adam's wheelbarrow on the pavers below.

"Fuck yeah, you do," Adam grunted before moving quickly away from the incoming castle guardian horde. Cam stayed behind, pouring enchantments into the horde, while I followed Adam to make sure he didn't steal the duchess out from under our noses.

Getting her back to Kev's homestead wasn't easy, but as soon as we got her behind the fences and golden pips began raining down from the sky, we all cheered in relief. And I set my headset on the desk with a clatter.

"Thank fuck."

"We did it!" Kev said with a brilliant smile on his face. He threw off his headset and tackled me, throwing his arms around my neck and hugging me so tightly my chair flipped over.

We tumbled to the ground in a laughing heap. Having his body against mine, having him in my arms, was as much of a relief as completing the mission. Maybe more. He felt so fucking good, like he was supposed to be there all the time, that it was hard to remember all the very good reasons why he wasn't.

I tightened my arm around his back and brushed a smiling kiss against his cheek. "Duchess-napper extraordinaire."

His eyes were bright, and a dimple popped on his cheek. "No one bailed on us, and we got the job done!"

I pushed his glasses back up his nose with my fingertip. "You were calm under pressure. You kept everyone together."

Kev's smile faded as he realized we were pressed against each other, but he didn't move away. Our mouths were inches away from another kiss. "I couldn't have done it without you," he said softly.

It wasn't true. He was a true master of the game, better than I would ever be, but I appreciated him saying that. My chest tightened, and my eyes strayed to his lips.

"*Are you even listening to us anymore?*" Adam's tinny voice came out of both our abandoned headsets, causing Kev to jerk and scramble up from the floor.

"Uh, yeah, sorry," Kev said, clearing his throat. He focused on the monitor and neatly avoided looking in my direction. "I'm back."

I slowly stood up and righted my chair before slipping my headset on.

A distinctive chirp sound came through comms, and I froze. Was that…? It sounded like a Grindr notification sound, and it for sure hadn't come from Kev or me. Was Adam seriously trolling for ass right now while online with his supposed boyfriend?

I glanced over at Kev, who seemed like he hadn't heard or hadn't recognized it, and ground my teeth.

It was no secret that I didn't like Anomaly, had gotten a bad feeling from the guy when we'd interacted over the defense of Kev's homestead, and had suspected all along that he was trying to manipulate Kev somehow while also profiting from Kev's glory. But this…

"Sorry, guys," I said, trying to sound calmer than I felt. "I gotta go. Good work. Thanks for letting me join you."

Before I clicked out of the chat, I heard the distinctive chirp again and felt my blood pressure spike. I waited for Kev to notice—to flinch or wince or lose his mind and kick Anomaly to the curb right then and there—but he was calm and efficient as he doled out the prize pips equally and congratulated Cam and Adam on their new rankings.

Cam signed off, clearly buzzing at having leveled up to Ascendant's Class, after offering to buy us all drinks if we were in Vegas for HOGCon, and that was when I set my headset down and turned off the game... but I didn't leave the room. I pretended to be engrossed in text messages on my phone—apparently, the IRS was looking for me, *and* I needed to buy an extended warranty for my car—while waiting for Kev to finish.

For a long while, I could only hear Kev's side of the conversation, which amounted to grunts and hmms. Then his fingertip began tapping the side of his thumb. "Yeah, no, I... Uh-huh. I didn't think of that. Good idea. Thanks for the suggestion. Maybe I'll try it next time..."

I didn't mean to eavesdrop—oh, who was I kidding? I was fully, shamelessly eavesdropping—but I got the sense that Adam was critiquing Kev's game play, which was ridiculous. Not only was Kev an amazing player, but he was also an adult, for fuck's sake. One who hadn't asked for feedback. One who was riding the high of a victory.

I waited for Kev to clap back, the way he did with me. To tell Anomaly exactly where he could shove his unsolicited advice and to call him out for nearly killing us all.

But he didn't.

My jaw began to ache with the effort of keeping my mouth shut.

"Oh, right. I forgot about the article. Uh... Well, I would probably keep something like that offline? Like, if it was critical data you really wanted to protect, it would be safest on a drive in a safe somewhere. It's not easy to access that way, but the safety is worth the inconven—oh. Uh-huh. Yeah. Is this data you need to access regularly or just store?"

I turned to look at him. Why was Adam asking Kev about data security?

"Yeah, but wait. This is data someone else has? That you want to find? Like… what kind of data?" Kev's eyes flicked to mine. I couldn't tell if his expression was one of embarrassment or concern. "Oh, phew. Yeah, no. That would be fine with 256-bit encryption. Standard stuff. I mean, unless you have like the NSA on your tail," he said with a laugh.

They talked for a few more minutes, and then Kev said, "Uh, no. I think at this point we should wait until next weekend. Yeah. Yeah. Well, I guess we *could*, but— Wait! I'm not agreeing! I— Adam?"

Kev blew out a breath and threw down his headset. It sounded like Adam had cut him off midsentence—probably rushing out to get dicked down—and I felt more enraged than I'd maybe ever been.

My skin crawled with annoyance at the rude internet stranger who tried to claim more of Kev than I could. If someone was lucky enough to get close to Kevin Rogers in any kind of relationship, they should have been treating that privilege like a gift.

"Everything…" My voice didn't sound quite right, so I cleared my throat. "Everything okay?"

Kev looked away and crossed his arms in front of his chest. "Yeah. He had to go do something for work."

"What does he do for work?" I asked, trying not to sound like I cared nearly as much as I did.

"Uh. I'm not really sure? He's a writer. I don't know the specifics."

I frowned. "He hasn't told you what he does? Not once, in all your chats? Has he told you where he lives? What kind of car he drives? Any identifying information at all?"

My mind conjured images of Anomaly living in a van by the river, luring sweet, helpful gamers into his web of lies.

Asshole.

"You mean his mother's maiden name and the last four digits of his Social Security number?" Kev scoffed. "No. You're making it sound secretive, but it's not like that. It's just... never come up. I haven't asked for details, just like he's never asked for details about my work." His face went pink. "He did ask for my help with an article he's writing just now, though, so maybe I'll ask him when I see him. In Vegas." Kev busied himself unhooking my devices and straightening up the cables.

As if I needed another reason to dread the op in Vegas.

Noting the tension in Kev's shoulders, though—the half-defensive, half-embarrassed way he leaned over the desk—I knew he wouldn't appreciate my comments about Anomaly. Instead, I tried to be casual. "I guess you guys aren't monogamous, huh?"

I pressed my lips closed in a grimace. *Way to be casual, Huxley.*

Kev's head whipped toward me. "Excuse me?"

"No judgment." I held my hands up. "Lots of people are cool with open relationships. Just... all the Grindr notifications there at the end made me wonder."

He turned toward me fully. "What Grindr notifications?"

Unease twisted my stomach. "That *brrt* sound. The ones coming through Adam's comms at the end. That's Grindr. Surely, you..." My voice trailed off as I remembered something Carter had said that implied Kev didn't have much dating experience. But I couldn't imagine a gay man who hadn't at least tried Grindr. Unless…

My heart stuttered as I remembered the way I'd pressed myself against him in the club. Had Kev never had a casual hookup before? Was I the first guy who'd ever corralled him against the wall of a bar and gotten him hard?

The idea wakened a primal, possessive, protective urge inside me that I felt more and more often around this man. One I had no business feeling for a guy who was Riggs's family, who was my coworker, who could have literally any guy in the world, the way Kev could.

"I thought that was a video game or a text chime," Kev mumbled. Red slashes burned on his cheeks, and he wouldn't meet my eyes.

"Oh. Uh. I mean. Maybe he…" No. I refused to consider that Adam was using a Grindr sound for any reason besides the most obvious one, even to make Kev feel better. "I'm sorry," I said instead.

"No, it's… it's good that you said something," Kev said, throwing me a fake-ass smile that made my skin crawl. "I actually thought that I remembered hearing Jordan's and Elvo's phones make that sound, and I was gonna ask them what game they were all playing." He laughed without humor. "So you saved me from that humiliation, anyway. Such an idiot."

I picked my words carefully. "I'm not trying to tell you how to feel, but I think if anyone should feel like an idiot, it should be the person doing the cheating."

Kev cut me off with a shake of his head, still not meeting my eyes. "No. It's not like that. Adam and I aren't exclusive. He said the other day that he wanted to be, but I… We hadn't made anything official yet. Looks like he wasn't willing to wait around for me to catch up." He shrugged offhandedly.

"Fucker," I bit out, sounding angrier than I'd intended. "He doesn't deserve you, Kev."

"Eh." He waved a hand dismissively and even managed a small, sad smile. "That's nice of you to say, but we both know the truth. I can be annoying, Huxley. A pain in the ass who's always looking for attention, remember?"

"Stop it," I growled. Without pausing to think, I grabbed him by the shirtfront and hauled him close, cutting off his words. I hated hearing him talk like that. Hated that he *thought* like that. Hated that I'd made him believe that I actually felt that way too.

Truths I'd barely acknowledged to myself fell from my lips, and for once, I didn't try to stop them.

"I only said that shit because I couldn't stop giving you *my* attention," I said, low and urgent, willing him to really hear me. "Because whenever you're around, you're the only person I can see. Doesn't matter if I'm in the middle of a game or the middle of a critical mission. Doesn't matter if you've just said something insulting that slashed my ego to ribbons. When you open your mouth, I can't *not* listen for your voice. When you're in the room, I can't *not* follow your every movement. When you're anywhere close to me, Kevin Rogers, I can't *not* wish that you were right here in my arms, and when you're in my arms, I can't help but wish I… *fuck*."

I kissed him, licking at his lips until he parted them, allowing me to taste his sweetness. I wanted to swallow him whole, lose myself in his body, and beg him never to leave.

Most of all, I wanted him to believe, down to his bones, that he was desirable. He was worthy.

He was everything.

I kissed him until we were breathless. When I pulled back, his eyes were dazed behind crooked glasses. "You… you wish what?"

"Tell me to stop," I whispered, peppering his cheeks and chin with smaller kisses. "Tell me to leave you alone."

I moved my hands around to his slender back. The muscles shifted under his sweatshirt as his arms reached up to circle my neck.

"What if… what if I don't want you to leave me alone?" he murmured. The flags of embarrassment still painted his cheeks, and now his nose was pink from my beard. My heart hammered in my chest. "Tell me what you wish, Hux."

"When you're in my arms, I wish that you were even closer," I admitted in a whisper. "Under my lips. Under my hands. In my bed."

Kev's whole body shivered in my arms, and his eyes widened, but just when I worried that I'd freaked him out, he pushed himself closer to me. "Hux…"

"I'll do anything to make you feel good. Just tell me."

The corner of Kev's mouth turned up. I could still see shock and a little fear in his eyes, but when he bit down on his lower lip, his whole face took on a teasing light, and it called to me like a fucking siren, luring me even closer to him. "So, just for the record, you don't hate me?"

I held him closer to my body so he could feel the press of my hard dick against his lower belly. "Does it feel like I hate you?"

"And you're saying I *don't* annoy you."

I shook my head, even as my insides lit up at his challenging tone. He wasn't going to make this easy on me, which only made me prouder of him.

"Oh, no, you do. You annoy the fuck out of me, every moment of every day. You're annoyingly sexy. So annoyingly sweet. And really annoyingly intelligent. I can't stop thinking about you. Can't stop wanting you. Drives me insane."

His teeth sank further into his plump lip, and my dick literally pulsed against my zipper.

"Let me touch you," I said in a rough voice, my hands caressing up and down his back, trying to map every inch of his body. "Let me kiss you all over."

Maybe then I'll get you out of my system once and for fucking all, I thought a little desperately, even though I already knew better.

"Like… naked?" Kev pretended to sound shocked, though his eyes danced.

I held back a snort of laughter. "Naked! God, no. What kind of guy do you think I am? I meant I wanted to taste your cotton-blend hoodie." I buried my nose at the join of his shoulder and bit him through the cloth.

"O-oh," he stammered. "I had no idea you had a fiber kink."

"You should see how crazy I get when I get my tongue on worn denim," I purred in his ear.

Kev pressed himself against me with a shiver. "Can we… can we go to my, um, bedroom?" he asked, looking over my shoulder at the doorway through which my boss had only left a few minutes earlier.

"Yes. Definitely yes."

"But I don't want…" He paused as if trying to figure out the right words. "It's not that I don't want to… I'm just not sure I want *everything.*"

I cupped his cheek and met his eyes. "Kev. I don't want to do anything you don't want to do. If it doesn't feel good or you don't want to do something, just tell me to stop, and I will." *Even though it will kill me.*

He blew out a breath and smiled in relief. "Yeah. Okay. Yeah."

God, he was adorable. I wanted to fuck him into the floor, but I also wanted to put him in my pocket and keep him safe for all time. I wanted to protect him from all the assholes in the world, starting with Anomaly451 and ending with… well, *me*. But I was too selfish for that.

I grabbed his hand and pulled him toward the closed door at the far end of the room. "This way?" I asked belatedly, acting like I hadn't snooped through the exterior windows at the back of the house one afternoon.

His hand was warm and damp in mine. Clearly he was nervous, but I'd also felt his own hardness against my own, so I knew he was as turned on as I was. I silently vowed to take good care of him, to make him feel good.

When I opened the bedroom door, I was surprised by how messy it was. Kev kept his gaming lair spotless. Everything had a place, and he seemed meticulous about keeping things tidy. His bedroom, on the other hand, looked like a tornado had ripped through it. Clothes were piled on the floor, and the navy-and-white comforter was in a tangle at the foot of the bed. The pillows looked like they'd been used to fight a war, and one of the corners of the fitted sheet had long given up the fight and surrendered to the center of the mattress.

And in the center of the bed was a very worn, very bedraggled stuffed duck.

"Oh no," Kev said under his breath. "I… uh… hang on a minute!" He turned and shoved me back out the door, slamming it closed between us.

I placed my palm on the closed door and fought a grin. "I don't care if it's messy," I said through the barrier.

"It's not usually like this," he swore. "It's usually very neat! It's just… fuck," he muttered. His voice lowered. "I wasn't expecting anyone to see. Ever. But that's fine! No problem. I can do this! I'm just going to straighten the bed, and then I can…Wait! Henry Cavill! Play Marvin Gaye's 'Let's Get It On' —"

I opened the door and strode through it, grabbing Kev up, yanking the duck from his hands, and depositing him on his back on the unmade bed before following him down and crushing his mouth with mine.

"I'm not here to see your room, Kev," I rasped out, yanking his head back so I could meet his eyes. "Okay?"

"Playing Chris Isaak's 'Wicked Game,'" a deep, cultured, oddly satisfied voice said, moments before haunting, aching guitar chords began playing softly in the background. The lights dimmed automatically.

Kev made a soft exhale of agreement, and his eyes went liquid. Then he lifted his head up to kiss me back.

After kissing all thoughts from his head, I tore off my shirt and began stripping him down methodically, starting with his glasses.

"So sexy," I said as I placed them safely on his bedside table. The way his pale skin flushed made me feel supremely powerful.

I dropped kisses on every single inch of that skin until each of his exhales became a small whimper or a grunt, and his eyes turned glassy with need.

"Gonna come," he squeaked a few times too early, but I simply grabbed the base of his cock and squeezed firmly.

"Not. Yet," I warned. "I want to make it last. I've been waiting a long time for this." Longer than I'd let myself believe.

He panted into the air, his chest heaving with the shallow breaths. "Can't... can't..."

"You can," I said. "You will."

"Jasper," he begged, using the name I'd so rarely heard out of his mouth. It was enough to nearly unman me. My cock begged for relief, but this was for him, for Kev, and I wasn't about to take my hands off him to give myself pleasure.

Kev's fingers threaded into my hair and gripped it tightly when I finally took his dick in my mouth and swallowed it down.

"Ahh! Oh God, oh. Oh! Oh God. You're... you're *sucking me*." The pure wonder in his voice made me redouble my efforts. "Oh my God."

I fondled his balls with one hand and ran the other one up his stomach to his chest before tweaking his nipple with my thumb.

"Can I come? Oh, Hux, please!"

I met his eyes and pulled off long enough to make an affirmative sound before dropping down on his cock again and trying to make it the best orgasm of his life.

Pretty sure I succeeded.

11

KEV

Proper blow job etiquette was not one of the things I'd learned during the year my grandfather had sent me to cotillion, and I wasn't sure I had the brains to ad-lib at the moment.

"You didn't come," I said stupidly to the man who'd collapsed on the bed beside me. Damn, but Hux looked good on my rumpled sheets.

Hux's laugh was pained. "Give me about half a second, sweetheart."

I glanced down and saw him pulling open his fly. My stomach swooped with excitement, and I put my hand on his wrist to stop him. "Can I?"

Hux flipped our hands over and shoved mine into his underwear with a groan of relief. My fingers automatically wrapped around a surprisingly girthy cock, and I made a sound so needy I might have been embarrassed if Hux hadn't moaned my name and thrust up into my grip in a way that suggested my noises were really working for him.

I scrambled around on the bed to get a better angle. "Lie back," I said before yanking his pants and boxer briefs all the way off. I had never touched a guy this way before, but Jesus fuck, I'd fantasized about it so often that if there were a tournament for hand jobs, I would be at the very top of the Ascendant's Class.

"What's that smile for?" Hux demanded.

"Just thinking about what I'd like to do to you," I said, which was in no way a lie.

"You're going to kill me," Hux muttered at the same time I looked down at him for the first time, and all the breath left my body in a very loud, "*Ohhhhh.*"

His cock was huge—at least, it was much thicker than mine and a little longer too. The hair around the base was neatly trimmed, and I tried not to think about who he trimmed it for. Hopefully himself. And no one else.

I wanted so many things I couldn't decide what to do first. I wanted to run my hands all over his thick, muscled thighs, to trace every inch of the tattoos on his chest and flanks in the dim light, to taste his salty skin. But his cock was flushed deep red, and so hard it looked painful, so I decided the rest could wait temporarily.

I reached over to the bedside table to grab my tube of lube, not realizing I'd flashed him my bare ass until his hand landed on it with a stinging *smack*. I gasped, and he groaned again, even deeper this time.

"No, seriously. *Killing me.* God, this ass. No amount of health diamonds could bring me back," he said, giving my flesh a firm squeeze.

Hux slid his thumb between my cheeks to graze my hole, and I squeezed the lube so hard the bottle nearly sailed across the room. My entire body flushed hot, my recently satisfied dick gave a hopeful twitch, and the urge to push back against him was so strong I barely stifled a whimper.

Wait, what was I supposed to be doing?

Oh. Right. Touching Hux's monster cock.

Holy shit. I—nerdy, slightly weird, forever awkward Kev Rogers—was about to touch Jasper Huxley's cock. I really hoped that I could do this right.

I grabbed his hand and turned back around to face him. His eyes were hot and hungry, roaming every inch of my naked body with obvious appreciation.

"Hands off, Huxley," I warned, pressing his wrist to my mattress, hoping I didn't sound as nervous as I felt. "This is my quest now. I call it 'Make HogMaster lose his mind.'"

"Oh, *really*? Then by all means." Hux's face split in a wild, challenging grin, and my nerves fled as quickly as they'd come. I wanted this man so badly—wanted to give him pleasure, wanted him at my mercy.

Hux made a big show out of moving his hands to stack them behind his head, and he spread his legs slightly, the very picture of relaxation… except for his cock, which was steel hard and begging for my touch. But when I stroked one finger down the length of him, the smile slid off his face immediately, and his mouth opened in a wordless groan.

Oh, yeah. *Game. On.*

I poured out twice as much lube as I needed and started jacking him off with the combination of intuition and scientific precision I applied to most things. I tugged his balls gently with one hand while the other worked his smooth shaft in long strokes, first hard and fast, then quick and light. I tried to catalog his every reaction—the tightening of his eyes, the arch of his back, the hitch in his breathing—but when Hux started panting and keening my name, it was impossible to stay focused and detached.

The man was too fucking glorious. And not everything had to be a competition.

"You're amazing," I whispered hoarsely, honestly.

"Fuck, Huxley, I want you to come for me so badly. I want to see you."

Hux pushed his heels into the bed and thrust up into my hand, unreservedly begging for more, and I picked up the pace, using two hands to jack him off. The squelching of the lube mixed with the slinky thrum of the music—what the hell song was this? Who told Henry to access my Sade playlist?—was more erotic than anything I could have imagined in my wildest fantasies.

I had no idea how the hell we'd gotten here, but if this first time was my only time with Hux, I wanted to make the most of it. I braced my hand beside his head so I could lean closer and inhale him, filling myself with his sandalwood scent, and when his messy head tipped back on the pillow, revealing the corded lines of his neck, I didn't resist the urge to slide my lips over that taut flesh, tasting and savoring his flavor.

Hux cursed and hissed, gripping my arm with strong fingers. "Kev. Oh, shit, Kev, don't… don't stop."

As if I would. As if I *could*.

When his orgasm blasted over him, he roared out my name, and I watched him come with fascination. The long ropes of his release fell onto my fingers and into the hair below his belly button. I ran my fingers through the mess, then let them drift further, tracing the lines of script and the slightly faded compass rose tattoo that twined over his hip. I made out the words *No Roots* and then a tattoo that was darker, maybe newer, that said, *No Shortcuts*.

God, this man was fascinating. The greatest puzzle I'd ever encountered. And here I was, the world's luckiest, newbiest newb, watching him gasp and shiver his way back to earth.

"If this is a dream," I murmured, "I will kill anyone who wakes me up."

Hux turned his head on the pillow and regarded me solemnly—almost… expectantly—and I began to feel incredibly awkward. How did you end an encounter like this?

Hey, man! Good Game.

Come back soon!

Would you mind posing for a pic so I can remember this moment?

My face heated, and I ducked down to hide it by his hip, pretending to peer more closely at the ink. Hux would probably hop up any minute and stammer his excuses before bolting back upstairs where the normal people were. He wouldn't want to stay here with me for any length of time. He didn't even really like me.

You're so fucking sexy. So damn sweet. I can't stop thinking about you. Can't stop wanting you.

I blinked and swallowed past a lump in my throat. Had he really said that, or was that a heat-of-the-moment kind of thing people said during sex?

I snuck a glance up at his face and discovered Hux was still studying me with the barest hint of a teasing smirk on his lips.

"Hey," he said in an obnoxiously sexy voice.

"Oh. Hey." I cleared my throat and reached for my comforter to hide my pale, skinny body. I tried to make it look casual, but I got the feeling Hux saw right through me. "Thank you. That was very nice."

"Nice," Hux said thoughtfully, like he was tasting the word. He rolled his top lip between his teeth to try and hide a grin, but he wasn't fooling anyone. "That's one word for it."

I threw up my arms, accidentally naked-ing myself again. "I don't know how to do this, okay? I don't… I don't understand the protocol. No one ever told me how to make polite chitchat after a… a *sexual encounter*, or if they did, I don't remember."

"It's been a long time since I've done this too," he said softly. "Half a year. Maybe more."

I bit back a hysterical laugh. "Yeah. It's, ah… it's been a little longer for me."

Hux lifted a curious eyebrow and shifted his weight so he was more comfortable on the bed. Then he lifted one of my hands—which had begun tapping wildly at some point —and smiled almost… affectionately. "So what do you *want* to do?"

I hesitated for a moment, but that sweet smile was like a DragonFire Dagger, burning through all my defenses. "I want to be like some kind of romance heroine and lie on your chest," I admitted. "But that's stup-*ah*!"

Hux yanked on my hand, pulling me down so that my head rested on his chest, and wrapped his arm around my shoulders. I felt stiff and awkward.

"Wait a minute," he grumbled, sitting up and dislodging me back onto the mattress. He pointed a finger in my direction. "Stay right there. Not kidding. Don't move."

I blinked once and nodded, because when the naked, sexy badass tells you to stay still, you… well, you probably get so hypnotized by the sight of him that you'd agree to just about anything.

Without another word, he disappeared into my bathroom, giving me the most incredible view of the muscular slab he called an ass.

"*Ohhh*," I breathed, watching it like a hawk. A very lucky, almost horny again, hawk.

When he returned, I noticed he'd cleaned himself off, and he carried a damp cloth. When he got to the bed, he reached for my hands and cleaned them off before tossing the cloth in the direction of the bathroom. Then he climbed back into the bed and settled himself again.

"Now," he said, sounding like a Bossy McCommander-face, "get back over here."

This time, I didn't hesitate. I rested my cheek on his chest and let my arm settle over his defined abs. Even though it felt cheesy and stupid, it also felt incredibly good.

But what did it mean? Were we... um, fuck buddies? Or was it a one-night stand? Was this the beginning of something more than that? Or was I reading too much into it?

Hux's fingers lightly raked lines up and down my bare back. "Take a breath," he said softly.

I grunted. "You say that a lot."

"Only to you."

"I just..." I tried to think about the right way to word my question without sounding clueless. Or desperate. "I don't really know..."

"The protocol," he finished. I could hear a smile in his voice, but he didn't sound mocking. That was something, at least.

"Well, yeah. I don't want to make assumptions. Or say something stupid."

Hux shifted me a little and used his free hand to tip my chin up until I met his eyes. "For starters, I'd like to stay in your bed tonight. All night."

I stared at him without blinking. "Really?"

"Yes, but only if you're okay with it. I meant what I said earlier that I don't want you to feel uncomfortable."

"I'm okay with it," I said, playing it cool. "Really very extremely okay with it." Well, maybe not as cool as I'd thought.

"And if you want more... sexual encounters, all you need to do is tell me. Okay?"

I swallowed. Tell him? In words? Like, *take me now, Huxley?* Or *if you're not busy, could you pencil me in for something for later today?* "Uh… pretty sure I can go ahead and authorize any future encounters right now," I mumbled into his pec.

Hux tugged my head back to look at me. His fingers smoothed the hair back from my forehead. The look in his eyes was surprisingly… fond. "Maybe give me a few minutes to recover first. That first… *encounter*… was pretty mind-blowing."

I nodded like a bobblehead. "Yeah. Yes." I looked around the room, wondering again what a normal person would do in this situation. "Would you like a drink?" I asked politely. "Or a snack?"

Hux's smile grew, but so did that fond look, so I figured that was okay. "Do you have a drink to give me?"

"No. But I could always go upstairs and get something. I mean, I have some soda and coffee in my lair, but it's a little late for caffeine. Unless, of course, you're one of those people who aren't sensitive to caffeine. Did you know that fully ten percent of people don't —"

Hux grabbed my chin and leaned up to kiss me, cutting off my awkward chatter and replacing it with something infinitely hotter.

I lost myself in the feeling of giving over control to him. I was learning very quickly that I loved the feeling of surrender. Nothing would have pleased me more than for him to take over and just tell me what to do.

He rolled me over until I was on my back on the bed and he was halfway on top of me. We made out like teenagers—well, not the kind of teenager I'd been but the kind I'd heard about. The kind that got up to no good in their parents' basements.

I loved every minute of it and didn't want it to end.

Making out with Jasper Huxley felt like winning the lottery. Or finally getting a stolen duchess back to my homestead.

Or... my brain stuttered and flatlined, unable to dredge up a single fitting analogy, maybe because nothing in my entire life compared to this.

We kissed and felt each other up for a long time, long enough to make me secretly giddy that one good session seemed to be giving me years of the experience I'd been lacking. Every place I touched or kissed or nipped was a new experience, and I hoarded them all greedily.

"Oh, fuck. You're burning me up," he moaned when I accidentally rubbed my face against his hardness while worshipping each of his many, many abs with my tongue.

I jumped back and started apologizing before Hux leaned up and put his hand over my mouth. "Stop apologizing for turning me on, Kev. I want you to touch me. I crave it. You can do anything you want to me."

"But what do *you* want?" I demanded.

His tongue touched the corner of his mouth, and his eyes flicked down to his cock, almost on instinct. He didn't say a word, but it was enough to tell me exactly what he wanted. His hand fell away from my mouth.

"Oh, fuck yeah," I blurted. "But, like, I'm not experienced. I mean, that much is probably painfully obvious, heh." I swallowed thickly. "But, I... I'll probably be terrible at it and embarrass us both. Heh."

This time, I slapped my own hand over my mouth to stop the unpleasantness.

Hux tried to stifle a laugh. "There's no possible way you could put your mouth on me, *anywhere* on me, and not have it be incredible." He tapped my forehead with one thick finger. "Consider the inverse, Dr. Rogers."

I blinked. The inverse? Hux's mouth on me? Oh. *Ohhhh.*

Yeah, I couldn't imagine there was such a thing as "terrible at it." And considering how badly I wanted him in my mouth, I figured I'd be an extremely motivated learner.

My stomach vibrated with nerves, but I moved forward anyway, letting the tip of my tongue come out just enough to feel the smooth skin of his hardening cock. The ragged breath Hux dragged in emboldened me to do it again.

And again.

I ran the flat of my tongue over his shaft until I got brave enough to suckle the head. Every porn video I'd ever watched rolled through the back of my mind in an effort to cram some last-minute training for the big test.

I passed.

As soon as I was brave enough to brush my fingertip over his hole, Hux lost it, arching up and groaning before warm salt flooded my mouth. I sputtered and panicked for a minute before swallowing experimentally… and then more enthusiastically, swallowing down every drop and licking up the remainder.

"Oh fuck," Hux breathed. His fingers carded through my hair. "Fuck."

I knew better than to ask if I'd done okay. I could tell he was more than pleased by my inaugural attempt, so I grinned up at him instead. The cat that ate the canary.

"Proud of yourself?" Hux asked with a laugh.

I climbed on top of him and kissed him hard, reveling in the idea that he could taste his own release on my tongue. "Mmhm."

Hux's hands moved over my skin, touching me everywhere. I fantasized about waking up again in a few hours to experiment some more. I wanted to try everything with him. Maybe I wasn't quite ready for anal without more of a conversation about what exactly was happening between us, but I definitely wanted to suck him again. And I wouldn't have minded him sucking me.

"Thank you," Hux said softly into my hair. "That was even better than I'd fantasized."

I smiled into his chest with pride and happiness. It wasn't until I was on the very edge of falling asleep that my brain finally picked out the critical information from that sentence.

When in the world had Jasper Huxley fantasized about a sexual encounter with me?

12

HUX

Thank God for Kev's meticulous security. When my boss tried to find me at five in the fucking morning, at least he wasn't able to barge in on my naked tangle with Kevin Rogers.

No, instead, he used the alert feature on our group phone app to make my phone start blaring from my pants on the floor like the safe house was being invaded.

Kev jerked in my arms and knocked his head against the underside of my chin. "Wha?"

"Shh. Go back to sleep," I said in a sleep-roughened voice. "That's Champ. Something must have happened." I moved out from under him, taking one last chance to inhale the sleepy vanilla scent of him and nuzzle his messy hair.

When I pulled my phone out of my pants, I blinked against the bright screen. Then I blinked again at the message.

Champ: *Grab Kev. We need both of you in the van to Nashville.*

I tapped out a response.

Hux: *What's happening?*

Champ: *An opportunity to get Vince's Horn. We need all hands on deck for this one.*

I glanced over at Kev, who'd curled up around the pillow I'd been using. The urge to protect him was overwhelming and instinctive… and I didn't even try to talk myself out of it anymore.

Hux: *You sure we need Kev? What if he's busy? What if he doesn't want to come?*

Not that I could envision a scenario where Kev didn't leap at the opportunity to help the team, no matter what it cost him.

Champ: …

I sighed. He always responded with those three dots instead of saying, "Who's in charge of this mission, Marine?"

Hux: *ETA 15 mins.*

I shut off my phone and sat on the edge of Kev's bed, letting my eyes adjust to the semi-darkness. Then I took an extra second to let my mind adjust too.

I'd hooked up with *Kev Rogers*—the man who'd gotten under my skin, gotten into my blood, and driven me crazy for months. And maybe in another time, with another guy, I could have convinced myself that I'd only done it because sex was a convenient way to relieve the tension between us, or because he was hot as fuck and I'd been high on adrenaline, but today, with Kev, I… couldn't.

Last night hadn't been like any kind of hookup I'd ever experienced. There were moments when our eyes had met and I'd been almost sure he could read my mind, maybe better than I could.

It was like I'd strapped in for the sexual equivalent of a carnival kiddie coaster and had suddenly found myself strapped to a rocket, hurtling through the stratosphere, upside down and laughing my head off. But it felt too good, too right, for me to regret it.

In fact, I wanted to enjoy the ride as long as I could.

A security light from outside gave just enough illumination for me to see Kev was awake and looking at me. I reached over and smoothed a thumb over the light stubble on his jaw.

"Hey. Champ wants you on a mission with us to Nashville."

His eyes widened. "Today?"

"Right now."

"Oh! Yeah!" He grabbed the edge of the covers to pull them back. "I'll be ready in—"

I stopped him with a gentle hand on his throat. "Wait," I said softly. "I just… you don't have to do this if you don't want to."

He searched my eyes. "But I do want to. I want to help."

I ran a thumb along his thrumming pulse. His fine skin was reddened in places where I'd held him too firmly, sucked him too hard, and that possessive feeling swamped me again.

I was becoming familiar with that too.

"Just promise me you won't feel pressure to do anything you feel uncomfortable wi—"

Kev surged forward until his lips touched mine. "If you're going, I'm going," he said, and then he kissed me enthusiastically. It was awkward and clunky but so damned sweet I wanted to pin him down and reward him for his confidence. Unfortunately, there wasn't time.

I pulled back and grabbed his glasses off the nightstand before settling them on his face. "I think it would be more efficient if we showered together. Save time."

"And save the planet," he agreed piously.

Showering together turned out to be a mistake. As soon as I got my hands on him under the hot spray, my dick thundered to life. I fumbled us through a quick frot before rinsing off and throwing yesterday's clothes on.

Thankfully, I had a change of clothes in a guest room upstairs. I raced through my usual pre-op checklist of dressing, then feeding Rodrigo and cleaning his cage, and by the time I hit the kitchen for coffee, I was only three minutes late. I definitely didn't have enough time to brew a fresh pot of coffee, but maybe I could—

Kev was already there, holding two travel mugs and bags of something that smelled like Mrs. Carmody's breakfast sandwiches. He shook one cup and a bag in my direction.

"I added that gross syrup you like," he began, but I cut him off with a fierce kiss.

There were definitely some upsides to having Kev on the team.

Maybe a *lot* of upsides.

We quickly made our way out to the driveway, where the team was assembling. I was surprised to see Quinn in the group. "Is it Bring Your Boyfriend on the Op day?" I muttered under my breath.

Kev frowned. "Sorry, did you say something?"

I blinked and felt my face heat. Shit. Had I actually just thought of Kev as my boyfriend?

Jesus Christ.

Kev was supposed to be the less-experienced one of the two of us, but suddenly, I was acting like a teenager who'd just exchanged promise bracelets with his first crush. I needed to slow the fuck down.

"Nothing," I said, annoyed at myself.

"Huxley," Champ said, glancing pointedly at his watch, "nice of you to join us. Did you have trouble finding Kev?"

"Uh. No." I knew my face was getting even redder. "Nope. He was… right in his bed." It was harder than it should have been not to add, "*with me.*"

"Thanks for coming, Kev," Champ said much more warmly. "Okay, let's move."

Kev seemed strangely shy as we loaded up. He didn't meet anyone's eyes, including mine, and deliberately chose a seat in the back of the surveillance van, away from everyone else. I must have glanced at him in concern one too many times because Riggs side-eyed me.

"What'd he do to piss you off now?" he asked in a low voice.

"Who? Oh, Kev? Nothing."

Riggs tilted his head and smirked. "Then why do you keep glaring at him?"

"I'm not glaring at him," I hissed. "I'm worried about him. He's being unusually quiet."

"You? Worried about Kev?" Riggs's smirk widened. "Sure, bro."

I tightened my grip on my coffee. "I'm serious."

Riggs's eyes narrowed on me for a moment, and then he shrugged. "It's five thirty in the morning. Maybe he's half-asleep like the rest of us."

Except I knew that wasn't it. Something had gotten in his head between the time we'd left the kitchen and the time he'd gotten in the van, and whatever it was, I wanted to fix it for him. Hell, I wanted to grab the front of his shirt and yank him toward me, wrap my arms around him, and reassure him. But that was definitely not happening here in front of my team, my boss, while on a mission.

Besides, I didn't know what Kev even wanted. Yesterday, he'd been calling that cheating asshole Anomaly his boyfriend, about them maybe becoming exclusive in Vegas —

"Hey." Riggs nudged me. "Are you eating that sandwich or turning it into a smoothie?"

I looked down at the crumpled breakfast sandwich bag in my hand. "Neither. Just… thinking."

"About?"

I bit my tongue. I was absolutely not going to tell Riggs about what had happened with Kev. For one thing, Kev was an adult, and his sex life was none of Riggs's business, even if he did think of Kev as a brother. For another… how the hell could I explain what was going on when I didn't know, myself?

Fortunately, before I had to reply, Champ's voice filled the van. "Listen up. I had a long talk with my mom last night."

I glanced around at my teammates, wondering if we were being trolled, but no one seemed to bat an eye at the idea that Champ was suddenly having heart-to-hearts with the Nashville socialite he'd been almost estranged from for years.

Maybe I wasn't the only one whose world had turned upside down.

He continued. "Quinn called her to talk about a gala she's planning in the fall, and over the course of the conversation, he told her that we were investigating Vince—"

"Ah, shit," Elvo groaned.

"Excuse you. You make it sound like I blurted it out, and I didn't. I *suggested* to Bunny that continuing to have a relationship with her son's ex-boyfriend was inadvisable for several reasons." Quinn lifted his chin in the air and sniffed delicately. "Then I *encouraged* her that distancing herself from Vince would go a long way toward healing the breach between her and her beloved son."

"Uh-huh," Champ agreed dryly. "And then…?"

Quinn sighed, and his shoulders slumped. "She kept

acting like Vince was a lost puppy who needed her maternal guidance and affection and would be really hurt if she stopped sending him birthday cards… so I dropped a truth bomb on her. I told her Vince was dangerous, that he'd almost kidnapped me, and she needed to stay away for her own good."

"Uh-huh." Champ nodded. "And *thennn*?"

"And then she got all worried, so I had to tell her the basic details of Vince going rogue," Quinn admitted. "And then she asked if her Percy was going to stop him, and I said of course, but that Champ was gonna have to confront Vince somehow first, and it might get messy. And that's when she… well, she offered her assistance."

Everyone perked up. Champ's ex was not only a villain, but he was a villain with a badge and someone we needed to be very careful with. Getting the data off his Horn was arguably going to be the hardest op of all because Vince knew Champ… and would probably see us coming.

"She called Vince last night and invited him to brunch this morning," Champ explained.

"And didn't take no for an answer." Quinn sounded admiring. "Every time he tried to get out of it, she pretended not to understand, and when he insisted he was too busy, she said she couldn't wait to see him so she could give him his invitation to her next gala."

"Vince is a sucker for a gala," Champ said.

"Champ was supposed to notify the team last night, but he, ah… got distracted."

By the smoldering look on Champ's face, it was pretty clear who had done the distracting.

"Uh-huh," Champ said yet again.

"Anyway," Quinn continued with a laugh. "We're going to play it safe. If it doesn't work, it doesn't work. But I have a feeling Bunny's actually going to be able to pull this off."

Champ looked over at his man with pride tinged with exasperation. It was the kind of look that usually made me roll my eyes, but for some reason, today I had a different reaction.

Understanding.

He looked like I'd felt yesterday after watching Kev successfully complete the mission to distract Camila Dacosta, despite nearly losing his shit. I'd been impressed with his abilities, not only in the game but with the people he'd had to wrangle. I'd been proud of his achievement. And I'd wanted to shake him for continually putting himself in that position.

I glanced back at Kev again, because I couldn't resist, but when I felt Riggs's eyes on me, I turned back around and tried to focus on what Champ was telling us.

"So we're going to get there early. Quinn and I are going to crash the brunch as a distraction while Riggs and Elvo wait in the guest room to receive the Horn. Hux and Kev will run point on surveillance from the van and be ready in case we have a problem accessing the Horn data. Yolanda, Katie, and Jordan are en route to Georgia to target the hunter, so I appreciate the extra assistance today from Kev and Quinn."

He didn't mention that Riggs and Elvo would be armed, but I knew that had to be a large part of their role in today's mission.

Kev's voice was almost too soft to be heard over the group chatter. "At least he has his Horn with him."

I glanced back to find him tapping away on his tablet. He had the coordinates up for the Horns we were targeting, something I should have thought to do the minute Champ told us whose Horn we were going after.

I spun around in my seat and began powering up the computers in the van and organizing earwigs for Riggs and

Elvo. I knew from experience Champ wouldn't allow them for him or Quinn since Vince was way too savvy to the tech we used.

Once we arrived in Bunny's fancy neighborhood outside of Nashville, we dropped everyone off and moved the van around the corner to the parking lot by the country club tennis courts.

I climbed into the back and found Kev already at home in front of the monitors. "I'm surprised Champ is willing to involve his mother in an op," Kev said without looking at me.

"It's definitely not like him," I agreed. "They're not particularly close, but I think Quinn's been trying to change that. And Bunny cares about Champ a lot... even if she doesn't know what to do with him half the time."

To my surprise, Kev laughed. "Oh, God. Relatable."

I frowned as I dropped into the chair beside him. "In what way?"

Kev glanced in my direction for the first time since we'd left his house. "In all the ways? Remember, I was raised by a socialite too. My grandfather lives in a neighborhood just like this one."

"No kidding. But your grandfather adores you—dotes on you, I think Carter said—and is incredibly proud of your achievements."

"Oh, yeah. All of that," Kev agreed, sitting back in his seat. "He loves me a ton, even if he secretly worries that I'm a vampire because I spend all my time in my lair, avoiding sunlight and humans." He grinned. "At least he tries to understand, though, which is more than I can say for my parents. They decided I was too weird for them back when I was in middle school, so they left me in Tennessee and went off to work for a medical mission to Africa. But they pray for me," he added solemnly.

I stared at him blankly as all the pieces of the privileged childhood I'd imagined for Kev Rogers rearranged themselves in my mind. "I… I had no idea."

"Well, no, how would you? I'm just saying, I understand what it's like to be the black sheep of a family."

"The black sheep," I repeated, still stunned. "Because you like computers and don't like to socialize?"

"Not just that. I mean… my whole family are cardiologists, you know? *Brilliant* ones. Handsome, golden-haired, charming, giving ones. People who save other people's lives daily. And I'm not just talking about Carter and my grandfather," he went on. "I mean, my own dad, and Carter's dad, Grandfather's father… heck, there was probably some Neanderthal Rogers painting hearts on the wall of a cave somewhere." He paused. "And then there's… me."

"Yeah, *you*. Brilliant, charming, kind, giving… The apple didn't fall far from the tree, as far as I can see," I said stoutly.

Kev's cheeks went pink, but the look he gave me was nearly pitying. "Easy to say when you weren't the one who had to tell your grandfather that you couldn't bear to dissect a frog in ninth grade biology and watch his premed dreams for you evaporate on the spot. And I don't remember you finding me all that charming either until, like…" He tapped his lip thoughtfully. "Yesterday?"

"It was longer than that," I said gruffly. But he was right. I'd been lying to myself, and to him, for a long while. And it was silly for me to think that me telling him the truth just once or twice would make up for that.

In fact, I had a lot to make up for where Kev was concerned.

I leaned toward him. "Well, fuck 'em."

"The frogs?" he said lightly, turning back toward the monitor. "Because I don't think—"

I reached out and spun his chair toward me, then gripped his chin, forcing him to look at me. "Fuck anyone who'd want a bland, predictable carbon copy when they could have someone as smart, and fun, and enthusiastic, and just plain *good* as you in their lives. You didn't have to be out here today, Kev. You're not trained for this stuff, you're not emotionally prepared for it, but you got out of a warm bed and you showed up because you *care* about people. You care about doing the right thing. And I think that makes you a fucking incredible person. An incredible teammate."

Kev's eyes got wider and shinier with every word that tumbled out of my mouth. "You think that? Really? I… I got worried that I was going to let you down." He motioned toward the monitors and surveillance cameras. "Let the team down."

"You won't," I said. I hoped he could read the sincerity in my eyes.

"I'm just afraid you'll change your mind back again," he blurted. "That you're gonna remember how awkward and overwhelmed I get, and you won't want me." His eyes widened, and his face went deep red. "Want me on the team, I mean."

"I want you," I told him, suffusing the words with meaning. "That's not going to change." I cleared my throat. "Even though I still think you need training before you do fieldwork."

Kev opened his mouth to say something—probably something I really wanted to hear, like how he was feeling about last night and this morning—but at just that moment, a sleek, black sedan pulled up.

"He's here," I said into the team comms.

Kev murmured, "He's alone. I wonder where his accomplice is." He pulled his tablet onto his lap and began tapping and swiping. "Wait, what if there's another van around here with that guy in it doing surveillance on us?"

"Shit," I said, sitting up straighter. He was right. We needed eyes on Vince's motel buddy, the other guy from the DEA. "Can you look for traces of anyone in the security system?"

"On it."

We worked together for several minutes until Kev pulled out his phone and made a call. "Hi, I was hoping to be connected to room 114. Thanks."

I glanced over at him. "Calling the motel. Jesus." Simple, yet effective.

"I'm looking for Linda…" he said, taking on a much heavier Southern accent than I'd ever heard from him. "Oh, are you sure? She's not there? She gave me this room number and said… okay, sorry to bother you."

He hung up the phone and grinned at me, which made my stomach tumble. "We know *someone* is in that room. Now all we need to do is hack the hotel Wi-Fi and make sure he's not snooping on our op."

"Can't say I mind working with an evil genius," I admitted with a chuckle.

We both went to work on the countersurveillance efforts while also keeping an eye on the cameras and mics inside Bunny's residence.

Vince wasn't happy to see Champ and Quinn at brunch, that much was clear. But I was happy to see that Quinn was able to give Vince an icy nod and smile, looking exactly like a man who'd been hoodwinked into brunch with his boyfriend's ex… and not like a man confronting his would-be kidnapper.

"Quinn's holding it together," I said almost proudly. "He's strong."

"It's all those years he spent smiling at bridezillas and

never telling them what he *really* thought about their *Twilight*-themed weddings." He laughed.

"Uh-huh. Almost like his differences make him a *benefit* to the family?" I teased.

Kev blushed again and got very busy fine-tuning the zoom on the camera feed. But after a moment, he shot back, "So how come you're not complaining that Quinn needs training?"

"Because Quinn's not my... uh." I muttered a curse under my breath. "Because Quinn's not getting involved as often as you are. And it's not really training so much as... experience. Not being thrown in the deep end, where you're feeling responsible for mission-critical intel. You need to work up to things."

"Unlike you, a natural-born badass."

I snorted. "Yeah, no. Back in high school, I was so thin I was practically transparent, and I had my nose in a Dungeons and Dragons book any moment that I wasn't gaming."

I felt Kev's gaze on the side of my face before he broke off with a head shake. "No. Don't believe you."

I laughed. Part of me wished we were anywhere but here so I could give him my full attention and hear all his stories. But another part of me loved every minute of sharing this small space with him, of sitting together with the tense atmosphere of an op surrounding us.

"It's true. I didn't bulk up until I joined the Marines. My dad was this big, physical guy—he was a Marine too—and he wanted me to play football, so I tried, but my football career lasted one whole game. Couldn't throw, couldn't catch." I shook my head. "In the end, one of the guys on the team pretended to be my friend, then got me in trouble with the coach, just so I'd get kicked off."

Kev pushed his glasses up and slid his chair back

angrily, like he was ready to go out and hunt Marc down. "What the hell? That's terrible."

I pulled his chair back beside mine. "Don't you worry. Karma is real. Last I heard, Marc Pine got flagged for multiple IRS audits."

"*Multiple* tax audits?"

"Mmm. Isn't it weird how glitchy some systems can get?" I asked innocently.

Kev laughed delightedly, and the sound warmed me all the way through. At least momentarily.

"And what does your dad say when he sees you now?" Kev demanded. "You glowed up."

"Oh, um." I scratched my head. "Well. He died last summer. No, don't get that face," I said quickly. "We weren't close. We just had nothing in common, really. Messed me up for a while there because I spent a lot of time regretting that we hadn't had a chance to *become* close. You know?"

Kev nodded, his eyes warm with understanding, and I realized that he really *did* know what that might feel like, maybe better than anyone. We were more alike than I would have thought possible.

"Well, for what it's worth, I think your dad would be really proud of you. You're trustworthy and dependable, and witty, and you have the most beautiful smile I've ever — uh. Not that I think your dad would notice that," he said in a rush.

Christ, he was adorable. Once again, I wished like hell that we were back in his bed, or my bed, or anyplace that we didn't have to worry about a —

"Horn," Kev said on a quick intake of breath, pointing at the monitor. "In Vince's back pocket. How the heck is Champ going to get it from him?"

I blew out a breath and focused more closely on the

monitors. I should have been thinking through ways to help the op. I should have been focusing on my teammates and making sure everything ran smoothly instead of low-key inhaling the warm coffee scent of the man sitting next to me and imagining what he looked like naked in bed with my greedy hands roaming over his soft skin.

"Ohhhh, damn. Holy crap, that's good," Kev said with a smile in his voice. My eyes flicked over to drink him in until I noticed what he was looking at.

Champ had somehow gotten Vince pinned against the wall in a hallway off the main living room, and they were arguing almost nose to nose. Through my comms, Elvo's whispered voice was downright giddy. "Target acquired!"

"What the hell happened?" I asked Kev.

"Champ shoved Vince against the wall, and Elvo snaked his hand out of that closet and grabbed the Horn out of Vince's pocket without Vince even noticing. Turn up the volume. I think Champ said something about not using his mother anymore."

Champ poked a finger in Vince's chest, angering the man even more. Vince's face turned a dangerous shade of red.

"Get the fuck out of my face," Vince hissed. We could barely hear it on the home's security system microphones. "You have no idea what I'm going through, so just... back off."

That got Champ's attention. "What are you talking about?"

Vince shoved Champ away. "You think I wanted to come to fucking *brunch*? Jesus, Percy. I'm in the middle of a... of a... I'm in the middle of a goddamned case that's the biggest of my career. I don't have time for this bullshit."

Champ studied him for a moment before saying, "Talk to me, Vince. Tell me what's going on. Let me help you."

Vince scoffed, an ugly ripping sound. "Sure. Big Champ coming to the rescue of good-for-fucking-nothing Vincent Parler. Yet again. No, thanks. I don't need your help, and I sure as hell don't want it either."

Champ put his hand on Vince's shoulder, carefully, as if Vince might throw a punch in retaliation. "If you're caught up in something…"

Vince shrugged his hand off. "This is bigger than you. You can't save everyone, Percival, even if you want to."

"No, I can't save everyone. But I can sure as shit save you. Or I can give you a good place to hide until stuff blows over. Just say the word, and I'll make it happen."

On the monitor, we could see Quinn creeping closer to the edge of the hallway. His curiosity was going to get him into trouble if he wasn't careful. We could also hear Elvo whisper that the Horn was ready to be put back in Vince's pocket.

"How?" Kev breathed.

How, indeed.

"Wait for it," I murmured. Champ and Elvo had played this game before. I knew what was coming next and could only hope Quinn did too, and that he refrained from stepping into the hallway to witness it.

"I care about you," Champ said to Vince, sounding like he truly meant it. Then he grabbed the man by the back of the head and pulled him in for an aggressive kiss, stepping forward until Vince was backed close to the closet door again. They grappled for a moment, Vince grabbing Champ's shirtfront to push him away before changing his mind and pulling him close. Champ jostled him against the wall and reached around to grab his ass right next to where Elvo was sneaking the Horn back into Vince's pocket.

"Oh my God," Kev breathed.

"At least this time, he's doing it on a gay guy," I said

with a smirk. "Most of the time, it's done on a straight man, and the results are way more violent but also way more effective as a distraction."

As soon as the transfer was complete, Champ took a big step back and pierced Vince with an intense stare. "Don't forget what I said. I can help you. Just say the word."

"Does your little boyfriend know you still want me?" Vince asked in a louder-than-normal voice.

Kev and I looked to the monitor where Quinn was. Thankfully, he rolled his eyes at the nearest surveillance camera.

"Why isn't Quinn upset?" Kev asked under his breath.

"Champ wouldn't have kissed someone else, even on an op, without talking to Quinn about it first," I said.

"Even so… I would… I would hate it if my…" Kev glanced over at me and then back to the monitors without finishing his sentence.

"You'd what?" I prodded.

He shrugged. "I don't think I'd like it if the guy I was dating kissed someone else. Even for an op. I'd be too possessive."

My heart thudded. "Even if it clearly doesn't mean anything? It's just business."

Kev pursed his lips to the side as if considering it. "I don't have much experience…" He looked directly at me with an embarrassed little shrug. "But I can't imagine a kiss not meaning something. It would feel… dishonest, I think. And I can't imagine dishonesty in a relationship."

It wasn't the first time he'd alluded to his lack of experience, and I really wanted to question him about that—preferably naked—but the second part of his sentence stopped my fantasies cold.

I can't imagine dishonesty in a relationship.

"W-work," I said firmly, facing the monitors once more. "Let's get this done and go home."

Because the sooner we were done with this op, the sooner I could figure out a way to come clean to Kev about Smitty without losing the fragile, vitally important connection that was building between us.

I should have known it wouldn't be that simple.

13

KEV

I wasn't sure exactly what I'd been hoping for, but Hux leaving town for three days for business—a job not at all related to the HOG case—wasn't it.

The house seemed oddly quiet without him there, and even though he'd left Rodrigo in my care, I felt strangely disconnected from him. Maybe this was standard clingy behavior after our night together. Maybe I was being an embarrassing cliché. But I felt a clawing need for reassurance. Despite all the kind things he'd said, part of me was convinced the night together had been a fluke or the result of a bet, that somehow it hadn't been real.

But another part of me simply wanted more. Okay, a big part of me wanted more. Much more.

Which might have been the reason I let out a loud *whoop* when Champ asked me to accompany him on another Horn mission to assist Hux on surveillance. This one was in a small rural town in Missouri, where someone at a boys' school had one of the Horns on the list.

Champ, Jordan, Riggs, and I flew to a small airstrip in a nearby town, where we were met by Hux in a rented minivan. The op itself was fairly straightforward. We spent the evening hours creeping around the campus with a Wi-Fi jammer and Hux's cell-enabled tablet to track when the Horn in question went off-line. When we finally narrowed it down to a room in the junior faculty residence hall that belonged to a Spanish teacher, Champ decided to break for the night at a nearby hotel until we could organize the op to retrieve the Horn data the following day.

Which was how Hux and I ended up staring at each other across a shared hotel room twenty minutes later, each of us poised on the edge of a double bed with a two-foot strip of carpet between us that might have been an ocean or an entire continent, it felt so vast.

Awkward.

"So… how's your week been so far?" I asked. My fingers wanted to knot themselves together in my lap, so I forced myself to sit on them. "Your texts said it was boring, but you, ah… you look…"

Delicious?

Sexy?

Hot as hell?

All true, but all implied a certain level of expectation and neediness.

"…rested?" I tried instead.

Hux nodded slowly. "Yep. That's true. Not much to do when you're by yourself."

"You could go out," I babbled, because I was a total idiot. "I'm sure there are bars and clubs around here." *Hot guys who'd find you hot, too, if they had eyes in their heads.*

"Sure," he agreed easily. He stared at me intently. "But I didn't."

"Oh." I swallowed around the ball of nerves stuck in my throat. It was still too early to go to sleep, but the only other alternative pinging around my muddled brain was to make out. Judging by the tense look on his face, Hux probably didn't have the same idea.

"We could play Horn of Glory!" I blurted.

Hux scraped his upper lip with his bottom teeth as if trying to hide a smile. "We *could*…"

I scrambled for my Horn and plopped myself back down on the bed, fluffing up the pillows to make a comfy backrest against the headboard and pushing my glasses into place. "This'll be epic. I'm challenging you to a terrain manipulation quest. First player to cross the Black-Bladed Hypnosis Quarry and capture a rebel harpy wins."

Hux played along, rooting his Horn out of his computer bag and climbing onto the other bed. "Excellent. What's my prize when I win?"

I let out a snort. "When you win? That's adorable. We don't need to worry about that. But when *I* emerge victorious, I win…" I tried to think of something good, something that didn't necessarily involve Jasper Huxley's naked body. "Um." I swallowed, making a clicking sound in my dry throat. All I could think of was the naked body thing. "Unlimited Rodrigo visitation without your sassy attitude."

Hux's smile was uncomfortably tender. He must have loved that rabbit a lot. "You love my sassy attitude. But those aren't good stakes because I already have unlimited Rodrigo visitation. So what about…" He tapped his chin and looked up at the ceiling. "You talking about your full-body massage the other day got me thinking. I've always wanted one of those."

"You want me to send you to my massage therapist?" I demanded, annoyed by the image of someone else's hands on Hux's body.

Hux scraped his upper lip with his teeth again. "Not exactly."

Suddenly, the image changed, and I pictured my own

hands on Hux's body… or, just as intriguing, his hands on mine. "Oh."

"Let's go. First one to capture a rebel harpy," Hux said with a laugh. His fingers flew over the controls on his Horn. "Eat my sparrowflox dust."

We battled viciously, trading insults through our laughter. And even though we were opponents on the quest, Hux tossed me some helium gumballs when I fell into the Vat of Regretful Choices.

It was the most fun I'd had in the game in a long time — maybe *ever*, even including the games I'd played with Carter. And it reminded me that I didn't only appreciate Hux for his hands and his smile and the all-consuming way he kissed me, but I genuinely liked him too.

We scaled the final spiny rock wall neck and neck and raced each other toward the herd of rebel harpies in the distance with Hux just a few paces in the lead — well within catching distance. But when he took his Impenetrable Livestock Lasso out of his pack, I swore loudly. His aim with that thing was legendary.

Hux laughed. "Good game, HogDoc. You fought valiantly."

"It's not over yet," I said through gritted teeth.

I couldn't let him win. It wasn't about the prizes — I'd love nothing more than to have to give him a massage — it was for bragging rights. I wasn't ready to give up my claim to being the better HOG player. And if that meant I had to play a little bit dirty… so be it.

"You're going down HogDoc," Hux cackled, clicking the game controls maniacally.

"No chance," I replied, playing my final pair of upgraded turbo boots and hoping for a miracle.

"I have turbo boots too, Kev," he singsonged, shooting

past me again. His victory was all but ensured. "I'm taking the harpy, and there's nothing you can do about it."

"I'm a virgin," I blurted. "And I was kinda hoping you could do something about that instead."

I saw him turn toward me out of the corner of my eye. My face flushed, but I focused on reaching the harpy herd. Just as I reached for the closest harpy, Hux's body tackled mine on the bed. My Horn went flying, and I squealed—*so mortifying*—milliseconds before Hux's mouth crashed down on mine... and I forgot all about the game.

I grabbed the back of his head and held it there, tangling my fingers in the long, silky strands of his hair, weighing my need for oxygen against my need for this kiss to go on.

No contest. I kept kissing him.

Hux mumbled something against my lips, but I couldn't make out the words, and I was way too invested in the kissing to want him to pull away long enough to repeat it.

We rolled around on the bed, our tongues tangling as we grabbed for each other's body parts. I wanted to touch him everywhere, memorize the size and shape of him with my skin so I could pull it back out in memories later.

"Want you," Hux croaked. "Want you so much."

His words made my head spin. How was it possible someone as gorgeous and commanding, sexy and capable, wanted me? I was a geeky homebody. People came to me to fix their iPads, not to have sex. Firsthand experience had taught me this after I'd spent many weekend nights tagging along with Carter and Riggs to bars with their gay friends.

Absolutely none of them had looked at me like a potential... anything.

So why was Hux doing it now? What exactly was this? Did it matter? Did I care?

"No," I huffed out on a laugh.

Hux stopped immediately and pulled back with wide eyes full of concern. "You want me to stop?"

"What? No! Gosh no. Why would you…" I realized what I'd said out loud a few seconds ago. "Oh, sorry. No, that was part of another, um… conversation."

Hux pulled back to look at me fully, and I felt my face go hot.

"Just so I understand… you're having another conversation in your head while I'm kissing you?"

"Well… yes?" I admitted in a strangled voice. "But the convo was also about you, so…" Sweet mother of minotaurs, had another human ever been born who was as awkward as me?

The slow smile that spread across Hux's face was warm as sunshine. I could stare at that smile forever.

"I missed you," he said softly. "I really, legitimately missed you the last few days, Kevin Rogers."

"Oh. Well, that's good. I mean, not *good* good, but good because… I missed you too," I admitted. "A lot. So now that you're here, maybe we could continue? With the kissing? Because the kissing is also good. Really good." I swallowed. "For me. It's good for me. Meaning, I'm good with it."

Shut. Up.

Hux's smile had grown wider with each ridiculous word out of my mouth. "So, you want me to stop?"

I closed my eyes and sighed. "I liked you better when you were kissing me. Silently."

Hux pressed me down onto the bed, his body propped over mine and his hands bracketing my face. The smirk faded into a serious expression. "I don't want to pressure you for sex. Especially if it's your first time. That's not why I kissed you."

I wanted to ask him many follow-up questions—for

example, why he *had* kissed me—but for once, I managed to stay on topic.

I swallowed. "I don't feel pressure. And I..." How did you tell someone you *wanted* to have sex with them? "I wouldn't mind having sex with you." Casual. That was good, right?

Hux tucked his upper lip between his teeth. "You wouldn't mind?"

I reached up to jab a finger into his armpit. The resulting yelp was particularly satisfying as I rolled the beefcake off me and sat up. "I'm being serious," I said, pulling my glasses off and rubbing the bridge of my nose where they'd been pressing at an odd angle during our kiss. "I... it's... it's awkward to talk about this. Possibly *every-thing* is awkward when I talk about it. But I'm not a virgin by, ah, choice. It's just... no one... there hasn't been..." I flapped my hand in the air and let my voice fade away rather than say the words out loud to him.

No one has wanted me like that.

Hux's face reddened, and his eyes narrowed. "Not possible. If I took you into any group of gay men, exactly one hundred percent of them would want you."

I snorted before clapping a hand over my mouth and shaking my head. "No. Definitely not. Believe me, I've been in groups of gay men. Heck, I currently *live* in a group of gay men."

Hux's eyes darkened. "And one of them wants you very, very badly."

The air thickened between us.

Part of me wanted to crack a joke to lighten the tension —ask him if it was Elvo or maybe Sasha—but I didn't dare take the chance I'd say something to change his mind about this.

About me.

"I want him very badly too," I admitted in a low whisper. Maybe I'd get lucky and he wouldn't hear me at all.

I hated being vulnerable around someone who had the power to cut me to the quick. And Jasper Huxley held more of that power than anyone else on earth.

Hux straddled my lap, leaning in until I was pressed back against the headboard. I felt the brush of his hard cock against mine and realized my breath was sawing in and out of me almost audibly.

"I want you, Kevin," he said in the same low whisper I'd used. "I want you more than anything. I've wanted you longer than you know."

The urge to give in and kiss him again, to let myself get carried away by the feelings between us, was almost impossible to resist, but I couldn't let it rest.

"You keep saying that, but I still don't understand," I said, almost apologetically. And I truly wanted to understand. I wanted to believe.

But why had he fought tooth and nail with me if he'd wanted me like this? Why had he acted like he despised me, both in the game and in real life?

His fingers came up to thread into my hair. "I know. I was so stupid. I fought my attraction to you because…"

"Because you thought I was an unmotivated freeloader," I supplied helpfully.

"No! Or… yeah. Maybe I really thought that at first, before I got to know you. But even after that, when every piece of evidence showed you were the opposite of lazy, I still tried to convince myself that you were, because…" Hux set his jaw and looked away, staring at the headboard behind me like the fake wood was fascinating.

"Because?" I prompted, tugging on his hair just enough so he'd look at me again.

"Because I already knew that you were way out of my

league," he said slowly. "Too good-looking, too successful, too rich to bother with someone like me. So I needed to believe—*Christ*, this is the most pitiful thing I've ever admitted to—" He shook his head, pulling away from my grip.

"Say it," I demanded, grabbing his cheeks with both hands this time, not letting him look away. "Tell me."

Hux took a deep breath. "I needed to believe that there was something wrong with you, because if it turned out that you were actually brilliant and hardworking and kind, then I knew I'd fall for you, immediately and totally, and it would kill me when you didn't feel the same way." His eyes searched mine. "So I pushed you away. I didn't want you near this op. I wanted to keep you away from my job, my team, my people. It was wrong, and..." He huffed out a laugh. "And seriously ineffective, because you shine so bright, I couldn't help but see the truth."

"Hux," I breathed. "*Jasper*. I don't know... I can't... what?" The words he was saying, the look in his eyes when he said it, were beyond anything I'd ever let myself imagine.

He laughed a little, and his finger traced the rim of my glasses. "You really don't get it, do you? How gorgeous and special you are. How valuable. Christ, I think Champ's ready to hand you my job," he said ruefully.

"He would *never*. Champ thinks the world of you. He thinks you can do anything," I assured him. "And he's right. You don't just have the skills, Hux, you have this... this calm, stillness about you. You make the team feel safe when they're out in the field. You make *me* feel safe."

But damn, this explained so much. All of those times Hux had pushed me away, had insisted he could do it himself, hadn't been about his ego or about hating me— they'd been about his own insecurities.

And if anyone could understand that, I could.

"I regret a lot of things with you, Kev. More than… more than I can even tell you right now." His eyes burned into mine. "But I'm truly sorry, Kev, if I ever made you think that you weren't good enough, when I was the one who—"

"I should never have touched your system," I blurted. "God. I knew it would piss you off. I just wanted you to see me and respect me. I—"

He grabbed my face and moved forward until we were nose to nose. "Don't apologize for being good at what you do. Don't be sorry for being smart and helpful when *I* was the problem. I realize what an ass I've been and how much it would have cost the team if you hadn't been as generous as you are. You deserve better. And I promise, I will treat you better from now on."

His words set off a strange bubbly feeling in my chest. My intellect wanted to deny his compliment, explain it away as some kind of joke or, worse, some part of the mission, but my heart was already breaking out the champagne, ready to savor this win after twenty-five years of consistent losses… and my gut concurred.

After years of overthinking things, I was ready to tell my intellect where to shove it.

"I want to have sex with you," I breathed. I didn't care if it sounded silly or unromantic. It was the raw truth, and I ached with it.

Hux's face lit up in a bright smile. He was the sexiest man I'd ever known in real life, and his smile had stopped my heart from the moment I'd met him. Having it this close to me, knowing I was the cause of it, was never going to be anything short of miraculous. It made my heart pound and my dick harden.

Please say yes.

Hux's lips brushed the skin below my eye before

moving across to my temple and down to my ear. "How did I get this lucky?" he said softly into my ear before pulling my earlobe into his mouth and sucking.

He moved slowly down the side of my neck, pressing kisses and sucking lightly here and there. By the time he got to my collarbone, he'd pulled up my shirt enough to yank it over my head.

When it got tangled in my glasses, I tried to remove them, but Hux pressed them firmly back onto my nose. "The glasses *stay*," he growled.

I nearly whimpered.

His eyes roamed over my naked chest, and I fought the urge to squirm and cover myself. Yes, he'd seen me naked before, but maybe he'd forgotten just how pale and skinny I was. And *fuck*, I hated that I was thinking these things when I should have been—

"Stop thinking," he murmured before taking one of my hard nipples between his teeth and sucking.

I pulled in a ragged breath. "Maybe you can teach me how to lift weights sometime."

He pulled off my nipple and met my eyes with an intense glare. "Or maybe you can just start hearing the words I'm saying. You're fucking beautiful. You turn me on more than any man on earth." His hands roamed up my arms, squeezing my biceps before doing the same to my shoulders. "Besides, you already know how to lift weights. Either that or you have a pull-up bar hidden in your lair somewhere. Your muscles are long and lean and sexy as hell."

Hux moved his mouth over to kiss across one shoulder and down to my biceps while his hands moved down my body to tug at the waistband of my pants. My brain intended to make a well-reasoned argument involving the lackluster comparison between a true weight-lifting program and desperate sets of secret late-night push-ups and pull-ups, but when he growled again and nipped lightly at my bicep, all that came out of my mouth was something that sounded like *mrpfh*.

"Uh-huh. Stop thinking," he said again, only this time, his tone was less teasing and more tender. "I want you, Kevin Rogers. I want you and only you."

I slid down until I was no longer propped against the headboard. Hux peeled my pants off before standing up to strip himself bare.

His eyes never left my body as he undressed. They skimmed across me like possessive hands, and I stared back at him, drinking in every new inch of exposed skin.

Jasper Huxley wasn't a tall man, but he was solid and strong. His body was a display piece, a sculpture adorned with defined muscles, colorful ink, numerous small scars, and that hot-as-fuck tragus piercing that constantly drew my eye. I wanted to know the story behind each and every one of those marks, both the ones he'd put there and the ones life had handed him. I simply wanted to know *him*.

"Hey," I teased hoarsely, holding a restraining hand against his chest when he made to climb back on top of me so I could keep my stellar view. "I distinctly remember that you mentioned another piercing the other day." In fact, I remembered that mystery had been a significant portion of my jerk session that evening.

Hux's knowing smirk was lava-hot and did all kinds of things to my blood pressure. "Yeah, no." He fingered the dark metal at his ear. "There's just this one... so far."

I ignored the "so far" part of his statement. The possibility of a future where Hux would get more piercings and I might get to see them was like a live wire—enervating, and way too hot for my mind to grab hold of. Instead, I focused on the matter at hand.

"Then why in the world would you let me think you had one?" I demanded.

"Hmm." Hux bit his lip and managed to get a knee on the bed. "Maybe because I wanted you to *distinctly remember* that conversation?" His teeth scraped his bottom lip as that sexy smile emerged fully. "Tell the truth. You thought about it, didn't you? In fact, I bet you thought about it *long and hard*."

I gasped in fake outrage, hoping it concealed my very real thrill. "That… that is neither here nor there," I said primly, still pushing half-heartedly against his chest. "I was lured in under false pretenses."

"Baby." Hux cocked his head to one side, then braced his hand on my chest and levered his other leg over to straddle my legs. "You saw everything there was to see last Saturday… remember?"

Oh, I remembered, alright.

"Poor Kev," he said, shaking his head sadly. "How can I make it up to you?"

I reached down to stroke myself, which made Hux's eyes flare. I groaned and closed my eyes, concentrating on how he made me feel. Restless, desperate… *desired*.

"You could hurry," I moaned.

"Fuck yeah, I can." His hand skimmed up my flank, then paused abruptly. His face fell. "Shit, wait. I don't have any condoms. I haven't had sex in a while."

I didn't want to think about Hux having sex with someone else. "Oh, right. Um… Well. I'm negative. I get tested at my annual physical because…" *I'm too embarrassed to tell my doctor I don't require testing.* "…because it's a good idea, and haven't had sex ever. Obviously. So…"

"The whole team tests regularly. I've probably had six negative tests since the last time I was active."

I nodded, trying to answer the unspoken question

without further conversation about his previous sexual encounters.

He lifted an eyebrow, and I nodded again. This time, he smiled and leaned down to kiss me before whispering, "If you change your mind, just tell me. If you want me to stop, just t—"

"I know," I blurted. "Shut up and touch me."

My erection had flagged, but the minute Hux scooted back and smoothed his hand up my inner thigh, it came roaring back.

He kissed me all over again as if his lips were seeking buried treasure and my body was the map, marking his territory with smooth lips and the scrape of stubble, finding erogenous zones I hadn't known existed, making me moan and shiver.

It took me a while to realize I wanted a share in the exploration, so I pushed him onto his back and took over, using my hands and mouth to touch and taste and tease every pleasure point he'd taught me. The noises coming out of Hux's throat made me hotter, but seeing his cock jump and twitch in response to my actions made me dizzy with lust.

Why had I waited so long to experience this with another man? Why hadn't I tried an app like other guys did?

Because it wouldn't have been Hux.

I closed my eyes and took a moment to express my internal gratitude for this experience. Knowing Jasper Huxley was a good man, a kind man, and I was completely safe with him. He cared enough to make it good for me, to listen to me and respect what I needed and wanted.

"You okay?" he asked, sitting up and cupping the sides of my neck.

I nodded. "Really okay."

Hux leaned in and kissed me hard, opening my mouth with his tongue and using it to own me along with the kiss. When he moved me off him, I was dizzy from the kiss and barely noticed him climbing off the bed to get something out of his bag.

He returned with a travel-sized bottle of lube.

"Lie back," he said.

I was an odd mix of relaxed and jittery. My body felt like molten goo, but my heart tripped over itself with nerves.

"It's okay," he murmured. "Tell me what feels good."

He focused on opening the bottle and pouring a little of the liquid over his fingers. I threaded my fingers into his hair. I loved Hux's hair. It was usually sticking up in a million directions as if he'd either slept on it for days or stuck his finger in a socket.

When the cool, slick sensation of Hux's fingers landed on the hot skin of my cock, I gasped and opened my knees. He quickly moved his fingers down past my balls to land on my hole. My face burned with embarrassment when I clenched against his finger.

"Sorry," I said.

"You're going to make me come," he grunted under his breath.

My eyes opened wider. "What?"

"So fucking hot," he mumbled. His eyes focused on what he was doing, but they looked a little glazed over. Could that be right? Was it possible my body made him as hot as his made me?

. I clenched again, this time purposefully. When he groaned, I saw his dick jump.

His finger pressed circles around my hole before finally popping inside. I gasped and clenched again. This was going to take forever. Maybe anal sex wasn't in the cards for us tonight. I couldn't stop tensing up and worrying about embarrassing myself.

"Fuck it," Hux said before diving down between my legs, shoving my knees up to my chest, and putting his tongue on my hole.

"Oh God!" I threw my head back. What… what in the… how could something possibly feel this good?

My reservations and nerves went out the window. There wasn't time or energy for any of that when all I wanted to do was memorize every sensation of his hot wet tongue on my tender skin.

Hux's mouth was aggressive. He licked and nipped and pressed until finally getting his fingers involved and stretching me for what felt like ages. When he lifted his head up to check on me, his hair was a rat's nest, his nose was pink, and his lips were spit-slick. He looked wild.

I remembered something Hux had said a while ago when he was teasing me about Adam.

Do you like the way he smells? The way he smiles? The way he looks at you? The way he carries himself? Does looking at him make your dick swell, even in a crowded room? Does he make you laugh? Does he know how to get under your skin? Does he make you want to be around him all day long? Does he make you think, 'Now, that is a man who could take me apart piece by piece and put me back together'?

"*God, yes,*" I said. The sound of my voice ripped through the air between us.

"Need you," he croaked.

I couldn't speak again around the guttural noises in my throat, so I nodded.

Hux slicked himself up before climbing up and pressing a kiss to my shoulder. "If you ride me, you'll be able to control things better."

I shook my head. I didn't want to control anything,

especially not now when I felt like I couldn't even control my own breathing.

Hux's hand brushed my hair back, and he met my eyes. "You still want —"

"Yes!" I cried. "Yes, I want you. Inside me. Please."

Hux let out a breath, and I could have sworn it was relief. Had he been worried I would change my mind at this late stage? How could I possibly have wanted to stop?

When Hux moved back between my legs and began pressing the head of his cock into me, all I could see was his face.

It was the face of deep concentration, the face of desperate need, the face of gentle concern.

And the face of something much, much more than a one-night stand.

14

————

HUX

Pushing into Kevin Rogers's body took more self-control than I'd ever needed in my life. I wanted to thrust my hips forward and take him, own him, pound him into the mattress until I shouted my release to the heavens.

But I couldn't do any of that. I was terrified of hurting him, and I wanted to make his first experience as good for him as possible.

As I felt his body's tight squeeze, I watched his face for any indication of pain or discomfort. His wide eyes stayed on mine while I murmured encouragement. I could feel his attempts to relax and focus on his breathing, and I loved him for it. He always wanted to do his part in anything he participated in, and I shouldn't have been surprised that this was no different.

Earlier, when he'd pushed me over and crawled on top of me, I'd been surprised and elated. I wanted him to take what he needed, to look out for himself and make sure he felt the same kind of ownership over the experience that I did.

I bit my tongue against asking if he was okay again. The

last thing he would want was to be treated like a delicate flower or, worse, a child, but I wanted so badly to make sure he was happy and feeling as incredible as I was.

"You feel so fucking good," I said, trying not to drool on him as his body continued to squeeze my dick.

I reached between us to grip his cock and stroke him back to full hardness. When I finally bottomed out inside of him, I stayed still for a moment, trying to give him a chance to adjust.

"So full," Kev groaned. His heels brushed my hips as he shifted and groaned. "Oh. Do that again."

I bit back a laugh, wondering if he was talking to himself. Instead, I pulled out a little and pressed back in slowly. He groaned again.

"*Jasper.*" It was all he said, but it was enough.

I began to pull out and thrust back in, slowly at first, until picking up speed at his urging. We found the right angle to turn his groans into squeaky whimpers, and I knew I wouldn't last much longer.

His cock was heavy and hot in my grip, and I shuttled my fist over it in hopes I could get him to come before I lost my control.

"*Jasper,*" he said again, only this time, there was a plea in it.

"*Fuck.* So fucking beautiful. Gonna make me come. You drive me crazy. You make me want things, Kevin."

I didn't know what the hell I was saying, only that I was feeling more whole in that moment than I'd ever felt. I wanted to stay with him there in his arms, in his body, in this connection we'd managed to find with each other. I was terrified something outside of us would pop this bubble of intimacy before it had a chance to solidify into something enduring.

Possibly even something permanent.

The next time I brushed his gland and stroked him in time to my thrusts, he threw his head back and choked out my name. Hot fluid spilled over my hand and lit me up inside. I released deep inside of him, realizing in that moment he was the only man I'd ever taken without a condom.

Aftershocks hit me hard, extending the blissful feeling of orgasming in the tight grip of Kevin's body.

When I was done and aware of my environment enough to realize I was going to crush poor Kev if I relaxed any more, I leaned up to kiss him gently.

"Hi."

His smile was lazy and soft. "Hey."

"You good?"

"Mmm."

I kissed him hard and pulled out of him at the same time, feeling his intake of breath at the sudden void. It wasn't a great sensation, so I'd hoped to distract him.

"Gimme a sec," I said before pushing off the bed to get a cloth. Kev followed me gingerly to the bathroom.

All of his nerves seemed to return in full force after I cleaned him up and moved him over to the other bed.

"You can keep the clean bed. I don't mind," he said, not meeting my eyes.

"I'm not switching beds with you, babe. I'm moving us both to the clean bed." I gripped his chin and forced him to meet my eyes. "If you're okay sharing a bed with me tonight."

"Oh, yes. Definitely. I… *yes*." He gave me a small smile. "Sorry, I didn't know."

I let go of him and nudged him over so I could slide into the crisp sheets next to him. "There's nothing wrong with not knowing the protocol."

His face relaxed into an eye roll at my use of the word. "Ha ha. You're hilarious."

"You want to know a secret?" I trailed one finger lazily over his sternum and loved the way he shivered closer. "I really fucking love that I'm the one who gets to teach you these things. It's… special." There were other words I could have used. *An honor. The greatest gift I'd ever received. Headier than any achievement I've ever earned.* All of those would have been true. But I didn't want to scare him off, not when he was so new to this.

Instead, I leaned over and kissed him, enjoying the fresh toothpaste taste of his warm mouth.

We kissed lazily for a little while until I laid my head on his chest—like the romance novel heroine Kev had mentioned the other day—and wrapped an arm around his middle. Kev's fingers sifted gently through my hair, and the affectionate movement lulled me halfway to sleep.

"Thank you," I said after a few moments of comfortable silence.

He huffed out a laugh. "Pretty sure that should be the other way around."

"Thank you for trusting me," I continued. "Whether it was a big deal for you or not, your trust in me was a big deal to me."

Kev's hand came down to brush across my cheek. "You're welcome. But I wouldn't have trusted you if you weren't trust*worthy*."

His words should have made me feel good and power-ful, and in a way, they did. I'd worked hard in the Marines to become someone my friends and teammates could depend on while still being easygoing and accepting. The kind of person that young Jasper Huxley growing up in small-town Pennsylvania with stern, sometimes absent parents had needed in his life. Hearing those words from

Kev's lips was a benediction I hadn't expected, making me feel truly seen and understood, and it went straight to my heart like an arrow tipped with a healing salve, making me care about him all the more...

Until I remembered all the ways I hadn't done right by Kev in the past. All the things I still hadn't quite come clean about.

"I don't know how you can trust me when I've been such a jerk to you," I admitted. I worried about bringing it up, but the words had shoved themselves forcefully off my tongue, as if we wouldn't be able to move on unless I cleared the air about this.

"You explained everything to me earlier." His face was open and trusting, his words relaxed and sleepy.

I nodded, enjoying the light scratch of his chest hair against the side of my face. "I know. But the same way you keep thinking I'm going to blink and suddenly realize that I'm not in bed with one of the Hemsworth brothers, I'm scared you'll realize what a selfish ass I am and how much better you could do with someone else."

"No way. I mean, no one else gives me a run for my money in Horn of Glory like you do," Kev teased. Then his smile faded, and the light in his eyes dimmed. "I would have said my friend Smitty was pretty good too, but he's ghosting me now, so... I'm not sure if we're really friends anymore."

My stomach dropped. Here it was—the moment when I really had to out myself as SmittyKitty, the moment when a simple omission became an outright lie that would come back and bite me, the moment when I could be the trustworthy person he thought I was and put him before the op.

"Kev..." I began.

"No, it's fine." He lifted a hand from my head to wave it dismissively. "Really. It's just... *this* is why it's hard for me to believe you when you say you like me, you know? I thought Smitty and I were becoming friends. We've chatted a lot about the game, and I told him some stuff about me growing up, and we had a whole conversation about rabbits, I guess 'cause he works at a pet supply store, plus a bunch of other conversations too, and I thought... Whatever. It doesn't matter. I guess he changed his mind about me."

I held him tighter and swallowed down the confession that had been on my lips. Kev was hurting—*again*—and that was my fault—*again*. Telling him the truth might relieve me of the weight of the secret I was carrying, but would it make him feel better? Or like he'd lost yet another person who claimed to really care about him?

The idea of right and wrong didn't seem so simple anymore.

All I wanted, in that moment, was to make Kev stop hurting.

"That's not possible," I said firmly. "Maybe he's busy at work."

"Not to diminish the importance of his job, but he can't be working at a pet store twenty-four seven. How long does it take to send a chat message? No, I think I probably did or said something that offended him. I'm kind of awkward sometimes when I'm trying to make friends."

I sat up and nearly bumped his chin with my head. "You're the best friend a person could have," I said with a little too much growl. "There's no chance in hell you did or said something that offended him. It's not possible."

He gave me a weak smile. "That's nice of you to say, but what I really want to know is... how do I fix it? Do you have any advice for what I could say to find out what's wrong?"

I took his hands in mine while frantically thinking through what I should say. I wanted to punch myself for not coming clean a long time ago. For trying to rectify the mistakes I'd made as HogMaster last summer by becoming someone new, like the challenges of building up a new game avatar from scratch were a good substitute for apologizing and trying to be a better player moving forward.

"Just… tell him you miss him, I think. Ask him how he is. Give him a chance to explain. And then… when he does explain, I really hope you'll listen to his explanation and forgive him, if you think he deserves it."

Because I would explain. I owed him that much, and he deserved the truth. But he didn't deserve to have the memory of this night ruined by the discovery that someone he thought was trustworthy had been lying to him. Not while things between us still felt so fragile and new.

Kev peered at me curiously, but after a moment, he just nodded.

"Thank you," he said with a sweet smile, pulling me down onto his chest again. I fell asleep feeling like the lowest scum of the earth and knowing without a shadow of a doubt that Kevin Rogers deserved better than Jasper Huxley.

The following day started off much like the last time we'd ended up naked together, though fortunately without the rude predawn wake-up call. Instead, we woke up naturally, still cuddled together in the bed, and I got to kiss his drowsy form for long moments while the light coming through the curtains brightened the room. I washed his body in the hotel shower with the kind of attention a brain surgeon would use while operating on a world leader.

In the process, I found several tickle spots and even more surprising erogenous zones. I could have stayed in there with him under the hot spray for days if we hadn't had a job to do.

But we did. So we dressed and packed and joined the rest of the team for breakfast before heading back over to the boys' school to gather the Horn data from our target.

I was getting sick of this damned mission, to be honest. I wanted this Horn of Glory situation off our backs once and for all, and if I felt that way, I could only imagine how Champ was feeling about it. I knew he'd been having regular phone calls with Jacob Horn and that he emerged from each one looking grimmer and more concerned. He had to be stressing big-time about leading his company's largest client into a PR disaster and potential criminal complicity in a massive money-laundering scheme.

When we got to the school, our target was working alone in his Spanish classroom deep in a basement where our surveillance tech wouldn't reach. Fortunately for us, getting into the school was as easy as five of us throwing on utility worker uniforms—the secretary not only failed to ask for proper ID but offered us *coffee*, for heaven's sake—but I had half a mind to call the parents paying exorbitant tuitions and warn them of the security nightmare at Jolly-Brook Residential School for Boys.

Kev and I would be providing OPSEC—essentially acting as backup in case of communication failures—so we needed to huddle together in a supply closet next to the Spanish classroom and monitor comms, while Champ and Riggs created a distraction in the hallway to lure the professor away from his Horn long enough for Jordan to sneak in and download the data.

Getting into position was simple enough. But the blueprints of the school I'd found hadn't prepared me for just how snug the little room would be.

"Here we are back in the closet in high school," Kev snickered.

He wasn't trying to start anything, but his breath tickled my ear anyway, just due to his proximity. That, combined with the vanilla-and-coffee scent that seemed to be infused in his pores, made me want to grab him and kiss the fuck out of him.

"This time, I'm with the hottest kid in school," I whispered back. "Not sure I'd have been able to stay in the closet much longer after being alone with you back then."

Kev's cheeks reddened. "You wouldn't have looked twice at me."

"You're right." Kev's smile began to fade until I pressed his glasses up his nose with my pointer finger and let my rapidly hardening cock ride against his thigh. "I would have looked three, four, five, twelve times. And then I would have touched."

As I spoke, Kev's face reddened even more, and his eyes went wide behind those glasses. Champ's voice hissed in my ears. "Initiating distraction sequence."

Kev muttered under his breath about uselessly formal language. "Why can't he just say, 'Let's go,' or something?"

"Darling, I told you Jeremy isn't in this school building!" Riggs exclaimed in a loud, worried voice from the corridor on the other side of the door. "His friend said he was being held captive in a room in the basement of the… what was it called? The big Johnson building!"

Kev snorted, and I shot him a wink. "Pretty sure it's just called the Johnson building," I admitted. "But Riggs has been living in the Thicket for a few months now. The puns become a way of life after a while."

"For God's sake, stop whining," Champ demanded in the voice of a man who had no patience for his partner's whining, let alone his puns. "Did you take your supplements this morning, Benedict? You know how cranky you get when you're undernourished."

Riggs gasped. "Percival, how could you?"

If Riggs's use of a pun hadn't been enough to get under Champ's skin, using his hated first name was a sure way to do it. Score one for Riggs. Their fight would turn extra authentic now.

"What did you just call me?" Champ growled.

Riggs let out a high-pitched shriek. "Oh, *stop*, Percy! You know how that mean face you make scares me! Our precious baby boy is being held in a *dungeon* somewhere on this godforsaken campus, and you are lecturing me about using my pet name for you? Focus, dearest. Jezzy needs us!"

I heard the rapid footsteps of several people coming out of school rooms along the hallway. Muffled voices demanded to know what was going on, and Riggs did us proud.

"What's going on? What's going *on*? I demand *answers*!" he raged in a mournful voice, as if someone was pulling out his hair one follicle at a time. "I demand *action*! That's what's going on! Someone, find me my baby! You there, in the polo! Find me my Jeremy! I can feel in my very *bones* that he's not well. *Jeremy*!" he shouted. "Jezzy, baby, call for Daddy! Daddy will come find you!"

Kev was laughing so hard tears were streaming down his face. I had to reach out to cover his mouth to keep him quiet.

Champ joined the verbal fray in his even louder voice. "Jeremy? Bang the walls if you can hear us. Bang once to tell us you're hurt and twice if you're alright. Bang for us, son!"

Kev's eyes were so alive I wanted to pull my hand away from his mouth and kiss him stupid. Instead, I leaned in and pressed a hard kiss to his temple before pulling back and keying my microphone to Jordan. "Status."

"Thirty seconds…"

I keyed the mic to Champ. "Give us another minute and a half," I said.

Champ's voice boomed through the thin door of the storage closet. "Get your hands off me, sir! I will not be treated in this manner. I want to see my *son*. You cannot keep him from me. Why are you all standing around in this useless manner? Where is Jeremy! We pay thousands of dollars to send our son here, and I will not be silenced!"

Muffled teacher voices talked over each other with questions and assurances while Riggs wailed in the background. "He's gone! Gone forever! Probably dead by now! They said he was being held in a room with another boy, but now he's been *murdered by the school*, just like in that episode of *The FBI Files*!" He paused. "Or was it *Blood, Lies & Alibis*?"

"I think it was *Cold Case Files*," Champ said thoughtfully. "*Blood, Lies, and Alibis* had that episode about the Poughkeepsie killer, and you got so upset you wouldn't rest until we liberated your mother from her retirement community, remember?"

"I think you might be right," Riggs agreed. Then, after another pause, "But either way, *dead*! Our boy has been murdered!" he sobbed. "Oh God. How will we go on?"

Kev shook silently, tears streaming down his face as he giggled madly against my palm.

Jordan's voice came over comms. "Clear."

A new voice came on the scene, louder and more outraged than Riggs's. "I'm Principal Halloran. What is your son's name, sir?" he demanded.

I keyed the mic to Champ and Riggs. "All clear."

Riggs sniffed loudly. "Jeremy, obviously. Jeremy Octavian Kirby-Edgewater! And I will remove every nail and cinder block from the Parson School for Wayward Boys with my own manicured hands until he is found!"

The principal cleared his throat. "Sir. This is the Jolly-Brook School. The Parson School is over in Kirkland."

There was a single beat of utter silence before Riggs spoke again. "Oh. And that's, uh… not affiliated with your school, I take it?"

"No, sir."

"You don't, say, share a dungeon?"

"A dungeon? Good God, no."

Champ sighed heavily. "Jesus Christ, Benedict. How could you get the name of our son's school wrong?"

Riggs sobbed. "Oh, it's all *my* fault, then? How typical of you. Just like the incident with the housekeeper was my fault—"

"You told her you'd seen the ghost of your murdered grandmother in our bathroom! Of course the poor woman quit on the spot! And your grandmother wasn't murdered."

"Well, that ghost was *someone's* grandmother! If you ever bothered to watch *Ghost Hunters* with me, you'd understand that those of us who are deeply empathic—"

"We apologize for the disruption, Principal Halloran," Champ interrupted loudly. "You've, ah… you've got a fine operation here. Excellent facilities. I don't suppose you have any openings for a sophomore with a talent for dramatics… No? Well." He sighed again. "Come on, Benedict. We're going home. *Now*."

"But what about Jeremy?" Riggs cried, his voice sounding further away. "What about the *dungeon*! Because I would never forgive myself if…"

The crowd in the hallway began to murmur and giggle until the principal shushed them all and herded everyone back into their classrooms. Kev and I grinned at each other in the tiny closet.

My comms clicked on, and Champ's voice spoke in my ear. "We're out. Give it seven minutes for things to settle down and the next class to begin, then meet us out on the road. I'll try to keep Benedict from any further hysterics in the meantime."

Riggs's chuckle echoed through Champ's mic.

Once the comms clicked off, I set a silent alarm on my watch.

"Seven minutes… however should we pass the time?" I whispered.

After a single beat, Kev and I launched ourselves at each other and made out like high schoolers in a closet.

Seven minutes in heaven, indeed.

Having Kev on the team seemed like a better idea every day.

But when we returned home to Licking Thicket, I realized immediately that my temporary reprieve wasn't going to last as long as I'd hoped, because my SmittyKitty Horn was already blinking with a message.

HogDocKev: *I miss playing with you. If there's something I did to cause you to pull away, please let me know. And I'm sorry.*

I blew out a breath and curled a fist over the center of my chest to press against the tightness there.

It was time to do some damage control.

15

KEV

When we got back to the house after the op in Missouri, Champ and Riggs relaxed around the kitchen table with Elvo, Yolanda, Carter, and Quinn, talking in low voices and filling everyone in, while Hux excused himself to go check on Rodrigo. Carter called out from his spot under Riggs's arm for me to join them, and Quinn waved me over eagerly, but I shook my head with a smile and slipped out onto the back porch instead.

The mission hadn't been particularly difficult or dangerous, and my part had been especially easy, but there was a kind of contact adrenaline high that came from being part of a winning team. I felt wired.

The night air was bracing, and a full moon dappled the trees silver. I took a deep breath of cold air and held it. From behind me came loud peals of laughter, and through the large kitchen window, I watched Carter bury his face in Riggs's shoulder while Champ acted out some part of today's adventure that involved a lot of hand-waving—the Benedict part, no doubt. Riggs made a rude gesture over Champ's head that set Quinn and Yolanda off again, laughing until they were leaning against one another to hold themselves upright.

This was my family now. These folks, along with Elvo and Jordan and Sasha, even Yolanda's wife, Katie, and the ancient guy with the kilts and the military jackets who acted as Champion Security's receptionist, were my people, and I loved every single one of them. After years and years of not feeling like I fit anywhere, I was living the dream, and I was freaking ecstatic.

But.

Somewhere in that house, Jasper Huxley was tending to his rabbit. Probably feeding Rodrigo the organic strawberries I'd asked Mrs. Carmody to buy and telling him his own version of today's story in his soft bunny-talk voice. And I was realizing—as in, an oh-shit-the-earth-has-stopped-turning kind of realization—that as great as it was to have *people*, what I really wanted most was one specific person.

My person.

Hux.

I wanted Hux to kiss me again, to fuck all the energy out of my system, then sleep with me all night. I wanted him to be there the next morning, and the next, and the one after that. I wanted to tell him about every project I was working on, to get his thoughts and feedback. I wanted to play every Horn of Glory quest with him and compete against him in every HOG tournament, because winning was always more fun when I won against him, and losing wasn't so bad when he was the one I lost to. I wanted to know more about his family and his years in the military and his opinions on mayonnaise versus mustard.

I wanted, more than anything, to know that he wanted those things also. But despite all his sweet, comforting words the night before, despite the way he'd claimed the seat beside me and kept his knee pressed against mine on the flight home from Missouri—claiming me as much as he could allow himself to while we were on a work trip with the team—I still wasn't totally sure that he wanted something with me that lasted longer than the op.

This felt like a failing on my part—like I was being extra needy, constantly asking him for validation—and I didn't want to be that guy, but my feelings were real, even if they were illogical, and I didn't know how to overcome them. I didn't know how to make myself believe when this situation had seemed utterly impossible just a few weeks ago.

My Horn yodeled with an incoming chat message, and I pulled it out of my pocket, grateful for the distraction from my overthinking. My pulse leapt when I saw who it was from.

SmittyKitty: *Pip! It's so good to hear from you. So, big news—I'm kind of seeing someone. Someone incredible. And I'm falling hard for him. I'm sorry I'm not spending much time in the game anymore, and that I won't get to see you in Vegas, but thank you for caring enough to notice. You're a good friend.*

Oh. Wow. My heart was a mix of happy and sad. Happy that my friend was happy. Happy that he considered me a friend too. Happy that I hadn't somehow run him off by awkwardness and oversharing. Sad for myself because Smitty reminded me of Hux, in a way that didn't involve any of the overwhelming attraction but therefore also didn't come with any of the uneasiness. I'd miss having him in my life.

HogDocKev: *That's exciting! I actually started seeing someone amazing also, except my guy is a HOG player.*

SmittyKitty: *Cool! Well, I hope he treats you right. Best of luck with everything. *fist bump emoji**

Shit. I leaned against the porch railing and thunked my Horn against my head. I was the worst. The actual worst.

Smitty probably thought I was talking about Anomaly, and why wouldn't he? A week or so ago, I'd been calling Anomaly my boyfriend—which was absolutely ludicrous in retrospect, because now that I'd started dating someone in real life, I understood that the casual chat friendship he and I shared was nothing like a romance—but I still felt bad that I hadn't officially told Adam we were done.

How had I suddenly gone from having no relationships *ever* to having too many relationships for my friends to keep track of in such a short span of time? I felt like I understood reality TV so much better now.

HogDocKev: *I don't mean Anomaly! I mean, he's a nice guy, but I actually fell for someone else.*

HogDocKev: *HogMasterHux.*

HogDocKev: *I know, I know! I know exactly what you're going to say. Wasn't he the guy I warned you away from? Isn't he my arch nemesis? Didn't he just recently burn my kelp forest and loot my jam cellar? Yes, yes, and yes. And I can't condone any of that, which makes our relationship a little complicated.*

SmittyKitty: *All relationships are complicated in one way or another, Pip. I hope it all works out for the best. He's a lucky guy to have you.*

Smitty wasn't usually one to hold back his opinion, so this bland reaction made me wince. I guessed I'd expressed my opinion of Huxley a little too well in the past, and now I felt the need to correct that.

HogDocKev: *No, I'm the lucky one! Hux is gorgeous. And witty. And fun. And steady, you know? He makes me feel… invincible.*

The dots swirled by Smitty's name for a long moment, but his reply was short.

SmittyKitty: *You have no idea how glad I am to hear that.*

But… I am not the guy you should be talking to about this. And I really do have to go.

HogDocKev: *Right. Okay. Remember I'm here if you need a friend. Otherwise, good luck with your new boo.*

SmittyKitty: *Thanks. I'll need it. He's the best man I know, and he could probably do a lot better than me, but I'm not letting him go. Have fun storming the castle, Pip!*

Well, fuck.

Just then, the door behind me opened, and a loud burst of laughter spilled out. Carter shut the door behind him and came to stand at the railing beside me.

"Shit, it's cold. You must be freezing."

I shrugged.

"Sounded like a pretty fun op. Champ said you handled your shit well."

I shrugged again.

"And Elvo said something about a really cool quest you completed with Hux the other day in Horn of Glory. You should tell me about it. You rescued a duchess, or—"

"Captured her," I corrected, because I couldn't allow the inaccuracy to stand, but then I shrugged once more.

"Okay, that's it. Who are you, and what have you done with my cousin?" Carter's eyes narrowed. "And don't waste my time telling me you're actually Kev, because there's no way the Kev I know would resist an opportunity to spill every detail of that game, especially if I specifically asked about it. You're obviously a pod person… and frankly, not a very good one."

My breath huffed out in a fog. "I'm definitely still me," I informed him glumly. "Inescapably me."

"Why the heck would you want to escape being you?" Carter demanded. "Dude, you're living the *dream* right now. Helping out on missions, an essential part of the team." He bumped his arm against mine. "Talk to me, Kev. You've seemed down for days, but I figured it was just stress. Now you're worrying me, so spill. Is it Hux? Riggs said he's been all up in your business—"

I couldn't help snorting at that… and then sighing.

I didn't really want to talk to Carter about this, not when he knew Hux personally, but I had to admit my list of available friends was exceptionally short… especially since one of them had just politely and gently excused himself from my life.

"Okay, so, let's say that there was this… this orc. Kinda shy. Awkward."

Carter blinked. "Uh. Okay…"

"And a really smart, brave, and physically fit… troll."

"An orc and a troll." Carter rolled his tongue over his teeth. "Got it."

"And let's say that these two creatures had a very complicated history. A sort of… adversarial history. One where they tried to piss each other off as frequently as possible through a combination of treachery, trash talk, and profound disdain."

"I think I know where this story is going," Carter said with a nod. "In fact, I think I lived it."

"So, like, imagine that one day, out of a clear blue sky, the orc realized that the troll wasn't horrible. He was… horribly wonderful. And chivalrous. And good. And patient. And when the orc told him about his family stuff and work stuff, the troll was really supportive. And the troll saw the orc's stuffed duck and didn't make a comment about it. And apologized profusely for all the stuff that happened when they were being archnemeses. And reassured the orc like *three times*, when the orc was freaking out, that he found the orc hot and smart and likable and amazing, despite his orc-ness. And then they, uh… they engaged in multiple phenomenal sexual encounters."

Carter's eyebrows winged high. "Multiple sexual encounters?"

"Multiple *phenomenal* sexual encounters," I stressed. "The phenomenal can't be overlooked."

"I see," Carter said faintly. "And the problem is…"

"The problem is… how is the orc supposed to believe it?"

"Oh."

"Like, he wants to. Quite badly. So much that he keeps pretending to believe it. Assuring the troll he believes it. But he can't control his feelings, Carter. And he doesn't know what the troll thinks about their future as a couple or if they even have a future beyond the next couple of weeks. And I can't ask Hu—I mean, *the troll*—about this again. It's already painfully obvious that he has way more relationship experience, and I don't want him to think the orc is weak or needy or too much effort or… or any of that. So, how can the orc know what the troll wants without bothering him?"

"Ohhhh. Yeah, no, I see," Carter said, his tone full of understanding. "I've been there, Kev. And I'm here to tell you…"

I straightened slightly in surprise. Carter knew what this was? Had felt it also? Really? I watched him closely, prepared to receive the relationship cheat code that would help me unlock Hux's psyche and—

"… you can't."

I blinked at Carter disappointedly. Wait, what?

"And you shouldn't have to. In fact, anyone who thinks you're too much effort shouldn't get a single second of your time. Real talk, Kevin, I know your parents. I know they taught you that it's not okay to be who you are. That you need to hide yourself from the world. I could kick their asses from Africa to the Thicket and back again for that," he said matter-of-factly. "But it's not *true*, cuz. The failing is in them, not you. And if Hux is the kind of person I think he is—"

I squawked in protest, and Carter rolled his eyes. "Fine, if the *troll* is half as great as the orc thinks he is, the troll won't be thinking that. I guarantee it."

I blew out a breath. "Yeah, but…"

"But nothing. So maybe you don't believe him right away when he says you're amazing. Maybe he hasn't earned that from you yet. That's fine. Give him the chance to prove it to you. To keep showing up for you. To keep accepting you, insecurities and all. To keep reassuring you. To help you be the best version of yourself. You deserve that. Hell, you deserve a lot more than that."

I swallowed hard as Carter's words rocked me to the core. I knew Carter loved me always, but there were times when it hit me how very lucky I was to have him.

"Thank you," I whispered. "I just… I really needed to hear that."

"Good. Now, stop freezing your ass off and go find your orc… troll… whichever one's not you. Okay? Doctor's orders."

"Yeah," I said softly. "I might just do that."

But when Carter slipped away, I stared down at the Horn in my hand for a long moment, gathering my courage.

"Hey," Hux said from the darkness behind me. "I was looking for you."

I jumped so high I nearly fumbled my Horn and turned my head to glare at him. "Jesus! You nearly gave me a heart attack!"

Hux's lips twitched before he stepped toward me, wrapping his arms around my waist and burying his face in my shoulder. "Mmm. My bad. Startling people is so *rude*, isn't it? Can you believe that sometimes, certain people startle other people *on purpose*?"

I snorted and relaxed back against him. "*Pfft*. You secretly love it. So, ah… Rodrigo's okay?"

"Yep." Hux leaned up so he could hook his chin on my shoulder. "He's chomping a couple of those organic strawberries Mrs. Carmody got him hooked on. Gonna be a rude awakening when he goes home and remembers he's but a poor little bun who has to make do with limp carrots and pellets."

My heart began skittering around wildly. I didn't want Hux to leave. I wanted him to spend the night in my bed. With me. I wanted Rodrigo to be at home here, sorta-kinda-permanently, so that he'd never be a lonely bunny again.

And if Carter was right, I needed to ask Hux for what I wanted.

"Hux…" I began. I licked my dry lips.

Through the window, I saw Carter loop his arms around Riggs's neck and smile up at him. The two of them hadn't stopped touching since Riggs entered the house, and soon, one of them would lead the other up to their bed, without either of them having to question it. My chest tightened with envy.

"So, I was thinking…" I started again.

"Where's Hux?" Champ asked, loud enough to hear clearly. "Did he go home already? He didn't say goodbye to Yolanda or Elvo."

Hux stiffened behind me.

"Maybe? I think he was checking on his rabbit," Riggs offered.

"And where'd Kev disappear to? I wanted to thank him before we left."

Carter darted a glance toward the window. Though he couldn't possibly see us through the darkness, I got the feeling he knew exactly where I was… and who I was with. Carter was smart like that.

"Oh, probably in his lair," he said casually. "Plotting world domination. Like he does."

Riggs's voice grew wary. "You don't think Hux is harassing him, do you?"

"What? Of course not," Carter laughed. "Kev wouldn't let him."

"It's just... they don't seem to like each other very much. I told Hux to leave Kev alone, but I don't think he listened."

Carter pushed his lips together and mooned up at his husband like he was fighting a smile. So was I... especially after Hux grumbled low in his throat. "Interfering assholes."

It was really sweet that Riggs was being protective... even though he didn't need to be.

"They've worked together just fine on the missions," Champ said easily. "They're getting the job done. Let it go, Riggsy."

"Champ's right. Kev can take care of himself, babe. He could drop Hux where he stands if he wanted to. Let the two of them sort it out," Carter advised.

Riggs looked torn for a second, like maybe he wanted to take a quick detour downstairs, but Carter caught his arm.

"Come upstairs with me instead," Carter urged. "I swear I saw a stampeding capybara up there earlier, and I'm feeling very... unsafe."

Riggs's head swiveled toward Carter with almost comical swiftness, and he raised his eyebrows. "Is that so? Are you saying you need your body... guarded?" he demanded with a leer. "Hot damn. Later, people. Duty calls," he said over his shoulder before moving Carter bodily out of the kitchen.

"We'll see ourselves out!" Quinn called after them. "Just in case you were worried about it! Don't miss us too much, guys! We'll lock up! We—*ahhh*!" An audible *crack* split the air, and Quinn jumped and spun. "Percival Champion, did you just smack my ass?"

"You gonna do something about it?" Champ growled.

"Gonna leave you here while I go home alone, that's what I'm gonna... *ooof*! Put me down, you oaf!" Quinn giggled as Champ hauled the smaller man over his shoulder toward the entry hall...

Leaving me alone with Jasper Huxley.

"They don't know you very well, do they?" he asked softly. "Carter, maybe, but the others don't get you at all."

This was so close to what I'd been thinking myself that I couldn't help but smile as I turned in Hux's arms. "You don't think so?"

He shook his head. "Carter thinks you're completely in control. Champ thinks you're all about the work. Riggs thinks you can't handle me."

I looped my arms around his neck. "And you know better?"

"Oh yeah." His nose nudged my jaw. "You're all about *helping*—that's what drives you to work as hard as you do. You're not always in control either..." His teeth scraped across my chin, and I shivered uncontrollably.

"And can I handle you?" I breathed.

Hux pulled back so he could look at me. "Better than anyone else in the world," he said candidly.

"Stay here with me tonight?" I asked. The words seemed to tumble out so easily when I was looking into his eyes instead of getting caught up in my own brain. I should probably try to remember that. "It's protocol," I added. "I looked it up."

Hux's lips widened into a giant smile, transforming his entire face and setting off my heart again. "Well, if it's protocol..."

He brushed his fingers over my lips.

"Can we order pizza, though? I'm starving." His words sounded casual, as if it was a simple hangout with friends, but his eyes were the complete opposite. They locked onto mine and pulled some kind of Medusa magic. I stood frozen in place, completely unable to move, the only thought in my mind *I need this man alone. Now.*

Hux's hand trailed down my chest. "I'm going to take that as a yes," he said softly.

Pretty sure I let out a squeaky noise just to make sure he knew I was on board with the plan and grabbed his hand, towing him toward the basement door and down into my personal space.

"Henry, don't let anyone in the lair without alerting me," I called out. "And could you order us a pizza. The usual order."

"Yes, sire," the AI replied in his calm voice.

Hux stopped in his tracks, nearly dislocating my arm from the shoulder. "Who the fuck is Henry?"

"Oh dear," Henry said.

Hux, who'd been glancing around like he expected a man to pop out from behind the curtain, stood still in the middle of the room. "Wait, is this your AI? He has a name? Holy shit, Kevin."

I flushed. "Surely you heard me talk to him the other night when we were here. Remember?"

Hux's attention snapped back to me like a rubber band, and the force of it made me catch my breath. "I was a little bit distracted by other things last time we were here. *Remember?*"

I opened my mouth to tease back, but a visceral memory of the two of us together in this room swamped me. The things he'd said, the way he'd touched me, the way he'd made me feel.

Be honest, Carter had said. So, I thought about the most honest thing I could do at that moment.

I launched myself at Hux's face and kissed him like it had been years rather than hours. I kissed him like I needed to make up for all the times I hadn't kissed anyone. Hux's strong arms banded around me like I might try to escape, but the joke was on him because I wanted nothing more than to stay right there, tightly held against his body, for as long as I could. For as long as he'd let me.

When he sank to his knees, I misunderstood and sank down with him. The feeling of his laugh against my mouth made me ebullient. I felt like I could float away and roam untethered across the earth with a stupid, dopey grin on my face hereafter.

We ended up humping each other on the floor. It wasn't pretty or poetic, but it was frantic and claiming and hot as hell. It was perfect.

His strength—the way his body weight pressed me down, his muscles tense and firm and somehow commanding—turned me on. His every move seemed possessive in a way that made my pulse quicken and my breathing stutter in ragged, erratic gulps.

In no time at all, I felt my release narrowing in on me, racing toward an inevitable embarrassment. Did adult men come in their pants like an uncontrollable young teen? And if so, how did they escape gracefully to change out of goopy clothes—

"Oh god, *fuck*. Coming." Hux's broken voice was all the permission I needed. My orgasm ripped through me as my body arched against his thrusting cock.

It took only seconds for the blissful release to turn into uncomfortably wet pants and for his delicious weight to become suffocating.

"Can't. Breathe," I wheezed dramatically.

Hux did a push-up to lift his body weight off me, but he leaned down to press a gentle kiss under the edge of my jaw. "I feel like I just splooged in my pants like a teenager."

I got the feeling he was trying to break the awkwardness and make me laugh. It worked.

We made our way to my bathroom and began to strip. "Another shower?" I asked when Hux opened the glass door and turned on the water.

He bounced his eyebrows. "I'll take any excuse I can to get you naked."

Once I was in his arms under the heavy stream of unlimited hot water, I allowed myself to set aside my fears and believe. I believed this was real, it was permanent, it was normal.

I let myself believe Jasper Huxley was really and truly mine.

"What you do to me," he murmured into my wet hair as he pressed his lips against me over and over.

This didn't feel like pretending.

"Tell me," I urged.

"I never thought I would find someone I craved morning and night. I never thought I'd meet someone as kind and genuine and forgiving enough to put up with my prickly bullshit. I just… I want to be with you like this all the time."

The pounding of the water on my upper back echoed my galloping heart.

"What does that mean?" I was afraid my newfound bravery was going to expire and leave me without answers.

Hux's strong hands grabbed my face, lifting it up until I had no choice but to meet his eyes. Thankfully, he'd pulled us out of the stream of water.

"Kevin, it means…" He took a breath as if making sure his words were right before sharing them. "I really like you. I think about you all the time. First thing in the morning, last thing before I sleep, even when you're not with me. Sometimes I see you jumping in to help where it's needed, or joking with Carter, or explaining some complex HOG maneuver to Elvo, or discussing politics with Jordan, and I just think, 'Holy shit, that's… that's *my* guy.' I want to protect you. I want to know all the thoughts in your brain, and I want to tell you all of mine, even if they're stupid, because I think maybe they won't feel as stupid if I share them with you. I…" Hux's words sputtered to a stop like an engine that had run out of gas. He wiped the water from his eyes and shook his head in frustration. "I want you to be mine. That's all. That's… that's it."

I was struggling to process the fact that this was happening, that I was hearing this declaration that was more wonderful than any dream I'd ever let myself dream, from a man I hadn't ever imagined could want me this way. More than that, I couldn't believe this was happening while his thick cock was pressed warm and wet against my leg. While he smiled his killer smile and his strong hands moved possessively up and down my arms. While my very own naked body was being perused lazily by a pair of mesmerizing eyes in the face of the sexiest man I knew.

"Okay." I blinked. That hadn't been as eloquent as I'd hoped. I tried again. "I'd like that. Thank you." I bit my lip. "Wait. *Fuck*. One more time."

Hux started laughing so hard I slipped out of his grip and nearly fell over. I couldn't hold back a laugh after seeing him lose it like that, and when we both ended up sitting on the floor, gasping for breath through our tears, I wondered if this was what it felt like to fall in love.

When we finally caught our breath, Hux reached out a hand. I placed mine in his and felt like I was grabbing onto more than just his hand. I was accepting his offer of something that would last longer than tonight.

This wasn't pretend. It was real. I didn't need to make myself believe it because finally, *finally*, I did.

It wasn't until much later, when we were tangled in my sheets and each other, that Hux showed his vulnerability.

"You didn't totally answer me before. Can we at least try this? Are you open to that? Even though I was such an ass to you?"

"I thought we already—"

"Yeah, we did. It's just…" He licked his lips. "Sometimes a person needs to hear a thing more than once to really believe it."

I pulled back from my spot snuggled up against his side. Why did it continually shock me that he and I could feel so similarly when I knew we had so much in common? Why did I always mistakenly think that I was the only one who had insecurities?

"You know," I said slowly. "You weren't the only one who was an ass. I mean, yes, maybe you said more unkind things. Maybe you even thought more of them. But I wasn't an innocent victim, Hux. You knew it then, and you know it now."

If he really thought I was smart and capable, he had to know that I could hold my own.

He nodded.

"So… of *course* I want to try this with you. Besides—" I grinned, trying to lighten the moment. "—this way, I can stare at that butt for days without being arrested. You're really pretty, you know?"

Hux huffed out a laugh, but I could see the worry still in his eyes.

I ran a hand down the middle of his chest and paused over his heart. "But your heart is what really drew me in," I admitted. "It bleeds for the people you love. It bleeds for justice. And it's terrified of being mangled."

His eyes widened, and he took in a shaky breath. "Terrified? Me? *Pfft.*"

I wanted to laugh again, but I didn't dare. "All that stuff you know about me? All the *why's* behind the things I do? Well, I know a few things about you now too. You had your own family expectations that you had to break away from. You had to find your own purpose, just like I did. You're scared of getting hurt, of being abandoned. You don't want to let anyone else down ever again or prove yourself unworthy of their love." I ran my fingers through his wild, wet hair. "Did you ever think that someone whose love is conditional on your perfection isn't someone worth loving?"

Instead of responding, he took the words in and tasted them, rolled them around in his mouth to determine how he felt about them and how they fit into his reality.

"I can't afford to lose Champ and the team." His words were so soft I could barely hear them over the sound of the furnace on the other side of the bedroom wall. "They're all I have. They're my family."

"Mine too." I brushed a thumb across his cheek. "Do you know why Riggs was assigned to Carter's protection detail in Venezuela instead of a junior security agent?" After living with Riggs for a few months, I'd picked up on plenty of stories of Champ and his team.

Hux's forehead crinkled in confusion. He probably thought I was changing the subject. I wasn't. "He fucked up. Offended a client. He was being punished."

I nodded. "He fucked up badly. He lost the firm's largest client. He put the entire company in jeopardy."

Hux's eyebrows remained furrowed. "Yeah. Well, it turned out okay, and we got the client back, so...?"

I cupped his face. "My point is, Riggs lost Champ

millions of dollars in annual revenue. He put the entire company at risk. And Champ didn't fire him. Didn't stop caring about him. Didn't *for one minute* stop trusting him to do the job."

The frown melted away from Hux's face. "Ah. I see what you're doing now. You think you're smart."

"No. I know I'm smart. A very smart man I respect and trust told me so just recently," I teased, moving closer to him so I could feel him in my personal space.

Hux pulled my hand away from his heart and kissed the center of my palm. His eyes never left mine. "Did I?" he teased. "I don't recall saying that."

"Oh, no, I didn't mean *you*. I meant Carter." I grinned and poked Hux gently in the ribs. "I meant to tell you, Smitty finally wrote back and explained why he was leaving the game." I huffed out a laugh. "And then Carter and I talked. He explained many things, like a shit ton of things. So many things I feel like I'll be mining his sleep gems for years just to thank him." I bit my lip. "But I think my biggest takeaway was this: the past is done. You and I were both immature idiots who didn't know how to acknowledge what was going on between us. We were scared. We tried to protect ourselves. It's what we do from here on out that matters. And I believe you. I trust you. I trust *us*. Okay?"

"Ah, Kev. *Fuck*." Hux's words seemed anguished. "You are the best thing— I don't know what—"

"Hush," I said, leaning up to kiss him, grateful that I got the opportunity to reassure Hux this time—and finally understanding that it wasn't a burden to reassure the person you cared about. "It's gonna be okay."

We didn't speak again for a long time. Our mouths were too busy drinking each other in, sipping each other's secrets and tasting the promise of a future.

The next morning, when Hux disappeared upstairs to

work and I hopped on my own computer to catch up on messages and emails, Henry Cavill threw me for a loop.

"You have three unread messages from Anomaly451, sire. Shall I read them?"

My palms began to sweat, and my knee banged the underside of the desk.

It was time to have a hard conversation. That was the absolute last thing I felt like doing, but I couldn't put it off any longer. Adam felt like unresolved business. Like the killer in some low-budget slasher movie who kept resurrecting himself to torment the heroine. Which was a grossly unfair thought when the man's only crime was *liking me*.

"Yes, please read them," I said, with more confidence than I felt.

"First message. Received, 6:53 p.m. Yesterday. 'I'm qualified for HOGCon, exclamation point.'"

The tone of the message lost something when read by my very unimpressed AI. I couldn't help but think that if Henry approved of Adam, he would have spoken with enthusiasm rather than voicing the punctuation.

"Next message. Received, 6:53 p.m. Yesterday. 'Can't wait to see you in Vegas, baby, period.'"

Ugh. My stomach dropped. "And the third?"

"Next message. Received, 6:54 p.m. Yesterday. I have a special night planned for us, ellipsis." Henry paused, then recited, *"Eggplant emoji. Eggplant emoji. Eggplant emoji."*

Damn.

16

———

HUX

Less than a week into my tenuous new relationship with Kev, the two of us were on a commercial flight to Vegas for HOGCon, and I felt grossly unprepared.

The op itself had been meticulously planned by every member of our team. We had identified the players, we had compiled files on their habits and affiliations, and I was confident that our talented group could carry it off.

What I hadn't yet figured out, though, was how the fuck I was supposed to let Kev—the untrained, enthusiastic, *helpful*, gorgeous man I adored—walk into the heart of a double-Horn op involving two Cartel de la Luna operatives without losing my goddamn mind. My stomach felt like it was being chewed through with acid, and poor Kev's fingers were practically broken from being squeezed too hard every time it was in reach of my hand on the plane.

"You, ah, have a very strong grip," he said after I returned from the lavatory and clutched his hand again.

"Sorry." I tried to relax my hand without letting go.

"What's going on? Are you scared of flying? I didn't notice this before any of the other ops."

I let out a laugh. "No."

"Then what's this about? Not that I'm complaining about holding your hand in public. It's really…" His smile turned a little dopey. "Nice."

I leaned over and kissed his cheek. "Understatement," I murmured into his warm, sweet-smelling skin.

I took a breath and tried to hold my temper. Champ's cutting words to me a few hours earlier still rang in my ears. *Stop treating Kev like a child who needs Daddy's protection. He's a grown man, and no one is forcing him into this. He'll have protection. Your protection. Are you telling me you can't protect him?*

Riggs's warning had been no less severe. *Carter says he has a good feeling about you and Kev. I don't know what the fuck that means, but you better not upset him. Be a true teammate, Hux, and don't let your private feelings—whatever they are—get in the way.*

I'd wanted to punch the two of them for backing me into a verbal corner, but that was nothing. I also wanted to beat the shit out of him for putting Kev on this op in the first place.

"You're worried I can't do the job," Kev said, as if suddenly realizing what I was so upset about.

"Absolutely not," I said a little too loudly. The older woman across the aisle snapped her head over. I ignored her but lowered my voice. "Babe, you are the most competent tech specialist I know and for damned sure the most capable Horn player. I'm not worried about you not being capable. I'm not worried that you'll let us down. Ever." *I'm worried about someone hurting you.*

His smile was accompanied by pink cheeks. "You're worried about my safety."

I took a deep breath and squeezed his hand again. "Mmm."

Kev leaned his head onto my shoulder. The sweet,

familiar scent of his shampoo helped settle my nerves. I'd spent the past few nights inhaling it as he'd slept in my arms. It was early days between us, I knew that. But it felt right. It felt necessary. It felt real.

I still needed to tell him I was SmittyKitty. It wasn't fair to have that deception between us when I wanted a serious relationship with him. But I also didn't want to throw our fragile new understanding into chaos at the same time we were expected to focus on this op.

Also, I was a coward.

Kev had talked the other night about the past being in the past and how it was what we did moving forward that mattered. I wanted that to be true. But I was more terrified of losing him than I'd been about any mission I'd ever been on—even the ones where bullets had flown—and I wanted to try to control the outcome as best I could, which was the fine-print bullshit no one ever explained about really falling for someone. The more you cared, the more you had to lose.

When all of this was over, I told myself I'd take Kev somewhere quiet, set a romantic scene, and come clean in a way that would let him know I'd never meant to hurt him. I'd promise him anything, *everything*, and pray that he forgave me.

Kev lifted his head off my shoulder and pulled his hand out of my grip to run his palm down his thigh. "I didn't tell you what happened with Adam. Anomaly451, I mean. He, uh… I… We planned to meet up in Vegas to…" He cleared his throat and finished in a strangled voice, "…get to know each other."

The idea of Kevin "getting to know" his cheating asshole online boyfriend made the edges of my vision jagged and dim. I bit my tongue to keep from interrupting him.

"But then stuff happened. With us. I mean, you and me, *us*. And I don't want to do that anymore. Obviously."

His hands continued rubbing up and down the fabric of his pants. Why the hell was he nervous? I grabbed his hands and held them gently in mine.

"Did you tell him that?" I asked softly.

He nodded. "I messaged him and told him that I'd met someone in real life."

I exhaled and tried not to grin in happy relief. "And what did he say?"

If he said anything to hurt or disparage Kev, I'd have to find the fucker in Vegas and have a talk with him. A physical talk.

Kev grimaced slightly. "He said he understood I was nervous, so we could take it slow with anything… physical. He said he wanted to meet and share a drink."

"Did he now?" I grunted. It was better than what I really wanted to say. "And what did you say?"

"I told him no," he said, shooting a glance at me through his dark-framed glasses. "I told him I didn't want anything physical at all because I was going to be there with my new b—" He made a clicking noise in his throat before clearing it and trying again. This time, it came out in a whisper. "Boyfriend?"

I leaned in and kissed him, using my mouth to remove any doubt in his mind that his use of the word was anything other than perfect with me. When I finally pulled back, he blinked a few times before straightening his glasses.

"Yeah, so, that's what I said."

"Good," I said firmly.

"And I said we could meet as friends, but that's all."

This was less good, and I wanted to complain about it — why the hell did he need to meet Anomaly at all? — but I didn't want to be the kind of asshole who policed his boyfriend's friends.

"Besides, I'm going to keep you too busy for any of that

nonsense. When we're not working, I'm going to need to examine your body for…" My imagination failed me at the last minute.

The tips of Kev's ears turned red. "Piercings?" he suggested.

I smirked. "I can say with one hundred percent confidence that you didn't have any piercings last night, baby. Not sure how you might have acquired any new ones this morning."

"*So far,*" he whispered, eyes dancing behind his glasses as he called back our conversation from the other night.

Icy-hot prickles danced up and down my thighs at the idea of this sweet man getting himself pierced. Of me watching. Of the two of us getting pierced at the same time.

"In that case, I think we need to study your body *thoroughly,*" I growled into his ear. "Scientifically, one might say. Making sure to consider all possibilities."

He shuddered against me like he wished he could fuse himself into me, and at that moment, there was nothing I would have liked better.

We teased and flirted and touched for the rest of the flight. I was secretly grateful Champ and the rest of the team were in California on the horse breeder mission and wouldn't be meeting up with us until the next day. For the moment, at least, I could have Kev all to myself.

I felt so much for the man that I figured I was glowing like a nuclear reactor, and I knew at least Champ and Carter—and therefore Riggs—had to have seen it by now. If they hadn't, the fact that I'd been parked outside of the safe house for days and kept turning up for breakfast would have clued them in. Kev had been right, though. Champ trusted his teammates and clearly trusted me not to fuck things up, no matter who I was sleeping with…

As long as I could keep my protective urges in check.

After we landed and caught a ride to the conference hotel, I realized just how big HOGCon was. Hundreds of people decked out in everything from HOG-branded T-shirts and ball caps to actual cosplay creations swarmed through the large open lobby.

Kev's eyes lit up like he'd just arrived at the gates to heaven. "Oh my God. Hux, look," he hiss-whispered, tugging on my sleeve. "The Wool Isle Sorceress is coming right toward us. Just look at the ruffles on her coat. Excuse me! Love your spindle dagger!" he called happily, earning a grin and a regal nod in return.

"And look over there! Is that person holding a cat dressed up as a LynxQuester? I need to get closer. Holy crap! Holy crap, it *is*. We are *so* bringing Rodrigo next year. Omigod, *hiiii*!" he cooed, making a beeline for the cat and his owner. "Can I pet him? Would he mind? Oh, wow. Hi, sweet baby! What a ferocious LynxQuester you are! I need someone like you to guard my jam cellar from looters. You busy later?" The cat purred, his owner preened, and Kev laughed delightedly, chatting animatedly for several moments before dragging me off toward the sales booths.

Two foam gourd hats, one tin sword, a souvenir program, and thirteen HOG friend requests later, I finally forced Kev away from the crowd toward the check-in desk to collect the keys to the suite HOG Corporate had sprung for, and I came to a hugely important realization.

There wasn't a single awkward or shy thing about Kevin Rogers. He'd simply needed to find *his* people, like we all did, and once he had, he shone.

"*Mmmpfh*," Kev moaned as I pushed him up against the mirrored wall of the elevator. "Dear God, Huxley, what's gotten into you? Is it my Sword of Enchantment? It is, isn't it? You're a fan of the sword—"

"It's *you*, Kevin," I breathed against his lips. "Just you.

But give me ten seconds and imma show you *my* sword of enchantment."

Unfortunately, when we got to the suite, Kev was all business. And not sexy business.

"That's weird," he said, clicking the keyboard of his laptop while I put in an order for a room service lunch. "Did we know Vince was going to be here? He didn't qualify. At least, according to my research."

My head snapped up from where I'd been double-checking my options on the menu. "What? Vince is here?"

"Yeah. The data only shows that his Horn is here in the hotel. I can't even figure out what floor he's on or anything."

After confirming our room service order, I hung up and called Champ to give him an update.

"Can you hack into the reservations system and find out where he's staying?" Champ asked through speakerphone. "Or tap into the cameras in the hallways and monitor him?"

Kev laughed.

I cautioned Champ that it wasn't that easy. "It's easier to hack most government systems than to tap into the security operations center at a Vegas casino. Even social engineering is far from a sure thing. We're gonna have to do this low-tech. Getting eyes on him and following him. Dropping a tracker into his pocket, if we can get someone here that Vince won't recognize. Kev and I will brainstorm."

Champ updated me on their op before asking if I was sure I was okay without backup until they arrived tomorrow.

"We're good. Just doing surveillance until you get here. Kev has a meet and greet tonight and an early information session in the morning. By the time game play begins, you should be here with the team."

I'd already kitted Kev out with a tracking chip in his

pocket and a tiny button camera and mic set in his shirt to pick up on any conversations he had with our targets. He'd rolled his eyes at me, but I could see affectionate understanding in those eyes too.

When the call with Champ ended, I joined Kev in tracking down the current Horn locations for all the targets on our list. Everyone was where we expected, with the exception of Vince and Camila Dacosta. Vince's shouldn't have been here but was. Camila's was supposed to be here but was somewhere in Arizona.

I wasn't going to worry about her, though, while we were in the middle of targeting our two final Horns and trying to keep Vince off our tail.

"Did you find anything interesting in the data we got off Vince's Horn?" Kev asked after the room service attendant had delivered our food. He shoved a french fry into his mouth before taking a sip of ice water.

"Nah. We've been so busy, I haven't had a chance to do a deep dive with it yet. I added the data to our offline storage and downloaded a copy to my laptop to look through later tonight."

"While I'm at the meet and greet?"

"Mmm," I said noncommittally. Leaving him alone to attend the meet and greet along with *several* known cartel operatives wasn't on my agenda. I'd have to tackle Vince's Horn data after we got back to the suite later.

Kev pinned me with a look. "I can read your mind, you know."

I imagined fucking him from behind over the back of the suite's sofa with the hot lights of the strip visible through the large bank of windows.

"Don't think so," I said in a rough voice.

Kev's eyes heated. "Not that." He hesitated. "Although, put a pin in that one for later. Go back to the other thing.

The one you're trying hard not to think about anymore." He leaned into my space, grabbed a fry off my plate, and waved it in my face pointedly. "You're not tailing me to the meet and greet."

"Incorrect." I took a big bite of my burger.

"I'm not going to do anything other than scope around and get footage on the button camera and possibly slip a tracker into someone's pocket. You'll be able to see it all on the computer right here. And these are my friends, Hux. I've played with most of them, I know how to talk to them. This is my strength."

"Mmm," I said again. I knew he had a good point, but it didn't matter. I focused on eating my lunch and not being an ass.

"You're being an ass," Kev said with a laugh. He threw my french fry back at me.

I caught it in midair and bit into it with a feral snap of my teeth. "You might have underestimated what it's like to date a professional bodyguard, sweetheart."

His cheeks turned pink, and it spread down his neck to his collar. "Unfair to pull out the *sweetheart* at a time like this. It's like bringing an Atomic Yam Launcher to an Orc Jousting competition," he muttered.

After a few minutes of enjoying watching him try to decide whether or not he should continue arguing with me, I put him out of his misery. "Fine. I won't tail you to the event. I'll back you up from here. But you need to come up with an easily recognizable code word that alerts me to any problems without alerting anyone else."

"Like... margarita or pigs in a blanket? It's a casual cocktail party, Hux."

"It's a HOG cocktail party," I reminded him.

His grin was adorable. "Jam thief? Kelp forest arsonist? *Orc hoarder?*"

"Rodrigo," I said, trying to stay serious. "Act like you see someone you know across the room and call out his name."

"Fine. But, just so you know, that's not going to be our safe word for sex."

I nearly choked on my food. The burger went down the wrong way and made me sputter and cough until I could catch my breath again. By the time clean oxygen reached my lungs, Kev had raised his arms in victory and could barely breathe from laughing.

I waited only long enough for him to finish his meal before dragging him into the bedroom and deflowering him again and again in the hotel bed. He was dead asleep when my phone buzzed on the nightstand with a message from Champ.

Champ: *Missed our chance at the Horn tonight. Will leave partial crew to try again in AM. Riggs and I are inbound. Status?*

Shit. Delays were not a good thing in an operation that required as much manpower as this one.

Hux: *Preparing for Meet and Greet. Kev is going to try and identify each target and set trackers.*

Champ: *Good luck. Keep me updated and don't do serious shit until I get there in a couple of hours.*

I closed the text app and looked over at Kev. He looked sweet and innocent in sleep, so different from the sexy, teasing man who'd tormented me during lunch, the confident, assured operative who insisted on going to the meet and greet alone, or the focused, competent professional who'd helped me prep for the mission. It was like each time the light shifted, it revealed a brilliant new facet of the man. It fascinated me and made me crave him more.

"You're being a creeper," he said sleepily.

"Yes." I leaned over and pressed soft kisses on his bare shoulder. "Promise me you'll —"

Kev's hand shot out and grasped my wrist. Within three seconds, I was on my face on the mattress with my hand twisted up behind my shoulder blades and Kev's knee on my lower back. Once I realized what had happened, I could have easily gotten out of his hold, but there was no arguing he'd gotten the drop on me with that unexpected move.

"I'm not powerless," Kev said, not sleepy any longer.

"Kevin," I breathed into the coffee-and-vanilla-scented pillowcase.

My sweet, adorable boyfriend had just incapacitated me when I'd least expected it. I outweighed him by seventy pounds and should have outmaneuvered him after years of Marine PT and specialized training. Baby had untold depths.

"There are things I'm not trained on when it comes to this stuff," he said. "Handling multiple things at once when the stakes are high. Compartmentalizing so I can stay focused. I have things I need to learn, and I know it. And I appreciate that you're protective, Jasper. It really works for me most of the time. Like, *really*. But when I tell you I can do something, you need to believe the words I say."

"Okay," I agreed.

"Good. Don't underestimate me again," he warned. There was an edge to his calm voice this time. "And don't treat me like a junior member of the team either. It's starting to piss me off."

He let go, and I shook out my arm while rolling over to face him. "Starting to?"

Kev gave me a reluctant smile, but I could tell he wasn't completely okay with what had happened. And he was right. That was exactly how I'd been treating him.

"Okay," I said, sitting up and reaching for his shoulders. "You're right. I'm sorry."

He nodded. "Thank you."

"Can we talk about where you learned—"

"Sorority self-defense class," he said, a little too fast for me to catch.

I opened my mouth before his words sank in. Then I closed my teeth with a clack.

Kev climbed off the bed and began shuffling toward the bathroom. "Long story," he called over his shoulder. "I'll be telling it in the shower if you'd care to hear it."

I didn't hear much of the story, to be honest, but I heard enough to understand I needed to avoid all Vanderbilt Chi Omegas from now on. What I did hear was the gasping whimpers of a wet and hard Kevin Rogers when I went down on him.

This time, he knew better than to sink to the floor with me.

Doing surveillance on Kevin was not hard work. Imagine getting paid to stalk your crush. My eyes stuck to him like duct tape until I realized he was geeking it out with our fellow HOG superfans, who were all dressed as spelled mushrooms, magical ponies, and fruit orcs.

Meanwhile, I dove into the data from Vince's Horn. We'd prioritized the financial transactions and drug movement history data on all of the Horns because going through the chat logs was extremely time-intensive and not very rewarding. Several of Champ's lower-level agents had been combing through the chat logs in an attempt to identify additional people of interest. It wasn't easy to differentiate between a benign in-game contact and a communication associated with the cartel.

It took me forty minutes before I recognized a name that was out of place in Vince's chat logs.

"What the fuck?" I slowed my scrolling and scanned back up the log.

Anomaly451: *Return to homestead.*

Anomaly451: *Exchange power beacon for sparrowflox powder!*

Anomaly451: *Pumpkin Butter Booster is compromised.*

Anomaly451: *Target NaboEnojado7 for exchange.*

Anomaly451: *Return to homestead.*

Anomaly451: *Abandon homestead.*

My heart began to pound wildly. As it so often did, this one piece of information was the linchpin, the crucial missing key to the code that brought the whole puzzle into focus.

And once it was, my heart raced even faster.

I checked the surveillance monitor and saw Kev still happily chatting with a woman in a Marigold Fairy costume. She was waving a magic wand in one hand and a drink in another.

He was safe. For now.

I quickly dialed Champ's number, never taking my eyes off Kev's video feed.

"Boss, I got something." My voice sounded steadier than it felt. Inside, I was horrified. My brain scanned at Mach speed through every memory and snippet of information I'd learned of Anomaly from Kev. "Vince is targeting Kev… or, or… he at least knows Anomaly451, who's tried to befriend Kev in the game. They—Anomaly and Vince, I mean—have been exchanging power beacons for sparrowflox powder and talking about Pumpkin Butter Boosters, and I think they might share a homestead."

There was a beat of silence. "Jesus Christ, this fucking game. *English*, Huxley. Lay it out for me without mentioning a single fairy-tale creature or magical tuber. This plane is getting ready to take off."

"Actually, Champ, a pumpkin is a gourd, not a—"

"*Huxley.*"

"Right. Okay. So this guy, Anomaly, has cultivated a friendship with Kev in the game—talking to him, questing with him, et cetera—for weeks, at my guess."

"And he knows Vince?"

"According to Vince's Horn chat logs, they've communicated *repeatedly*."

"Why would he want to play the game with Kev? You think he knows Kev's related to us? Does he want access to Horn of Glory Corporate?"

I grabbed my hair and yanked. "No, I think it's way more targeted than that. I don't know exactly when they started chatting, but I'd bet it was right around the time that Tommy Drakes got Buck Nutter's Horn from the flea market, or maybe... maybe when we got involved by bringing Buck home from Venezuela. I think while Vince was trying to convince Quinn to give him information about you, Anomaly was trying to find out what we knew a different way. Through Kev."

"Shit. Did Kev give him anything?"

"No," I said with no hesitation. "Kev knows better than to fall for a phishing scheme. If Anomaly had ever mentioned Champion Security, Kev would have caught him out instantly. But he kept asking Kev rando, semi-related questions, like how he'd secure digital data. And Kev told me that Anomaly kept trying to score an invite to Kev's house. When Kev backed off, Anomaly insisted on meeting him here, probably hoping to soften him up so he'd get an invite later."

Champ grunted thoughtfully, which was a wholly inadequate response to the situation.

I found it necessary to repeat this last part in case I wasn't clear the first time. "He's insisting on meeting with

Kev, Champ. Kev, who is all alone downstairs at the meet and greet right now."

"Yep. I heard you," Champ said easily. "Who said you can't get lucky in Vegas, eh?"

I blinked. "Lucky? What the fuck?"

"Kev can get the data off this guy's Horn. Flip the scenario. Scam the scammer. Grab the data off this Anoma-whatsie's Horn and see where he fits in the cartel hierarchy."

"You want… you think he should…" Was Champ *out of his fucking mind*? "That's… not going to happen," I said as calmly as I could. Which wasn't very calm.

Silence came from the other end before Champ finally said, *"Oh?"* in that way of his that brooked no disobedience.

On the monitor, Kev moved away from the Marigold Fairy and pulled out his Horn device. It looked like he was checking his messages, but I couldn't read the words on the screen through the button camera view.

He glanced around the room, and I was positive—like, 96 percent sure—that he looked apprehensive. What if it was a message from Anomaly insisting on a meetup… If so, it meant the man I was falling in love with was in danger.

Which meant disobedience be damned.

"Gotta go," I said before hanging up on my boss and bolting for the door.

17

KEV

Normally, I was a nervous weirdo at parties like this where I didn't know anyone. But as soon as I saw all the costumes and felt the shared passion for my favorite game, it felt more like entering a room of friends I simply hadn't met yet.

I'd put on a nicer pair of jeans and my "Proud Homesteader" shirt—the limited-edition one, with the Coral Reef Princess and the Double-Eyed Gatekeeper pretending to be friends, even though everyone knew they were mortal enemies in real life—before coming down here to look for our targets. All I had to go by were some photos of the people we *thought* were connected to the Horns in question, based on Horn location data and the surveillance that a few of Champ's operatives had conducted. The two likely suspects didn't look nearly as easy to engage as Camila Dacosta had been.

Luis Estrada was a baggage handler at DFW, the largest international airport in Texas. Despite earning just under twenty bucks an hour at his job, Luis was known for the six-thousand-dollar Nike Air Yeezy sneakers he wore when he wasn't at work. He was also known to me as the man with the terrifying face tattoo.

Camden Mallon, on the other hand, wasn't physically intimidating, but he was backed by an incredibly wealthy and influential family. He was a slight gamer-geek like me, but his family were the Mallons of Mallon Shipping fame. They owned one of the world's largest cargo container logistics companies, which meant they basically owned the docks at America's largest ports.

As soon as Champ had learned the various identities of the people on the Horn's list of cartel contacts, he'd put one of his data analysts on each of them. He'd hoped to be able to give the DEA a detailed dossier on these players to speed their own investigation when the time came.

I was secretly relieved not to see either Luis or Camden at the party right away. I'd meant what I'd said to Hux in the hotel suite earlier—this was the area where I thought I could help this operation best, I didn't want him to underestimate me, and I really could take care of myself—but I wasn't quite as confident as I'd wanted him to believe. I was employing the fake-it-until-you-make-it mentality that had helped me break out from my lair over the past few months.

No lie, though, slipping a tracker into someone's pocket —heck, just getting close enough to do that—was fucking scary. My hands were sweating just thinking about it.

Thankfully, enough people came up to compliment me on my shirt that I ended up having some enjoyable conversations while continuing to scope out the room. It wasn't until I was in the middle of discussing my recent Duchess of Moon Flower Quest with a high-ranking healer in a gorgeous fairy costume that I saw a man who looked like Camden Mallon across the room.

Okay, I could do this. I was as capable as I'd told Hux I was. As brilliant as Hux believed me to be. And I was going to prove to him I was a contributing member of this team who didn't need handholding.

As I moved away from the Marigold Fairy, my Horn buzzed with a message.

Anomaly451: *Angel-face, are you here? I'd love to meet up. Even a quick hello. I'm standing by the table with the chocolate fountain.*

My hands started sweating again as I glanced in that direction. There were too many people between me and the food tables to be able to see much, especially when I didn't know who I was looking for. Suddenly, the whole let's-promise-not-to-Google-each-other, let's-see-each-other-for-the-first-time-in-person thing seemed ridiculous rather than romantic. At the time, I'd been thinking that I could never be brave or stupid enough to have chat sex on-camera with someone, but now I realized how shortsighted I'd been.

How the heck was I supposed to be in a relationship with someone I couldn't pick out of a lineup? More importantly, how was I supposed to avoid my almost-kinda online boyfriend if I didn't know what he looked like?

You'd have on-camera sex with Hux, my brain helpfully informed me. *In fact, you'd really like that.*

I closed my eyes and concentrated on breathing. This was true, but then again, I'd probably do anything for Hux. He was my forever exception to the rules.

The Almost-Definitely-Camden-Mallon guy was busy talking to a thirty-something-year-old woman with long dark hair pulled back in a sleek ponytail. Their conversation looked flirty, which would help me with distraction.

As I fingered the tiny tracker in my pocket, I thought through the steps Hux had shown me. *Bump, slide, grab, apologize.*

"And if you can spill your drink on their shoes, even better."

I had ordered a soda water with lime just for this

purpose, and luckily, my hands were shaking hard enough to make the bump and spill effortless. The nearly empty cup tumbled to the carpet by his shoes.

"Oh my gosh! I'm so sorry," I said a little too loudly, sliding the tracker into the man's pants pocket with one hand while grabbing his upper arm with the other and squeezing.

"When a stranger touches us, we can't help but zero in on that touch to assess friend or foe. It's a guaranteed distraction from a much lighter touch near the pocket."

Hux's words tumbled through my mind as I continued the ruse, bracing me as they always did. I let go of the man and stood up straighter, clasping my chest and inhaling to keep his attention for another beat. "I am so, so sorry. These kinds of things make an awkward gamer even more awkward, am I right? Heh." I leaned over to retrieve the cup. "At least it was soda water instead of a strawberry daiquiri," I added with an embarrassed laugh. "Enjoy your night."

I strolled calmly away, knowing without a shadow of a doubt I could not do that a second time tonight without taking a break first to bring my blood pressure back into healthy limits.

Maybe meeting Adam would be a good distraction. I could say hello and wish him luck in the tournament, at least. After all, it wasn't like I wanted to sever our friendship. Even though I was with Hux, I still enjoyed having friends. Wasn't that a sign of a healthy relationship?

Would Adam even want to remain friends even if I didn't want more?

Only one way to find out.

HogDocKev: *Hey, Adam. I'm heading your way. I'm wearing dark-framed glasses and a Proud Homesteader t-shirt.*

I moved toward the food tables, catching sight of the

one with a chocolate fountain on it. But instead of seeing anyone who could be Anomaly451, I saw a completely unexpected—and horrifyingly familiar—face.

The man from the motel. Linus Dixon, Vince's partner in crime. The man I'd casually delivered a pizza to and caught on my button cam all those nights ago.

For some reason, despite all the people around us now and the utter lack of witnesses back then, this situation felt infinitely more dangerous.

My heart rate took off again, and I fumbled for my phone to call Hux. Thankfully, there was still a crowd of people between me and the motel guy, so I was able to switch directions easily and blend in with another group.

"Baby, shit," Hux said, sounding oddly out of breath. "I just tried to call you. You've gotta keep your ringer on when you—"

"He's here," I hissed. "Vince's accomplice."

"I know. Wait, how do *you* know?"

"Because I saw him. I recognized him. I—"

"Okay, stay where you are. I'm coming. Getting in elevator right—" The connection ended.

I scurried around a ten-foot-tall troll balloon near the bar and joined the crowd queuing for pictures with the Tin Archer. While I waited for Hux, I messaged Adam. He might not be boyfriend material—not for me, not in real life —but I also didn't want him to end up anywhere near Linus Dixon. Not only that, but I didn't want to wait alone in this room while Hux traversed the enormous hotel to get to the conference center on the opposite end.

HogDocKev: *Hey, sorry. Can we meet on the other side of the room by the bar under the square chandelier? I'm thirsty.*

Anomaly451: *I'm gonna be the thirsty one, baby. *flame emoji* Heading that way now. So glad you changed your mind. I can't wait to hold you!*

My brain translated "hold" as "hug" to keep me from completely losing my nerve. Adam was going to have to accept I wasn't interested in that anymore. And if he didn't… things were going to get very uncomfortable when Hux showed up.

I waited a solid three minutes before leaving the picture line to join a throng that was heading toward the bar while loudly arguing about the use of flamethrowers to battle pernicious Kudzu Creepers.

As soon as I approached, though, I saw that the guy from the motel had moved too, damn it. There he stood, in a black button-down shirt, black slacks, and slicked-back hair, by the bar under the square chandelier, right where Anomaly was supposed to be.

For a supposedly brilliant person, it took me a really, really long time to figure out what this meant. Thirty seconds, at least.

"No," I breathed. Tingling numbness crawled from my fingers up my arms. "No," I said again, trying desperately to come up with a scenario that would explain the coincidence. Any scenario besides the one most likely.

Adam, Anomaly451, was Vince's accomplice.

Linus A. Dixon.

"Kevin? Darling, is that you?"

My eyes snapped up to his face, now split with a wide, friendly smile. A messy combination of fear and anger strangled me. How dare he approach me like this? How dare he have approached me in the first place?

How dare he *target* me. Because that's what it had to be, right? He'd never actually liked me. That was too easy. Now that I thought about it, the whole thing had been too easy. Why else would someone be interested in a random player in an online game? He'd come out of nowhere, chatting me up and flirting with me before ever even knowing I was gay, or what I liked, or anything else of substance greater than my superior ability to farm ensorcelled kumquats.

My feet were glued to the carpet, unsure whether to fight or flee.

I finally chose the third option: fake it.

"Hi!" I said, moving forward, even if it was as slowly as I could possibly move. If I approached slowly enough, maybe Hux would arrive and figure out how to handle this. "Adam?"

He nodded. "It's so good to meet you." He held out his arms like he was expecting a hug, but I held out a hand for a shake instead. It was clumsy and bumbling, but that was on-brand for me, and at least it kept me out of his embrace. He finally took my hand with a slight frown. His grip was strong and dry, which should have reminded me of Hux, but it didn't.

Nothing about this man reminded me of Hux.

This was the guy who'd taken Quinn hostage. Who'd almost gotten him *killed*. Whose bosses had held Carter and Riggs prisoner. Who probably had freaking murderers on speed dial.

My Chi Omega self-defense classes seemed incredibly inadequate.

"Come, let me buy you a drink," he said, turning toward the cash bar. "You look nervous." His hand landed on my lower back, which made the hair stand up on my neck and arms. Where the heck was Hux?

"Not nervous, just overwhelmed by the excitement of being here. When—" My voice cracked, so I cleared my throat. "When did you arrive?"

"A couple of hours ago. I was hoping to have time for a quick shower, but getting a ride from the airport was a disaster. Maybe you can help me clean up later." He winked before turning to the bartender.

Had he always been this smarmy? Oh, dear God, I was pretty sure he had, and I'd tried to convince myself it was charm. The thought literally nauseated me. I pressed a hand to my stomach, trying to keep the french fries I'd consumed at lunch from making a reappearance.

I craned my neck in hopes of finding Hux. Even though the convention center ballroom was packed with people, I felt alone and untethered.

"What room are you in?" he asked, handing me a cocktail I hadn't asked for and taking a second one while handing the bartender some cash.

"Oh, ah… fourteen twenty-seven?" I said, making up a number out of thin air. "I think? This place is huge and a little confusing." Okay, that wasn't a lie, but I was hoping the dopey act would buy me some time.

"You haven't been to Vegas before, have you?" He clucked his tongue. "Poor baby. Stick with me, and I'll guide you." He held his glass out to me as if wanting to clink it in cheers. "To new memories."

I clinked my glass to cover the shudder running through me and then held the drink up to my lips. The sharp smell of strong alcohol hit the tender skin of my nostrils before the glass even reached my mouth. There was no way I was drinking whatever that was. My original plan had been to fake a sip, but at this strength, I feared a contact high.

"Mmm," I said instead. "How was the flight from DC?"

Hux was right—I wasn't trained in this. That was a stupid question.

But he hadn't necessarily come from DC. I racked my brain to remember what we'd learned about the mystery man. This was the DEA tech guy, the hacker.

Our message history scrolled through my memory, flashing reminders about his questions on data storage and security. What kind of information had he been trying to get from me? What did he think I could do for him?

My phone buzzed with a message.

"Sorry," I said weakly. "My grandfather. He worries. Just give me one quick sec."

Hux: *Make an excuse. Say you're sick. Delay till tomorrow.*

Thankfully, there were enough people around us to keep Adam — or whatever his name was — from seeing my phone screen. I tapped out a response.

Me: *Shouldn't I learn his room number? Or get him to confess? Something?*

Hux: *No. Get out of there.*

But I didn't want this encounter to be for nothing. I remembered the second tracker in my pocket.

Hux: *Kev, I've got eyes on you, but I can't get too close. He might recognize me if he has intel on the team. Move toward the elevator. Do it now.*

Hux: *You've got this.*

My hands shook even worse than before. Hux wasn't coming. Couldn't come. So it was up to me.

I slid the phone back into my pocket and fingered the tracker.

I could do this.

I swallowed. "I'm… not feeling well. I think I need to…" I leaned against his shoulder suddenly, like I was feeling faint. My drink tipped just enough to dribble on his shoes, but instead of grabbing onto me to keep me from falling, Adam shoved me away from him.

"What the fuck? These are seven-hundred-dollar shoes."

I blinked at him in shock. The tracker fell from my fingers back into my pocket. "Sorry," I said again. I probably looked as nauseated as I truly felt. "I'm so sorry. I think I need to go back to my room and get some rest."

When I turned away from him, his hand darted out to grip my elbow. "I'll walk you back. You shouldn't be alone."

I hope Hux is still listening to the microphone feed.

"That's not necessary," I said faintly. As I moved through the crowded room, I thought I recognized my other target, Luis Estrada. It didn't matter. There was no way I was pulling the drink-spilling maneuver a third time tonight. I kept walking toward the doors and tried again to shake my escort. "Stay and enjoy the party so you can tell me about it tomorrow."

"Linus? Is that you?" a young woman's voice called out in surprise as she noticed the man nearly dragging me through the ballroom.

He ignored her.

"Linus! It's me, Darla. From the Philly division. Remember? We met at the GovTech conference last year?"

"You're confusing me with someone else," he said without looking at her.

She frowned. "No, I—"

By the time she second-guessed herself, we were out of the ballroom and striding down the wide corridor. Hux was nowhere in sight.

My mind scrambled to come up with a plan. One that would shake him loose while stroking his ego enough that I could try again with him tomorrow... though the very idea of spending more time with this almost-mistake made me shudder.

What I knew for sure was that I couldn't let him get me upstairs alone. I didn't think he'd kill me—as long as I kept my mouth shut and played along, he had different plans for me. But if I went upstairs, Hux would come after me, I knew it. Then the whole operation would be blown, and Hux could be seriously injured.

All that uncertainty made my knees weak.

Instead of fighting to control my body's reaction, I leaned into it—leaned into *Anomaly*—and pretended I was as excited by the idea of being with him as I would have been if I hadn't fallen hard for Jasper Huxley in the meantime.

"Adam, stop. I'm really not feeling well. I'm exhausted, you know? What with the travel and the excitement of coming here. I wanted to wait and meet you tomorrow when I looked fresher, but then you messaged, and the temptation was too great to resist. I… I've been so confused about you and me. I convinced myself that what you and I shared wasn't real." *Because it wasn't.* "So I started seeing someone back home. But now that I've met you in person, I finally understand what real attraction is." *And it's not this.* "I'm overwhelmed by the, um… the strength of my reaction to you. And I… I want to be with you." I forced myself to set my hand on his arm. To widen my eyes and glance up at him soulfully. "But I think a man's first time should be perfect." The way mine had been with Hux. "Don't you?"

Adam straightened and puffed out his chest. "Of course. I want that too. But we're together now, honeybunch. I'm committed to that. Come back to my room so I can take care of you," he said. "We can talk until you feel more settled. You can tell me all about your life in Tennessee. We can plan that visit we talked about. And when you're feeling calmer…" He smiled that smarmy smile again. "I'll be gentle, I promise."

Shit. Lesson number one: appealing to a man's sense of honor only works when he has one.

I quickly changed tack.

"Oh, that would be wonderful. Only…" I sniffled feebly. "I didn't want to mention this because I wanted to make a good first impression, but now that I know how you feel about me, I feel like you should know." I batted my eyelashes just a little. "See, when I'm overwhelmed, I get certain, erm… symptoms?" I glanced around the empty hallway and whispered, "*Toilet symptoms*. It's not contagious, of course! Not at all. But I do need Gatorade. And Imodium. And saltines. Then *more* Imodium, and so forth, kind of in a cyclical pattern? At home, my cousin sings me this song from *Moana* in between bouts and does the voices? I could… I could maybe find YouTube video of it for you if you don't already know the words. It lulls me to sleep… at least for a few minutes before I'm up and at it again. But I'm perfectly fine again after six, maybe eight, hours or so." I smiled at him gratefully. "I've never had a boyfriend before, but it'll be so nice to have someone to call to for more toilet paper while I'm incapacitated. This will be such a bonding experience for—" I clapped a hand to my stomach. "Oh. Oh, gracious. We should really head upstairs now."

His face morphed during my little speech until he finally decided I was too much of a hot mess to deal with.

"Actually, I ah…" He moved his arm out from under my hand. "I wonder if you'd feel better in your own room. Just for tonight."

I tried not to let out a giant breath of relief. "Oh? Well… I suppose, if you think it's best."

He nodded. "I do. But you message me later to let me know how you're doing, and then we'll meet up tomorrow. Stop by the hotel gift shop on your way through the lobby to get that… medicine." The edge of his lip curled up.

"Sure," I said with another sniff. "You'll stay and tell me how the party goes? Fill me in on everything tomorrow?"

"Yep. No problem."

"If you change your mind," I began, but Linus was already beating a hasty retreat to the ballroom.

"Get some rest," he called over his shoulder.

I shuddered again but lost no time in getting away from there. I hustled around the corner and whipped out my phone. Before I could dial Hux, I was body-slammed by someone I hadn't seen.

Suddenly, warm bands of iron locked around me, and the scent of Hux's sandalwood deodorant was in my nose. *Safety. Familiarity. Comfort.*

All the fears I'd held back with Adam… *Linus*… crashed over me in a wave, and tears sprang to my eyes.

"Shh, shhh. Got you. You're okay. You're fine," he murmured in my hair. "You did so good. So, so good, Kev. You were amazing."

He babbled reassurance while we held each other and tried to calm down. Part of me wanted to be stronger, worried that Hux would go back to handling me like glass if I showed him how truly afraid I'd been. But the other part of me needed comfort too much to care.

"I wasn't." This time when I sniffled, it wasn't part of any act. "I sucked. All my tough talk with you upstairs and I couldn't even get the tracker on him. I blew this opportunity. I failed the team."

Hux pulled me back and gripped my face between his hands. "Stop," he said firmly. "You didn't fail anyone. I knew that Anomaly had to be part of the HOG cartel ring, but *you* were the one who just positively ID'd him as Vince's accomplice at the motel. That's a huge deal. And as for the rest… Shit goes wrong, Kevin. That's the number one rule of every mission. Why isn't Champ's group here right now with us? Because shit went wrong on their op, and they need more time to try again. That's all this is." His fingers tightened, forcing me to look at him. "I was close enough to hear everything. You weren't alone. And if you'd needed me to, I would have laid that fucker out before he got a glimpse of my face. But you handled it. Do you hear me?"

I nodded as much as I could around his fingers, and Hux must've seen the truth in my eyes because he nodded once also. He dropped his hand away from my face only to grasp my fingers instead and pull me toward the elevators. His grasp was like an industrial-strength rubber band, and I relished the feeling of protection it gave me.

Jasper Huxley was angry. He was trying his hardest to hide it from me, but there were enough little indicators to alert anyone who knew him well that he was seething with rage on the inside at how close we'd come to disaster, thanks to fucking Linus.

I kept my mouth shut and decided I'd let him stew, at least until we got back to the suite. His brain was probably processing data a mile a minute like mine was, assessing the situation while keeping an eye out for threats…

Which had to be why we nearly missed the opportunity of a lifetime standing to one side of the lobby.

"Omigod." When I gasped and yanked Hux to a halt, he immediately spun around, ready to confront whatever new danger threatened. But I merely pointed, wide-eyed, at the man on the far side of the lobby.

"That… that's Buck Nutter, Huxley! *The* Buck Nutter, inventor of the Horn of Glory. Holy crap. Do you think he'd sign my T-shirt?"

18

———

HUX

I slow-panned to Kev. Was he messing with me? Buck Nutter was the cause of this entire clusterfuck. In the time it took me to register Kev's obvious hero worship, I realized he was being serious.

Buck Nutter—the original inventor of the Horn Of Glory game, a former unwilling guest of cartel leader Gustavo Santiago, and the man who'd smuggled cartel data out of Venezuela in the unlikely form of a gaming device—was standing in the lobby of the hotel, decked out in purple jeggings that clung to his skinny frame, a green Hawaiian-print shirt, a Horn of Glory fanny pack, and bright red cowboy boots with sparkles on them. As we watched, he nodded thoughtfully at the man beside him and smoothed down the corners of his sandy mustache.

I stood and stared like a fool until my brain kicked into action and my muscles tightened. "Fucking Christ," I muttered, pulling out my phone to call Champ. "Do not take your eyes off him, Kev. Better yet, maybe you should try to place a tracker on him. He'd recognize me, but he probably doesn't know you."

"Tracker? What... oh. *Ohhh*." I could tell Kev had forgotten all about Buck Nutter's role in this operation. To be fair, Kev hadn't been working with the team back when Buck Nutter had disappeared. Kev had been on comms with us when we got Carter, Riggs, and Buck out of Venezuela, but he hadn't been on the scene. And afterward, he'd gone back to his regular life while we, Champion Security, had lost our asset.

Buck Nutter had left his Horn with a money-hungry ex-girlfriend and bolted to parts unknown. From the tanned skin and wrinkled Hawaiian shirt, I could assume it had at least been a tropical unknown part.

"Champ," my boss barked in my ear.

"You're not gonna believe this, boss, but I have eyes on Buck Nutter."

The silence over the line was reassuring. At least I wasn't the only one to freeze upon receipt of this unexpected windfall.

"You shitting me?"

I snapped a quick pic with my phone and sent it to him. "Nope. And unless you say otherwise, he's about to become a guest of Champion Security's hotel suite whether he likes it or not."

"Do not take your eyes off that wily fucker," Champ growled. "I'm on my way."

"Permission to take him in?" I begged.

"Do what you have to do. I trust you."

More proof that what Kev had said was true. Champ respected my ability to get the job done. To do the right thing.

I turned to Kev. "Do you think you can drop the tracker on him?"

Kev was pale and nervous. I wasn't sure if it was left-over from the interaction with Anomaly or fear of what I'd asked him to do with Buck. Before I could pull my request back, he stood taller and pushed his shoulders back. "Yes."

I blinked at his manufactured bravery, his willingness to try. His dedication to the mission and his team.

I'm in love with you.

The words fell into my mind like Thor's Hammer striking the ground. The resulting vibrations unsettled my stomach and jangled my heart. This wasn't the time for incredible, life-changing realizations. I didn't have room in my mission plan for this.

Instead of saying the words out loud, I grabbed the front of his shirt and pulled him toward me, crashing my lips on his with a ride-or-die kind of desperation. He needed to know, to *feel* the intensity of this moment even if I couldn't explain it in words right now.

Kev's eyes widened comically, and he nearly fell over when I released him. His fingertip jabbed the center of his glasses to shove them back up his nose while he stammered. "Oh. Well. Okay, then. So…"

"You are…" I scrambled to think of something other than the declaration of love echoing loudly in my mind. "Mine."

Lame. What I should have said was that I was his. That I wanted us to be each other's.

But Kev didn't seem to mind.

His goofy grin set my heart rate back to a steady rhythm. This was my familiar and beloved Kevin. My partner in this crazy op and the man I trusted most with my heart. And when this mission was over, I was going to tell him all my truths and then ask, *beg*, for him to be my partner in everything.

"I'm going in," he said in a teasing tone that didn't fool me. He was nervous and exhausted. If he could do this one thing, I was planning on taking him back to the suite and fucking him into a coma.

As I watched Kev make his way across the lobby toward the Hawaiian shirt, what happened next seemed to unfold in slow motion.

Buck's face lit up in recognition as he spotted someone coming from Kev's right. My eyes tracked what he was looking at and saw Vince Parler striding purposefully toward Buck.

What the fuck?

I lurched forward to try and prevent Vince from spotting Kev while I scrambled to determine whether or not Vince knew Kev and would recognize him as part of the Champion Security family. Vince wasn't an idiot. He was also smart enough to recognize a tracker drop if he saw one.

Before I could reach Kev and stop him, Vince noticed him and definitely recognized him.

"Kevin Rogers," Vince said, studying Kev as if trying to decide whether he was friend or foe, which was exactly how I was feeling about Buck Nutter right about then.

Was Buck working with Vince? And if so, since when?

What did that mean for the data we'd taken off his Horn after Venezuela?

Was Champion Security some kind of pawn in a game we didn't even understand?

Kev stopped his progress so quickly he nearly tripped over his own feet. His lack of forward motion helped me catch up to him quicker, and I stepped up next to him with a hand on his back. I felt the tension in his muscles release a little.

"Vince," I said in a hard voice. "Fancy meeting you here. Taken anyone hostage recently? And you." I turned back to Buck. "What rock did you crawl out from?"

Instead of answering, Buck lifted an eyebrow at Vince. It was Vince who answered.

"Not here, Huxley. We need to go somewhere private." His voice was low and serious. Vince no longer seemed like Champ's smarmy ex-boyfriend or the villain he'd been the last time I'd seen him at Bunny's house.

"We're not going anywhere private with you," I seethed, saying the exact opposite of what I'd just finished saying to Champ on the phone. Only two minutes had passed, and I now felt like I was holding a bag of venomous snakes.

The tension came back in Kev's body a split second before an attractive blonde woman stepped up and put her arm around Vince. "I agree with Vince," she said with a sultry smile. But her eyes were all business.

Camila Dacosta, drama mom and truly terrible spell-caster, was dressed like she was heading out to a nice dinner on the Strip. My bag held more snakes than I'd anticipated.

"Cam?" Kev asked, obviously confused as hell. That made two of us.

She lowered her voice as she leaned closer. "My name is Laurel Whatley, Special Agent with the FBI's Criminal Investigation Division. And we need to talk before you fuck this up any more than you already have." She leaned back and smiled again, the elegant darling in a group of half-angry, half-confused men. "Shall we head up to your suite for a nightcap?"

My eyes shot to Vince to see his reaction to her revelation. Had he known her as an agent or as a member of the cartel's infrastructure? He was hard to read, too distracted by scoping out the people around us as if being caught with any of us would be his downfall.

And, if Laurel was who she claimed to be, he might very well be right.

Strangely enough, it was Vince's hesitation that made me decide to comply.

We followed her like four of the seven dwarves trailing after a very cranky Snow White. Buck Nutter was clearly Dopey while I had a lock on Grumpy. Oddly, Vince seemed Happy as we got out of the crowded lobby and into a more private elevator nook. Kev, of course, was Doc.

"How did you know where we were staying?" I demanded. Camila—*Laurel*—simply rolled her eyes.

"You're really asking how the FBI found you when you're staying in a HOG Corporate suite without attempting to use a fake name?"

FBI. Right.

When we entered the suite, she helped herself to the room phone to order an obscene amount of food and coffee. I narrowed my eyes at her. "Help yourself," I muttered.

"I haven't eaten since this morning," she said with a shrug.

Kev had reached for my hand in the elevator and hadn't released it since. He continued to side-eye the agent as if trying to determine if she was part of an elaborate ruse.

"One of you needs to start talking," I demanded, trying to sound more commanding than I felt at the moment. "And show me some ID that I can verify. What the fuck is going on?"

Laurel's casual grin dropped, and I got another flash of the special agent underneath as she took out her badge and threw it on the table in the center of the room. "What's going on is a certain cartoon duo—" She glared at Kev and then at me. "—turning an operation I've spent months planning into a fucking circus. So sit down and be quiet, sunshine. This isn't a Duchess of Moonflower quest, and you're not in charge now."

Vince held his hand out as if to calm her down. "I told

you when you recruited me that Percy Champion was not going to leave this alone. And thirty minutes ago, you were telling me we needed a miracle if we wanted this case to pull together now that your informant backed out. How about you ask him what they're doing instead of pissing them off."

Laurel turned her glare on Vince instead, but after a moment, she blew out a breath.

"Fine," she said, folding her arms over her chest. "Impress me."

Kev's hand tightened in mine. *Right.* We didn't exactly have a battle plan other than collecting the last of the Horn data to hand over to someone who had the authority to actually *do* something with it.

Enter the FBI.

"Yes," I said, clearing my throat. "We do have a plan. But first, we need to know what Vince's role in this is."

"And Buck's," Kev added, seemingly remembering that Buck was in the wind the last time we'd checked.

"And I need to verify your identity. No offense, Laurel. I mean Camila. I mean OnCallWidow."

Vince's eyes kept flashing toward the door. "Yeah, well, I need to get back down there soon to meet up with Luis. Can we make this fast?" He turned back to meet my eyes. "Where's Champ? He should be in on this conversation."

"He's on his way," I said, assuming it wouldn't be secret for long once my tall boss strode into any room where Vince happened to be.

He sighed and ran a hand through his hair, looking rumpled for the first time since I'd known him. "I cut a deal, okay? I'm working with the feds."

"What kind of deal?" I asked.

He picked at a spot on his cuff. "The kind that keeps me out of jail."

There was a knock at the door, and half the people in the room reached for weapons they weren't carrying. Kev simply strode over to answer it before I could stop him. When the room service attendant laid out the food instead of opening fire, we all let out a collective breath and settled around the suite's dining table.

Laurel started explaining. "Vince approached a trusted contact of his in the agency—"

"The FBI," Vince muttered. "The DEA is an agency too, you know."

"Fine. Whatever." Laurel waved half a veggie wrap in the air as she spoke. "The FBI connected him with my boss since I was already undercover on the Cartel de la Luna case."

Buck Nutter hadn't uttered a word, but he kept dropping his fork, losing his napkin, and nearly knocking over his bottle of water. Squirrelly didn't begin to describe the man, but I wasn't sure whether that was because he was involved in a deeper con… or it was just part of his personality. I tried to keep one eye on him while the other was split between Laurel, Vince, and Kev.

Vince interjected. "Linus crossed too many lines. It wasn't worth it anymore."

Buck nodded around a mouthful of coleslaw. "That's how I felt, bro. Too many. You know?"

No. I didn't know. None of this made any sense to me. Thankfully, Champ showed up before I could lose my temper and scream the place down in frustration.

"What the fuck is going on?" Champ growled, walking into the suite like he owned the place. In a way, he did since he was the one paying for it.

"You made good time," I said blandly.

Champ grunted in acknowledgment. "One of my team members hanging up on me after telling me Vince and his partner were on the scene and then threatening to go rogue tends to motivate me," he replied without looking away from his alpha staredown with Camila. "We'll be discussing that later."

I shrugged, though he wasn't looking. Champ could discuss it all he liked, but I was perfectly comfortable with my actions. I'd known Champ would head here immediately once I'd told him about Anomaly, and I was starting to understand that no matter how pissed off Champ got, he trusted my instincts and wasn't going to fire me for using them.

Kev leaned a little closer to me. Vince sighed in resignation. Laurel sized up Champ's tall, imposing form. And Buck grinned a goofy smile at Riggs, who'd entered the room on Champ's heels. "Well, hey there, kidnap buddy! Long time no see."

Riggs's eyebrows furrowed. "I thought Champ was pulling my leg when he said Buck was here."

Champ stood at the head of the table and pegged Vince with a glare. "Talk. Now."

It took less than ten minutes for them to lay out the situation. Most of it was exactly what we'd theorized, but they filled in some holes for us.

Vince's coworker Linus A. Dixon—A for Adam—had hacked into Vince's personal finances and discovered some illegal money movement several months before. He'd used this information to blackmail Vince into tracking down the smuggled Horn. When they hadn't been able to get at the corrupted data Kev and I had put on the Horn, the blackmail had continued. But when Linus had suggested that Vince should take Champ out in a late-night assassination, Vince had known real fear.

"I'm sorry," Vince said to Champ. "That was when I… when I realized things had gone way too far."

Champ didn't seem moved at all by his apology, and I could imagine he was thinking about what Vince had done to Quinn. I knew nothing Vince could say or do would make up for that because I felt the same way about Anomaly.

"So you approached the FBI for a deal," Champ sneered, still pinning Vince with laser eyes. "Do I even want to know how the fuck you got involved in illegal money movement in the first place?"

I'd known he wouldn't let that part of the story slide. Champ would hate to know he'd almost married a criminal.

Buck was the one who answered. "Vince here skimmed a little off the top of a couple projects he was assigned to in the Middle East." He wiggled his bushy eyebrows and belched lightly. "Ain't that right, Vincey boy?"

Vince's cheeks flamed, and his jaw worked, but he neither confirmed nor denied.

"How the hell do *you* know?" Champ asked, turning his stare on Buck.

"I had a lot of downtime in the compound in Venezuela before you two arrived. And I'm a good listener." He shrugged. "I learned a lot. And I wrote it all down and saved it in my Horn."

Kev and I exchanged a glance. We had not seen any notes on the smuggled Horn.

Laurel's lip curled up with a knowing smirk. "Not *that* Horn," she said. "His personal Horn."

I shook my head. Buck Nutter had smuggled *two* Horns out of Venezuela on the hijacked flight from hell? Not only the sparkly peach first-gen one but his everyday one too? How? *Why?*

"Two Horns are always better than one, am I right, boys?" Buck pronounced solemnly like he could read my thoughts.

He went on to explain that when he'd disappeared from the Thicket, he'd headed for Hawaii—hence the shirt. Not fully understanding how government alphabet agencies worked, Buck had approached a local FBI field office to inform them that he had information about two rogue DEA agents, along with a list of suspected American citizens associated with the Cartel de la Luna.

"And that's how I got myself put into protective custody in Hawaii," Buck said with satisfaction.

No wonder we hadn't been able to find the man if the FBI had been blocking our attempts.

Champ's gears were turning, and if he was anything like me, he was having a hard time giving Buck credit for anything productive or good. "Why steal the sparkle-Horn if you already had the data on your own Horn?"

Buck shrugged. "I knew the cartel would come looking for me, and I wasn't sure who to trust. I figured if I left the valuable one behind with a little stolen data on it, the cartel folks'd think that was all there was."

Laurel gave him an approving smile. "When in reality, he had much, much more."

Buck grinned. "Heap loads."

Laurel's smile disappeared, and she was all business once more. "We have enough to take down Linus right now, but Linus is small potatoes. We want Gustavo Santiago. In addition to crippling the drug supply he's flooding into the United States, we need to know if he has other assets in the US government."

Riggs was keyed up, the way he got when he was building up a head of steam. "Gustavo is a ghost. He owns even more government assets in Venezuela than he does in the United States, and he lives in a guarded compound—"

Vince shook his head. "Except when he leaves the compound under the care of his brother and comes to the

United States for medical treatment… plus a little business on the side. He's meeting with Linus here in Vegas."

Laurel corrected him. "Not *in* Vegas. He's not stupid enough to risk coming into the city with CCTV everywhere. In the past, they've met in remote desert locations. He'll message Linus the GPS coordinates shortly before the meeting."

It was all starting to come together now. Kev must have realized it at the same time I did because he asked the question. "So you want to get the data off Anomaly—I mean, *Linus's*—Horn to figure out where and when they're meeting so you can arrest Gustavo?"

Laurel nodded. "That's the goal. Unfortunately for us, Linus's record is spotless. Not so much as a parking ticket. In fact, he has several commendations for his excellent work on behalf of the DEA. No judge is gonna sign off on a warrant to obtain his Horn on the basis of a cartel-informant testimony, even if he was a DEA agent." She tilted her head to indicate Vince. "We were hoping Linus would trust Vince enough to give him access to his Horn, but Linus has made it pretty clear that Vince is a loose end he'd prefer to tie up. So if you people have a plan…" She lifted one meticulously groomed eyebrow. "Now would be the time to share it."

No one said a word. We all stood around the room exchanging glances, letting the situation sink in.

Then Kev's body tensed, and he dragged in a huge breath. I knew what he was going to do before he even opened his mouth, and I wished like hell I could stop him, but the words were out before I could move a muscle.

"I can get his Horn."

19

KEV

I deliberately didn't look at Hux. I knew he'd be mad and worried. Instead, I looked at Champ. "I know I can do this. I have a relationship with Ad—*Linus*, and he thinks I'm naive enough to go along with him."

Hux's body thrummed with tension, so much that it vibrated the air between us and coiled all my own muscles in response. I knew Hux was going to freak out, especially coming on the heels of my last interaction with Linus, but at the same time, I wasn't going to sit by when I was the team member best placed for this particular op.

"You know it's true," I added.

Thankfully, Hux kept his mouth shut. Meanwhile, Laurel's eyes glittered like a sacrificial lamb had just dropped into her lap... because I had.

Champ rubbed his chin thoughtfully. "Let me think about this."

"There's nothing to think about," Laurel scoffed. "The kid has an in, so we use him."

Hux's muscles had turned to steel, and anger radiated off him in waves. "This *kid* is a brilliant programmer who's not trained for this shit," he snapped. "And he doesn't work for you—"

"No," Champ said firmly. "He works for *me*."

"And he makes decisions for himself," I added in a much softer tone.

Champ nodded. He exchanged a look with Hux, then Riggs before turning back to Laurel. "What's the risk assessment entail? What do we know about this Linus guy?"

Laurel winced and shot me a look that was almost guilty. "Nothing good. Let's just say that if Vince had carried out the hit on you the way Linus wanted... it wouldn't have been the first murder he was involved in."

Oh. Good. *Great.*

Hux pushed himself back from the table so quickly his chair toppled over. "I need... *fuck*." He stalked toward the bedroom and slammed the door behind him.

Riggs ran a hand over his face. "Kev, have you really thought this through? What you're risking for yourself... and what you're asking *him* to risk?" If there was any doubt in my mind whether Carter had shared his suspicions about me and Hux with Riggs, that confirmed it.

I looked at the closed door over Riggs's shoulder. The part of me that still wanted to protect myself felt like I should say something self-deprecating about how Hux and I were new, about how Hux's reaction said more about his protective streak than about his feelings for me. But it felt wrong to deny or minimize what had grown between Hux and me in such a short time.

While the conversation at the table turned to discussion of Linus's service record and the crimes they suspected him of, I stood up and walked toward the bedroom. The door wasn't locked, so I entered without knocking, then leaned back against it, closing out the rest of the world for a moment.

The bedsheets were still crumpled from where Hux and I had lain on them earlier—shit, was it just a few hours ago?—expecting to have the entire suite to ourselves all night, and now here we were, plotting to take down my supposed online boyfriend, who was actually a corrupt DEA agent acting on behalf of a crime lord.

Hux stood in front of the large picture window, his muscular frame a dark shape that blocked out the night sky and the colorful lights of the Strip beyond.

"Hux?" I said softly, stepping toward him cautiously.

He spun from the window and met me halfway, dropping to his knees before me in front of the bed and grabbing my hand in his. "I'm sorry. I know how hard this is on you, and I don't want to make it harder. I just… I'm sorry."

My knees suddenly felt like jelly, and I sank down onto the bed with a bounce.

I knew what he meant. He was sorry I was still involved in this mess. Sorry that someone I'd considered a friend—or maybe more—had betrayed me. Maybe even sorry that he'd freaked out.

I was sorry too. Sorry that I was so fucking naive that I hadn't seen Anomaly for a smarmy asshole when he'd done a really shitty job of hiding it. Sorry I couldn't find a genuine friend to save my life, since even Smitty had peaced out of my life at the first opportunity. Sorry I'd been taken in by someone with an agenda. Sorry that I couldn't sit this op out, even though it would cost both of us.

Hux laid his head on my lap. "You don't have to do this. I don't want you to do this."

"Hush." I ran my fingers through Hux's crazy hair. "I'm going to do it. You know that."

"You're going to have to… to… *be* with him," he said

brokenly, speaking aloud what we both already knew. The only way I'd be able to get Linus away from his Horn would require me to change my mind and tell him I was ready to spend the night with him. My "in" with Anomaly was going to have to be a seduction.

I remembered sitting with Hux, watching Champ kiss Vince—watching *Quinn* watch Champ kiss Vince—and telling him firmly that I was too possessive to watch my boyfriend kiss someone else. Now here I was, putting Hux in that same position, but with an added twist of awful. Linus was a murderer who'd probably be expecting far more than a single close-mouthed kiss.

I blew out a breath. "But then it will be over. Then we can move on. You and me, Hux."

He lifted his head, and his eyes glowed, not just with the reflected light from outside but with all the things he felt for me. Affection and fear. Tenderness and concern.

Love.

The truth of it was so potent it nearly stole the breath from my lungs. Hux loved me. *Loved* me. Maybe as much as I loved him.

I bit back a whimper. The need to tell him, to say the words, was nearly painful. But a niggle in my gut, or maybe the last thin layer of self-protection I held stubbornly around my heart, told me this was not the time.

I wanted that to come later, when the danger was past. I wanted him to look at me—plain old Kev Rogers, complete with black glasses and endless awkwardness—and make his declaration so I'd never have to wonder whether he'd spoken too quickly in the heat of the moment.

Hux's gaze searched my face, and then he nodded. "You and me. I like that." He pressed a lingering kiss to each of my palms before pulling back.

He got to his feet, ran a hand through his hair, and

inhaled sharply. "Okay. So we're doing this. I'm gonna be with you every step of the way, in your ear and on the button cam—"

I shook my head. I understood what he was saying, the overwhelming protectiveness that made him say it, but just the thought of that made me want to puke. "No way. I'm not wearing standard surveillance gear with a federal agent who may have been trained on the same stuff. Not to mention..." God, I really hated that I had to bring this up. "Button cams only work when you're wearing buttons, and earwigs only work when someone's not gonna be up close and personal with your, um... ear."

Hux looked close to vomiting. I was really, seriously hoping that I could accomplish this without losing a stitch of clothing or getting anywhere near Anomaly, but I had to be ready, and Hux knew it.

"Maybe you guys can get in beforehand and set some bugs or cameras? Or can you, like, snake things in through the vents?" I forced myself to shut up before I made it even more apparent that I didn't know the difference between movie tech and real-life tech when it came to spy gear, because that only highlighted the other truth we both knew—I wasn't trained for this.

My mouth stretched in a rictus grin. "Gonna be fine."

He stared at me for a prolonged moment before leaning down to kiss me. It was gentle and slow, sweet and somehow heartbreaking. Like a just-in-case goodbye or a heartfelt apology.

I broke it off with a small smile when Hux would have deepened it. I didn't have the emotional energy for a sad goodbye. Not when it was taking everything I had to be a strong, brave Champion Security team member who had his shit together.

"Let's go," I said, standing up. "Let's do this."

We spent the next several hours coming up with a plan. It was clear from the way they contributed that Laurel, Vince, and Buck were on our side. Their eagerness to bring the perpetrators of this scheme down was obvious in their willingness to stay and hash out even the most boring details.

Through the night, we learned more about how this clusterfuck had come to be. About how Buck had been leery of trusting Champ since he worked for HOG Corporate, the company Buck claimed had "stolen" his life's work and then kicked him out. About how Vince's anger and spite over Champ's insistence on moving to "the backwoods" and the ensuing breakup had led him to start skimming money in the first place, leading to his involvement with the cartel, but that it wasn't until Linus Dixon had ratted out an associate who'd ended up very dead at the feet of Gustavo Santiago that Vince had agreed to do what he did to Quinn that day at the farmhouse last month.

"I'm sorry," Vince told Champ in a rough voice. "I didn't know what he meant to you."

As though that could be an excuse for hurting someone.

"I don't forgive you," Champ growled back. "And I never will."

The tension between the two of them wasn't the only tension in the room.

Riggs carried a massive grudge against Buck Nutter for disappearing after they'd saved him in Venezuela, which came to a head after Buck made the mistake of asking Riggs about "that cute doc fella you were so chummy with."

The looks Riggs shot him across the table made the entire room feel like it might implode at any minute.

"Don't talk about him. Don't even think about him. Had you come to us for help, we could have avoided all this shit," Riggs said, eyes flashing. "Heck, if you hadn't gone around trying to sell your... your *seed*—" He darted a look at Champ, whose jaw tightened at the pun. "You wouldn't have gotten kidnapped, and we wouldn't have gotten involved."

Buck finally threw up his hands. "That's bull puckey, and you know it. Your mission's always been to save your client, and your client's been profiting off these transactions for the better part of a year. Oh, poor Jacob Horn wants to avoid a public relations scandal. *Wah wah wah.* Maybe he shouldn'ta promised me we'd be partners, then cut me outta the game while takin' nary a step to prevent his ass from hangin' in the wind. Meanwhile, here's me, put right in the dragon's mouth when I'm the one who single-handedly developed the danged game in the first place."

I glanced at him, wondering if I should let that falsehood stand. "Single-handedly? Huh. That's not entirely accurate, is it?"

Buck's face flushed as he glared at me. "You don't know jack."

"No, but I do know Darlene Louderbach. She and I go way back. Back to the days of Frogs and Guardians, in fact."

The blood drained from Buck's face. "You keep your damned mouth shut."

I shrugged. The bloom was a little off the rose now that I could see Buck's true cowardice in this situation. "Know what would go a far distance toward keeping my mouth shut? A matching set of limited-edition Candy Cane Horns for me and my... Huxley," I concluded with only a minor stutter.

Hux snorted and sputtered, just having taken a sip from his water bottle. Champ grinned outright, and Riggs flashed me an air fist bump.

Laurel ended a call and dropped her cell on the table

with a clatter. "As soon as we have actionable information from Linus's Horn, I've got a local federal judge ready to sign a warrant. But," she warned me, "you'll have to keep him there until we can get the right paperwork to justify the arrest."

I let out a shaky breath and nodded. "I'll do my best." *And hope I don't have to actually sleep with the guy.*

When the planning was finally done, Champ refused to let Buck or Vince leave the suite. While Laurel returned to her own room to confer with her support team before returning in the morning to run op support from the suite with the rest of the incoming Champion Security team, the rest of us tried to get some sleep.

This was easier said than done.

Hux and I were forced to share our room with Vince, who bunked in a nest of blankets on the floor but at least remained quiet. Meanwhile, Champ and Riggs had to share their bedroom with Buck, who talked incessantly—and loud enough to wake the dead—until dawn.

If I hadn't spent the night in Hux's tight hold, I might have fractured from the stress during those sleepless hours I spent watching the outside lights spill across the ceiling. Usually planning helped put me at ease, but after learning more about Linus Dixon, I was well and truly terrified. Adam had never existed, and the man I'd thought I'd known was actually a cold-blooded murderer and the right-hand man of one of the most dangerous drug lords in South America.

I tried not to think about what the morning would bring but what would happen after that. Hux and me, together for good. Rodrigo having the run of the mansion. Our family safe at last.

I knew there were awkward conversations to come—like, would Hux want to move in with me? Would I be willing to share my lair for the long haul? Was I gonna let him ride my motorcycles? Would he continue to raid my jam cellar with impunity whenever I pissed him off? —but I was no stranger to awkward. And while I thought the answers would be yes, probably, maybe, and unfortunately, I was willing to give him a say in the matters.

As long as we were together, the rest would sort itself out.

The next morning, I put on my game face and made my way to the conference center for the information session. Late the night before, I'd messaged Adam on my Horn to tell him I was feeling much better and hoped we could sit together at the session.

When I saw him sitting among the other gamers, my stomach almost erupted. My phone buzzed in my pocket with a message from Hux.

Hux: *You got this. Laurel's agents are close and you have your panic button.*

Me: *I'm fine. Take a breath.*

Adam stood and waved me over with a big smile on his face. "There you are. I'm glad you're feeling better."

When I took the seat next to his, I leaned my shoulder against his. "Sorry again about last night. I feel like an idiot."

He chuckled. "It's okay. Nerves and travel can throw your body out of whack."

"Thank you for being so understanding." I swallowed and lowered my voice to barely a whisper. "I've never… done it with anyone, you know? And… I was nervous."

Adam's eyes flared like I'd hoped. Cartel villain or not, it was hard for a man to resist the siren song of a virgin. "Oh, sweetheart," he murmured, reaching over to take my hand in his. "We can take it slow, okay?"

I nodded. "Can we... I mean... I'd like to get to know you better. Maybe later tonight, or...?"

He pursed his lips in thought. "There's actually some more security stuff I wanted to ask you about for my article. I was hoping you could bring your laptop to my room so we could work together on it. Maybe we could skip this afternoon's practice session and..."

"I'd like that," I blurted. The sooner we could get this over with, the better. "Yes."

He grinned like the Cheshire cat. "Excellent."

If the information session had anything of value in it, I didn't notice. None of the words penetrated my gut-clenching fear. Knowing that Hux and Champ were around somewhere keeping an eye on things meant I was less afraid of Linus, at least for the moment. But I was very afraid that I wouldn't be able to stay in character as sweet, naive Kev, and Linus would realize something was amiss. The stakes were high for Champion Security, for the FBI, for my family, and for the future I wanted to build with Hux, and I desperately didn't want to fail.

"So, lunch in my room, sweetness?" Linus said once the session ended.

"I, um... think I need to go back to my room to take another shower," I admitted, trying to look a little embarrassed. "And... stuff like that."

He shot me a knowing look. "Sounds good." After giving me his room number, he leaned in and pressed a kiss to my cheek. I could almost feel the cloying scent of his cologne—something that might have been incredibly expensive but smelled exactly like the body spray I'd used as a teenager—attaching itself to the fibers of my shirt.

Suddenly, the shower wasn't just an excuse.

"I'll be waiting," Linus promised, smoothing a fingertip over my cheek. It was a gesture Hux had done to me several times—a claiming, affectionate gesture—and the overwhelming wrongness of having someone else touch me that way made my skin crawl.

How the fuck was I going to endure him touching me intimately?

I imagined that if Hux were anywhere in sight of this, he was going to go nuclear, which would make all my worry a moot point.

"Later!" I mumbled, and then I rushed out the door and down the wide hallway to the hotel lobby, not looking around me for familiar faces even though I wanted to see one desperately.

When I opened the door to the suite, someone grabbed me and yanked me into the room before covering my mouth with their... mouth?

My hammering heart slowed to its Hux-pace as the familiar taste and feel of him sank in.

"And here you thought they weren't getting along, Riggsy," Champ teased.

"Trust Huxley to go from 'I want to punch his face' to 'I want to eat his face' without pausing anywhere in between." Riggs's eye roll was audible, but he didn't sound unhappy either.

Hux pulled away but didn't go far. His arms remained banded around me. "You good?"

I nodded, and it wasn't a lie. Being with Hux grounded me, calmed me. Reminded me why I was doing what I was doing.

"All set for this afternoon. He's waiting for me to..." I wasn't going to mention showering or douching to put any of those images in Hux's head. I'd learned that lesson last night. "Change."

Hux knew what I wasn't saying. Anger simmered behind his eyes, but he kept his mouth closed. Instead, he led me to a chair at the table, where tons of laptops were already set up and unfamiliar agents were busy at work. One of the new agents walked me through their successful attempt to place mics and cameras in Linus's room while we were at the morning information session.

"We got the room number from Vince and bribed a member of the housekeeping staff to let us in. It's not legal, though," she explained, "so nothing captured will be admissible in court. It's only for your protection."

I nodded as they explained that if I was willing to wear a wire, that recording *would* be admissible in court. "All it takes in Nevada is for one participant in the conversation to consent to a recording, and that's you," Laurel explained.

I glanced at Champ. There was no reason to look at Hux when I knew he was practically jumping out of his skin in an effort not to derail this mission.

"I'm leery of that. I didn't want to be on comms or to wear a button cam because Linus might… spot those things. But I also want to get the best possible evidence to put him away. Either way, I don't want to put myself in more danger than necessary." Hux would kill me if I did. "What do you suggest?"

Champ shared my businesslike tone. "We assume he has a handgun in his room, but we also know he's not going to corner himself for no reason. Shooting you—no matter what goes down between you—would make him a sitting duck. He's miles away from a clean exit."

Hux made a wounded noise that Champ ignored when he continued. "The most dangerous scenario would be him discovering you're working with the feds. In that case, he would know he's most likely surrounded. I think you can safely carry a hidden recording device. If things between you turn bad, we can be in there in moments."

The agent added, "The housekeeping lady gave me a key."

Champ's eyes flicked to Hux before landing back on me. "A wire in your clothes won't work in case he… or you…"

"Right," I said softly.

Champ cleared his throat. "So anyway, we have one that looks like a USB key. Since he wants you to bring your laptop, it won't be a problem. Worst-case scenario, let him think the Horn data is on it."

As soon as Champ had implied I might be undressing in that room, Hux shoved his chair back and strode out of the main room and into the bedroom.

I glanced at Champ, who'd closed his eyes and clamped his lips shut in annoyance. "Motherfucker," he muttered under his breath. "Is my team cursed to always fall in love during a goddamned op? Why? And why me?"

When I stood up to follow Hux, Riggs shook his head at me. "Give him a minute. Let him get his head back in the game. Otherwise, he's going to say a few things you'll both regret."

"And fuck up our op," Champ added.

The agents walked me through the recording device and gave me a few minutes to clean up my laptop and run a script to put my important files in the cloud so Linus wouldn't have access to them.

When I was finally ready and Anomaly451 was lighting up my device with messages asking where I was, I ignored Riggs's headshake, entered the bedroom, and closed the door. Hux stopped pacing the carpet in front of the bed as soon as he spotted me.

"Hey. I'm about to head out, and I wanted to say—"

"I love you," Hux blurted, looking red-eyed and wild, like he'd been on the run from an escaped horde of angry bees. "And… you're going to do great! I just know it!"

I'd never seen him this way. He looked like he was barely holding on, like he was one silken thread away from snapping clean in half.

"Jasper? What the —"

He grabbed me and pulled me in, not even for a kiss but a full-body bear hug. He squeezed the breath out of me and murmured something against my collarbone too softly for me to hear. It sounded like he was making deals with himself or God.

I was stunned by his admission but freaked-out by his delivery. I'd expected him to be protective, to be worried, but this seemed over-the-top. I wished I could ask about it, to find out what was making him lose control so badly… but we were out of time.

"I'm going to be fine," I said into his hair, trying to reassure him. "You'll be listening in. The agents have a key."

He pulled back with a manic grin. "Yeah! Absolutely. Gonna be fine. You got this."

Now his anxiety was infecting me, which was the last thing I needed. "Stop acting weird," I snapped. "This is an op. You've been on a million of them, and you've worked comms on a million more. Let me do this without worrying about you worrying. Okay?"

He nodded and straightened his face. "Yes. Absolutely."

My teeth tightened as I pushed him away from me. "Stop saying absolutely."

I moved back out into the big room before Hux could initiate anything that smacked of goodbye. I didn't want another hug or a kiss, and I was steaming mad that he'd picked that moment to drop the L-word.

Instead of waiting for any final information, I grabbed my phone and laptop and bolted out of the suite. The USB voice recorder was already in my pocket, so I reached inside to flick it on.

I stalked down the hall toward the elevator and jabbed the button angrily. My stomach was still a bit queasy with anxiety, but the annoyance from the interaction with Hux was enough to temper it and calm my breathing.

The man couldn't tell me that I was capable and brilliant one minute and then lose his shit like I was a precious, fragile vase one misbehaving teenager away from crashing into a million pieces on the ground the next. It made me feel like I couldn't tell him about my fears or moments of weakness without him taking them on.

I didn't need a partner who'd coddle me, who'd keep me in my safe little lair forever, hiding from the world. I needed one who'd help me step out into the light and face whatever challenges life threw at me—and all the anxieties and awkwardness they brought—by my side.

Maybe I wasn't trained by Champion Security, maybe I wasn't a world-renowned, life-saving doctor like everyone in my family, but I was trained in self-defense, and no one knew their way around a Horn device better than I did.

I could get this data. And I would.

As the elevator doors opened, my Horn buzzed with a message.

Anomaly451: *Babe?*

I gritted my teeth and typed a response.

HogDocKev: *On my way.*

I slipped it back into my pocket and stepped into the elevator. The faint jazzy instrumental version of *The Girl from Ipanema* seemed at odds with the seriousness of the situation. When I exited the elevator two floors below, my phone buzzed.

Hux: *I'm sorry.*

Hux: *I really do love you.*

I couldn't not reply. Not when I loved him too. I stood outside the elevator and pecked out a message.

Me: *You have shitty timing. That must be why you can't ever harvest a damned greenberry before it gets stolen.*

The three dots danced for a few long moments.

Hux: *That was a low blow.*

Me: *Kinda busy right now, baby.*

Hux: *I know. Have fun storming the castle, Pip.*

I grinned and felt the familiar affection I always felt when Hux used that phrase.

I knocked on the door to Linus Dixon's room. Just as he was opening the door, my entire world paused, came crashing down.

Hux wasn't the one who used that phrase.

SmittyKitty was.

20

HUX

I realized what I'd done the minute my finger hit the Send key. The blood drained from my head so fast I felt like I was going to tip over.

I could only hope that Kev was too nervous to notice my fatal error.

"Fuck," I breathed, quickly typing another message.

Me: *I can explain.*

It was too late. Kev's voice came over the surveillance speakers. "Hi. Sorry I'm late."

"Not late, precious," Linus purred. "Right on time."

Listening to a man sweet-talk my Kevin would have been excruciating under any circumstances, but this was nearly intolerable. I stood up and turned toward the window, trying to ignore what was happening floors below me, only to turn again and stomp toward the door, ready to pull the plug on the whole mission and tear Kev away from Linus bodily.

"Sit your ass down, Marine," Champ snapped at me.

I glared at him but stomped back to Riggs and took a seat beside him anyway. I forced myself to look at the camera feed on the monitor and told myself to be a fucking professional.

Still, when Linus gave Kev a hug, I closed my eyes.

The fear I'd felt a few minutes ago when Kev and I were in the bedroom hadn't subsided. If anything, it had intensified with every passing second. I'd never known pure panic like this in my entire life. Not when my friends had been kidnapped, not when their partners had been threatened, not when I'd had a gun held to my head one time long ago by a Russian guy who'd turned out to be double-crossing us. Always, *always* I'd held myself a little bit remote. Aloof. Studying the data, making the calls. Compartmentalizing and following the training I kept preaching to Kev about.

But it turned out training meant fuck-all when the one person you'd finally let yourself love wholly and completely was walking his ass into a murderer's hotel room… and compartmentalizing was fucking impossible when you knew that *you* and your relationship were part of the reason your lover was putting himself on the line.

Having faith in Kev wasn't the problem—I believed in him completely, and he'd proven himself time and time again, despite his fear. But fucked-up shit happened on ops all the time, and loving Kev meant that I couldn't distance myself from life. Love had cracked me open, and now I was vulnerable.

How the fuck did people in love manage to go through life feeling so *powerless*? How could they stand it?

"So glad you're here. I thought maybe you'd run into another friend downstairs and changed your mind," Linus continued.

"No, I… I was looking forward to having some time alone with you. I'm not all that great in big crowds."

When I didn't hear any other conversation, I squinted

one eye open to see Linus pulling Kev over to a small desk in the room and sitting him in the chair.

"First, I was hoping you could help me with the data security issue we talked about," Linus said. "It'll give us a chance to get to know each other better. Plus…" He grimaced ruefully. "Well, the deadline for my article is this weekend, and I'm starting to panic. You started explaining encryption, but then we were interrupted. If you were going to secure critical information, how would you do it?"

Kev shrugged. "I'd put copies on multiple hard drives and stow them in various safe locations. Safe-deposit box at the bank, hidden safe in the house… you know. That kind of thing. You definitely don't want them connected to the internet."

A muscle in Linus's jaw tightened. "But what if you… needed to work with the data? And you couldn't afford to have it out of your sight?"

The next part had been rehearsed several times the night before. I held my breath.

Kev pretended to consider it. "Oh… well, for example, there's some really important data I'm working on for a friend of mine. I have it saved on my laptop, but I use 256-bit encryption. If you're not logged in as me on the machine, it would take forever to hack it."

Linus fell for it. His eyes lit up. "Can you show me?"

Kev bit his bottom lip and looked away nervously. "I'm not really supposed to let anyone see it. I could get in a lot of trouble."

Linus moved behind Kev and rubbed his shoulders, leaning forward to speak next to his ear. "But this is me. I'm not just anyone, am I? I'm your boyfriend." He paused coyly. "Unless you've changed your mind again. Decided to pursue things with that other guy you're seeing."

Kev's nostrils flared. I recognized the sign of his annoyance, and I knew this time it wasn't aimed at Linus. "I was seeing someone else. But it turns out he was lying to me the whole time about who he was."

My throat closed up, and my fingernails dug into my palms. So much for hoping he hadn't noticed my slip.

Kev was brilliant. Why did I keep forgetting that?

"Oh, no! You deserve better than that, sweetness," Linus murmured, getting closer to Kev again to look at the laptop over Kev's shoulder.

Kev shrugged. "I'm used to it. It's one of the reasons I was so happy when you reached out to befriend me in the game. I have a hard time trusting people. I feel like a lot of people only approach me to use me."

I felt the worried glances of Champ and the others zinging back and forth. This was *not* something we'd rehearsed, and it cut too close to the truth of Kev and Linus. *Dangerously* close.

And it was all thanks to *me*... the guy who'd been too worried about fucking over the op to tell Kev the truth and was now about to fuck over the op because I hadn't.

Linus froze for a beat before speaking. "Not true. How could you think that?"

"Oh, I don't mean you." Kev wrinkled his nose as if wondering how Linus could imagine such a thing. "Of course not. I just mean players in the game who see my advanced level and want to play with me to earn better access in the game. You're not like that. You're already a great player. In fact, do you... do you want to play something together now? It might be a fun kind of way to... I dunno. Break the ice?" Kev let out an embarrassed laugh. "Sorry. Ignore me. I just wanted an excuse to see your Horn. Sometimes I think about you lying in bed playing with it, and I thought..." He caught his full lower lip between his teeth and looked up at Linus from under his lashes. "…now that we're here together…"

"Fucking fuck," I croaked.

Champ tried to hide his smirk and failed. "I changed my mind. I love this game. The puns are delightful."

Linus moved around Kev to rest his ass on the edge of the desk next to Kev's laptop. "Why don't we trade for a few minutes? Let me poke around in your security setup while I let you see my Horn?"

Laurel let out a relieved breath and spoke through her comms microphone. "Distraction team, be ready."

Kev seemed to hesitate again, as if truly unsure whether or not he should let Linus see any of the Horn data. From what everyone had decided last night, there was no reason not to load the stolen Horn data onto the laptop. According to Buck, Linus was already well aware of the names on the list and who they represented.

"I'll show you the security I set up, but please try not to look at the data…" Kev said. "Or I could get in big trouble."

Linus gestured for Kev to give him the chair, but Kev held out his palm and made a flirty request for the Horn first. Once Linus handed it over, Kev stood up, but Linus didn't move aside right away. Instead, he made Kev, who was blushing madly, brush past him chest-to-chest before taking his seat, and laughed softly at the way Kev scurried toward the bed.

I made a silent vow that I was going to break every one of Linus's tiny fingers so the man would never be able to play with his Horn again.

Kev ducked his head shyly and took a spot on the bed where the light was dim and Linus would be less likely to see what he was doing.

"I can't believe you have a Silver Cloven Horn!" Kev

said excitedly. "You never said. So sexy! I sort of imagined you with one that's smoky black. Or maybe deep red. But this is even better. I mean, at least it's not green or blue!" Kev's laughter sounded forced to anyone who knew him, but Linus didn't. "I always say you can't trust a man with a green Horn. They'll turn on you every time."

Riggs glanced at my green Horn, which I'd left lying on the table, and then at me. He didn't ask for an explanation, and I didn't offer any.

Linus seemed to be ignoring Kev entirely, which was probably Kev's goal with his relentless chatter. He was turning on his awkwardness full blast and expecting it to repel the asshole at the desk, like it had so many people. I wanted to clap for him. I wanted to cry for him.

I wanted him to hurry the fuck up.

"C'mon, c'mon," I murmured.

Kev snuck a Wi-Fi-enabled transfer dongle out of his pocket and slipped it into the side of the Horn before tapping away at the Horn as if pretending to play it. "So, were you still interested in being allies in the tournament? Now that we completed the duchess quest and you leveled up, I don't see any reason why we can't! Oh, but remind me that I need to transfer you an Apple Butter Booster before the games start tomorrow. My boyfriend deserves *allll* the boosters. I'm a very loyal sort of person that way," he chirped happily. "Meanwhile, those who cross me will find their homesteads—and I mean any and all of their home-steads—pillaged entirely, their villagers relocated, and their fields salted. If they think burning a kelp forest was bad, they should buckle their tattooed asses up and fucking tremble, because they have no idea how truly vicious I can be when I'm motivated." He gave a light little laugh that might have suggested he was joking.

He wasn't.

The suite went silent, and when I glanced up from the monitor, I saw multiple pairs of eyes watching me warily. Even Laurel gave me a sympathetic grimace.

"Huxley," Champ asked conversationally. "What the fuck did you do?"

"Could we focus on the op, please?" I demanded. "A man's *life* is on the line here, people."

The female agent in front of me perked up, drawing everyone's attention. "Data incoming."

Laurel and two other agents raced over to get a better view. Normally, the data would be 100 percent my wheelhouse, but at that moment, I couldn't move my eyes away from the source of the danger... and the most precious person in my life, who was sitting right behind him.

Linus was typing quickly, probably searching Kev's computer to see if there was any other Horn-related data on it. He was quickly disappointed.

"How much data have you had to secure on this machine?" he asked over his shoulder. "Any other, ah... examples you could show me for my article?"

"Nope. Just that list of usernames. That's all they gave me so far," Kev said without thinking, not realizing his answer took away Linus's need to continue focusing on the laptop.

"*Glk!*" I said in Laurel's direction. I'd meant to say something like, "Get someone in there, he's looking," but it came out as a choked cry.

She was already in action, grabbing her radio. "Go!" she told the distraction team. Immediately, a strong knocking could be heard on Linus's door.

Kev still had the transfer dongle in the device. Thankfully, Linus stood up while keeping his attention focused on the door and didn't notice. Unfortunately, before he moved away from the desk, he took a weapon from the drawer.

"Fuck," Champ said. "We need to go in."

Laurel shook her head. "No warrant yet. Stand down."

"Tough shit," Champ barked. "We got the data. That's my guy in there, and I'm not gonna wait around while an armed suspect decides whether to—"

"Wait, look!" I cried, pointing at the monitor. "He's signaling us."

Kev kept his chin pointed down at the game, trying to pretend he hadn't spotted Linus's gun. And against his thigh, where Linus wouldn't notice, my brave, intelligent man held out his hand with all five fingers splayed in a "wait" gesture.

"Give Kev a chance," I told Champ roughly. "Trust him. He hasn't said our code word. He's asking us to hold off. He… he wants to do this."

More than that, I thought he *needed* to do this. To have this chance to prove something to himself. After all I'd taken from him over the past few months—fuck, all that I'd taken from him *today*—I wouldn't let him lose one more thing if I could help it, even if my worry for him was tearing my heart to ribbons.

And, I supposed, *this* was how people in love managed to live their lives, despite the fear and vulnerability. Because holding back or caging their beloved, even when trying to protect them, would smother them. And you couldn't do that to someone you truly loved.

"Who is it?" Linus demanded through the door.

"Bobby! Come out with usss! We have ticketsss to the shhhow!" a slurring voice called from the hallway. "Kelly s-said to come get you. Come on!"

Kev kept his eyes on his screen and counted us down. Four fingers, then three, then two, and just as the computer in front of me beeped to signal the completed transfer, Kev closed his hand into a fist.

"Got it!" the agent at the table called excitedly. "Emailing it to the judge. Procuring the warrant."

Kev quickly whipped the dongle back into his pocket and laid the Horn next to him on the bed so it didn't even look like he was all that interested in it. He stood and took a step toward the door while Linus shifted his body to hide his weapon. "We should tell them they have the wrong room."

Linus looked annoyed. "No Bobby here!"

"Yo, Bobbyyyyyyy!" another drunken voice called again, again accompanied by knocking so loud the door vibrated in its frame.

Kev laughed nervously. "Maybe open it up so they can see we're not Bobby and go away? I don't know about you, but it's kinda killing my romantic vibe."

I forced myself to take a deep breath. It was almost over. We had the data, and any second, Linus would open the door. Kev would make an excuse and escape to safety… which was when my other mission would begin. The one where I explained to Kev why I'd lied to him, and begged him not to hate me.

All around me in the suite, agents bustled here and there, talking to the judge, to the person waiting at the judge's office, to the agents in the hallway outside of Linus's room.

Meanwhile, Laurel's eyes ate up the data on the agent's screen. "There. Location coordinates. That's Gustavo's user-name. *Yesss*. We have the location of the meeting, people!"

I didn't care about any of it. My eyes never left the screen, tracking Kev's gorgeous face… and the weapon in Linus's hand. Which was why I was the first person to notice when Linus turned away from the door and faced Kev instead.

Gone was the smarmy, seductive expression he'd worn

when he was impersonating a man in love. Instead, his eyes were hard and his jaw set.

"Tell me what Champ knows, Kevin."

"Oh, fuck," I breathed.

It took a minute for the people in the suite around me to realize what was happening.

"What?" Kev squeaked. "Who?"

"No," I said, shoving back from the table. "He's been made. I think Linus knows we're onto him."

"Christ," Champ said. To Laurel, he added, "Get your people in there *now*." He grabbed two earwigs from the table and thrust one into my hand. "Let's go."

We were both armed, but the FBI SAIC had threatened us to within an inch of our lives not to draw down unless mortally threatened.

I wasn't sure about Champ, but I felt mortally threatened. My heart was beating out of my chest.

"Stay on surveillance and relay intel," Champ barked at Riggs. "Hux! With me."

Later, I would remember to be grateful to Champ for what he'd done in that moment. It wasn't like him to misassign roles, and by rights, it should have been Riggs who went in with guns blazing while I stayed behind with the techs and data. But ever since Champ had fallen for Quinn Taffet, the wedding planner who'd gotten under his skin and kept him up at night, he'd been a changed man.

One who knew I wasn't staying in that suite for anything.

We raced to the end of the hallway and threw ourselves down the stairs. All the while, Riggs kept a running stream of chatter in our ears. "Warrant here in less than five minutes. Try to wait."

"What's he doing now?" I begged, hoping that Linus had put his gun away. Christ, I'd watch a video of them kissing a billion times on repeat if it meant Kev would be safe and whole and—

"Impressing the hell out of us," Riggs replied before putting his mic up to the surveillance speakers.

Kev's voice sounded terrified, but there was something underneath it that gave me pause. I'd heard Kev scared, and that wasn't what I was hearing now.

That sounded like Kev when he was *enraged* and trying to cover it up.

"Adam…" Kev sniffed. "I… how did you know? I'm s-so scared. I think they're… I think they're into something bad. I think they have information about something impor-tant and I'm somehow caught up in it. I'm innocent, I swear. All I did was protect the data!"

Champ keyed his mic. "Where's the weapon?" he asked in a low voice as we neared a couple in the hallway on Linus's floor. I could see the distraction agents further down the hallway, still acting drunk and silly outside of Linus's room.

"At his side."

Sweat beaded on my forehead and lower back. "Ten bucks said the sorority didn't teach weapon neutralization," I muttered.

Champ looked at me like maybe I'd lost my mind. "We going in?"

My heart screamed yes, but my brain knew better. "Not… not yet. Let him finish this. Get everything on a recording. *Then* we go."

Champ nodded once as we approached the agents in the hallway and stood waiting.

"Warrant in elevator," Laurel said over comms.

Riggs's voice took over. "Weapon down for now. He set it on a table and is approaching Kev."

"Oh, my poor baby," Linus's voice cooed, dripping with insincerity. "I'm so sorry. Come here."

Bile rose up in my throat. Kev had no idea how close we were. He didn't know if he had one more minute in that room or twenty.

"Are you caught up in this?" Kev asked in a soft voice. "Is that why you're asking me about this stuff?"

"You don't know what you're talking about," Linus replied in a fake pleasant tone barely holding back an angry growl. "I suggest you tell me what you know instead of asking me questions."

Kev's voice got stronger, his anger rising to the surface. "I know you're really a DEA agent. I know you're suspected of murder. And I know you're planning to assassinate Gustavo Santiago while you're here in Vegas."

Champ's eyebrows rose into the sky. "What the fuck?" he mouthed at me. I shrugged stiffly.

Kev was poking the bear. And the bear was made up of C-4 explosives. I hoped like hell he knew what he was doing.

"Kill Gustavo?" Linus asked with a huff of laughter. "Why the hell would I take out the source? Where would we get the drugs if we took out the head of the damned cartel? The drugs bring the money. I'm this fucking close to being able to quit and retire to a private damned island. No more fucking Horn for the rest of my days. And I didn't kill anyone — Gustavo did. I just told him where to find the guy."

Laurel's voice over comms was reverent. "He's getting us confessions on top of everything."

The elevator at the end of the hall dinged, and an agent in a suit came out, waving the warrant. The "drunk" agents straightened up and pulled their weapons out of hidden holsters. "Back away," one of them said to us.

Champ pulled me back when I wanted to lunge forward and be the first to breach the room.

"Get him out of there clean," I urged them, voice cracking with fear. "Please."

I sent a message to Kev's phone, which was the breach signal we'd previously agreed upon...

Me: *Rodrigo.*

And then a second one that had fuck-all to do with this op.

Me: *I'm sorry. I love you.*

I knew he wouldn't see them, wouldn't take the time to pull his phone out of his pocket when his job was to find cover instead, but maybe later he'd notice them and know he continued to be loved fiercely regardless of how he felt about me.

Chaos ensued. Clatter and shouts, gasps and cries. One odd moment of silence before a single gunshot went off in the tiny room.

I broke out of Champ's hold and bolted for the door.

For Kevin.

21

KEV

When I'd entered Linus Dixon's hotel room, I'd felt nothing. Discovering Hux—my Jasper Huxley—was really SmittyKitty had been an unexpected blow. The kind that swept aside all of the false bravado and anger about Hux's overreaction that had carried me down the hall.

My brain scrambled to process the totality of his deception. Honesty from here on out, we'd said. All the shit we'd said and done in the past would stay in the past, and we were a team moving forward.

So what the hell had he been thinking?

When Linus began playing me, my words came easy. No nerves, no overthinking. Too much of my heart and soul was wound up in razor wire to worry about this manipulative asshole when I was so distracted by the *other* manipulative asshole.

I was going to kick his ass. Unleash every self-defense move the Chi Omegas had ever taught me, complete with the bloodcurdling screams, and maybe add a few of my own besides. The kitchen laser plan was back on, complete with extra lasers, and I really hoped that no one I liked planned to ride in Huxley's vehicle anytime soon because they would soon realize that his stereo only ever played "Cotton-Eyed Joe" and "Who Let the Dogs Out" on an endless loop, at volume eleven, *forever*.

Also, his homestead was mine. I wasn't gonna piddle around with his jam cellar or steal his precious greenberries; I was going to annex the whole lot and train Hux's former villagers to blow razzberries at him on sight. And as for his alter ego, Smitty…

As I sat at the keyboard in Linus's hotel room, pretending to worry about showing him the cartel data, whole swaths of my conversations with SmittyKitty came streaming through my memory. His rage at Anomaly's overstepping. His pride when I told him about the dick rocket. The way he'd tattled on Huxley—on *himself*—when Hux had looted my jam cellar. His cheerful "Have fun storming the castle, Pip"s that had made me smile, made me laugh, made me feel good about myself, even when Hux and I had been too entrenched in our pride and insecurity to bridge the gap between us.

While I waited for Linus's Horn data to download, I remembered my most recent Smitty conversation—the first conversation we'd had since Hux and I had declared a truce, a conversation that *conveniently* had happened just hours after I'd confessed to Huxley how much I missed Smitty's presence in my life—and Smitty's confession that he'd stopped playing as much because…

Because he was falling for someone. Someone amazing. The best man he knew.

He loved me.

I held back a laugh. He hadn't just fallen in love with me last night, in the suite, in a moment of danger. It had happened days ago, even before I'd realized my own feelings. And when he'd blurted it out earlier, it hadn't been because he'd wanted to do some kind of tearful goodbye before I walked into danger because he didn't think I could handle myself. That wild look on his face in the suite had been the terror of a man who knew the man he loved was going into a dangerous situation, and he wanted me to carry that into battle with me because he trusted me to get the job done.

He trusted me to storm the castle.

My heart felt huge behind my ribs, like it would burst out of me and fling itself up two flights of stairs to Jasper's own chest. Knowing Jasper loved me that much, *trusted* me that much, made me feel invincible.

Which was probably incredibly bad timing, what with the whole bringing-down-a-cartel thing happening *literally in the room with me.*

I wanted this bullshit to be done even more than I had before, if that were possible. I wanted the cartel out of our business and off our minds. And I wanted Linus Asshole Dixon to go down.

In order to do that, he needed to confess where my recorder could catch it. There was no way for me to know if we'd gotten any incriminating evidence on his Horn. I didn't have a comms unit in my ear. So I had to get as much evidence as I could before leaving the room.

Which sounded great and totally doable... until he pulled out the gun and approached the door.

Stay calm.

I took a breath and let it out. We'd known he probably had a weapon. Champ had laid it all out for me, along with the likelihood of him using it. As long as he didn't realize that I was working with the feds, I was safe.

Safe-ish.

Kinda.

"Tell me what Champ knows," Linus demanded, turning

away from the door—and the FBI distraction team on the other side of it.

Oh, damn. My vision went squidgy on the edges. Our conversation after that seemed like it was happening underwater or through thick glass. Everything was slow and weird.

Linus kept stalking closer to me, and I kept backing away, and all the while, he explained his crimes like a mustache-twirling villain at the end of a B movie. Worst of all, he spoke about these horrors in an oddly soothing sort of voice, like this was all some bizarre kind of virgin seduction foreplay.

Did this shit actually *work*?

What kind of guys had he been sleeping with?

It wasn't until he'd fingered Gustavo for a different killing that I finally pulled out of my fugue state and thought, *Holy shit. We did it.*

He'd accused Gustavo of a murder. He'd admitted to his involvement with the cartel.

That meant this whole nightmare was… was *over.*

When the door opened and agents streamed in, life seemed to speed up again. By then, my hindbrain was chanting one word over and over, like a magical incantation. *JasperJasperJasper.*

I looked to the door, too numb to move my body, but out of the corner of my eye, I saw Linus lunge for his gun on the table where he'd set it down.

When the shot hit my ears, I wasn't sure who'd fired it. Had it been Linus? An agent? But then Linus's eyes got wider for a split second before he crumpled to the ground, knocking the desk chair over on his way down. Agents raced to get his gun.

Behind them was Hux. *Finally.* And then I could move.

I reached out my arms and felt the tears come. Within

seconds, I was in his arms, held tight with the familiar bands of muscles that I hoped never ever let me go.

"Baby," he cried into my hair. "Are you okay? Are you hurt? Kevin, talk to me."

"I'm okay," I managed to croak. "Not hurt."

I held on to him so tightly I could barely breathe. He murmured words of approval against my head, about how proud he was of me, what a good job I'd done, and how impressed everyone was.

I didn't care about any of that.

"I love you too," I breathed.

Hux pulled back and took a ragged breath. "Oh, fuck, Kev, *how*? After everything I—"

I shook my head to stop him. "I'm not happy you lied to me, and we're going to talk about it. Tolls will be levied. Penalties *will* be paid. But I…" I swallowed while I tried to get my thoughts together. "I see now how you tried to end it after we started something in real life. And I didn't let you." I smiled at him. "Because I wanted to tell you about this amazing guy I was with. And I still feel that way."

I wasn't making much sense, but the adrenaline was still rushing through my system, and I couldn't feel my hands and feet.

Hux held my face in his hands. "I love you. With everything I am. I promise I will never lie to you again."

"I love you," I said again before burying my face in his neck and inhaling his familiar sandalwood scent. Agents scrambled around the room, shouting commands and blocking off the area around the body.

"Let's get you out of here." Hux hefted me under the legs and carried me out of the room and down the hall before setting me down, but he still didn't let me go, even when Champ came over to congratulate me on a job well done.

"You can be on my team any day, Kev," Champ said, squeezing my shoulder.

Riggs came blasting out of the stairwell and sprinting down the hall, ripping me out of Hux's arms to hug me tightly. "Thank fuck. Carter's breathing down my neck asking for confirmation you're unharmed."

"Hey." Hux elbowed Riggs out of the way with a glare to enfold me in his embrace again. "Get your own Dr. Rogers. This one's mine."

Jordan and Elvo appeared and slapped me on the back, uttering their own kudos while Riggs looked on and smiled.

All of that was great. Wonderful. But the only prize I wanted was the man who held me tight against his side.

It wasn't until much later, after hours of FBI interviews and debriefings, that I was finally able to shower off the stress of the day. I was practically dead on my feet, but Hux was there to hold me up, keeping my head above water in more ways than one.

He washed my body reverently, taking his time to caress every part of me with his loving touch. Meanwhile, I ran my fingers through his crazy hair, caressed his piercing, and traced the tattoos on his chest with my tongue, basically doing everything possible to stop him from washing me efficiently, but he didn't seem to mind. Not one bit.

"Champ told me you held him back from barging into the room before I'd gotten the confession."

Hux looked up from where he knelt on the tiles. A soapy washcloth made its way up the back of my calf. Just looking at him naked, wet, and on his knees for me made my dick hard.

"Yeah," he said.

"You trusted me to see it through."

"Yeah," he repeated, focusing back on my legs.

"It must have killed you," I teased.

"Yeah," he said for the third time. "That's… an understatement right there."

I tackled him to the ground, where we ended up exhausting ourselves with a sloppy, wet, but incredibly satisfying sixty-nine. In a matter of weeks, I'd gone from a virgin to someone initiating advanced sexual maneuvers in Las Vegas.

"I think… you've corrupted me," I said in a gasping breath while still coming down from my orgasm.

Hux pressed a kiss to my hip before sitting up and pulling my damp body into his lap. I slumped against him. There was nothing more in my body to give.

"I'd like to apply to fill that role permanently," he said, sounding more serious than usual. I glanced up at him.

"Huh?"

"The timing is bad, I get that. Maybe you need more time to figure things out, once all this chaos is done, and that's… that's fine. I'll follow whatever timeline you're comfortable with. But I need you to know you're it for me, Kevin." He took a breath. "I thought I was in love with you yesterday. Last night. This morning. But with every new thing I learn about you, I swear I fall in love just a little bit more. So I would really like the chance to move forward with you. To get to fall in love with you over, and over, and over again. Forever."

After all that had happened that day, I hadn't thought I could get emotional again for… God, hours at least. But it turned out I had a fresh supply. I felt so much for the man that it wrecked me, then built me up again in the best possible way. And I knew there was no one I'd rather have as a partner, in Horn of Glory or in life.

I couldn't possibly compete with the poetry Hux had uttered, so I didn't try. Instead, I leaned my head on his chest again and closed my eyes with a grin. "Okay… but I'm only doing it because Rodrigo deserves two parents."

Hux yanked me up and kissed me so hard I almost choked on shower water. We kissed long enough to turn pruney, long enough for Hux to wrap a towel around us both and drag us both to the bed, long enough for him to wrap his strong arms and legs around me… and for Hux to fall asleep, still kissing me.

Before I closed my eyes, I blinked at the lights from the strip that danced across the ceiling. I might have wondered if I'd stepped into a fantasy world, but Hux's solid weight grounded me and reassured me that I was right where I belonged—in a world where magic didn't come from health boosters or enchanted swords, trolls or potions, but from the man who'd chosen me, the man I'd chosen, and the beautiful future that lay before us.

It turned out love was the craziest and most wonderful game of all.

And I was playing to win.

EPILOGUE
HUX

Six Months Later

I had lived in many places and seen many things over the past thirty years. Broad rolling rivers and endless mountains. Vast, lonely deserts that scorched and froze in turns. Oceans so wide and empty it felt like I was the only creature in the universe, and cities so crowded that it felt like all of humanity was sharing the same breath.

Some of those places I'd loved, and others I'd hated, but not one of them had been *mine*. None of them had been *home*. Until the road I'd been traveling had bent, unexpectedly and randomly and not altogether welcomely, and I'd found myself plunked down in this tiny, green corner of Tennessee, where the cows outnumbered the people, and the puns outnumbered the cows, and my soul had stretched and sighed and put down roots.

Because that was what happened when you found the place where you were meant to be. The people you were meant to be with.

And it was, I reflected as I sat atop a long wooden

picnic table and let my eyes roam over a grassy field littered with summer dandelions and laughing children, a beautiful, beautiful thing.

"You know, boys," Buck Nutter said thoughtfully from a nearby lawn chair. "The best part of a Lickin' is just sittin' back and enjoyin' the sensation." He took a sip of his beer and swallowed with a long, drawn-out *aaaahhhh*. "Doncha think?"

I ignored him. I'd gotten quite good at ignoring Buck over the past six months of depositions, case meetings, and the random, almost daily encounters that came from living in the same small town. In fact, Kev sometimes said it was my superpower.

"Gonna have to disagree with you there, Buck." Quinn, who sat on the bench near my feet, leaned over to take a big bite of Champ's Lickin' Horn—the HOG-sponsored deep-fried, sugar-dusted ice-cream cone that had become a fan favorite at this year's Lickin' festival. "Best part of a Lickin' is the taste."

Champ shook his head sternly at his boyfriend. There would be hell to pay when they got home for Quinn's egregious pun usage, and the impish smile on Quinn's face said he both knew this and *welcomed* it. "If you're gonna make me try one of these," he grumbled, taking a large bite of his own, "I'm glad we're doing it with an actual cardiologist on hand."

Carter sipped from his water bottle and watched in fascination as Riggs inhaled his second hot dog in under twenty seconds. "Pretty sure I'm going to be too busy resuscitating my own husband to save Quinn's twinky ass. Baby, maybe *chew*? Just a thought."

I held up my beer stein and tilted it in Riggs's direction. "Don't listen to the haters, Riggsy! Just ten more and you'll beat Elvo's record from that Fourth of July in Lejeune."

Carter groaned and dropped his chin to his chest. "Don't egg him on. The last time you guys threw down a food challenge, he was up all night crying and trying to pick out a name for his 'cake baby.'"

Champ snorted. "He wasn't crying because he ate a whole birthday cake. He was crying because he was another year older."

Riggs shot Champ the bird without pausing his hot dog consumption.

Kev came bustling over from a nearby art booth and dropped a lingering kiss on my lips before leaning against my side. The collar of his T-shirt—a limited-edition HOG design that depicted a troll prince and the Duchess of Moon Flowers in front of a homestead in a parody of American Gothic—was damp with sweat when I nuzzled into his neck, but he still smelled like Kev. Bracing coffee and wholesome vanilla and everything I liked best.

"Hey," he chuckled hoarsely, pushing me away half-heartedly while also tilting his neck to give me better access. "Stop distracting me. You won't believe what I just saw."

I pulled away just slightly. "Was it those pizza sticks with the parmesan cheese? Because I was stunned too—who puts pizza on a stick?—yet they were surprisingly good. I ate two—"

Kev covered my mouth with his palm, and his eyes danced. "Better than pizza sticks. I just saw the metal sculpture of our logo that Mal made. It's *perfect*. Come see!"

No lie, the words "our logo" hit me hard, the way it always did when Kevin talked about something that was ours. Our bed, our rabbit, our future. Our development company, which we'd officially incorporated three months ago. Our game, which we'd already started to develop by taking some of the aspects we loved best about Horn of Glory and making them exponentially more inclusive and equitable. Our life in the Thicket, with its weddings and funerals, near-weekly fundraisers and festivals, barbecues and potluck dinners.

The whole thing made a person sentimental. And really, really grateful.

Still, since I'd helped design the logo and had custom-ordered the sculpture, I'd seen it many times during the build and design stage. Mal's art booth was all the way on the opposite side of the fairgrounds, at least a hundred feet away. And those pizza sticks, while delectable, sat heavy on a person's stomach, especially when mixed with the better part of three beers.

I licked Kev's palm, and he snatched it away with a laugh. "Can't I just… appreciate it from afar?"

Kev tilted his head in a little gesture I'd come to recognize as trouble and ran his tongue over his teeth. "I believe I see what's happening here."

I scratched at my forehead. "Baby—"

"Someone—it's *you*—has forgotten simple respect for rank." Kev took the beer stein from my hand and sipped from it slowly.

I tilted my head back so that the sun made brightly colored fractals whirl and shift against the back of my eyelids and tried valiantly not to laugh. Had I known it was possible to be as happy as I was with Kevin Rogers in my life? I wasn't sure I had. "Not this again, I beg you. I have respect. So much respect."

Kev hummed sympathetically. "And yet…"

"I gifted you that Temper Turkey when you mentioned that Oprah needed a sister, remember? And now you can calm entire orc hordes in seconds. That was a gift of respect." I also hadn't said a word when he'd named his golden duck in the game after the ancient stuffed duck that sat on our bed, even if I'd privately laughed my ass off, but I knew better than to mention either of those facts.

"I suppose you did," he admitted. "Though I'm deducting points because anyone could see that Matthew McConaughey the Temper Turkey was a male turkey, what with his epic plumage."

"And let's not forget last night." I lowered my voice, though the other guys were all busy in their own conversations. "When we did the Cloud Maven Javelin Toss to decide who got to top, and I lost that one crucial throw at the end…"

"How was you losing a sign of respect?" Kev hesitated before gasping. "You *didn't*."

"Weeelllll…"

"You absolutely did not lose that game on purpose! I don't care how many hours of practice you've put in, you've never managed to toss your Enchanted Javelin through the Ring of Evenlore, which means I won fair and square." He scowled. "Didn't I?"

I shrugged helplessly and lied my ass off. "What can I say, baby? I wanted you to, uh, toss *your* Enchanted Javelin at my…"

Kev slapped his hand over my mouth again. "Jasper. Theodosius. Huxley."

"Nah mah acshal nam," I muttered against his skin.

"Irrelevant. I am… I am *outraged*. I am *incensed*. I am…" He sucked in an enormous breath through his nose. "Champ! Riggs! Everyone! Who won in the Ascendant's Class at this year's Conqueror's Tournament?"

"*You* did, HogDoc," several amused voices sang in unison.

I shook my head, fighting laughter.

"Yes, I did. And would you say," Kev continued, his

eyes hot on mine, "that means that I... *ascended* to the highest level of HOG stardom?"

"Yes, HogDoc," they said again, though Quinn almost ruined it by laughing.

Kev pursed his lips and tilted his head, so perfectly, deservedly smug that I wanted to throw him down on the picnic table and taste him like my own personal Lickin' Horn. "One would think that Huxley would appreciate being my Ascendant's *Consort*. One would think that he would appreciate being leveled up in the game and getting that fancy custom hoodie with his new title on the back. But noooo. He's never worn the thing."

I grabbed his wrist and pulled his hand away from my mouth easily. "I've worn it."

Kev blushed profusely. "I... I mean, outside of our bedroom."

"Has he been disrespectful again, Doc?" Riggs asked sadly. "I'm afraid you need to punish him."

I shot him a laser-eyed glare. "Butt out, asshole."

"Riggs is right," Champ pronounced. "This attitude wouldn't be tolerated in the Marines."

"Et tu, Percival?" I demanded. "What happened to never leaving a man behind?"

"I'm feeling like he needs to recite the fealty pledge," Carter decided, tossing me a knowing wink. "It's the only way."

Champ and Riggs hooted with laughter. "Remind us again what the pledge says, Huxley?" Riggs asked. "I forgot."

"No you didn't." I grabbed Kev around the waist and dragged him up so he was partly on the table beside me and partly on my lap. "Ascend your ass down."

Yolanda walked over from a nearby lemonade table and straddled the picnic bench. "Shit. Tell me I didn't miss him doing the pledge," Yolanda said with a grin. Her wife, Katie, wrapped her arm around Yolanda's shoulders and kissed the side of her face.

"Nope." Champ dropped an arm over Quinn's shoulders and hauled the man against his side. "You got here just in time."

"Not saying it," I grumbled, leaning in to sniff Kevin's neck.

"Pretty please?" Kev's voice was full of laughter and light, and it was enough to make me feel like I'd say anything just to keep him happy and free.

The past few months hadn't been all joy and ease, as much as I'd wanted them to be for his sake. The FBI investigation had been long and difficult, forcing Kev to relive some of the scariest moments of his life over and over. Moving in together, which had seemed so easy and natural at first, had involved melding the finances of one happy-go-lucky bajillionaire and one poor-and-frugal Huxley, which meant a *lot* of discussion and compromise—two of my least favorite things. For a while, even Horn of Glory hadn't been as fun for Kev as it usually was, almost like peeling back the curtain on HOG Corporate and the cartel, Anomaly and Smitty and all the lies, had dulled its shine.

But we'd stuck together, Kev and I, and the rest of the team too. We'd held tight to the things we loved, and we'd let the rest of the storm blow over us. And now I could confidently say that we were a tighter unit than ever. Happier and more settled than ever too.

Jordan was dating someone. Sasha too. Elvo, while still happily single, was busy showing his younger sister around town, now that she'd moved here to take Herman's receptionist job and my spot in the apartment with Elvo. Herman, meanwhile, was living his best life at Thicket Sunset, the area's very own senior community, which, according to local lore, featured such unique activities as Naked Bocce and Swingers' Saturday Bridge Nights. Herman fit right in.

HOG Corporate was still thriving since the FBI had managed to keep the company's name out of the media. Jacob Horn hadn't been pleased, at first, upon learning that he had to change their financial systems as a condition of the deal, but he'd been happy with the result. He'd even given Champ a secret wink-wink during one meeting, implying he'd already made out like a bandit in the short time they'd been rolling in cartel money. Thankfully, Champ had been too much of a professional to knock the man's teeth out.

The cartel members on the original Horn list had been rounded up and taken in. Once Laurel's team had managed to capture Gustavo Santiago, the rest had fallen like dominos. Unfortunately, Gustavo had died of a severe heart attack in jail while awaiting trial.

If only he'd had a cardiologist nearby.

And as for me… well, the past few months had worked a lot of changes in me too. I'd started talking to my mom a lot more, making steps to bridge the gap that I'd never managed to cross before my dad died. I'd lost a good chunk of the chip I'd been carrying on my shoulder when it came to money and self-worth. I'd accepted that some people really could love me unconditionally. And I'd redefined what success and *winning* really looked like.

It looked a lot like a smile on the face of the man beside me.

I watched Kev's grin grow wider as he joked around with the team. My love for him was like a magical beanstalk that continued growing, twining around everything in its path, nurturing those who needed it, drawing connections where there'd been none, thriving in the light.

"I love you," I said, low enough that only he could hear.

He turned away from everyone's hooting and teasing and dazzled me with his grin. "I know what you're doing, and it won't work, my love. There *shall* be a fealty pledge. I won't let you change the subject."

My heart beat faster, and my breath got tangled in my chest. I felt like I was standing on a precipice, high atop a mountain. Below me lay all the heartbreaks and misadventures, the lessons and the failures, that had gotten me to where I was. My whole life had been building toward this… and there was no fear in my heart, only joy.

"*Pfft*. If I'd wanted to change the subject, I'd show everyone my new T-shirt."

Kev's eyes drifted down to my much-loved, often-worn, navy blue Michigan alum T-shirt. "Uh-huh."

"Oh, Kev of little faith." I hopped down from the table and pressed the softest kiss to the lips of the man I loved. Then I whipped off my top T-shirt and showed him the custom shirt I wore beneath.

I saw his eyes widen as he recognized an aerial view of his own HOG homestead—with its brand-new luxury jam cellar—and the smile fall from his face as he read the words below.

Dr. and Mr. Ascendant. Two hearts. One homestead.

And then I dropped to one knee in the grass and reached a shaking hand into my jeans pocket for the ring.

"Kevin Rogers," I recited. "I pledge fealty to you. And I—"

"Oh my God. *Oh* my God. Oh my *God*," Kev chanted. And then he fell to his knees in the grass, too, grabbed my face, and kissed me.

"Good Lord, Kevin, let the man get the words out," Kev's grandfather teased with an affectionate smile from behind his phone camera. I'd made the drive to Nashville earlier in the week to ask for his blessing before proposing to Kevin, and he'd burst into tears.

"He's the best man I know," I'd told him with tears in my eyes.

And I couldn't wait to tell Kev about how his grandfather had gotten teary-eyed, too, then looked at me over his turkey club sandwich in the middle of his crowded golf club lunchroom and said, "Hurt him and there will be no rock large enough for you to hide behind," in a terrifying gravelly voice. He and Kev were more alike than they knew.

Now here he was, making sure Kev would be able to watch this whole thing again later. Which meant I needed to make it good.

"You humble me," I began. "You teach me. You've changed my life for the better. You love like you're trying to fill the world with it, like loving others is the air you breathe, and you make life magical for everyone around you just by existing. Please marry me. Share a homestead with me. Let me spend the rest of my life showing you how much I love you." I shook my head ruefully, my careful speech now seeming totally inadequate. "Love seems so small a word for something that feels this big. It's impossible for four letters to contain how much I feel in my heart."

Then Kevin Rogers, the light of my life, shot me the challenging grin that had first drawn me to him, first sparked the flame in my heart that now burned for him. The grin I hoped to see every day for the rest of my existence.

"I think you'll find I can do it in *three* letters, Huxley." Then he pressed his lips to mine and murmured… "*Yes.*"

Up next: Meet the feuding Honeycutt and Wellbridge families in the

brand-new Honeybridge series! Turn the page for a sneak peek or grab Firecracker here → https://readerlinks.com/l/2613083

Want more Licking Thicket romance? Check out more hilarious reads set in the punniest small-town in America…
Fakers (Brooks and Mal
Liars (Diesel and Parrish)
Fools (Dunn and Tucker)
Turkeys (Charlton and Hunter)

SNEAK PEEK OF FIRECRACKER

JT

"I feel like you left here in a *mood*." Alice's voice through the Porsche speakers sounded way calmer than I felt at the moment.

My assistant wasn't wrong. She rarely was.

"Mood. *Mood*," I said through my teeth. "Yes, I think you could call it that. After three fucking years of working my ass off for Conrad Schaeffer with his promise of a promotion to vice president, I actually believed it was finally going to happen."

"No shit, JT. The man's an..." She lowered her voice. "An insufferable ass. But rumor has it he said you'd get promoted to VP as soon as you close the Honeybridge Mead account up in Maine. Which, let's be honest, is practically a done deal considering you grew up in Honeybridge. Surely you have connections that can help..."

Her voice faded away while my head took me to a million places, none of which were compatible with my sanity.

Green eyes bright with arousal.

Bare, freckled shoulders.

A smile rarer than a sun-shower in June.

Anger so hot it burned, even in my memories.

Connections? I definitely had connections. But they were the opposite of helpful.

"Conrad made it sound like you know the guy who owns it, right? You two went to school together or something?" Alice continued, breaking me out of my memories.

Or something.

I swallowed around my nerves. Flynn Honeycutt was six feet of walking temptation wrapped in a barbed-wire coating of *stay-the-fuck-away-from-me.*

My boss couldn't have given me a more difficult challenge if he'd tried. Not that Conrad Schaeffer knew anything about Honeybridge Mead or Flynn Honeycutt. No, he'd most likely found out about the brand the same way the rest of the world had—through some viral social media posts.

Frankie Hilo had made several posts from the Honeybridge Tavern and Meadery. One duck-faced mirror shot of the singer being her ridiculous self in the men's room. One orgasmic selfie of her holding a half-empty glass with the simple caption "bussin." And one reel she'd shot in front of the Tavern, in which she panned the entire length of sleepy, old-fashioned Fraser Street, declared that she was "absolutely sliving the savage vibe" of Honeybridge, Maine, and instructed her Hilo-lovers to come see for themselves.

And apparently, they had. According to my mother, who served on every town development committee (because god forbid that anything should happen in Honeybridge without her input), tourism in the quaint lakeside town was up eighteen percent over the town's best summer previously, and new artisans and chefs were moving in, bringing their talent and entrepreneurial spirit. "The club has even had to hire an extra gate attendant," she'd sniffed, which was Patricia Wellbridge's genteel way of saying the town had been overrun with riffraff.

If this was true, that was great. Flynn Honeycutt deserved the boon to his business, and Honeybridge itself could use the additional tourist traffic.

Personally, though, I had my doubts. Honeybridge was a tiny town that was a little too proud of its quaint traditions and local legends. Nothing ever changed there, including the people. The life you were born into was the life you were expected to lead, forever and ever amen.

That was the reason I'd deliberately escaped the place years ago in search of bigger and better things—a life on my own terms. It was a large part of the reason I hadn't even been back for a visit in three years, too.

Now here I was, tasked with spending time in Honeybridge—"A few weeks at least, Jonathan. Heck, maybe the whole summer!" Conrad had suggested, to my utter horror —to court a new client into signing a distribution deal with me at Fortress Holdings.

A client I'd known my whole life and who'd hated me nearly as long.

A client whose naked body felt like it had been crafted to fit against mine.

A client whose prickly exterior hid a vulnerable underbelly of need.

A client whose soft cries in bed still haunted me most nights as I took myself in hand and searched for relief.

I had strong suspicions about why I, of all the people Conrad Schaeffer could have chosen to represent Fortress, had been chosen for this mission, and I was extremely displeased.

"Alice," I said, clearing my throat and trying to put the past where it belonged—deep, deep down in a lead-lined vault. In the ocean. On another planet. "I need you to get me everything you can on Honeybridge Mead's competitors. If we take them national, I want to know who they'd be up against besides Lotus and Fairchild."

This was *business*, I reminded myself, no matter how personal it felt. A deal like any other I'd done for Fortress over the years. Sure, it was way more important since Conrad was so fixated on this particular deal that he'd placed it squarely between me and a VP title, but a deal nonetheless. And I was really, *really* good at closing deals.

Alice's keyboard clacked in the background. "Will do. I've already put together a dossier on Flynn Honeycutt. He's—"

"Don't need it," I said sharply. "I know Flynn. I've got that part handled."

This was, of course, a giant lie. I might *know* Flynn, but I'd never understood the man. Still, no dossier was going to give me any additional insight.

What I knew for sure was that my usual methods with clients—building a relationship, figuring out what they truly wanted, and making sure they got a fair deal—were not going to work here. Not when we had a lifetime's worth of misunderstandings and antagonism between us…

And one incredible night of the opposite.

Instead, I was planning to go for shock and awe. Throwing out my most generous, most unrefusable offer first so there'd be no need for any back-and-forth.

"Okayyy," she said hesitantly. "So I'll pull together comps and keep an eye on everything else in progress. I'm assuming you'll be working from there for the time being? Mr. Schaeffer implied you'd be out of the office for a long while."

I clamped my teeth together to keep from shouting an expletive into my poor assistant's ears. "Conrad's wrong. I plan on being back in New York with a signed contract in a week at most."

The smile was obvious in her voice. "Ah, there's the Rainmaker talking. Go get 'em, JT!"

After ending the call, I added the stupid office nickname —*Rainmaker*, gah—to the vat of shit I was irrationally angry about.

That anger was the reason I'd chosen to drive to Maine instead of flying to Portland and taking a helicopter to Honeybridge, like my father often did. I needed to take out all that negativity on the winding two-lane roads and let the sun and wind wash it away before I gave in to my desire to tell my boss where to shove it.

As much as I disliked certain things about Honeybridge, I couldn't fault the natural beauty of the place. Skirting the edge of an enormous lake in the middle of the Maine woods, where the moose outnumbered the people three to one, it was half a day's drive—or a billion light-years, depending on your point of view—from the city I called home. And as I cruised down the sun-dappled road, inhaling the deep, heady pine scent that was like no other fragrance in the world, I couldn't help but leave a tiny portion of my New York stress behind.

Before I had a chance to put the top down on the Porsche and really enjoy it, however, my phone rang again.

"Jonathan, darling, how are you?" My mother's voice was loud enough to make me jump and nearly knock my iced coffee over. "Things here are *wonderful*. Rarely have I had a better day."

I contemplated ending the call. Dealing with Patricia Wellbridge's socialite melodrama was a frustrating experi-ence at the best of times. Since I'd had to cancel my trip to an all-inclusive Mexican resort (and deal with the theatrical rantings of my friend with benefits, Massimo, who'd now be enjoying the trip without me) before banishing myself to this place, it was safe to say this was not remotely the best of times.

And given the mounting evidence that my mother had been involved in that banishment—the sharp uptick in her hounding to "come home for a nice visit, darling," added to my parents' brief visit to the city recently and multiplied by Patricia's need to control things she had no business controlling—my anger ratcheted high enough to make the steering wheel leather squeak in my tight grip.

We're getting rid of anger, I reminded myself. *Anger is not productive here.*

"Mother," I said carefully. "I've got to be honest. I've had better days. In fact, I need to get on a very important business call right now."

I wasn't proud of the lie, but if I stayed on the phone with her for long, it wasn't going to end well.

"Nonsense." Her laughter sounded breathless, and she punctuated each word with a loud puff of air. "Nothing's... more important... than family." She panted heavily. "In fact... most of *your* family... is coming home... for the summer kickoff this weekend. Redmond. And Thomas. Your brother, Reagan. You know your *brother* always makes an effort to get back home."

Easy enough for Reagan since I wasn't sure he'd ever officially moved out. My brother was a sweet guy but way too caught up in my parents' social sphere.

"Good for them," I grumbled. "But I really do have to go."

"I understand! I understand! You're focused on your career. You're a Wellbridge." She heaved another breath. "Success. Is in. Your blood. But *family* is our strength, sweetheart. Why, your father, the Senator, often says —*ooofumowowow*!"

She let out a bellow like the warbling wail of a loon, and I sat up straighter in my seat, my temper yielding to concern.

"Mother? Are you alright?" I demanded. "Are you having chest pains? Should I call —"

"No, darling, I'm fine! Just doing my yogaerobics. It's a newer, more *refined* form of yoga. I'm simultaneously meditating to lower my heart rate *and* doing cardio, all while talking to you," she said proudly.

Yogaerobics? Had she made that up herself?

"But if you're doing cardio, doesn't that defeat the whole…" Belatedly, I remembered why it never paid to engage with my mother. You couldn't have a productive conversation with a person who refused to hear you and could never admit they were wrong. It was as useful as… well, as screaming your frustration at the inside of your car.

Which I badly wanted to do just then.

"Never mind," I sighed.

"Where are you, sweetheart? You sound perturbed. Are you perturbed? You're not still driving, are you? Driving while perturbed can be *so* dangerous. And I do believe it's illegal in Maine."

Aaaaand there was my suspicion confirmed.

I narrowed my eyes at the pastoral country road ahead of me. Cows dotted the field past the tree break to my right, and bright green leaves shivered in a gentle breeze to my left, but I was only peripherally aware of any of that. "I live in New York, Mother. Why would you assume I was anywhere near Maine?"

"Well, I… Er. Didn't you say so?" Mercifully, the huffing and puffing cut off.

"No. In fact, why would you assume that I'm driving at all?"

"The, ah…" She cleared her throat noisily. "Mothers just have a sense about these things. We love our children so deeply and want their happiness—"

"Mother," I interrupted with saccharine sweetness. "What have you done?"

As if I didn't already know.

"There's no need to take a *tone*, Jonathan," she tsked. "I didn't *do* anything." After a brief hesitation, she admitted, "It's possible that when your father and brother and I were in New York last week—at one of your father's political fundraisers, you remember? The fundraiser you were too busy to attend?" She gave a sad little pause. "The governor's race won't be for another year, of course, but everyone in Augusta thinks the Senator will be a shoo-in for lieutenant—"

"*State* senator," I corrected automatically, rolling my eyes. "Dad is a *state* senator."

"My goodness. There's no need to be uncharitable, Jonathan," she chided. "After all, it's only a matter of time until—"

"Still waiting for the explanation," I gritted out.

"*Hmph.* Well… as it happens, we ran into your boss while we were there, and would you believe, Conrad and the Senator knew each other back in college! He wouldn't have made the connection to you, of course, since your father hadn't taken my last name yet back then. But he said you never even mentioned you were related to the Senator."

I ran a hand over my face. Conrad had said something during our conversation earlier today that had tipped me off to this, but I'd hoped to god he'd been joking.

He hadn't.

"Why on earth would I?" I gritted out.

"Darling, why *wouldn't* you? You're proud to be a Wellbridge, aren't you? To have a father who's a senator?"

I gave up correcting her dubious use of the word "senator." She was never going to change. "Of course I am. I just…"

Having a family with wealth and connections was a privilege, but I'd wanted a life where it didn't matter that I'd been born Jonathan Turner Wellbridge III, the firstborn son of Patricia and Trent. The only way I'd managed to get away from their hopes and expectations for me was by moving to New York after college and staying there.

Though apparently, that hadn't worked either, damn it.

"So, of course, Conrad and your father got to talking," she continued, undeterred as ever. "Conrad mentioned how very well you're doing, bringing so many vineyards and craft breweries under the Fortress Holdings umbrella for distribution deals. How you've made them the fastest-growing consumer products group in the country. How they call you the *Rainmaker*, the man who can close any deal with ease—"

"Not any deal," I said grimly, thinking about my most challenging prospect yet, the one waiting for me at the end of this drive.

"—and I may have mentioned how very difficult it's been for us, having you so far away and too busy to visit the way you once did. Reagan would do so much better with your influence. I told Conrad how very grateful we'd be if there was any way he could manage to get you home."

I thumped my head back against the leather seat. Sometimes I worried that my mother was delusional. But then I remembered that, no, she was just Patricia Wellbridge.

"The truth is…" Mother hesitated for a long moment, then admitted, "We miss you, Jonathan. We love you."

I sighed, my anger easing a fraction.

I knew she genuinely missed me. And I missed my family, too.

Sort of. Sometimes.

But there were very good reasons why I'd avoided Honeybridge for as long as I had… including one incredibly hot, unforgettably passionate, very poorly timed night that my mother didn't—and absolutely *wouldn't*—ever know about.

"I love you, too, but—"

"Which is why," she cut in, innocent as a lamb, "it was absolutely *providential* that your brother happened to mention to Conrad that some *upstart brewery* here in town has gotten a small following on the social medias. That piqued Conrad's curiosity enough to agree to send you home for the *entire summer* to sign a deal or whatnot. Isn't it delightful, darling? I have *so* many events and entertainments planned."

Reagan had put this idea in Conrad's head? I changed my mind—he was not a sweet, decent guy deep down; he was a mischief-trolling curse of a sibling, from his five-hundred-dollar haircut to his pedicured toes.

My mother wasn't any better. She knew exactly which "upstart" brewery Reagan had mentioned to Conrad Schaeffer—and exactly who owned it.

"I wouldn't call Honeybridge Mead an upstart," I said, mostly to provoke her. "Not when Flynn's Grandpa Horace started it forever ago. And according to everything I've read, it's doing a booming business under Flynn's leadership."

"Yes, well," she scoffed. "Perhaps amongst the *tourists*."

"After ordering samples, Conrad said this could be the most important contract I get all year."

"Oh, surely not."

"Mmhmm. I'd think a loyal Honeybridger like yourself would be proud that a homegrown business is so successful—"

"Proud? Of a Honeycutt-owned business?" My mother sniffed. "Not hardly. Though I'm sure those Honeycutts are thrilled to have gotten one over on us yet again."

I rolled my eyes. There it was. My mother's *raison d'être*. The Wellbridge-Honeycutt feud.

The rivalry between the two largest families in Honeybridge was hardly new. It had been raging since seventeen-hundred-and-who-the-heck-knew, when a pair of best friends had traveled north from Boston to settle the fertile land near a lake and make their fortunes. Sounded wholesome and idyllic, and it had been... until Peregrine Wellbridge had decided to dam up the town river to irrigate his crops, cutting off his best friend's water supply, and January Honeycutt had lost his ever-loving mind and chopped down Peregrine's favorite oak tree in retaliation to make a mantle for his fireplace.

Since then, the Wellbridges and the Honeycutts were required, by birthright, to disagree on absolutely everything, from the color of the sky to the name of the lake near the town, which was known as either "Kiss Me Quick Lake" or "Lake Wellbridge," depending on who you were and which camp you found yourself in.

As a result, competition in the town was fierce. I'd like to have said that the people my age weren't as obsessed with the feud as the generations before us had been—and they were definitely less mean-spirited about it—but the competition between the clans raged on intensely, and the other folks in town knew enough to stay out of the way.

I'd never bought into it and had always had plenty of Honeycutts in my Contacts list. But the most important two had always been Pop Honeycutt, who ran the General Store, and... one other number I should have deleted three years ago.

A number that belonged to a man with green eyes,

freckled skin, and the prickliest disposition I'd ever encountered.

"Ah, well. I'm confident the *Rainmaker* will carry the day at the negotiation table," Mother assured me proudly. "Even if it means getting in bed with Flynn Honeycutt."

It was a good thing no one else was on the road around me, otherwise I might have run head-on into oncoming traffic. The images those words conjured—lean muscles and sloppy kisses, the scent of mead and sex thick in the air, Flynn's low voice urging me to *"Use your mouth. Just like… fuck."*—were ones I'd thought I'd purged from my memory years ago.

"The important part," my mother said, "is that you'll be home for weeks and weeks. You can see your friends. Revisit all the places you remember best—"

"God, no," I squeaked out.

"Pardon?"

"I won't be staying that long," I said more firmly. Calmly. *Controlledly.* "There's no reason. I'm going to make Flynn a very fair offer, so this should all be settled very quickly, and I'll be back in the city again before I know it."

I willed myself to believe it, no matter how much I might enjoy the summer sunshine on my arm and the clean air blowing in through the windows.

"Nonsense. Once you get here, you won't want to leave. The softball tournament is starting Saturday, and you'll be here to lead us to victory. Redmond's girlfriend is coming for a few days, and Aunt Louise is in raptures. Oh, and I've invited the Penningtons to visit through Regatta Day, so they'll be here for the Fourth of July, too," she went on merrily, as if perhaps all the yogaerobics had destroyed her powers of comprehension. "You remember the Penningtons, Jonathan. Brantleigh is such a lovely, lively young man and the heir to his father's real estate investment portfolio. And then, of course, this weekend…" She paused dramatically. "…is the third weekend in June."

"The… oh, *fuck*." I squeezed my eyes shut.

Box Day.

"Jonathan! *Language*."

I came around the final curve into town and saw a long row of taillights backed up in front of me. Dozens and dozens of cars were stopped on the country highway, trying to take the main Honeybridge turnoff.

"The Box Day Parade is today, isn't it?" I sighed, banging my forehead on the steering wheel.

"Why, yes. Obviously." Mother sounded almost offended that I might not have remembered the festival during which the good citizens of Honeybridge went to great lengths to create lavish floral arrangements for their window boxes, which were then judged by a mostly impartial (which was to say completely partial) panel of other Honeybridgers, all for the glory of earning a small rocker on the bottom of the Welcome to Honeybridge sign. "Your cousin Henrietta and I have been working on our theme for ages."

Right. Good old Cousin Henrietta.

Box Day was my mother's personal Valhalla, during which she tried in vain to best Willow Honeycutt at something, *anything*, generally by bringing in a rotating cast of professional floral designers from the city, pretending they were long-lost Wellbridge cousins, and getting them to put together her boxes.

It still never worked.

Remembering the town welcome sign reminded me of the hidden road behind it. I had just enough time to veer off quickly on the small side road as I passed the Welcome to Honeybridge sign. Dangling from twin chains below it were smaller signs that read "Honeycutts: Ice Festival Heroes" and "Honeycutts: Blueberry Day Winners" and "Honeycutts: Softball Tournament Champions," which really was laying it on a bit thick when I thought about it.

The lone "Wellbridges: Best Leaf Peepers" rocker seemed extra pathetic in comparison. Since when was Leaf Peeping a competitive thing? Was that really the best we could do? Surely there had to be some sort of—

Whoa. No. I brought that train of thought to a screeching halt as the tourist traffic disappeared behind me. I was not here in Honeybridge to get sucked back into the competitive fray. No way.

I was here to sign a distribution deal with Flynn—with *Honeybridge Mead*, which was not the same thing—and get the hell back to my real life. The life where eventually Massimo would get over being angry, and Alice would help me remain at the top of the Fortress sales ladder.

The life where Patricia Wellbridge didn't get to boss me around.

I took a deep breath and slowed the car to put the top down so I could truly enjoy the drive through town despite my mother's continued babbling about the Outdoor Lantern Supper, the Intimate Cocktail Fete, and the Joyous Summers-End Regalia she was planning. It was a gorgeous day, and the sight of all the familiar landmarks gave my heart a tiny, nostalgic squeeze.

Okay, maybe there were *some* things I'd forgotten I'd missed about this town.

As I drove behind the redbrick town hall and caught glimpses of children and parents laughing and eating ice cream cones from the General Store along Fraser Street, I gave myself a firm talking-to.

I would not fall back into old habits of letting my parents control where I went and who I spent time with. I would not let the old family feud lull me into an *us* versus *them* mentality. And I would not, under any circumstances, allow myself to look at Flynn Honeycutt as anything but a former classmate and current potential client.

Apple Street was closed to traffic, and Pinehurst was blocked with delivery vans. I finally had to acknowledge to myself there was only one reasonable way remaining to get to Wellbridge House.

I turned onto Fraser Street and took a deep breath.

I almost didn't recognize Honeybridge Tavern when I came upon it—a gleaming white clapboard building with a jaunty sign where a dilapidated pile of brown shingles had once stood. And I sure as hell didn't immediately recognize the man unloading a box truck on the sidewalk outside, even though he had shoulders that looked extremely familiar.

Suddenly, one of the children outside Ollie's Fudge Shoppe—a boy with curly, Wellbridge-blond hair—began screaming in panic as the puppy he'd been holding jumped out of his arms and darted into the street, trailing its leash like a comet's tail… directly in front of my car.

I hit the horn and slammed on the brakes. At the last second, I yanked the car to the right, away from the pair, plowing through a gigantic pothole right outside the Tavern, and rocked to a stop inches away from the sidewalk.

Muddy water sprayed up like a mushroom cloud, blanketing the hood of my Porsche, the windshield, the sidewalk… and the man standing there with a wooden crate in his hands.

Horrifying.

More horrifying still was the way my stomach clenched and the whole world faded to white noise as my brain thought, *Yes. Fucking finally. There you are.*

It had been three years since I'd laid eyes on that face.

On that dark hair and defined jaw, those broad shoulders and tree-trunk legs. On the man who'd forever be at the heart of my personal I-knew-I-was-gay-when story.

Flynn Honeycutt looked good. Better, even, than he had three years before. The kind of good that even a dousing of filthy water couldn't wash away. And for the faintest nanosecond, as he shifted the crate to one huge arm and lifted his hand to wipe the mud from his eyes, his biceps bunched, and his lips twisted up in a half-smile, like he was ready to laugh at the ridiculousness of it all.

In short, he was devastating… and doing business with the man was the furthest thought from my mind.

But then the moment passed, and time sped up again. Flynn's eyes—leaf green, emerald green, *Honeycutt* green— flared in recognition and then flashed with rage.

"*Frog!*" He growled my silly childhood nickname like it was the dirtiest curse he knew.

He took a single threatening step toward my car before one of his coworkers rushed up to pat him with a towel and blocked my view.

"Jonathan? Jonathan, are you alright? What's happening?" my mother demanded.

Part of me wanted to get out of the car and run to him. To apologize and explain, preferably while toweling Flynn off. But I was pretty sure that would only make things more tense and awkward, which was pretty on-brand for me and Flynn Honeycutt, and would absolutely, positively ensure that I would never get him to sign the contract I needed.

So, instead, I did what I always did. I sighed and drove away.

"Nothing, Mother. I, ah… I just reached Honeybridge."

"Wonderful! So you'll be here shortly. The place never changes, does it?" she sighed fondly.

"No," I said, casting a glance in my rearview mirror. "Some things don't change at all."

Achilles had his one weak heel.

Samson had his hair.

And in an entire career built around closing deals and understanding what other people wanted, I had Flynn Honeycutt… the one person I'd never been able to charm.

At least not yet.

Grab *Firecracker* here → https://readerlinks.com/l/2613083

A LETTER FROM LUCY & MAY

Dear Reader,

Thank you for reading *Hacked*! We loved returning to the zany world of Licking Thicket and hope you enjoyed it as much as we did. For more stories set in this quirky small-town, be sure to check out the complete Licking Thicket and Champion Security series.

Next up for our co-written works is an exciting new series called Honeybridge! We can't wait to introduce you to the Honeycutt and Wellbridge families whose ancestors founded the town many, many years ago and who can't stop feuding to this day.

Grab *Firecracker* here: https://readerlinks.com/l/2613083

If this is your first book by one of us and you'd like to read more, we suggest you start with *Fakers*, book one in the Licking Thicket series, or Lucy's *Borrowing Blue* and May's *The Date*.

We would love it if you would take a few minutes to review *Hacked* on Amazon, GoodReads, or BookBub. Reader reviews really do make a difference and we appreciate every single one of them.

We've been friends and fans of each other's work for a couple of years, so we weren't surprised when writing our first collaboration went so smoothly. We were surprised, however, that it didn't end up being a standalone novel like we planned. There are plenty more stories to tell, so stay tuned!

Be sure to follow Lucy and May on Amazon to be notified of new releases, and look for us on Facebook for sneak peeks of upcoming stories.

Feel free to sign up for our newsletters, stop by www.LucyLennox.com, www.MayArcher.com, or visit Lucy's Lair and Club May on Facebook to stay in touch.

To see fun inspiration photos for this book, check out the Pinterest board for Hacked.

Happy reading!

Lucy & May

MORE FROM LUCY AND MAY

Licking Thicket

Flakes

Fakers

Liars

Fools

Turkeys

Peacocks

Champion Security

Hijacked

Hitched

Hacked

Honeybridge

Firecracker

Mr. Important

ABOUT LUCY LENNOX

Lucy Lennox is the USA Today bestselling author of over fifty gay romance titles including the GoodReads Hall of Fame winner Wilde Love. Born and raised in the southeast USA, she is finally putting good use to that English Lit degree she earned before the turn of the century.

Lucy enjoys naps, pizza, and procrastinating. She stays up way too late each night reading romance because it's simply the best.

For more information and to stay updated about future releases, sales and audio news and to grab some free and bonus reads, please sign up for Lucy's author newsletter on her website at LucyLennox.com or to stay in the know, join her exciting reader group, Lucy's Lair on Facebook.

facebook.com/lucylennoxmm

instagram.com/lucylennoxmm

amazon.com/Lucy-Lennox/e/B01N0IOYPT

bookbub.com/authors/lucy-lennox

patreon.com/lucylennox

pinterest.com/lucy_lennox

ALSO BY LUCY LENNOX

Find me online → https://linktr.ee/LucyLennox

Read my books:

Made Marian Series

Forever Wilde Series

Aster Valley Series

The Billionaire Brotherhood Series

After Oscar Series (with Molly Maddox)

Twist of Fate Series (with Sloane Kennedy)

Licking Thicket Series (with May Archer)

Champion Security Series (with May Archer)

Honeybridge Series (with May Archer)

Find a complete list of my stand alone romances and novellas at www.LucyLennox.com along with audio samples, freebies, suggested reading order, and more!

ABOUT MAY ARCHER

May is an M/M author who lives in Boston. She spends her days planning vacations, mainlining diet soda, avoiding the gym, reading M/M romance, and when all other forms of procrastination fail, writing it.

Visit her website at mayarcher.com to sign up for her news-letter to hear about sales and upcoming releases, freebies and behind the scenes info and more! Or join her Facebook group, Club May!

facebook.com/may.archer.author

instagram.com/mayarcherauthor

amazon.com/May-Archer/e/B075JQVGLX

patreon.com/MayArcherRomance

bookbub.com/authors/may-archer

ALSO BY MAY ARCHER

Find me online → https://linktr.ee/mayarcherauthor

Love in O'Leary Series

Whispering Key Series

The Sunday Brothers Series

Copper County Series

The Way Home Series

Licking Thicket Series

(cowritten with Lucy Lennox)

Champion Security Series

(cowritten with Lucy Lennox)

Honeybridge Series

(cowritten with Lucy Lennox)

For a comprehensive list of titles, audio samples, freebies, suggested reading order, and more, visit my website at www.MayArcher.com!